Silent Music

Kate Lord Brown

Contents

Also by Kate Lord Brown

The Beauty Chorus
The Perfume Garden
The Christmas We Met
The Taste of Summer
The House of Dreams

For Guy

"They who dance are thought mad by those who hear not the music."

Proverb

Author's note

'*Have I got a story for you.*' It's amazing how often people want to tell you their tales when they find out you are a writer. But Tess Blythe kept her secrets close to her heart. The moment I met her, I could see why everyone loved Tess. The door of her old Cape Cod house down in the East End of Provincetown was always open, something good cooking on the stove, her red lacquer table crowded with family and friends who had made the pilgrimage. Tess always said the shape of the Cape reminded her of a dancer's arm raised in fourth, and that's why she made it her home.

In her nineties Tess was frail, but she had that inner beauty which becomes more radiant over the years, even as some curl in on themselves and wrinkle like dried leaves. Her cool green eyes shone the way deep spring water shimmers over smooth pebbles, light catching and playful. I always had the feeling she hid a lifetime of secrets behind that quiet smile, but Tess wasn't the kind of person to talk about herself. I had so many questions, but she always wanted to know how you were, how your book was coming on, were you still in love, had you tried that dance class she had recommended? *You must dance, darling! Don't be so self conscious. Why, children are born dancing. Lighten up, have a little fun.*

You came away from a night around Tess' table feeling like you had shared your deepest self - it wasn't until later you realised that she had encouraged you to do all the talking. She was a mystery, for sure.

I must have been to her house in the winter, but in memory it is forever summer, doors and windows open to the warm sea breeze, sheer linen curtains billowing, sunlight filtering through the leaves. It was one of those homes which seems to embrace you the minute you step inside. It was nothing fancy, just a little shingled place near the water, but the house was crammed with Chinese antiques - tall wedding chests, an opium bed in the guest cottage, smooth pillow boxes filled with notes and treasures. Tess never talked about the past, so I was curious about her connection with the East.

Tess was the still heart of this kaleidoscope. The sparkling light, the laughter, the music seemed to come from her. When I think of Tess, I think of the glimmer of sequins, glitter, gold and diamonds. *I am a magpie, darling. Style is what matters - good taste is awfully dull, don't you think?* Her face in repose as she sat at the head of her old table watching everyone talking and eating reminded me of a lake when the wind drops and the surface becomes the mirror of the sky. I could never figure out what she hid below that beautiful stillness. I've seen footage and photos of her in the archives from the late sixties and she had the kind of striking presence which could leave a conversation hanging like a bird shot on the wing. Titian hair, alabaster skin. Everyone said she had what it takes to be a prima ballerina - so why did she never perform?

Now, she sat at the head of her table like a benevolent queen, tall spined, but relaxed, one graceful hand smoothing the head of the Pekingese on her lap, the other cradling her one Martini of the day. She was disciplined - in her habits, her housekeeping, her career. Talk to any dancer who worked with her. She expected the best of herself and everyone around her. Sure, her work as a choreographer was legendary, but she was kind. That's what I remember most about her. Her kindness. *Keep your mind open, your heart open. It will get better, trust me. The world is a magical place.* We were all a little in love with her.

There were always people around, young artists and dancers, and writers like me, who had come out to Provincetown to work in Tess' cottage down in the dunes on a grant from her Foundation - the shack, she called it - and loved it, and returned to the town again and again. It was almost as if when you fell into Tess' orbit, you couldn't stay away. I saw her and her son Robert walking the dog down on the beach most days, and we'd pass the time or she'd ask me to come up to the house on Sunday for lunch.

One night last year when I bumped into Robert at a party in town, I found the courage to ask him about his mother. *'Ah',* he said, 'don't you know? Hers is a great love story. Why don't you come over to the house for dinner tomorrow and we'll show you all her papers. She has boxes and boxes of letters and cuttings. You know, someone should write a book about her.' So that's what I did.

February 2018

Prologue

Hong Kong 1939

"Elizabeth Martha Montgomery, wilt thou have this man to thy wedded husband ..."

Will I? Tess is so unused to being asked her opinion the question floors her for a moment. She daren't look at Kit's hopeful face in case he sees her uncertainty. He is so handsome, so immaculate, so *good.* She imagines, fleetingly, taking a swing at him with her bouquet of white chrysanthemums. *Mrs Christopher Blythe, Mrs Christopher Blythe,* she repeats in her mind, her gaze darting around the cool blue shadows of St John's Cathedral, hoping to find a certain answer. She knows he is there, somewhere, in the congregation. Her gut instinct is to cry 'No!', to run. She pictures herself fleeing down the aisle, escaping through the humid precinct of banyans and palms, trailing chiffon, lace, petals, the bouquet flung into the air as cockatoos and parrots cheer her on. But look at all these people. The congregation has been spread evenly across the pews like picked out seedlings, given space, to disguise the lack of people on Kit's side. *Do I have*

14

any choice? She looks for the door, her heart fluttering like a bird trapped behind glass. *I can't go through with this. It's not fair on Kit.* She sees her parents. Her father's face is unreadable as usual, he stands with the proud posture of a naval officer of the China Station. Her mother, Elizabeth the First as Tess thinks of her in secret - always Elizabeth, never Liz or Lizzy let alone Tess, is trying and failing to disguise the expression of relief and surprise she has worn permanently for the last two weeks, casting gleeful surreptitious glances back to the congregation. Elizabeth Blythe fizzes with energy, head bobbing like a canary, checking the Colony notables have arrived rather than concentrating on Tess and Kit: *is everyone here? Are they impressed? What a coup to have Sir Percy at their daughter's wedding.*

The tight lace Juliet cap of Tess' veil presses against her throbbing temples, and heat crackles along her spine like flames taking in dry grass, a bead of sweat coursing along the curve of her back. She wishes her mother hadn't insisted on such a terribly heavy silk for the dress. Lights spark in her eyes, she feels faint. *I should have eaten some breakfast, whatever mother said.* Her empty stomach tightens, nauseous again. *I can't pass out.* She forces her self to concentrate on the words the priest is intoning. *Will I? Will I?* She takes a deep breath and flinches. In her haste the seamstress has missed a pin in the armhole of the heavy silk gown. The sharp, silver tip has pricked at Tess's tender, pale underarm from the moment she left her parent's house on the Peak.

Oh god, does it matter that I'm not head over heels in love with Kit? She is, as her mother pointed out with a regularity which would shame the speaking clock, not in a position to be picky. *I can grow to love him, can't I?* His proposal came at such a good time, was such a relief. She should be happy, shouldn't she?

Tess looks down at the toes of her silk shoes peeking beneath her skirts. *At least you can't see your great big feet in that dress*, her mother conceded.

'Will you ...'

What choice is there? I have to do the right thing. Fractured moments of conversations come back to her: '*Who would have thought it? How lucky you are. Seventeen, young and in love with the most eligible bachelor in Hong Kong. What a catch Kit is'.* Tess swallows down her nausea. She would give anything for some cold water, her dry lips parting at the thought of condensation on the glass. She senses Kit, waiting for her, and her gaze meets his steady, kind blue eyes at last. *He **is** kind, isn't he? And cultured, and so handsome in his naval uniform. Everyone says how lucky I am. Everyone.* Beyond, she sees the ashen face of the best man staring at them, red eyed. *Is he hungover? He looks like he's been crying.* Tess forces herself to focus on Kit. She daren't look at the congregation. She knows he is there, watching.

'... so long as you both shall live.'

The silence seeps across the church, pooling in the shadows, waiting. Tess stares intently at the tips of her white silk shoes, and a cold shot of anxiety pumps through her, the memory of a drop of blood, staining, spreading. She blinks, willing the image away. She feels a quickening in her stomach at the finality of it, the future stretching ahead of her indefinitely like the looping track of a rollercoaster to some unseen destination.

He's a good catch for a girl like you, one of her mother's bridge partners had said to her a couple of nights before.

A girl like me?

Independent, clever. He won't hold you back.

*He **is** good, isn't he*, Tess thinks now. *Too good for me. I'm bad, and I'm broken.* When Tess imagines her insides she thinks of shattered mirrors, shards of ice. It's as if the pin in her sleeve has worked its way free from her heart, pricking her conscience. *I'm broken.*

She remembers holding a goldfish underwater in the cage of her fingers as a child, the light flick of its shimmering tail. *A good catch.* The movement in her stomach beneath the steadying palm of her hand is that light, that urgent and full of life.

It's too late, she thinks. *What choice do I have?*

The silence seems to expand, blood singing in her ears. Then Kit smiles, and winks at her. She comes back to the moment, aware of the light from the nave windows, the sounds of the city she loves beyond the pale white walls. *Will I?*

When Tess dreams of this moment over the years, she hears the scream of a mortar shell, falling. Then nothing. She knows logically that Hong Kong did not fall until December 1941, that she and her son were safely in Somerset by then. But Kit wasn't. Nor her parents. Perhaps it is simply that from the moment of her wedding Tess has had the sense of something unexploded in her life. The threat of something about to blow up.

Act 1

Tess Blythe's debut *Dance of Life* reveals the pulse, the music of our secret hearts. She expresses something that can't be put into words. Yes, her choreography is beautiful, poetic but it is unflinching. It makes us face ourselves. She raises a mirror to our love, anger, loneliness. She strikes at false idols, figures of authority - warmongers, politicians, clergy. She takes her audience from a barren dark earth stage back to the hidden forest. Trees grow and blossom from the stage floor. Her images are archetypal, timeless, but ambiguous. Are her elegant horned male dancers stags? Are they cuckolds? Is her white dressed, red shoed principal dancer a virgin bride, a mother, a whore? 'It's never stated who the burning woman is,' she said. 'I'm always searching for the universal truths that unite us as human beings. The magnetic pull of desire powers this ballet. I hope that anyone watching it feels that silent music.'

Ballet Today 1968

Chapter 1

New York, October 1961

Perhaps Tess dreamt it. Everything seemed too normal. High above Central Park, Kit Blythe took breakfast at precisely 8.00 am just as he always did in the dining room of his penthouse apartment at 1040 5th Avenue the morning after he asked his wife for a divorce.

'I've a good mind to write to the Director,' Kit went on. 'Fancy hanging Matisse's 'Le Bateau' upside down. As I said to Mr and Mrs Hoffman, if the Museum of Modern Art can't get it right, what hope does the great unwashed have?'

He shook out the fresh copy of the New York Times obscuring his face from Tess's view, and reached out his hand to take another bite of toast, morning sun gleaming on the gold signet ring on his pinky finger, his neatly manicured nails. It had always annoyed Tess that Kit had such beautiful hands, it didn't seem fair somehow that his nails should be shell perfect ovals compared to her own which stubbornly refused to grow, and always split or broke. The newspaper headline: *Powerful Saturn Rocket is Fired,* caught her eye.

'I am glad that we are being civilised about this, old girl,' he said.

Civilised? Tess thought, taking her usual seat opposite him. She longed to grab him by the collar of his Brooks Brothers shirt and shake him. She longed to weep rivers of deep black kohl tears for her marriage and bury her face against his starched white chest. There had to be something to mark the destruction of their life, surely? That she had woken to a world which seemed so normal was unbearable.

'I wouldn't want-' Kit said.

'Do you really think there will be men on the moon by the end of the decade?' she interrupted.

'Ludicrous,' Kit said, dabbing a crumb from the corner of his mouth with a heavy damask napkin. The way Kit spoke the syllables of the word made her think of glass marbles. *Why, I could listen to your husband talk all day*, she remembered one of his clients telling her breathlessly. *Such a beautiful voice.* None of them knew what life with Kit was really like. Why, only last week a friend had said to her: *You're the only woman I'd trust with my husband. You and Kit have the last good marriage in the city.*

'I'd love to go to the moon.' Tess blew the steam from her cup of hot water and lemon.

'You?' he laughed behind his paper.

Why not? she thought. 'I can do anything I

want now.'

'Don't be like that, darling.' Kit took a sip of coffee. 'Eugh,' he said. 'No sugar.' The cup rattled in its saucer. 'Then again if Kennedy's telling us all to build fallout shelters, maybe you'd be better off on your moon.'

She stood, leaving an uneaten grapefruit on her plate, and dropped two sugar cubes into Kit's cup. 'You'll have to get used to taking care of yourself, you know.' She turned to the full length windows, watching the morning sun burning through the mist over the reservoir and the park. She imagined herself floating through space, the earth and all its petty problems receding, and a sense of stillness and peace filled her.

'Besides, last I heard, Bloomingdale's don't deliver to the moon.'

'Idiot,' she said, softly. Her titian hair was loose, falling over one shoulder, her eau de nil silk kimono pooling on the floor beside her. She raised the translucent porcelain cup to her lips and blew gently again, steam blurring the sun. *He eats quietly,* she thought. *That's one thing, at least.* Kit's manners had always been immaculate compared to the husbands of some of her friends. How many times had people told her: *you are so lucky to be married to Kit. Such a gentleman, such taste.* The embodiment of the Englishman in New York.

'How did you sleep?' she said, feeling anything but lucky.

'Not bad.'

'I didn't sleep a wink.' Tess rubbed at her temple. She imagined an army of tiny people mining away at the sparkling caverns of her mind with pickaxes. 'I heard your door-'

'My jailer now, are you?'

'Kit, don't start.'

'I tried not to disturb you.'

Tess closed her eyes, forced herself to breathe slowly before answering. She knew that petulant tone well. 'Are you not sleeping well either?' She said kindly. 'It's ... it's been a shock. There are some sleeping pills in my bathroom if you-'

'Heavens sake, Tess. I just felt like a walk.' Kit turned the page. 'I won't be able to relax until the Hoffman job is done. Did I tell you Mrs Hoffman is insisting on gold dolphin taps and a Tiki print paper for the master en suite? I had hoped I'd educated her a little-'

'So you weren't even thinking about us?' Tess shook her head.

'We are going to be civilised about this, aren't we?'

'Oh, *excuse me*.' Tess' hand shook as she sat down and put the cup on its saucer. 'Of course. Hoffman. Hoffman ... The one on Park Avenue? Gold dolphin taps and Tiki print paper? Good for her.' Kit grimaced. 'Oh, it will be beautiful. All your projects are.'

'As soon as it is finished and I can think

straight, we need to make arrangements.'

'Arrangements?' Tess looked down at her hands.

'The divorce, Tess. We have to decide what to do about Bobby, about this place.'

'It was you who wanted this ridiculous mausoleum.' She swept her hand wildly, the porcelain cup falling, breaking. 'You and your damn obsession with *The Age of Innocence*.'

'Clumsy.' Kit clicked his tongue.

She glanced down at the fine shards shattered in a pool of gently steaming water on the parquet. 'It was the last one from the Hong Kong set.' It seemed fitting, somehow. Tess fought the temptation to go to the dresser and fling every last precious porcelain and bone china plate like a Frisbee across the room. She pictured Kit ducking and diving, trying to save them, and smiled to herself. 'Kit, please, can't we talk about this-' She broke off, hearing a knock at the door, and glanced over her shoulder still expecting her dog's frantic clatter of paws across the parquet floor. 'I miss him,' she said.

'Who?'

'Bingo.' She heard Bessie their maid greet someone. From the lobby the comforting sound of the vacuum and the elevator bell muffled as the front door slammed close.

'Right on cue,' Kit said, folding his paper, and smiling up at Bessie, who carried a large wicker basket to the table. Kit's lightly tanned face was freshly shaved, his golden hair still damp from the shower. *Still handsome*, Tess thought. The realisation that there would soon be a day when he was no longer the first person she saw in the morning hit her like a blow to the chest, and she inhaled sharply. Once upon a time she had carried their marriage, their family in her heart like a gift, like a precious sea smoothed stone. Its weight was sure and true. It grounded her, steady, and certain. How had she not noticed it had gone? When Kit told her he wanted a divorce, Tess felt a fathomless dark hole bloom in her heart, pulling away everything she knew, everything she loved. She looked at him now, lightheaded, shaken. 'Thank you,' Kit said, taking the basket. 'Close your eyes,' he said to Tess.

'Kit, I'm not in the mood for games,' she said, close to tears.

'Trust me,' he said softly, waiting for Bessie to leave. 'Close your eyes.' A corona of light faded into darkness behind her eyelids, and Tess listened intently. 'There you are,' Kit said, and she started in surprise at the sound of claws pawing the basket, a pitiful whimper.

'Kit, what were you thinking?' Tess imagined a bundle of white fur, a red satin ribbon. 'You didn't-'

'I know how blue you've been since Bingo died, and with Bobby at college, and, well, now ...'

'You thought I'd be lonely.' She felt the

weight of the dog in her lap, its trembling flank, the fast beat of its heart through soft fur and fine ribs. 'This is so typical. Trust you to plan something like this and make it impossible to hate you.'

'I love you, Tess, you know that.' She felt Kit stroke the line of her jaw. 'I'll always love you but-'

'But that's not enough for you, any more.'

'For either of us.'

She kept her eyes closed as she leant in to his touch, trying to compose herself, to stop the tears. 'Kit, I can't bear it. You're not just my husband, you're my best friend. How am I supposed to-'

'Please, don't. Don't cry. You'll break my heart.' Kit knelt down beside Tess, and squeezed her hand, pressed her fingers to his lips. 'We will always be friends. You're strong, Tess. You will be strong, and you will be happy again. That's all I care about. We both need this.' Tess heard him clear his throat. 'Well, are you going to look at her?' Tess' eyes shone as she blinked and looked down at the Pekingese. It gazed up at her with one clear, dark eye. The other was stitched closed, a ragged row of dark thread lashes trembling, it's fur clipped short.

'Oh, you poor thing. What did they do to you?' Tess whispered, laying her palm against the dog's side. She felt the tension in the little animal seep away at her touch like rain into dry earth. 'Look at her, Kit. Imagine still trusting people after everything she's been through.'

'Remember the state Bingo was in when you adopted him? I figured if anyone can give this little one a good life, you will. They found her tied up in a yard on Canal Street. No sign of any owner.' Kit sat back on his heels. 'What will you call her?'

Tess thought for a moment. 'Looty II, after my first Pekingese. I named her after Queen Victoria's,' she said. 'Thank you. It's kind of you to think ...' *To think of me alone.* Tess bit her lip, anxiety welling in her stomach. *I don't know how to do this. I don't know how to be alone.*

'I searched every pound in the city for a Peke, made a hundred calls ...'

'What happened to her?' she interrupted.

'They think she was attacked, or kicked. Poor old thing. They couldn't save her eye.'

She looks how I feel, Tess thought, gazing down at her. *Damaged.* The dog cowered at the sound of a key in the lock and the hall door slamming closed. 'It's ok,' Tess held her closer. 'Don't worry, no one is going to hurt you ever again.'

'Morning! What a wonderful morning,' Bobby called, tossing his grey trilby onto the hat stand. He shrugged out of his jacket and hung it on the back of his chair at the table. 'What on earth is that?' He pulled a face looking at the dog.

'Cover your ears, Looty,' Tess said. 'She's a gift from your father. You know how I've missed having a dog. Bessie,' she called to maid, 'her nose is a little dry, could you give her some water - and there's some cold chicken in the refrigerator. Oh, and could you fetch Bingo's old bed from the storeroom?' She handed the dog to her. 'Thank you.'

'Good morning,' Kit said to Bobby. 'Or good night?'

'I was worried,' Tess said, walking towards her son.

'I'm a big boy, Mom.' He put his arm around her waist and lifted her hand, swinging her round. 'I've been dancing. Surely you'd approve?'

'All night?' Kit raised an eyebrow.

'What else are Friday nights for? Come next time!' Bobby said to Tess. He swung his hips, dancing away from her. 'The twist, Mom! All the kids are going wild for it. You'd love it.'

'I'm too old to twist,' Tess said, laughing. She settled at the head of the table, opposite Kit, the folds of her kimono gleaming like a mother of pearl shell. Looking at her husband's face, as familiar as her own, she thought he looked tired, his fair hair thinning, a plum bloom circling his eyes. She glanced at Bobby. When she first met Kit, he had the same youthful energy as their son. He was playing tennis. He was tall, with a swimmer's build - broad shouldered and slim hipped. His determination, his violent, elegant game thrilled her. A visceral shot of desire coursed through her at the memory. She had decided she wanted him before a word was exchanged. *What happened?* she thought. 'I can't remember the last time we went dancing, can you?' she said. Kit went back to his paper without looking at her, and her smile faltered.

'Guess what. I asked her,' Bobby said to his mother, dragging his chair out. Tess leant over to pour him a cup of coffee. 'I asked Frankie, and she said yes.' He took two slices of toast from the silver rack, and Tess stopped pouring, mid stream.

'You're getting married?' She filled the cup, settled the coffee pot back on its stand.

'Ah, now we'll hear it,' Kit said, glancing up briefly from his paper. Only Tess sensed the alarm hidden beneath his unchanged calm expression.

'Darling, are you sure this is the right time? You're just getting settled into law school in Boston,' she said.

'I told you, didn't I, in the summer.' Bobby sat back in his chair. 'I told you the day I met Frankie that she's the girl I'm going to marry.'

'Surely there's no need to rush?' Tess said, keeping her voice light and even.

'We're in love, Mom. I want her with me, in Boston. I can't stand being away from her.'

She remembered he said that the summer he turned eleven, when he went off to camp: *I can't stand being away from you.* Then he returned from the summer with a new reserve. Before, he had hugged her freely, snuggling his lithe little body to hers. She remembered the weight of his skull against her collar bone, the clean animal pelt of his hair, cupped in her protective hand. After that summer he needed her less. Bobby's laugh brought her back to the moment.

'Darling, the timing isn't great,' she said. 'Your father-'

'Has a lot of work on.' Kit stared at her pointedly. 'Your mother and I are rather busy to organise a wedding at short notice.'

Tess felt as if the room was falling away around her. He wasn't going to tell Bobby, not now. *What am I supposed to do? Just pretend everything is normal?*

'My project is at a critical stage, and the dance school has just reopened after the summer break, so your mother hasn't got time to-' Kit went on.

'You don't need to do a thing. Frankie's Ma is going to do it all,' Bobby interrupted.

'We haven't even met the girl, or her family-' Kit began.

'They're coming over tonight to meet you.'

'Tonight?' Kit and Tess said together.

'Why wait? I thought we could all go dancing. Break the ice.'

Tess pictured the evening, with Kit his usual charming self. Bobby and his girl, shining, golden, in love. She imagined herself smiling and smiling. *Break the ice.* She imagined her frozen heart, shattering.

'Dancing?' Kit said. 'Not in whichever sleazy rock and roll club you've been hanging out in Midtown? Is that where you met this girl?'

'No, I saw her before in a café near the university.'

'She's a student?' Tess said.

'Night school. She's going to be a translator.' Tess could hear the pride in his voice. 'She just works at her mother's café during the day.' Bobby took another piece of toast, loading it with butter. 'And at the Pep, once in a while. You should see her, Mom, Frankie moves among the tables like she's dancing.' He mimed carrying the toast like a tray above his head, swinging his hips, gliding around the room.

'A waitress, Bobby?' Kit folded his arms. 'Hear that, Tess? Our son and heir is going to marry a waitress. Well, isn't this a blast. What an evening of delights we have ahead.'

'Take no notice of your father,' Tess said, cupping her chin in the palm of her hand. If Kit could pretend everything was normal, then so would she. She could carry it off. She could play her part. 'Snob,' she said to Kit.

'Hopeless romantic,' he shot back.

'You'll get it when you see her,' Bobby said, biting into his toast.

'Fine, invite them over,' Tess said. 'Nothing formal. We have ...' She looked to Kit for confirmation.

'Four.' Kit paused. 'No, I'll postpone the Hoffmans. Under the circumstances. I believe Mrs Hoffman was planning a trip out of town tomorrow anyway, to the fat farm-' He puffed up his cheeks.

'Kit, don't be so cruel,' Tess said.

'Wait a minute - circumstances?' Bobby said.

'Your father just means we want to meet Frankie and her family in private-'

'I'm not ashamed of Frankie,' Bobby said, frowning at his father. 'Just you wait 'til you meet her. You'll see.'

'That's not what we meant.' Tess took his hand. 'I'm happy for you, darling. Really I am.' She glanced at Kit. 'Your life's just beginning.'

Chapter 2

Tess stands on the pavement of East 61st in front of Kit's building, traffic and people swirling around her. She stares at the red lacquer box in the window of the antique store. It seems she thinks more often of Hong Kong these days. Even after all these years in America, she carries the East in her like a melody - a misty light, a fetid incense heavy fragrance which coils through her dreams, still. Her mother had a collection of lacquer boxes, just like this one. It conjures a lost time for Tess now. A certain world of polished teak floors, and white plaster walls, of looping fans and green palms beyond the shutters. Blood red hibiscus and the scent of frangipani. The bustle of the Kowloon Ferry pier at the end of Ice House Street and the lap of star speckled dark harbour water on the ferry's sides. The scent of citronella on a summer night. Lavender mountains. Kit.

We were happy once, weren't we? Tess' focus returns to her own polished reflection in the plate glass window. She realises then that nothing has felt certain for years. She has been living in a floating world, and now she is utterly adrift, the last anchor, Kit, cut free. She had been walking aimlessly after the cinema, not wanting to go home to the apartment, and found herself outside Kit's office building. It is an unspoken rule that Tess does not come in to his workplace. The building is full of antiques stores and designers. It is Kit's domain. It has always been uncomfortable for him when home and work collide, but she had hoped to bump into him, to have a chance to talk before tonight. *I can't bear it. The only person I want to talk to about this is the one who has broken my heart.*

Tess hears the muffled sound of several clocks chiming in the building. It is nearly time for her class and she must focus. *I can do this,* she repeats in her mind, walking away. *I can. I can.* On the opposite side of the street she sees the slender figure of a young woman, the hem of her dark coat swinging wide from her hand span waist as she hails a cab. Tess smiles, recognising her. She can spot one of her girls at fifty paces - there is a cool poise to the alumnae of the Blythe Dance Academy, something about the elegance of their carriage which sets them apart from the sweating, hunch shouldered commuters thronging the afternoon streets. On the pavement by the lights - *Walk, Don't Walk* - she sees the girl raise her arm again in a graceful arc. She imagines an orchestral score swelling, the crowds parting to leave the girl dancing alone in the street. *Grade*

Five, with distinction, she thinks. *A natural.* The yellow cab pulls over, extinguishes its light. A man in a black fedora waiting for the crossing opens the cab door for the girl, tips the brim of his hat.

Tess smiles, satisfied, and strides along the autumn sunlit sidewalk like she carries a melody in her. *I can do this ... I will make my own way. My own life.* The initial shock of Kit's announcement has subsided and Tess feels a sense of determination rising up in her. Her metal heeled stilettos crack like sparks, like pistols. Her pillbox hat, white gloves and coat are like armour. She is at home in this world of steel and glass, familiar with its bright lights, its steam blurred edges. There are road works at the lights on 2nd Avenue, a construction worker leaning against his pickaxe, hard hat tipped back on his brow. Tess notices him notice her, and narrows her eyes, staring ahead.

'Cheer up, sweetheart,' he calls to her.

'Idiot,' she says under her breath. *Not now. Please, not now.*

'Hey, Red. Yeah, you.' He rolls the toothpick he is chewing to the other side of his mouth. Tess closes her eyes, imagines him choking on it. 'C'mon sweetie. You lose something? Cheer up - how about a smile?'

'Cheer up?' She says, calmly. The vertebrae in her neck pop as she raises her chin, cricks her head to the side. The man stops chewing, his eyes widen in alarm. 'Cheer up?'

'Hey, sweetie. Didn't mean nothing by it,' he says, raising his palm in defence.

'Has it ever occurred to you I might have lost something important? Something vital, in fact.' She raises her voice over the traffic, walking slowly towards him, her skirt swinging. 'What have I lost, you say? How about this?' Tess puts her hands on her hips. 'Say you meet someone. Say you build a life-'

'Woah ...' the man says, backing away.

'Say they have - oh - countless discreet affairs.' She stands close to him, her eyes shining. 'And you ask what's lost? You see, you put up with it because you made a promise. You made a vow. But every time something is lost. You lose your spark. You lose your hope. You lose a little piece of yourself every single day. You lose a whole life without realising. Because it happens day by day, little tiny spark by spark you don't see the light in yourself going out.' She raises her hands, fingertips miming small firecrackers. 'And yet you keep on day after day after day for the sake of your child, for your family - you do your best for husband and make yourself beautiful, and stay thin, and desirable, even though-' Tess pauses. 'And then, when they ask for a divorce - as my dear husband did only last night - one day you wake up and realise there is nothing left of yourself.' Her hands fall, fingers snaking like smoke. 'Pouf.' The man can't look at her. 'So I say to you next time you feel the urge to tell some poor girl to *cheer up, sweetheart, watcha lost?*' she says, her eyes blazing, 'why don't you keep it to yourself because maybe, just maybe she has lost the most important thing in the world. Herself.'

□

Tess unlocks the studio door in the alleyway at the back of the old brownstone on East 79th, and flicks on the strip lights. The air is still and dusty, warm with the taste of summer for now. She knows the days will come soon when it is dark outside and the skylights are blocked with snow, when the old radiators belch and gurgle heat into the room. Tess shivers at the thought of another New York winter as she winds the heavy coil of her auburn hair into a bun and pins it firmly down, bobby pins scratching at her scalp. She pauses, arms raised. *Everything's changed*, she realises. *Perhaps I won't even be here next winter.*

Her stomach freefalls, anxious. *I can do this,* she tells herself. *I can.* She checks the fine gold watch on her wrist. *Is that the time? The girls will be here soon*. Tess hurries to the dressing room. Tess tries to distract herself from the coiling, panicked thoughts racing repeatedly through her mind like the loop of a Mobius strip by humming *Moon River* as she eases her narrow feet into the foot of her pale tights. She wriggles into them, smoothing the fabric over the hard bone of her ankles and knees, the long firm

37

muscles of her calves and thighs. The leotard is freshly laundered. Tess thinks of the warmth of Bessie's workroom as she pulls it taught over her hips, her arms, pictures the door swinging open to the light, white tiled room at the heart of their apartment, the comforting loop of the drier, the scent of clean linen. *All that will be gone, soon.* Tess imagines herself walking away down a dark, rain-soaked Fifth Avenue, a small suitcase in one hand, Looty in the other.

Where will we go? Tess adjusts the shoulder strap, and checks her reflection. *I can go anywhere. Paris. Rome ...* She looks the same as ever but she feels as fragile as the last of the Chinese porcelain cups she drank her lemon and hot water from every morning. Translucent. Broken. *Home,* she thinks. *I just want to go home.* Her face crumples, and she presses one fist against her eyes, steadying herself against the mirror with her other hand. *I don't even know where that is, now.* She takes a deep, shuddering breath and cups her face in her palms. *Stop it. Pull yourself together. You can't let the girls see you like this.* She wipes a smudge of mascara from beneath her eye, and focuses on the silver print her palm has left on the glass, watching it fade. *That's it. That's how I feel. Everything I know, everything I love is ... it's going.* Tess fastens a slip of chiffon skirt at her waist, and reaches for her shoes. Several pairs are stacked in her locker - supple ballet pumps, and pointe shoes, black and pink.

How many days, weeks, months has she done that - put on her dancing shoes ready for class? There would be a last time, soon. A wave of uncertainty sweeps over her again. *The apartment will have to go, the school. Everything will have to change.* Tess hesitates, reaches to the back of the locker and takes out one red satin pointe shoe. The fabric is cool and smooth to touch, the ribbon snaking from the shadows, a provocation. A temptation. *Dare*, the ribbons whisper. She thinks of a favourite red silk cheongsam left over from the Hong Kong days which Kit deemed 'too much'. She kept it in defiance. Tess wears it sometimes when she is alone, imagining other lives. *That's what I have to do. Make a new life.* Tess remembers the thrill of the silk on her skin. *Now I'll wear it whenever I want.* She re-imagines her exit, pictures herself striding through the grey teeming crowds on Fifth Avenue, a scarlet exclamation.

The sound of the street drifts through to her, the door slamming as the first pupils arrive for the afternoon class. She hears Gladys warming up at the piano, scales and chords echoing through the studio. Tess tucks the shoe away and picks out a sensible pair of black flats, flexing the leather, hurriedly knotting the ribbons against the side of her Achilles tendon and tucking the ends in. *I can do this.* She is ready.

The girls, ten, eleven years old, skip and

run in to the class from the changing room, chattering. A few of the mothers fuss around them like hens, fingers pecking away loose hairs, twisted elastic. Tess notices a short plump girl with heavy tortoiseshell glasses standing alone, arms stiff, head tucked in. She can see from the tremor of her shoulders she is trying not to cry. Her gaze travels across the room. A group of three girls stand together in the corner casting glances like poison darts towards the girl. Tess' eyes narrow and she claps her hands sharply.

'Patsy, Betty and Matilda, begin warming up-'

A mother interrupts her. 'Mrs Blythe, may I have a word about putting Betty up a class-' The woman's light wool suit reminds Tess of the cloying taste of sugared almonds.

'After the session, Mrs Dean,' she says, not slowing her pace across the studio. 'Now,' she says gently, dropping to one knee in front of the lone girl. 'Let's sort these ribbons out, shall we, Hazel?' She glances up. The girl's face is red with hot, humiliated tears. 'Want to tell me about it?' The girl presses her lips together, shakes her head. Tess sees she is watching the three girls at the back of the class. 'Not there,' she calls. 'Betty, Patsy, Tilda, at the front of the class please.' Tess releases the ribbons around the girl's ankles and ties them again. 'Now,' she says softly. 'Have you heard the story of the Ugly Duckling, Hazel?'

'Yes, Mrs Blythe,' she says, blinking.

'Well, dear, I was that Ugly Duckling. When I was - oh - nine or ten, around your age, I had buck teeth, and a patch on my lazy eye, and these great long feet.' She flaps her hands like flippers, and Hazel laughs.

'You, Mrs Blythe? But you're beautiful. I don't believe it.'

'It's true,' she says, retying the ribbons and tucking in the ends. 'And in my experience some girls can be incredibly cruel.' She pauses. 'Do you want to know the secret I learnt?'

'Yes. Yes, please.'

'People who are mean, people who bully, they feel horrible inside. They pick on other people because they hate themselves so much. Isn't that sad?' She sat back on her heels. 'We should feel sorry for them. Stand up to them - firmly and kindly, never sink to their level - and believe in yourself, my dear. One day you will be a swan.'

'A swan?' the girl says, standing taller.

'If you keep your chin up, and look the world in the eye, you'll do your best, why, you'll fly. While they will still be flapping around, quacking away like the silly ducks they are.' She tilts her head and returns Hazel's smile. 'There, that's better.' She leads her to the back of the class, staring down the three girls. 'Now, you settle yourself here,' she says. 'That way no one is looking at you, no one is being unkind. You can just take your time until you feel confident.' The girl looks up at her.

'Thank you, Mrs Blythe.'

'My, what beautiful golden eyes you have. I can see why your mother called you Hazel.' She gently adjusts the girls' posture. 'Shoulders back, chin up,' she says. 'Imagine there is an invisible gold cord pulling your head, your spine up, up, up.' She backs away through the line of girls to the front of the class and signals to the pianist. 'Gladys, let's begin.'

☐

Gladys packs up her sheet music in a supple old leather case and slips it over her arm with her crocodile handbag. 'You hungry, Tessie?'

'Darling, I've been hungry for the last thirty years.' She shakes out her hair and eases the tension in her narrow shoulders. 'You go on without me. I'll lock up here.' Tess stands on tiptoe and looks out of the side window at the sound of laughter, women's voices. 'Besides, Betty's mother is still waiting to pounce on me in the alleyway. Go on, off you go,' she says under her breath watching the women leave. Gladys slides a silver hipflask from her handbag, and waves it in the air, a question. 'Scotch? You angel.' Tess takes a sip, and closes her eyes gratefully. 'Thank you. It's been a hell of a day.'

'The summer feels like a distant memory already, doesn't it?'

'It's crazy, Glad. Why do we work all

year to feel like ourselves for one month only?' Tess' heart fills with longing. She thinks of cool dawns, sea mist, sand on bare boards, salt tasting skin. She could just jump in the car now and be at her beach cottage in Provincetown in five hours. She pictures herself, driving out across the Sagamore Bridge, top down, breathing in the briny air, the scent of crushed pine needles. Her stomach rumbles at the thought of a plate of fried clams from her favourite roadside shack.

'You are funny. It's best not to think about it, we've all got to work. Day by day's the only way. Say, how did you enjoy the movie?' Gladys takes a long draft from the hipflask, and leans back against the piano.

'Oh,' Tess sighs. She picks up a discarded ballet wrap from the studio floor and sweeps her clasped hands to her breast, turning a slow pirouette. 'You must see *Breakfast At Tiffany's*, Gladys. It's ...' She frowns, thinking how she had sat alone in the cinema with tears coursing down her cheeks that afternoon. 'It's quite lovely. Audrey Hepburn looks divine.'

'Where's it showing?'

'Radio City.' Tess folds the small pink cardigan and places it on a chair.

'I'll go tonight.' Gladys clicks open her handbag and tosses the hipflask in. She takes out a gold tube of lipstick. 'Want to see it again?'

'I'd love to, but we have guests.'

'Spoilsport.' She puckers her lips. 'Can't

tempt you with supper, can't tempt you with a movie. Anyone fun coming over?'

Tess takes a deep breath. 'Tonight we are meeting Bobby's fiancée.' *The irony,* she thinks. *Typical Kit.*

'Fiancée?' Gladys turns to her, wide eyed, her lipstick poised.

'Apparently.'

'Since when?'

'Since our son and heir decided he can't bear to be at college without her.' Tess bites her lip. 'They're too young. Why he can't wait until he finishes law school, I don't know.' She pauses. 'Well, I do know. But what do I have to do with it? I'm just his mother.'

'Kids these days don't want to wait,' Gladys clicks her bag closed. 'I keep forgetting you're old enough to have a kid at college.'

'Bless you. I'll be forty soon enough.'

'You sure don't look it.' Gladys tilts her head. 'But you do look a little blue. Sure I can't help?'

Tess hesitates. She longs to tell someone, anyone, how Kit had calmly told her their marriage was over. They were dining alone in the Rainbow Room. *Perhaps he was afraid I'd make a scene? That's why he told me in a restaurant rather than at home. Kit had talked about his day, about a painting he had bought at auction. And then he just came out with it,* she imagines telling Gladys. '*I want a divorce'. I think I laughed. I thought he was joking. You know his sense of humour. I was just so shocked. It's normal, isn't it, to laugh when you're shocked?* Instead she takes Gladys' outstretched hand and gives it a squeeze. 'I'll be fine. Go on, run along. You'll catch the movie if you go now.'

'Breakfast as usual with the girls tomorrow?'

'See you at the diner.'

□

Once she is alone, Tess puts on a favourite single, Ray Charles' *The Right Time*. She runs her hands through her hair, and rolls her head, easing the tension from her shoulders, eyes closed. Her hair is silk soft. Kit doesn't like her to back comb her hair like the fashions, to spray it into submission. He likes her to wear it in a simple, elegant bun or chignon. It is their one enduring intimacy. Each night he brushes her hair for her. One hundred strokes. No more, no less. *Brushed,* she thinks, trying it out. *My husband- My ex-husband used to brush my hair every night.*

Tess lays her left palm against her breastbone, extends the other arm and begins to move as though she is dancing with a partner, slow, sinuous, letting the music move her. The rhythm rises in her, the familiar urge to dance like an answering pulse. She loses herself in the melody for a time, and closes her eyes. *I can do this.* For the first time, she feels a sense of relief. *It's over*. The pretence is over. She knows in her heart that Kit is right. The memories of the years flicker in her mind. The arguments. The silences. *Keeping up appearances*, she thinks, and her arm falls when she realises the time. Thinking of her conversation that morning with Kit and Bobby, she slides to the floor beside the record player with the careless liquid grace of a silk scarf falling, and lays her head against the speaker. She does not feel like playing the good wife, the good mother tonight. She wants to feel the music resonate through her. *My life*, she thinks, *is all treble and no bass.* She turns up the volume. The music surges through the still evening air of the studio, her fingers extending, arcing across the warm wood floor. The notes are deep, rich. She longs for her heart to pulse like this, the music inside her rising. She longs to be touched. *To feel alive.*

Chapter 3

Tess knocks on Kit's study door. 'The doorman rang, they're here.' When he doesn't answer, she steps forward, Looty following at her heels. 'Kit, it's time to go,' she says, easing the heavy wooden door open. It swings with some resistance against the thick gold pile of the carpet in the study, the fire in the marble hearth guttering in the breeze. Shadows dance around the Prussian blue walls, firelight warming the gilded frames of etchings of Somerset. Kit sits at the mahogany desk, a fine paintbrush in hand. A black shaded table lamp with an antique Doric column base spills light across a mood board. The inside of the shade has been hand finished with gold leaf. The effect is luminous, sepulchral. It is a signature touch in all of Kit's design schemes. He looks up at Tess and removes his tortoiseshell half moon glasses, laying them down on a copy of *The Captive*. He cradles a turquoise blue egg in his palm, dabbing a final touch of paint with a fine haired brush before placing it carefully on a stand.

'What do you think?' he says.

'It looks perfect,' she says, peering closer. Kit has sealed the ends of the blown egg and matched the colour exactly.

'Rather like our marriage, wouldn't you say, old girl?' He laughs sadly and wipes the brush, sliding it back into the canvas roll at his side.

'Please, it's not funny.' Tess passes the palm of her hand across her face. She thinks of a young couple she saw in the park that day when she was out walking Looty. She had seen the man several times before, imagined he lived nearby. He was a tall, dark, blank canvas for her desires. There had been others, nameless strangers who recognised something in one another. Whose gaze said: *would you? another time, another place, would you? Mirror, mirror, do you see me?* He was just her current favourite. But today he walked with a young girl, two or three years old, riding high on his shoulders, and a woman, clearly his wife from her arm in his. Sunlight filtered down on them like a blessing through gold shimmering leaves. Tess walked by unnoticed - no habitual glance: *I'm a woman, you're a man.* Today he only gazed at his wife. *Just as it should be*, she thought. Tess would not return his look next time they passed. It was no use to her when she knew the back story. She wanted romance, a secret daydream, not the reality. She envied the young couple, sensed the raw, missing thing at the heart of her own marriage.

'We *are* friends, aren't we, at least?' she says. 'We've always been that, and you've been a wonderful father to Bobby.' She realises she is already thinking of her marriage in the past tense. She feels dizzy, like the world is lurching and swaying, a rocket loosing from its moorings. She looks at the rows of birds' eggs in the immaculate mahogany display cases around Kit's study. *Which one was it?* It gives her a quiet thrill to know that somewhere among the perfect blown eggs is the one she caught Bobby playing with when he was a child. Bessie had startled him, and he had dropped it, cracking one side. Tess had simply replaced it, hiding the broken part. It was their secret. *No one would ever know, to look at them.* She picks up a blue lacquer box from Kit's desk.

'I saw a little pillow box in a store today. Do you remember, mother used to collect them.'

'Do I remember? I sold most of them to her.' He pauses. 'Life's funny isn't it? If I hadn't bumped into you that day on Hollywood Road, Bobby wouldn't even be here.'

Tess remembers. She was standing at the bottom of one of the steep flights of steps which led up to the narrow road of antiques stores in Hong Kong. The fetid smell of fish, drains, incense, noodles frying had made her nauseous and she was gripping the iron railing trying desperately not to be sick. Someone had placed a tiny statue there beside the steps, a makeshift altar, with pink incense smoking into the grimy evening air like the stamens of an exotic lily. She was clutching a paper bag of herbs in one hand.

'Tess?' Kit had said. 'Tess?' He had touched her arm, and she spun round in surprise. Kit shifted a heavy parcel wrapped in an old copy of the China Mail into his other arm, and led her towards the road. Tess tried hard not to cry at his kindness, forced herself to focus on the parcel: *Brink of War,* the headline said. She longed to throw herself into his arms, to bury her face in the reassuring crisp linen of his jacket. They paused to let the people crowding into the Man Mo temple push through the gates. She thought of the red lacquer walls, the coiling incense hanging from the rafters, the beady eyed gods, and pressed her handkerchief to her lips, fighting her nausea.

'What on earth are you doing over here?'

'I've been riding the ferries all afternoon,' she said. 'Mother's just been going on and on. I had to get out of the house. I just can't think straight. Kit, I don't know what to do?' Tears welled in her eyes.

'Come on,' Kit said, pushing a path through the teeming crowds for her. 'You look ghastly. Let's get you a glass of cold water. What on earth are you doing all the way over here by yourself?' He glanced down at the crumpled bag in her hand. 'Medicine? Are you unwell?'

'It's ... it's dong quai. And other things. I

don't know. I-' As she coloured and began to sob, Kit put his arm around her.

'What is it old girl? How can I help?'

'Have you seen them?' Kit says now. 'What are they like?' He swings his jacket from the back of his chair, and shrugs it on. She cannot remember the last time Kit took her in his arms, let alone comforted her.

'Not yet.' Tess blinks.

'You look beautiful,' he says, stepping back to check her dove grey taffeta dress.

'I can't do this, Kit. I can't pretend everything is-'

'Yes, you can. We can.' He looks at her, eye to eye. 'It will be fine. We really can't ruin Bobby's wedding with our news.'

'But-'

'Take off the necklace.'

'Too much?' Kit nods and unclips the heavy rope of pearls for her.

'Really? Jackie Kennedy said pearls are always appropriate.' She goes to follow him, and pauses, checking her reflection in the mirror above the mantelpiece, running her fingertips uncertainly along the naked plane of her collarbone. She has the unsettling feeling that she has got it wrong again, somehow. 'Kit-'

'Now now, Tess.' She waits for him to say it. 'There'll be time for us after the wedding.'

'This divorce-'

'Tess, not now.'

'Then when?' Her voice breaks. 'You can't just throw something like this at me, and then expect me to pretend everything is ok.'

'We have to think of Bobby. How would it look?'

'Who gives a damn what people think,' Tess said. 'I'm right aren't I? Is there someone else?'

'Yes.'

'Oh god.' Tess' legs weaken, she clutches at the back of the chair for support.

'Why do you always do this? Why ask me these things if you don't want to hear the answer? I've never lied to you, Tess.'

'Thanks. Very big of you.'

'Do you really want a fight now? Just as they are arriving? God, your sense of timing.'

'I just want to know the truth, Kit.'

'Truth?' He breathes a laugh, a short dismissal, and walks past her.

Tess touches his arm. 'Does she know about you ... about your-'

He hesitates. 'It's not a problem.' The words *with her* hang unspoken in the air.

'I suppose she has money.' Tess laughs, tears pricking her eyes. 'God knows she must have, you've spent all mine.'

'I was unlucky, that's all.'

'All those schemes, all those dreams-' Tess shakes her head.

'God knows I did everything for you, and for Bobby.'

'I know you did.' Tess exhales and lets her head fall to his shoulder. 'I know.'

'I tried and tried to give you the kind of life you were used to.' Kit turns to her, holding the door closed, speaking softly. 'It was just bad luck. We had an agreement - I kept my side of the deal. I have done the decent thing and stood by you-'

'Decent?' Tess steps back as if she has been struck. 'Oh, bravo, Kit. I had no idea that life with me and Bobby had been such hardship-'

'I adore you both, you know that. But Bobby has left home and after all I have done for you both, I deserve to think of myself now, to look forward to a comfortable future.'

Tess longs to cry out: *what about me? Bobby's gone, you've gone, where do I go now?* 'And she'll give you that? No strings?'

'She's older-'

'Of course she is. What will you be? A companion? That'll suit you perfectly.' Tess runs her thumb across her lip. 'Did you ever love me? I remember standing there in St John's and my gut instinct was to run. Do you know that?' She snatches up the pearls, defiantly clips them back on. 'The irony. I thought I was trapping you, that you deserved better.'

'We deserved,' he says carefully, 'one another.'

'Thing is, Kit, I grew to love you. I love you, and Bobby, and our life, and now it's all blown to pieces. You've broken my heart-' *It's true*, she realises. It's a physical sensation. She is wounded, and grieving. *Does he even care?* She scoops the dog into her arms. 'You *don't* care, do you? You want me to go through this - this *farce*, so we can throw a big party and suck up to all the great and the good so they carry on paying you thousands of bucks to redo their cottages in the Hamptons and their apartments on Park Lane? You want me to play happy families then give you a quiet divorce when it suits you?' Tess raises her chin. 'I won't do it.'

'Yes you will.'

'Why should I? Why should I pretend?'

'For Bobby.' Kit stares at her, and Tess hangs her head. 'We will both pretend for a little longer. Then, when the happy couple are settled in Boston we will separate amicably-'

'Amicably?' Tess' jaw flexes. 'Sure.'

'I want to be happy.' He tucks a strand of Tess' hair behind her ear. 'Is that too much to ask?'

'Maybe the most important things in life aren't always about making yourself happy. Ever think of that, Kit?'

'Oh, the sacrifices of St Tess of the Upper East Side-' he murmurs.

'Mom? Dad?' she hears Bobby, calling from the lobby. 'They're here.'

'I did, I sacrificed everything for you,' Tess says, lowering her voice.

'We both got what we needed out of this. Now Bobby is marrying, my duty is done.'

'Is that all I was? A duty?' Her cheeks flush.

'One only loves that which one does not entirely possess,' he says, and she frowns. He gestures at the book. 'Proust.'

'Proust can go to hell. You never possessed me-'

'Perhaps not.' Kit interrupts, cutting the conversation short. He swings open the door of the study with a flourish. 'Ah, there he is, our son and heir,' he says striding down the corridor towards Bobby. 'Let's meet this waitress, shall we? Are you sure? It's not too late. You could have done so much better for yourself.' Kit looks across at his son. 'I was hoping you'd go home for a spell after college, find a suitable girl ...'

Home, Tess thinks, following Kit through to the lobby. How is it that people like them who hadn't set foot in Britain for years, who had grown up in Asia, or Africa, or Australia still called it home.

'Dad, there's something I haven't told you,' Bobby says, leaning in to him.

'Let me guess. She's pregnant?' Kit says.

'Lower your voice,' Tess whispers. 'They'll hear you.'

'She is certainly not.'

'Then what's the hurry, with the wedding?'

Kit buttons his jacket, and they stand side by side in the lobby, waiting. 'A spring wedding would be charming. Who gets married in November?'

'Her uncle is going back to Italy soon, and as the head of the family Frankie wants him to give her away. That's all.'

'So we're rushing all the preparations just to accommodate some peasant?'

Tess flinches watching the lift ascending, lights illuminating. *A suitable girl.* She knew what Kit meant by that. Breeding. Money. *Just like me.* Her heart surged with defiant maternal love. *Good for Bobby. Good for them. May they live happily ever after and to hell with Kit's snobbery.*

The lift bell pings. She composes herself. She won't spoil Bobby's moment. She wipes quickly at the corners of her eyes, and raises her chin. *I can do this*, she tells herself, glancing at the profiles of her son and husband, one dark, one fair. She breathes deeply, centring herself as she used to before going on stage. The heavy gold doors slide open. *The perfect wife. The perfect mother.*

Chapter 4

'Welcome! Welcome!' Bobby said, embracing Claudia and Francesca, clapping Marco's hand in his. Tess noticed a flicker of uncertainty on her son's face, but he soon covered it. 'Mom, Dad, this is Frankie, Francesca,' he said, ushering forward a slender olive skinned girl, whose glossy black hair was swept simply back from her clear brow into a loose bun.

'What a beauty!' Kit said, kissing her hand.

'How do you do, Mr Blythe, Mrs Blythe,' she said, shaking Tess' hand. Tess held her gaze for a moment, felt the girl's calm, her self-assurance. She could tell from her posture she had danced as a child. *Good. You'll be fine*, she thought. *I was worried that Bobby had picked someone decorative but weak.* The girl was more than a match for him, she could tell. 'May I introduce my mother, Claudia, and my uncle Marco.'

Claudia sashayed towards Tess and Kit, a sumptuous mink stole framing the low neck of her black sheath gown. Her dark hair had been backcombed into an elegant Jackie Kennedy style. There was a generosity to her Tess loved immediately. *The woman has the looks of Sophia Loren and the energy of a panther.* Tess smiled to herself, picturing Claudia draped along the branches of a tree like Bagheera.

'Welcome,' Kit said, stooping to kiss Claudia's hand.

'Such manners!' she said, 'That accent!' Tess noticed Frankie blush. *She's embarrassed by her mother.* At first she was so focussed on Claudia, Tess didn't register Mr Affini. Marco stepped into the lobby just before the golden doors closed behind him like the panels of an altarpiece. His fine wool suit was so dark it seems to absorb the light. It made her think of charcoal, ashes.

'Buongiorno,' he said, acknowledging Kit, and offering his hand. 'I am Marco Affini.'

Marco, she thought. *Marco*. His profile reminded her of the illustrations in the Myths and Legends storybook she loved as a child. The grey black waves of his hair defied his pomade, curling loose above his high brow, his broken aquiline nose a dangerous punctuation to his full lips. *Broken and all the more beautiful for it.* She remembered tracing the silhouette of the illustration in her book with the tip of her index finger as she sat beneath the tent of her bed sheet, reading by torchlight. She remembered the visceral, melting pleasure it gave her. Now, looking at Marco, she felt it again. There was a slight stoop to his shoulders, a weariness, as if he had fought many battles on the way home.

'Kit Blythe,' he said, firmly shaking Marco's hand. 'How do you do.'

'May I take your hat and coat, sir?' Bessie said, laying them carefully across her arm with Claudia's mink.

'*Grazie*,' Marco said. Tess noticed the effect he had on Bessie, a flush to her cheeks.

'May I introduce my wife, Elizabeth,' Kit said, the light pressure of his hand on the curve of her hip calling Tess' attention back.

'Tess,' she said, looking up at Marco's clear dark eyes. It was a shock. A recognition. *You, she thought. You.* Something broke free in her like birds taking flight from a frozen lake. She was startled, pulse quickened. He noticed something in her. Tess was normally good at reading people, at sensing their feelings but she felt uncertain. Was that slight smile friendly, or not? His guard was up. The hubbub of voices echoing in the marble hall receded. In that moment it was as if they were alone. She was not a wife, not a mother, she was herself, stripped bare. 'How do you do.' Her hand in his made her think of something resting sure and warm underground. The urge to not let go was unbearable. She imagined stage lights falling dark around them, a spotlight on their faces. A melody - something plaintive - clarinet or oboe, and she turns a slow pirouette into his arms, her back against his stomach, his arm encircling her.

'And who do we have here?' Marco said, lowering his gaze.

'This is Looty II,' Tess said. 'Be careful, she was a little snappy earlier with the delivery guy, she's still settling in.'

'Aren't we all,' Marco said.

'Say, Marco, did you see the Cassius Clay fight on the television?' Bobby said, clapping him on the back.

'I hear Mitoff had a technical knockout in the sixth round?' Kit cut in.

'What do you know about boxing, Dad?' Bobby laughed. He mimed punching. 'Marco was a fighter, weren't you, Marco? A real fighter.'

'I won a few, lost a few.' He shrugged. Tess' eyes narrowed, though she still smiled. *Bobby is trying too hard*, she thought, looking from Marco to her son. *He doesn't like him,* she realised. *Marco doesn't approve.* She felt her heart swell for her son, protective and fierce.

Tess' hand went to the nape of her neck, her fingers touched the smooth pearls. 'Please, do come in,' she gestured towards the drawing room. 'Have you travelled far?' she said to Claudia.

'Nah, Queens,' Claudia said. 'Howard Beach.' Kit's expression behind Claudia's back reminded Tess of her old Persian cat when it had a fur ball lodged in its throat. She tried not to laugh.

'What a room!' Claudia said, walking

ahead, hips swinging like a pendulum. 'What views.' The sun was setting over Central Park, gilding the treetops, the sound of songbirds above the traffic on the street below. A warm breeze lifted the fine hairs on Tess' bare arms. She felt the restless weight of his presence just behind her as they all took in the view. *Marco.* She glanced over her shoulder. He was standing back from the group, his feet planted firmly, one hand hooked by its thumb in his pocket. With the other, he rubbed his thumb nail slowly against the index finger as if he were sharpening a knife. He was taller than Bobby, the same height as Kit, but broader, more muscular. Tess looked from one man to the other, on edge, worried how this was going to go for Bobby.

'This calls for champagne, I think,' Kit said, striding towards the bar. He nodded at Bessie, and she disappeared into the kitchen to fetch the canapés. Kit took a bottle of Krug from the ice bucket and wrapped a spotless linen cloth around it, easing out the cork.

'Allow me,' Bobby said, passing a glass to each of the women.

'Just a soda water, please,' Marco said.

'Of course.' Kit took a heavy tumbler from the bar shelf, and filled it from the soda siphon. 'What line are you in, Marco?' Kit asked, inspecting a bottle from the fridge.

'I make shoes,' Marco said. 'These days, not so much fighting.'

'How delightful.' Kit gestured at his own handmade shoes. 'I get all mine from Lobb. In London.'

'Of course you do. They are ...' Marco frowned, searching for the expression.

'You've got to excuse my uncle,' Frankie said, leaning towards Tess and Kit. 'His English isn't that great.'

'Neither is your Italian,' Marco growled, narrowing his eyes at her. He smiled slowly and glanced at Tess. She felt the hair rise on the nape of her neck. 'Classic, that is the word.'

'Where is your family from, Mr Affini?' she said.

'Marco, please.' His voice made her think of molasses, smooth, dark. 'We are from Florence.' Tess looked as though she was listening when Frankie cut in, chattering excitedly about the neighbourhood her parents grew up in, the family, but in her mind she drifted away picturing streets of stone and shadow, the Piazza del Duomo. She imagined young couples dancing together in the darkness, strings of white lights beneath the cathedral, and Marco walking towards her, his hand outstretched.

'Tess,' Kit said. 'Tess?' She blinked. 'I was just saying, we've been talking about doing a Grand Tour for years, haven't we?' He handed her a crystal coupe of champagne. 'That's the problem when you spend so long travelling as an expat, you miss all the normal European destinations.'

'There is nothing normal about Florence,' Marco said to Tess. She realised he had been watching her, and she felt the heat bloom in her cheeks. He gestured at the record player. 'You enjoy Italian opera, I see?' He picked up the copy of La Bohème. 'I like this recording very much.'

'Tess is the opera buff,' Kit said. 'Afraid I find it mawkish, all that-'

'Emotion?' Tess said, raising an eyebrow. 'Just for that,' she said, taking the record from Marco, and slipping it onto the turntable.

'Oh, me too,' Claudia said as the music swelled around them. 'It just goes on and on, weeping and wailing.'

'So,' Kit said, raising his glass. 'A toast. To Bobby and Frankie. Yum seng, as we always say-' He hesitated when Marco did not raise his glass in turn.

'Yum seng?' Claudia said.

'It's an old Chinese toast,' Tess said, chinking her glass. 'Bottoms up.'

'Uncle,' Frankie said under her breath. 'You promised.'

'Is there something wrong?' Kit said, turning the music down. Tess placed her glass on the cool marble bar, untouched, trying to gauge Claudia's body language. Marco had leant his head down and Claudia was whispering in Italian. She was angry about something.

'I'm so sorry,' Frankie said, taking Bobby's

hand. Tess knew her son's expression. She remembered an incident at school when he had stumbled running across the playground at the end of the day towards her, and a larger boy had laughed at him. Instead of crying in humiliation, Bobby had barrelled into the boy, raining punch after punch at him. Tess had to pull him away.

'Frankie,' Tess said. 'Bobby tells us you are studying at night school? That must be-'

'This marriage is too soon.' Marco interrupted, folding his arms. 'They are too young. I have to ask you,' he said, pointing at Kit, 'how do we know your Bobby is not just marrying Frankie for the money?'

'I beg your pardon.' Tess noticed Kit's unchanged poker face but she could tell from the high spots of colour on his cheeks he was livid.

'A - how you say - golddigger.'

'How dare you-' Kit said calmly. He placed his glass on the lacquer table at his side with precision, aligning the circumference of the base with the angle of the gilded line. He looked at the glass and moved it a fraction, the tendon in his neck flexing. 'Our son is a fine man, who comes from a good family-'

'A good pedigree, perhaps, but not a good bank balance,' Marco said.

'Say, I told you that in confidence.' Bobby turned to him. 'Besides, I told you, I'm going to take care of Frankie. I am! I'm going to be the best damn lawyer in the city-' Tess wondered if he was going to thump Marco. 'Write a pre-nup if you want. I don't want a damn cent of Frankie's money.'

'Forgive my husband's brother,' Claudia said, laying a hand on Marco's arm. 'Roberto is a good boy, Marco.'

Roberto? Tess thought. She wondered at this life of her son's, this family where she did not belong. Once her life and her son's were so intimately entwined there was no air between them. She was all he wanted, all he needed. She could still remember the weight of him on her hip as a baby, how he slept curled like a shell on her stomach. She remembered freckles and scarred knees, and cutting tiny perfect nails like slivers of silver moons. There was no one on earth she had been closer to, she realised. With her own mother there were always nannies to brush her hair and cut her nails. She wanted it to be different with Bobby. He was hers and she was his. *And now, he is hers,* she thought, looking at Frankie, a small, wistful smile on her lips. Over the years she had felt him drifting away, further and further. She stared out of the window, thinking of the rocket, of space. *Roberto.*

'You don't need to apologise for me,' Marco said, sipping at his glass of soda water. Tess watched his reflection in the window. He was staring grimly at the skyline, an impatient twitch to his fingers as if he was clicking to the beat of the music. Or was he staring back at her reflection? She looked away quickly. 'As head of the family, it is my responsibility to ensure that my brother's children marry well. I want to see them settled with suitable partners.'

A suitable boy? Tess could not help smiling at the turn of events. Bobby would be fine, she knew. He could charm and argue his way from the moment he could talk, a natural lawyer. *Kit, however*. Tess wondered idly if her husband was about to have a coronary.

'Mr Affini, I can assure you-' Bobby settled on one of the bar stools. Tess could tell he was trying to look casual, unaffected.

'Save it, Bobby,' Kit snapped. 'You don't need to explain yourself to some ... some cobbler.' Marco slowly turned his head to look at Kit. 'Your niece would be lucky to marry my son.'

'But, Dad, you don't understand,' Bobby said, swinging round in his chair. 'Mr Affini has every right to be concerned. You see, the Affinis own one of the most successful shoe companies in Italy.'

'You said they had a café!' Kit said.

'That's what I thought, until I spoke to Marco and Claudia to ask for Frankie's hand in marriage.' Tess remembered the time Bobby had broken one of Kit's prized Staffordshire figurines. *He lied then and he's lying now*.

'The bar on Mulberry Street is mine,' Claudia said. She glanced at Tess. 'What am I going to do now that my husband is dead? Sit around all day feeling sorry for myself?' She tossed her head and flicked away the ridiculous idea with a perfectly manicured hand.

'I have no children,' Marco said. 'One day the company will belong to Francesca and her brothers. She will be a wealthy woman.' Tess glanced out of the corner of her eye at Kit, thinking of cartoons where dollar signs revolved in the characters' eyes.

Bobby leapt to his feet. 'Mr Affini, as I said to you the other night, I love your niece-' he turned to Claudia, 'your daughter, with all my heart.' Frankie stood and took his hand. 'I wouldn't care if she didn't have a penny in the world. I want to spend the rest of my life taking care of her, and making sure she is the happiest woman alive. I'm going to work hard to give her everything you would want her to have - security, happiness, love.'

'That's enough, Uncle Marco. I love Bobby,' Frankie said, standing tall at his side, challenging her uncle. 'He doesn't have to defend himself, not does his family. I choose him, do you get it? If you don't like it, you can forget your inheritance-'

'Francesca ...' Marco said.

'No. I mean it. Bobby is a good man. Do you really doubt my choice.' Frankie's voice softened. 'I have looked up to you my whole life. Do you really think I'd choose anyone less than you?'

Passion, Tess thinks. *There it is. Good for them.* She turned to face Marco, placing her hand on Bobby's arm. 'I know my son,' she said steadily, looking from Marco to Claudia. 'We've raised him to be a good man, kind and true, with a strong moral compass. He's bright, and smart, and hardworking, and I am very, very proud of him.' She turned to Frankie. 'If you are in love with one another, then I am happy for you. So happy-' Her voice caught, and Frankie took her hand, squeezing it. Tess looked into Frankie's eyes. 'You have my blessing.'

'That is enough,' Claudia said. 'Frankie is marrying Bobby, but she is also marrying his family. Look, Marco - look how much love there is here.'

'*Allora* ...' Marco sighed, watching Tess in silence. 'I hope you know what you are doing,' he said to Frankie finally.

Do any of us? Tess thought, returning his gaze steadily. *When I looked at my parents they seemed so grown-up. They seemed to have it all figured out. I wonder if they were just as confused and lost as I feel now?* She said to Kit a while back: *we are the age my parents were when we met, when they died. I don't feel grown up, do you?*

Marco turned and faced Bobby. 'Just remember, Roberto, I may not live to see your children grow up, however the family-'

'Family?' Kit said, his voice dripping with

meaning like honey from the comb.

'Yeah,' Marco said, shrugging his shoulders. 'Family.'

'*Basta*, Marco!' Claudia said, getting to her feet. 'That's enough!'

Marco tilted his head to Tess. 'Not all Italians are Mafiosi. I simply meant that Francesca has seven brothers. I will be watching you - and then they will be watching you. You step out of line with Frankie-' He bunched his fist, cuffed Bobby's jaw. Everyone laughed, but behind the humour Tess saw something in his eyes that pulsed adrenalin through her. A stillness. Strength, violence. She thought of gunpowder, cordite, fireworks over the bay.

'There. That's enough. Frankie has made her choice. These kids are in love and they are getting married. It's settled. If you are in agreement,' Claudia said to Kit and Tess, 'we'd like the wedding to go ahead as soon as possible, while Marco is here. As the head of the family, we'd like him to give Frankie away.'

'You are Catholic?' Marco said to Bobby.

'Protestant. Church of England to be exact.' Bobby held his gaze. 'Is that a problem?'

'But we will marry in Our Lady of Grace,' Frankie interrupted. She looked quickly from Claudia to Marco, squeezing Bobby's hand. 'We'll marry where I grew up, where our family is, and our children will be raised as I was.'

'How do you feel about that?' Marco

turned slowly to Kit.

'Me? I'm an atheist, dear chap. In terms of venue, obviously we'd prefer Manhattan as so many of our friends are here. But we shall venture across to Queens.' Tess imagined Kit setting off down Park Lane in pith helmet and safari suit, and bit her lip to stop herself laughing. She glanced up at Marco and saw him watching her, a questioning amused crease to his eyes.

'Howard Beach is a good neighbourhood,' Claudia said steadily, staring at Kit. 'Our family, our friends are there.'

'Of course.' Kit waved his hand airily. 'All that concerns me is the here and now, that these two young people love one another.' *Rubbish,* Tess thought. *All that concerns you is whether the Hoffman's will be impressed enough with Howard bloody Beach.*

□

How do you feel about that? Tess thought, walking along the lamp lit corridor with a heavy linen wrapped bundle laying across her arms. *How do I feel about that? I'm the one who took Bobby to Sunday school every week, who had him baptised.* She thought of Reverend Hardy for the first time in a long time. *Philip.* She remembered their easy laughter. Making strings of paper chains at Christmas, of carols, lantern lit faces. She remembered the red of holly berries, the red of her lipstick. She had a photograph, somewhere, tucked in an old Georgette Heyer, a group photograph with her and Philip at the centre. She is lit up, smiling. *I haven't smiled like that for years,* she thought. *Happy. I was happy, with him. I could have been happy with him.* She remembered walking across the churchyard in February, a carpet of purple crocuses and snowdrops scattered before them like confetti. It was so beautiful. She stopped at the threshold of the drawing room and closed her eyes, composing herself, the past rushing and pulling at her from the darkness like a wave. *I can do this.*

'Just before we go, I have a gift for you, if you'd like it,' she said to Frankie, smiling. She looked across to the bar where Kit, Marco and Bobby were talking. 'Please, don't feel you have to, you may not like the colour, but I've been saving this. I guess I hoped I'd have a daughter one day-'

'And now you do,' Frankie said, taking her mother and Tess' hands. 'My Ma always said to me, watch how a boy talks about his mother, how he treats her. You can tell a lot about a man from the way he treats his mother. Bobby adores you, Mrs Blythe.' It jarred, somehow. Tess could tell this girl meant well but she wanted to yell - *I know that. Of course he adores me. We couldn't be closer.* Instead she smiled. 'I hope we'll all be good friends.'

'So do I,' she said, meaning it. 'And do call me Tess.' She knelt by the coffee table and unfolded the lavender scented linen. 'My mother bought far too much silk for my wedding dress. At last there's a use for it, but only if you like it.' The yards and yards of silk had sat, folded reproachfully in Tess' cedar trunk all these years. All those christenings which didn't happen, ghost daughters whose dresses were never made.

'Oh, it's beautiful,' Frankie said, lifting the heavy oyster silk, unfolding it.

'The quality!' Claudia said, taking it from her, draping it around her daughter's neckline. 'The colour's beautiful on you.'

'It suits you far better than it did me,' Tess said, gesturing at a silver framed photograph on the piano. Frankie leapt up and brought it over for her mother to see. 'That was taken on the steps of the Peninsula Hotel in Hong Kong.' The breeze had lifted the skirts of Tess' dress, a billowing cloud of silk and chiffon. Kit had turned to her, and they are smiling, laughing. *Carefree.*

'That's what I want,' Frankie said. 'Look how happy you are.'

'Is that you?' Marco pointed to a faded sepia photograph of a young girl in a sailor suit, standing outside an old black and white house.

'Yes,' Tess said. 'That was the house I grew up in, on the Peak.'

'I like these little dogs,' Marco said, calling to Looty. 'What are they called?'

'Pekingese,' Tess said. 'I've always had one. They're such loyal little fellows. Bingo, my dog, he just died, so Kit found Looty for me.'

'I am sorry,' Marco said, looking up at her. 'They are like part of the family.'

'Marco likes dogs more than people,' Claudia said, laughing.

'And this is Roberto?' Marco said, bending to look at a baby photograph. He was so close to Tess she could feel the warmth of him, the scent of sandalwood, clean linen.

'Hard to believe he fitted into the cradle of my arm,' Tess said. *Roberto?*

'Oh, Mom.' Bobby hugged Frankie to him.

'Mothers are allowed to be sentimental at a time like this,' Claudia said. 'Every one of my seven boys-'

'Seven?' Tess said. She felt inadequate, somehow. She imagined herself on stage, a tiny white stick figure dwarfed by a towering, voluptuous spot-lit figure of womanhood. Claudia, a Venus decked in furs and heels.

'Rocco is the eldest. Then two sets of twins-' Claudia went on, her casual tone not concealing her pride.

'Goodness!'

'Five children under the age of five.' Claudia shook her head. 'Sometimes I ask myself how I coped. Then the youngest two came along. They each fell asleep every night to the beat of my heart.' She tapped her chest. 'And then Frankie came at last, my little princess, my baby girl.' Claudia tilted her head. 'Don't you think she looks like Natalie Wood?'

'Ma, stop it!' Frankie said.

'Did you see West Side Story yet?' Claudia said, shimmying, clicking her fingers. Kit's eyes widened. 'You've gotta see it.' Claudia leant towards Tess. 'If you want a tip for a good hairdresser we can book you in with us at Alfredo's. He's a genius.' She tilted her head, thinking. 'I reckon a Florentine Madonna for you, Frankie. I just saw it in Good Housekeeping. They part your hair like this-' she mimed a centre parting. 'Then sweep it up, lifting it at the crown, and they tuck the ends into a French roll. It'd suit you, sweetie. Classy.'

'Oh, Ma,' Frankie said, looking at her hands. Tess glanced at Kit and he mouthed *'classy?'*, pulled a face. Tess narrowed her eyes, warning him.

'Nothing but the best for my Frankie.'

'I love your shoes,' Tess said to Claudia, helping her tuck the linen bundle closed.

'Aren't they swell? Marco made them for me, years ago,' Claudia said, turning her ankle, the light shining a corona around her patent court shoe, her silk stocking. Tess could hear the pride in her voice. 'Of course he doesn't make the shoes anymore, he just designs them. We have hundreds of people working for us in the factories in Italy.' She clasped Tess's hand. 'But he must make you some shoes for the wedding.'

'I couldn't possibly.'

'It's the least we could do after your gift.

Marco is the finest designer in the whole of Italy.' Claudia stared at Tess' feet. 'Kind of big, aren't they?'

'I have the most terrible time finding shoes,' Tess said, blurting out her secret. 'It's my Achilles heel, literally.' She laughed, feeling awkward as Claudia and Frankie stared at her feet, all the years of embarrassment kaleidoscoping in on her. How had this woman found her weakness so soon? Claudia strode across the living room, her trim heels clicking on the polished parquet. She chattered on in Italian to Marco who was diffident, shrugging, clearly embarrassed, Tess's anxiety contracted and crystallised in her chest, she wished she could expel it like a dart, to stun this woman into silence. *Oh god, shut up, please ... stop it.* She pictured the panther falling from the tree, engulfed by the jungle.

'Marco,' Claudia said finally in English. 'No discussion. I said, you must make a pair of shoes for Mrs Blythe.'

'Please, do call me Tess,' she called, trying to sound carefree.

'But my tools are all in Italy.'

'You've been using the workshop here, I know you have.'

'I just hoped I'd see a little of New York in the time left.'

'Maybe Mrs Blythe would be kind enough to show you around afterwards?'

'No, it's unthinkable. I can't rush a design.'

'Time's short,' Claudia said, softer now. 'Go on, have a little fun. We've all got to work, the kids are at college, Mrs Blythe's dance school doesn't open in the day, that's right isn't it?' Tess nodded, unable to protest. 'That would be ok, wouldn't it?' She looked from Kit to Tess. 'You can show Marco the sights before he goes back to Italy? Hey, maybe you could even give him a few dancing lessons. What do you say, Marco? You don't want to show the family up when you dance with Frankie, do you?' Claudia laughed at her own joke.

'I don't dance,' Marco explained.

'Talking of which, let's head to the Pep,' Bobby said, grinning at the confusion on Kit's face. 'The Peppermint Lounge. It's a club across town.' Bobby took Frankie's hand, and twisted away from her. 'Live a little. Come on, what do you say?'

Chapter 5

The line stretched down to Broadway, groups of teenagers huddling together in the chill night air, swaying to the rock and roll blasting from the open doors of the Peppermint Lounge. A couple of NYPD patrol cars pulled up, blue lights flashing. Tess watched the policemen, silhouetted figures against the steam rising from the sidewalks, arms waving, whistles blowing, trying to free the snarled up crosstown traffic. Snatches of music pulsed in her. She imagined the men leaping onto the roofs of their cars, raising their arms in time with the melody.

'Is it always like this, Bobby?' Kit asked, cupping his hand around his lighter as he lit a cigarette for Claudia. He stepped aside as a man in a tuxedo ushered his fur coated wife towards the front of the line. 'I'm in the wrong business.'

'Sure it is,' he said, raising his chin to see Frankie above the heads of the people queuing in front of them. She waved frantically, gesturing that they should come forward to the VIP line.

Tess allowed her white velvet stole to slide from her shoulders. The cool autumn evening air whispered over her throat. She felt alive, quickened by the scream of sirens, the throb of the city traffic at night, blaring horns, the pulse of the music from the club rising in volume the closer she drew. The bouncer unclipped the heavy red rope and ushered them inside.

'Well done, baby,' Claudia said, kissing Frankie's cheek as she shouldered her way in. Tess followed, her eyes adjusting to the dim light of the small club. The smell of whisky, smoke and sweat raised her hackles, the bass line of the music beating in her heart. On stage, Joey Dee and the Starliters blasted out 'Peppermint Twist' and beneath them the shimmying dance-floor heaved, a mass people, thrusting arms, gyr-ating hips. 'See, my Frankie has connections,' Claudia said, taking Tess's arm as they were led to their cramped table at the edge of the dance-floor. 'Shall we have cocktails?' Claudia said. 'Martini?' Tess smiled and nodded. Kit pulled back their seats, and settled down to enjoy the spectacle. Tess noticed Marco was talking to a couple of dark suited Italians at the bar. Be-hind them the three bartenders conducted their own dance with themselves, their reflections in the mirrored walls weaving around one another, bottles of Chivas held aloft.

'What is this racket?' Kit said.

'Dad, they were the hottest act in New Jer-sey-' Bobby began to say.

'I wish they had stayed there. It's obscene,'

Kit said, unable to tear his gaze from the dancers.

'You prude,' Tess said, leaning forward on her arm, her chin cupped on her palm. 'I think it's fun.'

'Look at that girl, churning away.' Kit crossed his legs, leaning aside to let the waiter place their drinks on the table.

What a spectacle. Tess thought, cold nausea trickling through her.

'I said-'

'I heard what you said.' She was angry, suddenly. 'I think it is marvellous. Why shouldn't young girls and boys dance to any damn music they want to.'

'Here, here,' Marco said, at her shoulder.

'Shall we show them how it is done, Mom?' Bobby said, swivelling his pelvis, his hands twirling. 'You've just got to imagine you're stubbing out a cigarette with your toe.'

'Oh, you kids run along and dance,' Tess said. 'I'm happy watching.'

'You should dance, Tess!' Claudia says, gesturing at Marco. 'Dance with her, Marco.' Tess smiled. Her face betrayed nothing but she was wary of him, still.

'I don't dance,' he said.

'I'm fine, really.' Tess sipped her Martini, trying not to look at him as Claudia spoke quickly in Italian.

'Say, I couldn't help overhearing.' A young blonde boy turned from the next table. 'May I?'

He asked Kit.

'I don't think it's fitting-' He began to say. Tess glanced at him and took the boy's hand.

'It's just a dance, Kit. For heaven's sake.'

'Good for you, go on,' Claudia said, shooing her towards the dancefloor.

'Frankie is a waitress here, too?' Kit said to Claudia, raising his voice over the music.

'Waitress, dancer, all the girls get up on the rails. I think that's when Frankie caught your Bobby's eye.'

'It's not the most salubrious of...' His voice trailed off. 'Good heavens, is that Tennessee Williams?'

'They even get Dukes slumming it down here,' Claudia said, laughing. 'Haven't you heard?'

'Dukes?'

'Listen, my Frankie is a good girl, a hard-working girl,' Claudia said. 'All these girls are. Most of them are at college. And anyway most of the people here are from society.' She gestured at the VIP area. 'There are plenty of people looking out for her here, don't you worry. I didn't want her growing up with a silver spoon in her mouth, if you know what I mean? I didn't want her to be spoilt. I wanted her to see what most people have to do for a living, how hard they work-'

'I can't imagine she will continue after the wedding.'

'If Frankie wants to work, she will,' Claudia said firmly. 'But don't you worry, she will be a good wife.'

'That was fun,' Tess said, settling back into her seat at the end of the song. She felt exhilarated, the heat of the dance floor and the rhythm of the music pulsing in her. Tess looked back for her son, but Frankie and Bobby had stayed in the crowd of dancers. The band struck up the next tune and Frankie span away from him, glancing back, daring him to follow. 'Thank you,' Tess said, as the blonde boy held her chair.

'The pleasure was all mine,' he said, backing away.

'It's obscene,' Kit said under his breath. He raised his head like a meerkat scoping the horizon. 'Excuse me. I think I've just seen a client.'

'Don't our children make a beautiful couple,' Claudia said, leaning towards Tess to let Kit leave the table. 'You know, sometimes I miss my babies, don't you?' Her hands moulded the air. 'The solid goodness of them.' She hugged herself. 'The way they fit against your hip like a shell. 'Course I've got a couple of grandkids now already.' Tess heard the pride in her voice. 'Just you wait, it's fabulous. You get all the fun *and* you get to hand them back.'

'It's funny. I was just thinking about that a while ago.' Tess' gaze followed Frankie and Bobby dancing across the room.

Claudia smiled. 'Oh, sometimes I look at them, I look at Frankie now, and I see the ghost of the baby they were in them, I remember ...' She blinked quickly. 'Don't you feel that physical joy when you're near them? I just love it when I have all my babies in the house together, and it's just us. It feels like everything's as it should be. When one of them is away it's like I've lost a piece of me. Something's missing.' Tess looked at Bobby and wondered if she had ever felt that uncomplicated pride and joy about him. She had always felt like she was defending him, even to herself.

'Yes,' she said. 'I know exactly what you mean.'

'Of course, we'll be grandmothers soon,' Claudia said, laughing with delight. 'This wedding is going to be perfect,' she said, her expression softening as she returned Frankie's wave from the dance floor. 'Unlike mine.' She pursed her lips and turned to Tess. 'But enough about that. Where were you married again?'

'Hong Kong,' Tess said.

'How romantic. Was it love at first sight?'

'Kit was the only one tall enough for me,' Tess said, deadpan. She saw the confusion on Claudia's face. 'Of course, I adored him. We were friends for a long time before we married.'

'How did you meet?'

'Kit didn't notice me for years, but I fell for him the moment I saw him. He was on parade, in uniform -'

'He was in the navy, like your father? Bobby said his grandpa was a Commander?'

'Kit was in the wavy navy as they called

it, the volunteers. But he was interested in antiques and design even then, and he set up an import export business.' Tess closed her eyes for a moment, remembering her chill horror when she realised that Kit had burnt through so much money. She felt sick, lightheaded at the memory. *All he exported was money from my bank account.* 'He helped design the house of a friend of my parents,' she said, clearing her throat, 'and I was there playing tennis one day.' She blinked. 'The first thing he ever said to me was 'you have the most elegant serve I've ever seen, Miss Montgomery.'

'It's like something from a movie! Isn't it, Marco? I said, it's like something from a movie.' Claudia raised her voice. 'I'm imagining Carrie Grant and Katharine Hepburn.'

'It feels like a lifetime ago,' Tess said. 'We honeymooned in the Philippines. It was rather romantic, I suppose. Days at sea, Cole Porter playing endlessly, sleeping on deck to escape the heat of the cabins.' She realised Marco was watching her, and she looked across her glass at him. He did not look away. 'There's a fragrance that hits you the first time you sail to the east, of blossom and spicy wood. I think it gets into your blood. It never quite leaves you. I still remember it, my first glimpse of Hong Kong harbour - all the junks and sampans floating on the moonlit water.'

'Hong Kong,' Claudia said. 'How exotic. I

bet it was beautiful. You must have looked be-yootiful.' She reached for a cigarette. 'Are your parents here? Will they be at the wedding.'

'No.' Tess paused. 'Sadly they died during the war.'

'Oh, *Madonna*. I am so sorry. And Kit?' She looked up as Kit joined them. 'You got family?'

'I am not close to my parents,' he said.

'But they are still alive? Surely they would want to come to their grandson's wedding?'

'I doubt they would be inclined to leave Berkshire. My father loathes me - or he did the last time I saw him in 1937. He disliked change so I imagine he hasn't altered - and my mother was maturing nicely like a cheap wine ...'

Bitter and unappreciated, Tess thought as Kit delivered the familiar line with a laconic smile. *Silted up with unfulfilled promise.* She bit the inside of her cheek. *I wonder what the real story is with Kit's family?*

'Oh?' Claudia raised one perfectly sculpted eyebrow. 'Ohhh.'

'You have brothers and sisters?' Marco said.

'No. I am an only child, though I imagine if I had brothers and sisters I would have fallen out with them too. I always say there is a reason you fall out with your siblings.' Kit said, raising an eyebrow. 'Helps to spread the gene pool.'

'Kit's not in touch with his family, and I was an only child, too,' Tess said, wishing he would shut up.

'We are a couple of happy orphans who found one another,' Kit said, taking Tess' hand. She hoped her smile looked genuine. *Smile like you mean it* - her mother's voice came to her again. *Smile with your eyes*. 'We have lots of friends who are like family who will be delighted to celebrate with Bobby and Frankie. Tess will give you a list, won't you, darling?' He turned to her. 'If you can't beat them, join them. Shall we?'

Kit guided Tess through the throng of people twisting to *'Ya Ya'*, leading her in a sedate two-step foxtrot. 'What is this drivel? What's a 'la la' when it's at home.'

'For god's sake, Kit. Loosen up.'

'Not something that you're having a problem with. Second Martini?'

'Marco ordered another round of drinks. It seemed rude not to.'

'There's no need to suck up to him. Imagine, the cheek of the man, suggesting Bobby wasn't good enough-'

'Look at them,' Tess said, and Kit turned his head turning to watch Frankie and Bobby.

'Aren't they marvellous?' She thought for a moment. 'Was that it? Was that what started all this, hearing Bobby had met someone?'

'Nothing like young love to make you feel old.' A fierce expression crossed Kit's face like sunlight glinting on the blade of a knife. 'And I'm not ready for that. Not yet.'

'Peter Pan.'

'Not now,' Kit hissed. 'They're watching. Smile.'

'Or?' She felt the weight of Marco's gaze on her. Every time she turned he was watching only her.

'Bobby's fine, now. Good on him. I knew he was too sensible to take on some penniless waitress.'

'Is that all you care about, the money?'

'Bobby, and you, are capable of supporting yourselves-'

'As I have always done.'

'I want one last adventure. Is that too much?'

'Adventure? We moved so many times, so many countries,' Tess said, her eyes pricking with tears unexpectedly. 'I feel like I've left a piece of my heart in every corner of the globe. I don't ... I don't even know who I am any more.'

'Oh god, you're getting maudlin.'

'I am not.' Tess sniffed and raised her chin. 'It's you. You never were able to talk about your feelings.'

'We are expats, Tess. We belong everywhere and nowhere. I wouldn't have life any other way. With every move you can reinvent yourself-'

'I disagree. You end up taking yourself wherever you go, unpacking the same faults and flaws along with the tea chests. People make the same mistakes time and time again. And it tests you, especially hard postings.'

'I'd hardly call Manhattan a hardship posting.'

'I'm not talking about us. I'm talking about the dangerous and difficult places - Asia, Africa, Arabia. How many relationships have we seen fail? How many affairs, and broken marriages?'

'Thank heavens,' Kit said as the song ended and the crowd broke into rapturous applause. 'Let's get you a glass of water.'

'Now, what will we wear?' Claudia said, leaning towards Tess as she sat down. Tess didn't recoil when she touched her hand. She had always envied women who had that much confidence in themselves. *It is like people who are good with animals,* she thinks. *That maternal sense of firmness, or is it dominance?* She saw it in Frankie, too, a natural confidence from growing up in a large, loving family. Tess had a nagging feeling she had missed a step, somehow.

'Tess will find a darling little nothing, won't you?' Kit said. She glanced at him, heading towards the bar. *He's the one who needs water. He's drunk too much, as usual.*

'We must co-ordinate, make sure we don't clash with one another or outshine the bride.' Claudia threw back her head and laughed. 'As if we could. Look at her.' Tess heard the pride in her voice. *Look at her.*

Tess watched Frankie dancing, lithe and free, glorious. *I've never felt like that,* she thought. *I've always felt self-conscious. I want to feel like that. I do.* She remembered the girl's embarrassment at her uncle's halting English, how quickly she stepped in for him earlier. *Like a bright spark, flaring up.* Tess watched her son, the practiced, sure way he reeled Frankie back into his arms. Something in that sureness scared her. *He is so certain of himself.* That calculated charisma. A sense of déjà vu swept over her like seasickness, like vertigo although she hadn't moved from her seat.

'Dance with her,' Claudia nudged Marco's arm, whispered out of the corner of her mouth too loud, enough for Tess to hear. 'Look at the poor woman, foot tapping like mad. She's dying to dance again,'

If only you knew how right you are, Tess thought.

'Can't you see? Marco, dance with her. God knows that stiff of a husband isn't any good. I feel sorry for her-' Tess stared fixedly ahead. *She? She feels sorry for me.*

'I don't dance,' he said. 'I told you.'

'Rubbish. You were a boxer. Of course you dance.' Claudia tapped Tess on the elbow. 'Say, you wanna dance, don't you, Tessie?'

'No, really, I'm happy just watching.' Tess stared resolutely at the dancefloor, trying to hide her embarrassment. *Poor man, won't she leave him alone? Why on earth would he want to-*

It took Tess a moment to realise that Marco had stood and was waiting at her side, his broad, steady palm extended towards her like an oar from a lifeboat. *Dance with me.*

Marco ushered her ahead, the crowd of dancers parting before them like water. She turned to him, and raised her right hand. He held her lightly, firmly. After Kit it was like the difference between dancing with a tabby cat and a tiger. Over his shoulder she watched Bobby leaning in to his girl, whispering something in her ear as they danced. Tess felt like the past already, sensed his future unfurling away from this moment to somewhere she will only be a footnote.

'You said you don't dance.' She raised her face to Marco.

'I didn't say I can't dance. There's a difference.' Marco said. 'You dance well.'

'It's what I do,' she said watching Bobby and Frankie, nearby. Her attention was like a spotlight following them around the dancefloor. 'I teach ballet.'

'You mean you work?'

'That surprises you?'

'I thought women like you spent all day at the salon.'

'Women like me?' Tess moved her head a fraction to look at him, close to. She could see he was smiling, teasing her. It was as if she saw him with his guard down for the first time. Desire pulsed, bloomed warm and low in her stomach.

'I'm sorry if Claudia embarrassed you,' he said.

'Embarrassed?' Close to, his eyes were flecked with amber. She thought of the tigers eye gemstone she kept in her bedside drawer as a child.

'I'm sure you can have whatever you want. You don't need me.'

'You're talking about the shoes?' Tess blinked, like waking from a dream. 'You think I'm the kind of person who can just buy whatever takes my eye?' She frowned. 'Well these shoes were a mistake. Do you mind if we sit?' Tess wondered what Bobby had told him about the family's money. Marco led the way back to the table and held out her chair. Tess kicked off the high grey suede stilettos and tucked her feet beneath her.

'Maybe you do need me, after all,' Marco said quietly.

'Maybe,' she said, her spine straight.

'It makes no difference to me. Come to the workshop if you like,' he said, shrugging as the song ended.

'Marco! I'm sorry, he has no manners.' Claudia said. 'Bobby knows the address. There's no time to waste if we're going to get this wedding organised.'

'Have we set a date?' Tess asked.

'Friday November 3rd,' Bobby said. 'Frankie's birthday!'

'Too soon,' Claudia said. 'End of the month, straight after Thanksgiving? You'd better choose your shoes quickly, Tess. Why don't you come round on Monday at ten?'

'I don't want to be any trouble,' Tess said, glancing at Marco.

'We're family now,' Claudia said. 'Cause as much trouble as you like.'

Chapter 6

Claudia bore the memory of her late husband's frequent infidelities like shrapnel. Deep bedded, once explosive, now a daily, dully painful part of her. The first time she caught Carlo cheating her heart exploded. That's how she thought of it. In the space in her chest where she had carried her love, there was a void now, an endless dark hole where the glittering splinters of her heart drifted, silently. She had given herself, devoted herself to him absolutely, once. *Do you know how many times I wanted to ask my friends for help*, she said to Carlo one night. *Do you know how many times I wanted to tell our seven sons who adore you so much what a lying bastard their father is? But I will never do that. I want our sons to be better than their father. Men with true hearts.*

She wore her accomplishments like gold jewellery, smooth from touching - mother, wife, businesswoman, friend. *Lover?* she thought, looking down the table to his brother Marco, her gaze drifting through the extended arms and plates crisscrossing the table like smoke. *Survivor.* Once she had been enough for Carlo. She looked at Bobby, sitting across from Frankie, a part of their family now. *I hope you are a better man.* Part of her wanted to tell Frankie, to warn her to hold something back. Keep a piece of her heart safe. Just in case. *But I can't do that.* She looked at her daughter's face all lit up with love, and Claudia's eyes welled with tears. She remembered how it felt. She missed feeling like that. Claudia stemmed a tear with a corner of the heavy damask napkin tucked into the neckline of her dress.

'You ok, Ma?' Rocco said, pausing with a forkful of spaghetti halfway to his lips.

'Yeah, something in my eye, that's all,' she said, patting his arm. Claudia took a sip of water.

That's the problem, she told Carlo, after the first time. *I love you. And I don't doubt you love me, you just can't keep it in your goddamn trousers. Me? I honour the vows I made to you in church. But in my heart I will always feel I wasn't enough for you. I am not enough.*

I am not enough. She watched Marco. She remembered their conversation on the porch the night before: *The only reason I stayed with your brother was the men in your family have weak hearts. No one makes it past their fifties. It was just a question of time.* Marco had folded his arms, and said: *You don't mean that.*

She remembered the first time she saw Marco, ambling out of the gym in Florence with one of her brothers, how her heart stood still and desire bloomed in the space between them. But then Carlo pursued her, and before she knew it she was pregnant with Rocco and engaged to him. She had hoped in her secret heart that Marco would ask first. She remembered how he was unable to look at her at the engagement party. So nothing would ever come of it. Over the years she thought of him sometimes, when Carlo was making love to her. She imagined it was Marco's broad, dark hands on her, her fingers tangled in the glossy waves of his hair. Had there been women, for him, she wondered? If there were, he was discreet. He had never brought anyone home, never gone out for the night with a fresh shirt on and a posy of violets. She remembered seeing him fight. He was savage. He was a star.

Marco turned to her now, staring at her across the chatter of the table. *I heard you,* she thought. *I heard you talking in your sleep last night. I heard you calling her: Tess, Tess, aaah.*

'Excuse me,' Claudia says, patting her lips with the napkin and scraping back her chair. Rocco stood to help her, but she gestured he should sit and finish the meal. In the silence of her bedroom with its good and heavy dark wood furniture, Claudia turned on the lamp and looked at herself in the mirror. 'Idiot,' she said. *I thought he came back for me. I hoped.*

She swung open the door of her wardrobe and ran her fingertips along the rack of dresses, touching fur, and silk. *Nothing fits*, she thought. They felt like the pelts of other women, relics of other lives. Sometimes she thought of herself like one of the Russian dolls with all the women she was stacked inside her, smaller and smaller, and in her heart she carried the slender girl who loved two brothers. She hoped those women would come back to her, one day, young and defiant and beautiful. Like Frankie, she thought, smiling wistfully. Claudia picked up a framed photograph of her at the same age her daughter was now. Marco and Carlo stand either side of her. Claudia put her thumb over Carlo's grinning face, and her mind lit up with a kaleidoscope of alternate pasts and Technicolor futures, dreams that were as real to her as the truth.

Would it really cause a scandal now, she thought. *Has it been long enough?* She thought of the beautiful gown Tess was wearing last time she saw her. *Have I worn widow's black long enough?* She imagined a rainbow of dresses, red silk, turquoise velvet, sumptuous gold satins. Claudia took off the thin rope of pearls she had put on because she had admired Tess. *Not that he noticed. Is it so bad to love his brother?* Claudia flung down the photograph and looked in the mirror again. *I'm forty-four, my eldest child is twenty-six. I was just a child when Carlo knocked me up.* 'I'm young,' she said under her breath. 'I'm still young.' She focussed on the reflection of her bed in the mirror. *I still sleep on my side.* Every night she felt the aching space beside her. In the darkness, she whispered Marco's name to the ceiling, to the rafters, hoped her words slipped through the cracks, that he heard her calling him back to her in his sleep.

Chapter 7

Frankie is taking breakfast to the workshop for Marco - a flask of espresso, freshly baked rolls, his favourite *soppressa*. She walks down the dark pavement in a white dress, the petticoats swinging like the bell of a snowdrop around her slim tanned legs. There is a new copy of *'To Kill A Mockingbird'* beneath her arm, a silver bookmark placed a couple of pages in. Several passages have already been underlined precisely in pencil. Tucked at the back of the book is a sheet of paper with a 'to do' list for the wedding: *collect invitations from the printers; stamps; order wine; menu?* Frankie loves the early morning pulse of the waking streets. Marco is working, his head bent over a supple pair of tan leather Oxfords, a pencil in his hand.

'Francesca?' he says, looking up.

'Uncle.' She bows as Marco kisses the top of her head. 'Mama sent breakfast for you.' She glances at the unmade cot in the corner of the room. 'Did you sleep in the workshop again?'

'Yeah, your mother's mad. Always nagging about something.' Marco yawns and stretches.

He takes the steaming cup of coffee Frankie offers him. 'Grazie.'

'She heard from the boys you've been working out at the gym again.'

'Did she now?'

'She just ... she worries, Marco.'

'You can tell your mother I haven't set foot in the ring. I'm just teaching a few tricks to the boys, that's all.' Marco hides the tremor in his hand from her, sliding his fingers into his pocket. 'And this,' he gestures at shoes on the bench. 'I'm enjoying getting my hands dirty for a change.'

'They for Bobby?' Frankie slides her hands into the shoes, dancing a twist across the workbench.

'I was just checking the boys have done a good job.'

'He'll love them.' Frankie watches her uncle's expression closely. She can tell he is holding something back. 'I'm grateful.' She puts the shoes side by side on their stand. 'I know you don't approve of Bobby, so this means a lot to me.'

'He's not good enough for you,' Marco says, wiping his hands.

'Hey, nobody is good enough for me,' Frankie says, standing on tiptoe to peck Marco on the cheek. 'Am I right?'

'You're the brightest and the best of all of them.' Marco turns his hand over, frowning in concentration. 'If you were a man, I'd be leaving the company to you to run, not your brother.'

'Rocco will do great, you watch,' Frankie says. 'He's just kind of scared of you. All the guys are in awe of Uncle Marco.'

'Not you, eh?' Marco flashes her a quick grin.

'Anyway, who says a woman can't run a company?' Frankie puts her hands on her hips. 'Look at Ma.' She looks at Bobby's shoes. 'I'm sorry she has got you making shoes for everyone. Who comes all the way to America to spend their time in some old workshop?'

'I'm happy to be doing something.' Marco unwraps his breakfast and cuts some sausage with a slim bladed knife. 'What time did you kids come in last night?'

'Late.' Frankie's ponytail swings as she moves her head in time with the tune she is humming.

'You were with your brothers?'

'Of course, Uncle. Didn't let me out of their sight.' Frankie lowers her gaze, smiling, thinking of Bobby. She remembers the heat of the dance floor, the mingled scent of fresh sweat and eau de cologne, the warmth of his tanned hand in hers. She remembers their bodies, moving together to the music in the darkness, feeling how badly he wanted her, and her stomach drops with desire, again.

Marco checks his watch. 'I should get over to the house and clean up. Your mother's fixed a meeting with Bobby's mother.'

'You don't mind, do you?'

'The shoes? Nah, I'll do the design and let one of the boys make them up.' Marco flexes his fingers, and frowns.

'I think Mom just wanted to show off. You know how proud she is of you.' Frankie helps him into his jacket, flattening his collar. 'We all are. You're a genius.'

'Hey, you'll make an old man's head grow large,' he says, leaning down to kiss her hair. 'Walk with me?'

Fresh morning sunlight filters through the copper leaves of the trees, dappling the pavement with a shifting carpet of gold. Marco pauses at the window of a toyshop and points at the display of Barbies, and the new Ken doll. 'He looks like your Bobby.'

'He is kind of cute.'

'He's plastic. Too good to be true.'

'Stop it.' Frankie punches his arm and they walk on.

'The last time I saw you, you were still playing with dolls. Tell me again the story of how you met this boy,' Marco says.

'I've already told you.' Frankie laughs, looking up at him as they walk.

'Tell me again.'

'You old romantic.' Frankie leans in to him. 'So I was working in the bar one day, and I saw this boy staring at me. His coffee got cold, he was so distracted-'

'Hope you gave him hell?'

'Of course.'

'Your mother gave your father hell.'

'Did she?'

'Yeah. He didn't stand a chance, once she'd decided he was the one. That's what she always says.' Marco offers Frankie his arm. 'Then what?'

'I was hanging around outside the Knickerbocker Hotel with Rocco and the boys one night. It was busy, a group of sailors and guys in leather jackets were causing some trouble in the doorway to the Peppermint Lounge.' She smiles remembering the cars gliding by in slow motion, like crocodiles in a dark river, chrome fenders and tail fins catching the light. The neon sign flickered above, reflecting in the slick pavement below. She remembers how it gilded Bobby's hair, how he smiled when he saw her. 'So he showed up-'

'Roberto?'

'Yeah. Bobby just calmed the whole situation right down. Charmed them so much they forgot what they were fighting about. 'You won't believe it!' he said, squeezing through. 'Marilyn Monroe is on the dance floor.' 'You're kidding?' this sailor said. 'Doing the twist, man.'

'And was she?'

'Yeah, she comes in once in a while. She's beautiful. Really tiny.' Frankie remembers fighting their way through the crowd to a table.

She sat between two of her brothers, and Bobby and his friends joined them. Frankie watched a petite platinum blonde woman dancing and laughing on the crowded floor, a reverent space around her. 'Everyone's here!' Bobby had leant over to her. 'I heard Greta Garbo was in here the other weekend,' he shouted above the music. 'Say, would you like to dance?'

Frankie had shaken her head but the rhythm was contagious. Her heart was already dancing. Joey Dee and the Starliters stomped and twisted on stage, the crowd jiving to the Peppermint Twist. Her foot tapped beneath the table in time with the music, but she turned him down every single time he asked her. She sat back in the booth, watching the arrival of the rest of the Affini brothers. The men were dressed identically in dark suits with narrow black ties, starched white shirts immaculate, a hint of freshly laundered white vests beneath, the glint of stage lights on their black pomaded hair.

'You know I've been going to the cafe every single day for lunch after college,' he said, leaning across the table to talk to her.

'It's true!' his friend confirmed. 'Poor old Bob lives for a tantalising glimpse of your petti-coats-' He broke off as Rocco placed a large fist on the table, and sat back.

'Good,' Marco says. 'I'm glad Rocco was looking out for you.'

'Bobby was clever though,' Frankie says. 'After that he ignored me. He got to know the boys, used to come round the house, playing cards, barely said a word to me.' She shakes her head. 'Rocco invited him out to Coney Island one day with a bunch of us.' She smiles, remembering the summer heat, the lights of the carousel, the taste of salt and spun sugar on his lips.

'That's what I thought about him first time I met him,' Marco says. 'Clever. Sly. Made me think of a fox prowling round outside a hen house.'

'I remember! I was hiding round the back of the door because I was still in my dressing gown when he turned up one morning with flowers. You gave him a really hard time.' She punches his arm, gently. 'Roses? My favourite. You shouldn't have,' you said, pointing at the bouquet.'

'I wasn't going to make it easy for him.' Marco raises his hand in thanks as a pink Cadillac slows down to let them cross the road.

'That's when he asked me, walking me to work that morning. It was spur of the moment. He'd been out all night-'

'Yeah? With who?'

'He's not like that,' Frankie says.

'All men are like that,' Marco says. 'Some of us are honest about it.'

'Not my Bobby.' She remembers their conversation that morning.

'Tell me about your family,' Frankie had said. 'You got brothers or sisters?'

'Nope, just me,' Bobby had said.

'Ah, that explains a lot,' she said, swinging her bag.

'Such as?' Bobby turned to look at her, walking backwards along the pavement. His shirt was loose at the collar, his tie pulled down and his tweed jacket hung from his finger over his shoulder.

'The easy charm, the sense of entitlement,' Frankie said.

'Hey, go easy on a guy,' Bobby said, clasping his heart before swinging around a nearby lamppost. 'You're killing me.'

'Tell me about your parents, then,' Frankie said, laughing.

'Mom's beautiful. She was a dancer-'

'Like a nightclub dancer?'

'No,' Bobby said, laughing at the thought. 'Ballet dancer. Dad is a designer. He does up places for people with too much money and too little originality.'

'Is that what he says?'

'Dad loves three things. Beauty, money and my mother.'

'What about you?'

'OK, four things.' Bobby jumped up onto a low wall, walking one foot in front of the other like a tightrope. 'And you. What do you love?'

'Me? I love my family,' Frankie said as he jumped down and joined her. 'I love the idea of having a family of my own someday.' She flashed him a quick smile. 'But I want to travel first, see Europe. That's why I'm studying at night school to be an translator. I want to work over at the UN.'

'Yeah? That's great. How many languages do you speak?' They paused at the foot of the steps leading to the cafe.

'Italian, obviously.'

'Obviously,' Bobby said, stepping closer.

'Spanish, French ...'

'How do you say 'I think you are the most beautiful girl in the world' in French?'

'Je pense que tu es la plus belle fille du monde,' she said, lowering her face. Bobby raised her chin with the tip of his index finger.

'Je t'aime,' he said, his lips brushing hers. 'I know that, at least.'

'Ti amo,' she said. 'Or te amo if you want Spanish.'

'I'll take it in any language as long as you're saying it to me.' A light went on in the lobby.

'I've got to go, Ma needs my help setting up.'

'Frankie, I mean it. I love you. I've loved you since I first set eyes on you. Then, when you let me kiss you on the carousel I fell hard for you. Real hard.'

'Bobby, you're crazy-'

'Crazy in love with you.' He grinned, and dropped to one knee. 'Marry me.'

'Not here!' Frankie's eyes widened and she looked around the deserted street. 'We hardly know one another!'

'Marry me. I promise, I'll spend the rest of my life making you happy. I'll take you to Europe, we'll travel through Italy-'

'Frankie?' A woman's voice from the cafe called out.

'I have to go.'

'I'm serious.' Bobby raised his arms to the treetops, to the birds singing in the dawn light. 'Marry me.'

'Then you got to ask my uncle.'

'I don't want to marry your uncle.'

'Stupid.' Frankie cupped his face in her hands, lifting him up.

'Will you? Will you marry me?'

She kissed him. 'Yes,' she said. 'Yes.'

'Yeah, I remember that day,' Marco says, standing in the gate to the house, one hand in the pocket of his charcoal grey suit. 'I said to him: D'you fight, Bobby?' He says: 'Not since I was at school.' So I said, 'C'mon, let's spar a little.'

'You didn't?' Frankie's lips parted.

'Hey, I'm not going to let any punk kid marry my niece.' Marco looks at his watch. 'I'd better go wash. Mrs Blythe will be at the workshop soon.' He kisses Frankie's forehead. 'You off to college?'

'Yeah.' She twirls away, her skirt swinging wide. 'Be nice, ok? I like her.'

'I'm always nice,' he says, flashing her a quick smile. Frankie walks away hugging her book to her chest. *Even when he smiles*, she thinks, *he seems sad. He's such a sweetheart, always looking out for all of us.* She stops at the crossing to wait for the lights to change. *Tough guy, that's what everyone thinks, but he's got a soft heart.* Frankie watches a bus driving past with an advert for a circus pasted on that side. *That's what he is. He's like a big old tough lion who's tired of fighting. I wish I knew what I could do to make him happy.*

Chapter 8

'You made me cry last night,' Elaine said, holding open the diner door for Tess. They waited on the sidewalk, red tail lights of the traffic stretching away from them, gleaming in the afternoon light as Gladys took her coat down from the rack.

'Made you cry? How?' Tess shielded her eyes from the bright autumn sun, turning to her partner. Looty looked up at them expectantly, and Tess leant down to straighten her collar.

'Our Grade Six class performed the piece you choreographed for the winter show in full. It's beautiful, Tess. You should be really proud.' Elaine slipped her arm into Tess' and the three friends strolled along the pavement towards the ballet school, the little dog trotting ahead.

'You talking about last night?' Gladys said. 'I've told you before and I tell you again, you'se wasted on a little bitty school, Tessie.' She swept her plump arm into the air. 'D'you remember when we saw Margot Fonteyn dancing Giselle at the Metropolitan Opera House a few months ago?'

'I'll never forget it,' Elaine said. 'Everyone said it was the greatest reception any ballet has had since they opened with Sleeping Beauty in 1949.'

'*That* is what you should be doing,' Gladys said, wagging her finger at Tess. 'You should be up there, centre stage-'

'Get away,' Tess said, looking down at her shoes. She was wearing a tighter skirt than normal, and had to adjust her stride. She remembered Claudia sashaying across their living room. *I wanted to feel like that,* she thought, smoothing down the skirt, self conscious suddenly. 'It's ridiculous. It's way too late for me to dance.' A glass jar of red and white peppermint sticks caught her eye in the window of a store on the corner as she looked up. She remembered dancing with Marco in the nightclub. *Is it? Is it too late?*

'Choreography!' Elaine said, pausing at the corner of their street. 'You'd be fantastic, Tess. If you can do that with a few teenagers, just imagine what you could do with a professional dance corps.'

'London, Paris ...' Gladys said, her face softening.

'Stop it, you're tempting me.' Tess' heart quickened. 'It's funny. For so long I dreamt of being centre stage myself, but lately I imagine creating roles for others.'

'Do it! Do it, Tess,' Gladys said. 'Everyone's

bored to tears of Swan Lake and Sleeping Beauty and all the usual suspects. Audiences love to see new ballets. Look at everything Martha Graham is doing.' She nodded her head in approval. 'Miss Graham said she doesn't give a damn about race, creed, colour she just cares about talent.' Gladys wagged her finger at Tess. 'That's what you've got - talent.'

'Know what someone said to me the other day? 'Choreographers are the rare jewels of the ballet world,' Elaine said. 'He should know. He's some kind of critic, helps compile the Ballet Annuals each year.' She took Tess' arm. 'That's you, darling. A rare jewel.'

Tess bit her lip. 'But where would I start? I've got no contacts. And what about the school?'

'Darling, I'm not going anywhere,' Elaine said, her hand resting on her stomach. 'Why soon I'll be the fattest ballerina who ever lived.'

'The most beautifully radiant pregnant ballerina,' Tess said, resting her hand on her friend's. Her heart swelled with longing, feeling the child move. *I remember that feeling,* she thought. *I'd give anything to feel it again*.

'You can count on us. Haven't we been saying for years you'd be better off ...' Elaine stopped herself.

Gladys pursed her lips. 'You know what we think of the way Kit treats you.'

'Anyway. Do whatever you need, darling. I can run this joint in my sleep.' Elaine thought for a moment. 'Which I may have to, soon.' She searched through her bag. 'Glad, have you got a key?'

'Sure,' she said, as they walked on to the school. 'Think about it, Tessie. With everything you've got going on maybe a new start, a new challenge is just what ... Oh, my.' Gladys fell silent, her eyes widening as she noticed Marco leaning against the lamppost by the alleyway leading to the school. 'Now I see why you've got that fancy new outfit on.' Tess felt Elaine stand taller at her side.

'Marco?' Tess said, smiling. 'What a lovely surprise. May I introduce Gladys and Elaine, who work with me at the dance school.'

'How do you do?' he said, shaking their hands. He turned to Tess, and she felt her stomach freefall. On the cool autumn air she sensed him - warm leather, starched linen, sandalwood cologne. 'We had a date.' Gladys glanced at Elaine and they walked on to the door, busying themselves with the locks, apparently unable to find the right keys.

'A date?'

'Well, an appointment.' Marco smiled at her confusion, and squatted down to stroke Looty's head. 'Your shoes.'

'Oh Lord, I thought you were just being polite.' Tess pressed her palm against her forehead. 'I'm so sorry. You really were expecting me to turn up this morning?'

'Of course.' He shrugged, straightening up. 'I didn't have your number so I thought it was easier to drop in on my way to the Museum.' He took a breath. 'I wanted to apologise in person, too. If I was-'

'Rude? Offhand with my son?' Tess' eyes crinkled.

'I am protective of my nephews, but particularly of my niece.'

'Good for you,' Tess said. 'Are you going to the Met?'

'Yeah. There's an exhibit of Chinese Art Treasures I want to see. Thought I might get some ideas, for designs. You know.'

'Oh!' Tess' eyes lit up. 'It's wonderful, you'll love it.' She remembered trailing dutifully through the exhibition after Kit and the Hoffmans, how a small crowd had gathered around to listen to Kit's scholarly comments about each piece. Tess had let them walk on ahead, exhaling with relief as Kit's voice faded. She imagined the museum filling with red balloons, fuelled by Kit's comments, each balloon expanding to bursting point, rising and rising to the shadows of the roof, and herself, dancing alone in white, pointing at them one by one, exploding them with sniper precision. Alone, she let herself get lost in the crowd, in the beauty of each fine embroidery, each dazzling ceramic, in her memories of Hong Kong and her childhood.

'I'm afraid I have a class, otherwise I'd love

to join you.'

'Another time, perhaps?' Marco took a black leather bound sketchpad from his pocket and wrote down an address in Queens, and a number. 'This is the workshop,' he said, tearing it from the book. 'I'll be there tomorrow at nine. He took Tess' hand, pressed her fingers lightly to his lips. 'I hope you'll come.'

Tess watched him walk away. 'I'll catch up with you,' she called to Gladys who was waiting for her in the door. Tess wanted a moment to compose herself. She strolled down the pavement swinging one leg in front of the other as if it were a catwalk, feeling as if each step lifted her higher and higher into the air. She reached into her pocket book and bought a newspaper from the vendor on the corner. Tess scanned the headlines, hardly seeing them, as she walked back to the school. *Soviet Union detonates 58 megaton Tsar Bomba ... Novaya Zemlya*, she read, pausing on the street. 'That's how it feels,' she said to Looty. *It feels like the world I knew has atomised. Everything has changed.*

Chapter 9

Tess goes to him. She is shown into the workshop by a young man with a black apron tied around his waist, and told to wait. The tools in the workshop are cared for, ranked by type and size. Burnished wood glows warm in the afternoon sun. The air is full with the scent of leather, polish and glue. She is lightheaded, off-kilter. She feels how she felt in church in Hong Kong as a girl. The studio is serene, light filled. She can hear voices somewhere in the building, but here she is alone. She feels at peace. The silence is broken only by the steady tap of a hammer, pulsing like a heart beat. She turns in a slow circle, sunlit dust motes dancing around her.

'You came,' he says, in the doorway suddenly. He is wiping his hands on a white cloth which he tosses onto the workbench. A supple leather apron is tied around his waist, the sleeves of his white shirt rolled up to his elbows.

'It seemed rude to stand you up again,' she says, holding her handbag in both hands at waist height like a shield.

'I see you brought your chaperone?' he gestures at Looty.

'Guard dog.'

He gently strokes the dog's head, and she stands on her hind legs, paws on his knee, licking his hand. 'Some guard dog.'

'She's a good judge of character, that's all.'

'You have no need to feel afraid, Tess,' he says, and looks up at her.

'Afraid?' The steady pulse of her heart accelerates, runs away with her. 'We're not afraid of anything, are we, Looty?' she says, making light of it. 'She was terribly brave when they took the stitches out,' Tess says, gazing down at the dark crown of Marco's head.

'I bet that feels better, eh, little one?' He stands and calls out to one of the girls in the office to bring a bowl of water. Marco turns to Tess. 'Sit, please,' he says, gesturing at a high leather chair with a footrest. He drags over a stool and sits before her. 'How is your husband? And Roberto ... Bobby?'

'Well, thank you,' she says, still clutching her bag on her lap. He reaches across her, for a notebook and sharp pencil from the workbench. She notices it has been sharpened with a blade. The graphite is dark, pointed like a spear, a claw.

'So,' he says, pencil poised above the clean white sheet.

'So?' Her breath is shallow.

'What do you need?'

Her lips part slowly. *What do I need? What?*

'I want ...'

'No. That's not what I asked you.' He looks up at her. His eyes are hooded, he blinks and exhales. 'Women like you have a closet full of shoes they thought they wanted and never wear.'

'Women like me? Now hold on a minute, Mr Affini-'

'Marco.' He sketches a line in the corner of the page, waiting.

'You are making a lot of assumptions, Marco.' Her grasp on her handbag tightens. 'You think you know me?'

'I think you are the kind of woman who has always got what she wants, that is all, *Mrs Blythe-*'

'Tess,' she says, waiting for him to look at her. 'And appearances can be deceptive.'

'The apartment overlooking Central Park?' He gestures at her bag. 'This Hermes handbag?'

'My husband has expensive tastes,' she says, and the implication settles between them like oil on water. She sets the bag to one side.

'A pump? Heel or flat?' he says, and bows his head, a lock of glossy blue black hair falling forward.

'Low heel. Kit's not that keen-' She pauses, surprised at the emotion she feels welling inside her. She feels like she is being disloyal. 'I'm too tall.'

'What is too tall? You are the most elegant

woman I have ever seen.'

Tess inhales. 'He - Kit doesn't like me to be taller than him.' Marco makes a note. 'I don't know what I want,' she says quickly, and then, before she loses her nerve. 'I've never been able to find shoes which are comfortable. My feet ... I hate my feet.' Her voice breaks. 'They're so big, and ugly. My mother-'

'Ah, always the mother's fault. Let's take a look, shall we?' Marco says, his voice gentle. He stands and offers her his hand. 'Trust me. My designs will feel as natural to you as if you are barefoot.' His fingers sculpt the air, the arch of an extended foot, the curve of a calf muscle. 'Beautiful. Sinuous. You can take your stockings off in the bathroom,' he says without missing a beat, and gestures at a door in the corner of the workshop. He senses her hesitation. 'I need to see your feet properly, to design something that will be truly yours.'

She closes the door to the bathroom behind her and leans against it, her palm flat on her chest, breathing fast. *It's just a pair of shoes*, she tells herself. She catches her reflection in the mirror - flushed, tendrils of hair loosening. Tess unfastens one stocking, then the next, peeling them from her slim pale legs like a second skin. She feels exposed, raw, hair bristling at the nape of her neck, cool air on her skin. The bathroom is simple but immaculately clean. She hangs her fine apricot wool coat on a hook on the rough wooden door and pads barefoot across the workshop. The polished boards are warm and smooth beneath her feet. She feels her gait loosening.

'There,' he says as she settles back into the chair. 'See? You relax when you are barefoot.' He rolls back on the stool and lifts her right foot into his lap, cradling it in the warm leather apron between his thighs. 'Of course.'

'Of course what? You sound surprised.'

'You have the feet of a real dancer. Just think of all these feet have been through with you, how hard you have worked.' He runs his thumb across the welt above her big toe where the shoe has rubbed. It is intimate. Shocking. Tess is alert, breathing shallow. His palm cups the arch of her foot, the other hand encircles her fine boned ankle, his thumb and index finger almost meeting. She trembles at his touch. 'You have lovely feet.'

'They're terrible,' she says, surprised. 'All those years of dancing en pointe.'

'No. It shows dedication. Every scar, every toughening meant pain and hard work for you.' He looks her in the eye, steadily. 'And joy, maybe?'

Tess laughs, relaxing. 'Yes, lots of joy. You don't notice the pain so much when you are dancing. Only afterwards.'

'How old were you when you danced like that?'

'Twelve - no, maybe thirteen? You have

to wait until you're strong enough and your bones aren't malleable. I studied ballet for years, danced three times a week.'

'Your feet are perfect.'

No, they're not, I-'

'They are perfectly proportioned.' He slides a sketchbook beneath her foot and looks up at her. 'I have to pencil the outline, and then we will take some measurements.'

'Sure,' she says. The fine hairs on her skin rise as Marco slides the tip of the pencil around the outline of her foot, the shaft caressing her instep. 'Where did you learn to make shoes?'

'From our father, and our grandfather. I fought it for a long time, wanted to get out of the business, like Carlo.' He shrugs. 'But after a while I came home.' Marco turns to the workbench where a wooden last is clamped in a vice. Sawdust dances in the beam of the lamp. He takes down a cloth tape and grips the pencil between his straight white teeth. The tape loops around her foot, slides tight again and again. It is like a pulse, the sensation of his fingertips on her sure and tender. His head is bowed in concentration, marking down the measurements but she closes her eyes still, afraid of giving away how his touch has ignited her, a searing heat glowing deep in her stomach. Outside, beyond the window, a tree branch taps against the window, deep gold leaves glimmering in the sunlight. The tape measure loops again, sliding against her naked foot. She grips the chair, thinking of the tight coils of paper she bought for Bobby when he was small, paper flowers which unfolded in water, blooming, sharing their secret colour. That is how she feels. She makes herself focus on the book lying face down on the desk. 'Are you reading *To Kill a Mockingbird*'?

'Francesca leant it to me.' Marco smiles, glancing up at her. 'She wants to improve my English.'

'Do you like it?'

'I like this man - Atticus Finch. He has ...' Marco searches for the word. 'Integrity. I like that.'

Integrity, Tess thinks. Only the sound of Marco's pencil strokes on the paper break the silence. *Who are you? What are you?* There is a weight, a sureness to him, a strength which draws her like the needle of a compass.

'How does it work? I mean, what happens next, with the shoes?' Tess says, forcing her voice to be light. The silence is too much, flowing intimately between them like nectar. She had to say something, to break the intensity of it. All she wants to do is run her hands through his hair, bring him to her. Her nails flex against the arm of the chair like a cat, stretching.

'One of the boys will make up your lasts, while I complete the design. There are many stages to creating beautiful shoes, Mrs Blythe.'

'Tess.'

'It is an expensive hobby.' Marco tilts his head, inspecting her foot and making notes of any lumps and bumps. 'A pair of shoes can take six months-'

'We don't have that long?'

'No. For you I will make an exception.' He settles his hands on her foot. 'Your other foot, please.' Tess bites her lip in anticipation of the pencil outline. 'For you we will make something beautiful.'

'How many people does it take?' she says. *What would it feel like to kiss him?* she thinks. Tess watches his hands on her foot, imagines how they would feel on her calf, her thigh. She imagines him on her, skin on skin.

'Many people. There is the clicker who cuts the leather, the closer who stitches the uppers-'

'Sorry?'

'The top of the shoes. On and on and on. Many, many hands will make your shoes.' He rubs the tip of his thumb across his index finger, and Tess notices how tough his hands are.

'You enjoy your work?' She gestures at his hands, and Marco turns them over.

'For years they were ingrained with polish and glue, I did nothing but work.' He shrugs. 'It is satisfying. And you?' he asks, looking up at her from beneath a stray curl of dark hair. *Am I satisfied?* Tess thinks, her eyes widening.

She looks at her pale, fine hands. 'I think

hands tell you everything about a person,' she said, trying to change the subject. 'Funny, isn't it, how we see our own hands day after day and rarely pay them any attention.' She raised her right arm in a graceful, slow arc. 'In ballet, hand gestures tell you everything about a person, how they are feeling, what they are afraid of-'

'What they desire.' He tilts his head, sketching a line. 'Tell me about your work. Tell me about your life, Tess.'

She realises no one has ever asked her that before. She doesn't know why - maybe it is the warmth of the morning sun through the sky-light, or the scent of the workshop, or the close-ness of him, his strength and gentleness, but she talks.

'No one has ever-' she whispers. She sees him turn his head, straining to hear and her eyes open in surprise.

'Deaf in my left ear,' he says, tapping his temple. 'One too many thumps.'

'Thumps?'

'I was a boxer, when I was younger.' He smiles, eyes creasing. 'That's why I sleep on my right side, only way to get any peace in that crazy house of my brother's.'

'A boxer?'

'I won a few titles,' he says shrugging. 'But my last fight was years ago in Florence, before the war.'

'I was in Florence in 1938. My father

thought a summer in Italy would complete my education.'

'Did it?'

'It impressed Kit, anyway. He's never been.' Tess bit her lip. 'Our guide wanted us to go see a boxing match. I thought the name Affini rang a bell. Surely it couldn't be?'

'Imagine that, if we had met then.' The moment, the possibility blooms on the air between them, petals unfurling. 'I would have remembered you.'

'I was seventeen, just a child,' she says.

'I cannot imagine you as a child. You have such ...' Marco struggles to find the word. 'Seriousness-'

'Thanks,' Tess says, laughing.

'No - poise.'

'Thank you.' She smiles. 'I think. Are you saying I have always been old?'

'Perhaps we both are.'

'Tell me, how do you live, in Italy? Do you have children?' *A wife?*

'No, I live like a monk in the house I was born in.' He holds her foot in both hands. Every cell in her body shimmers, a flame rising from her toes to her crown. She longs to let down her hair, to let her head fall back in release. She realises she is gripping the arms of the chair and forces her hands to relax. He doesn't seem to have noticed the effect he is having on her. 'Just me and my young dog,' he says. She sees his shoulders fall a little. 'My old dog, he died, like yours.' His gentleness surprises her. It makes her think of a great white bear she saw at Central Park zoo, that latent, shambling strength. Marco glances up at her. 'I never married, if that is what you are asking.'

'No, of course-'

'My older brother Carlo emigrated, then died leaving Claudia with seven children and Frankie on the way. I guess I ended up adopting Carlo's family.'

'So you've stayed put in the place you grew up in?'

'I travelled, naturally, for work, but it is my home. It's my roots.'

'That seems so exotic, somehow. To me, at least.' Tess looks out at the treetops. 'I've lived so many lives I don't know where I am from, really. I miss ... I feel homesick all the time for some-where that doesn't exist any more. The Celtic name is hiraeth. I remember my aunt telling me about that.'

'It is just nostalgia, surely?'

'It's more than that. The Portuguese word is 'saudade'.' Tess lets her head rest against the back of the chair.

'You speak Portuguese?'

'No. In Provincetown, I've got a little shack up there, in the dunes, there are lots of Portuguese families. I got talking to an old man in the Atlantic one night-'

'Do you spend a lot of time talking to men in bars?'

Her eyes open wide, and then she sees the slow smile on his lips. 'No I do not. I was with a group of friends, and this old man just looked lonely and sad. I asked him to join us and have a drink. I asked him why he was sad-'

'You are a kind person, Tess Blythe.'

'He told me it's about the love that remains after something is gone.'

'A place? Or a person?'

She feels the weight of his question. Tess glances at him and smiles. 'Both perhaps. It's a little sad, a little happy.'

'A little like you, I think.'

He knows, she thinks. *He understands*. 'Me? I'm fine. I just have a restless heart, is all. I'm always looking for home.'

'Where were you born?'

'In Somerset, in my aunt Aphra's house. Kit and I were born in the same county and travelled half way round the world to meet one another. Isn't that strange?' Tess hugs herself. 'My father was at sea when I was born, so my mother stayed with her sister. I still miss that house, sometimes. I went back during the war, with Bobby.' She folds her hands in her lap. 'Tell me about your home.'

'No, enough about me. Talk to me while I draw something for you, Tess.' Her eyes prick with surprised, grateful tears. She cannot talk about herself.

'But I'm interested. Were you and Carlo close?'

'He was my big brother.' He smiles, but she sees the raw grief still, just below the surface. 'After our brothers died in the war, there was just us two left and too many sisters bossing us around. I always looked out for him, you know, even though he was the eldest. Carlo was always getting in over his head. He never did anything by half. it's like he knew he didn't have long, you know? When he died ...' He exhales. 'Claudia needed help. Frankie was a baby. All those kids.'

'You never wanted a family of your own?'

'They needed me. What more could I do?' His thumb rests against the arch of her right foot, checking something. It is like a brand to her, searing, delicious. Tess is lightheaded. 'I work to help them.' *Integrity,* she thinks. *There it is.*

'Weren't you ever lonely?' she says.

'I was never alone.'

'That wasn't what I asked.'

'What woman would take me, when I am raising my brother's family?' He rubs the dark bruise of stubble on his jaw, then sketches a long fluid line across the page. 'As I said, we are not talking about me. Relax, Tess.'

'I am. This is ...'

'Tell me all about your life. If I don't know you, how can I design a shoe for you? Start at the beginning.'

The silence stretches between them until she gives in. She tells him about Hong Kong, and London, and the countryside, and coming to New York. For the first time all the fractured pieces of her life are restored, brought together in one piece as smooth and seamless as the bolt of silk she gave to Frankie.

'There,' he says at last when she has fallen silent. He shows her the drawing. 'There's an elegant English heart to the design, a ... court shoe, with a low heel,' he says, kneeling beside her, their shoulders almost touching. 'Here, chiffon ties, like a ballet shoe.' He points out an embroidered detail, a fine knot of silk at the heel holding the ties. 'This is for the East in you, and this,' he says, tracing in a fine silver line along the midnight blue arch, 'is for New York.'

'Silver? With diamonds on the sole.'

'Crystals,' he says, smiling. 'Like the lights of the city, the night I met you. Or the scattering of stars over the sea you love so much.'

'Oh, they will be beautiful. Thank you so much.' Tess turns the gold watch, loose on her pale wrist. 'Look at the time. I must go, I have a class.'

Marco stands and offers her his hand as she steps down from the chair. He takes her wedding ring between his thumb and forefinger, slides it loose around her ring finger. 'You wear a band?'

'Of course,' she says, afraid again suddenly.

'But this marriage does not make you happy, any more, I think. Maybe it never did.' He pauses, gives her a chance to disagree. 'I think you made vows your husband did not keep-' Her eyes widen in shock. 'You, though ... you. He is a fool.'

'How dare you? No one has ever spoken to me like that-'

'Yeah, well that's their loss. Most people don't know what they want, and when they do they don't have the guts to go after it.'

'And you do, I suppose?'

'I do. I want you-' he says, and Tess gasps. 'I think I can give you what you need.'

'How dare you?'

'I promise, you have nothing to be afraid of.'

'Afraid? I'm not afraid of you.' She raises her chin.

'Yes you are. You're afraid of how you feel.' Marco tilts his head. 'I see you. I see you watching me.' Marco raises his gaze slowly to hers. 'I feel your hunger like a heat coming off you-'

'You know nothing,' Tess says, snatching away her hand. 'I should never have talked so freely with you-'

'I feel it too,' he says, looking down at her. 'From the first moment I saw you, I wanted you and now I think of you-'

'Stop. Please stop,' she says. *He feels it too*, she thinks.

'Perhaps I'm wrong. If I am, forgive me. But I feel drawn to you, and I think you feel it too.'

'You're leaving, soon. So what is this? A fling? Is that what you are asking me for? Is that how little you think of me?'

He pauses. 'I will be leaving soon, and I want to feel alive. And I feel alive around you in a way I've not felt before. Is that so bad?'

'I'm married,' she says. 'We're practically family. You want some sordid, secret-'

'We all have secrets.'

Tess is scared to look at him. *Does he know? Can he tell, somehow, that I'm available?* The distance between them is nothing, everything. *If I cross that line, I can't come back ...* Her lips part, she imagines them together, embracing.

'If I assume too much, I apologise. If not, I am here. Know that I admire you, I am ...' He pauses. 'You are an extraordinary woman, and your husband is a lucky man.' Marco reaches across her to pick up a pencil. 'I will not pressure you, I give you my word.' He turns to the desk and flicks through a gold edged diary, running his finger down the page. 'Come back in a week. Tuesday 7th. I'll have the lasts ready for you and we can check the leather to make sure everything is perfect before we make up the shoes.'

'A week?' Tess is flustered by his directness. 'Of course. I can't ...' *I can't wait*, she thinks. 'I don't know how to thank you.'

'After we work, you can show me around a

little.' He glances at her. 'That is enough.'

The thought of time alone with Marco scares her, thrills her. 'I'm not sure that's a good idea-'

'You have my word as a gentleman, I'll behave. Unless you don't want me to?'

'Marco ...'

'I promise.' He draws a cross on his chest. Marco scoops up the dog and grins as it nuzzles in to his neck, nudging his chin with its nose. 'Maybe we are just two lonely hearts with an afternoon to kill. It might be fun.'

Chapter 10

It is raining when she comes and he is waiting at the wooden door of the workshop, watching the water cascading down. Her red umbrella is a bright flame on the grey rain washed street. He knows it is her, it has to be. The umbrella has shielded her from the worst of the rain but she is still breathless, her cheeks pink, her hair flecked with raindrops like crystals.

That morning when she bathed, she had run the water as hot as she could bear. She touched herself, thinking of him. Tess stood before the full length steamed up mirror in her bathroom, and swept her palm from the floor up, revealing herself, skin smooth and lily scented from the hot water, the fine gold electric fur of her body brought to life. She noticed a fine trickle of blood on her pale thigh, and wiped it, surprised between her thumb and forefinger. She rarely bled, over the years. 'Dancers often don't menstruate,' her doctor had said. 'Eat a little more, fill out some. If you want another child, Mrs Blythe, you need a regular cycle.'

'I thought maybe you wouldn't come,'

Marco says now, smiling.

'I almost didn't.'

'And on time,' Marco says now, smiling.

'I'm usually punctual.'

'Except for me. You stood me up.'

'Our first appointment? That was a misunderstanding!'

'You make me feel ... special.' He gestures, open palmed. 'No guard dog?'

'You said I didn't need to be afraid.' Tess flashes a quick glance at him as she catches her breath, and grins. 'Looty hates the rain. What a day,' she says, closing the umbrella. 'This weather.'

'I like it, the way the earth smells.' He steps aside to let her in to the workshop, and closes the door behind them. A raindrop courses a rivulet along his throat, pooling between his collar bones. She envies it. Longs to place her lips there. She is glad of the ache in her stomach. It feels like the earth thawing after a long winter. The rain is muffled, and soft, pattering down on the tin roof above them. 'So. Your shoes.'

'Yes. Shoes.' She smoothes back her hair. 'How did they ...' She breaks off as he presents her with the laths, two burnished, slender moulds. She turns them over in her hand, fascinated. 'These can't be mine?' she lifts one of the lasts to eye level, runs her index finger along the slender elegant arch.

'I told you. Perfect feet.'

'How did you make them so quickly?'

'I have little elves working day and night for you.'

'They're beautiful.'

'I thought maybe this leather,' he says, handing her a piece of the softest nude suede like a gift.

'It feels like velvet,' she says. 'I love the chiffon ribbons.'

'As I said, I thought like ballet shoes.' He gestures at the drawing. 'From the front the shoes are simple, classic, but then when you are walking down the aisle and all eyes are on you-'

'On Frankie,' she says. 'No one notices the mother of the groom.'

'I cannot believe anyone has ever not noticed you, Tess.' She inhales sharply, and puts the leather on the workbench, holding her breath. 'So people will see the embroidery, the flash of silver, of diamonds on your feet.'

'It's too much. They're too beautiful.'

'I like to make something simple, but with a secret.' He places the laths square on the workbench, his fingers leave them reluctantly. 'Beautiful shoes for a beautiful woman.'

'Marco, I can't-'

'Are you hungry?'

'Hungry?' *How does he know?*

'For lunch. I missed breakfast.'

'Yes, yes I am.'

'There's a café across the street,' he says,

taking his dark jacket down from the rail. They pause on the pavement. It is raining softly. 'Shall I fetch your umbrella for you?'

'No, thank you,' Tess calls, running across the street between the cars. She glances back from the opposite side of the road and laughs. 'I love the rain, too.' They are breathless by the time they reach the shelter of the café awning, and he opens the door for her, a brass bell ringing.

'Menu?' the waitress tosses a plastic folder onto the table and takes a pencil from behind her ear. 'How's Claudia?' the woman says pointedly.

'She's good.' Marco gestures at Tess. 'This is Mrs Blythe, her son Bobby is marrying Frankie.' The woman raises her chin in approval, and takes their order.

'So where shall we go after this?' Marco says, sipping his coffee the moment it arrives.

'Afterwards?'

'It was a deal. You promised to show me around, do you remember?'

'Again, I thought you were just being polite.'

'I want to get a present for Francesca. A piece of jewellery. Something special. Where would you go?'

'Only one place. Tiffany's.'

'OK, and then where? I think I would like to lose an afternoon with you, Tess. What do you say?'

Chapter 11

Tess pauses on 5th Avenue, and checks her reflection in the plate glass window of the jewellery store. She is unused to the low dragging pain in her stomach. She thinks of ice, melting. *Funny, how unaware we are of our bodies until something goes wrong, or hurts,* she thought, laying her palm on her stomach. She looks herself steadily in the eye. *All we see is the packaging while our hearts, and lungs and all the rest quietly get on with keeping us alive.* Her focus shifts to the crowds teeming along the pavements behind her. *Every single one of those people has a conversation going on in their minds right now. They're thinking about what sandwich to have, or making love to the person they adore but can't tell, or someone who hurt them in 1954. All these thoughts, and the past and present and future flowing backwards and forwards along the street like a current.* She hums *Moon River,* and tilts her head, watching the reflection of the city, of Marco paying for the cab. *What is he thinking? What does he think of me?* He comes and stands at her side.

'What are you thinking, Tess Blythe?'

'Of the movie. Have you seen it? Holly Go-lightly stands here, eating a pastry, and-'

'Wait.' Marco jogs across to a pretzel stand and buys one. 'Ok,' he says, joining her again. He offers her some, and she shakes her head, laughing. 'We have to create the whole experience, no?'

'Holly Golightly says that nothing bad can ever happen to you in Tiffany's.'

'Everyone needs a place like that,' Marco says, frowning.

'Where's yours?'

'Me? There's a cypress tree on the hill near my house in the country. I can go and sit there with my dog, and look back at my home, and at Florence on the horizon, and I feel perfectly at peace.' He takes a bite, then tosses the pretzel into a nearby bin, and brushes the crumbs from his hands. The doorman swings open the heavy stainless steel and glass doors, and they step into the atrium of the store. Their footsteps are silenced by the deep carpet, and the low light enfolds them. 'I can see why she feels safe here,' Marco says, looking around the high ceilinged room with its vast Corinthian columns. 'Holly has her jewellery store, you have your place at the coast.'

'Do you miss your home?' Tess says, walking at his side.

'Perhaps I am still looking for somewhere, or someone that feels like home.' Marco turns and watches her.

'We are looking for a bridal gift,' Tess says to the sales assistant, laying her gloves on the glass display cabinet.

'Diamonds? Pearls?' he says.

'Pearls, I think,' Marco says, lifting the heavy rope around Tess' throat, his index finger sliding against her collar bone.

'Your wife's are exquisite,' he says, peering closer. 'Let me see what we have that is similar.'

'I apologise,' Marco says to her once the assistant has gone.

'Why?'

'He said you are my wife. I thought perhaps you would be embarrassed.'

'Why on earth would that make me uncomfortable,' Tess says, gazing down at the glittering display of diamond rings, deliberately not looking at him.

□

Marco walks up 5th Avenue, swinging a pale turquoise bag in his hand. 'Are you sure you wouldn't prefer a cab home?'

'It's not far, and it's a beautiful day,' Tess says. 'Besides, I don't feel like going home, not yet,' she says. 'Have you seen the park?' Marco shakes his head.

'Come on,' she says, running on ahead across the road. 'I've got an idea.'

They cross the Bow Bridge, and Tess

pauses to catch her breath, glancing over her shoulder at Marco. The pale arch of the iron bridge shines against the copper and yellow leaved trees, its wood struts are a warm red from the rain earlier. 'I love this bridge,' she says. 'It's my favourite place in the park. I don't know why, I can always think clearer around water. Do you ever feel like that? I used to spend hours riding the ferries in Hong Kong.' She blushes, feeling she is talking too much, and walks on. At the Loeb Boathouse, they rent a rowboat. Marco jumps easily down into the hull, and offers her his hand.

'This was a wonderful idea,' he says, bearing down on the oars. The boat skulls out onto the open water. Gold leaves drift down from the trees around them, the white columns of the boat house shimmering reflections in the water.

'I love this place in autumn,' she says. 'I always thought it would be a wonderful place for a wedding reception.'

'For Bobby?' Marco pulls back on the oars and the boat skims forward. 'I think it must be difficult for you as the mother of the groom to let go.'

'Let go?'

'Of everything. Let Claudia and Frankie choose the wedding venue, the flowers.'

'I'm used to it. Kit never lets me choose anything.' Tess leans forward and trails her hand in the water, glittering in her wake. 'I've spent my whole life letting go.'

'Tell me, have you ever loved another man, Tess?

'Apart from Kit, you mean? No.' She raises her face in surprise, narrowing her eyes in the autumn sun. 'There was someone, once,' she says, shielding her face with her hand to look at him. 'Nothing happened.' She looks out across the water. 'It was during the war.'

'Everything is different in war.' Marco bears down hard on the oars and the small boat glides across the quicksilver lake. 'How do you say? All bets are off.'

'We were apart for some time, you see. Kit was very keen that our child should be born in Somerset, as he was, and his forefathers.'

'A good tradition.'

'A necessary one were he to inherit blessed Midchester from his grandfather.'

'Ah. I see.' Marco exhales. 'I believe your husband likes money.'

Tess looks down at the palms of hand. 'My aunt, Aphra, always said to be wary of men with gaps between their fingers.'

Marco laughs. 'Why?'

'No good at holding on to money.' Tess turns her hands over. 'Kit's hands are like sieves.' She holds her own neatly interlocking fingers to the light, as does Marco. He raises an eyebrow, waiting for her. 'Yes, well, Aphra would approve of you.' Tess hugs her arms around her knees. 'Kit made me fly home, he was so determined the child was born in Somerset.' Tess smiled sadly. 'It was an unheard of luxury in those days. Ten days travelling through India, Egypt, Greece, Italy ...' Her voice trailed off. 'I think I threw up all the way from Hong Kong to Southampton.'

'But Bobby was born in England?'

'Sorry? Yes, yes he was. Kit was rather worried about the storm clouds of war gathering, and he wanted us safely out of there.' She pauses. 'Sadly he decided to stay on in Hong Kong, so did my parents.'

'They were stuck there?'

Tess nods. 'My mother and Kit were taken as prisoners of war in December 1941. Mummy died in the Stanley Internment Camp. Malaria. She - I don't think she ever recovered from the brutality she had seen. She's buried in the Military Cemetery there. I hope- well, one day I'd like to go back to Hong Kong, to take some lilies to her. She always loved the scent of stargazer lilies.'

'Your father?' Marco says gently.

'He was killed early on during the invasion.'

'I'm sorry.'

"*The eyes of the world are upon you - resist to the end.*' I'll never forget hearing Churchill's words. I knew father would never give in. He was on HMS Tamar, part of the China Station. They merged with the East Indies Station in December 1941 to form the Eastern Fleet.' Tess looks down at her hands. 'You know, they were making evacuation plans even in 1939, but my parents and Kit refused to go. Hong Kong was our home. My father was prepared to fight to the last, and mother wouldn't leave his side.'

'She was very brave. And so was your husband.'

'Yes. It still surprises me. I don't know why ...' Tess hesitates. 'Why did he stay?' She rallies herself. 'The authorities let foreign civilians stay as long they took on an auxiliary role. Kit was called up in September 1939 for the HK-RNVR - the Hong Kong naval volunteers. Mother volunteered at St Stephen's College. It was being used as a hospital. She - there was an awful massacre after the surrender on Christmas Day in 1941. I can't bear to think of what she witnessed, how terribly frightened she must have been.' Tess falls quiet. 'HMS Tamar was scuttled in December 1941 so that the Japanese couldn't get their hands on her. God knows what my father went through before he died. My poor mother.'

'She sounds like a brave woman, and loyal.' Marco lets the oars rest on his knees. 'She would be proud of you, Tess.'

'Do you think so? She never got to hold her grandchild, that's a great sadness to me. She would have loved Bobby. Adored him. She always wanted a boy.' She smiles sadly. 'Sometimes, I think there's not a family in the world untouched by the damnable war.' Tess hugs herself. 'I thought for long time that Kit had been killed, too.'

'That must have been terrible.'

'It was something of a surprise when he showed up in Somerset in Christmas 1945, put it that way.' She gazes across the water.

'A regular Christmas miracle, eh?'

'Something like that.'

'Has he told you anything of his experiences?'

'He never talks about it.' Tess glances at Marco. 'Did you fight?' He nods 'Do you talk about it?' He shakes his head.

'We are all the same.'

'Kit was ... He was very changed afterwards.'

'Is that not a sadness to you?' Marco pulls down on the oars and they surge forwards.

Tess feels like someone had kicked her in the solar plexus. 'A sadness? It's *the* sadness,' she says angrily. 'We never stood a chance. My life, my whole life is ...' She thinks of Kit's collections, the rows of hollow eggs and pinioned butterflies. 'It's built around this dead and hollow heart.' She leans forward and hugs her knees. When she closes her eyes she feels like she is flying above the water.

'I am sorry.'

'Don't. Don't be kind. You'll make me cry, and I hate crying.' Tess breathes in sharply, and smiles. 'Oh god, I'm sorry. I never talk like this.'

'It is good, I think?'

'I just ... I can't help feeling like I missed a step somewhere along the line. Like I missed my moment. I've done everything that was expected of me. I married, I - I had a baby, a career. Why aren't I happy?'

'Who said being good would make you happy?' She can tell he is smiling from his voice. She is afraid to look at him.

'I don't know when it was that I realised I've dedicated my whole life to making my family happy, and lost myself along the way. It's all I wanted, to make Bobby and Kit happy, so why do I feel so lost? It feels-' She struggles to articulate the feeling welling in her chest. 'I just have this sense that it could be so much more. It's just out of reach.'

'What is?' Marco stops rowing and the boat glides on in silence.

'Depth. Passion. Love.' Tess passes the palm of her hand over her closed eyes.

'You know you do that when you are trying to see something, to say something.'

She looks up at him, surprised, then down at her hands. 'I remember an old friend of my mother's said that when you have children you become the frame, not the painting. I get that, you know. I am so proud of Bobby, so glad that he is marrying such a beautiful, remarkable young woman-'

'But you're still hoping you have time to be the masterpiece?'

Tess laughs. 'You're wicked.'

'You don't need to worry about your Roberto. Francesca will make him the best man he can be, mark my word.' Marco smiles and rows on. 'And you have time now, to become who you were meant to be all along, I think.'

Tess looks up at the sky, at a cloud of swifts whirling and stirring the clouds above the water. 'Fly the nest. What a funny phrase that is. Do you have that, in Italian? Empty nest.'

'It is what life is about, movement and change, and the young moving on to make a life of their own.' He pulls down on the oars. 'It is bittersweet, of course. You are proud, and yet your heart breaks a little all the same.'

Images crowd in on her, like flicking through an old photograph album known only to her. Bobby's face, the first time she looked into his fathomless black eyes when the nurse handed him to her in the maternity hospital. That love. That deep, fierce love which so took her by surprise. His exuberant first steps, running away from her down a sunlit dappled path, the sound of his laughter rising on the spring air like a babbling brook. Riding after him across the moor, his narrow shoulders lowered over the conker hued withers of his pony. She remembers watching him blowing bubbles on the beach in Provincetown on a cold day whose sunshine held the first false promise of summer. She stood just behind him, perfect, iridescent bubbles drifting up and away into a cloudless blue sky. She feels him faintly now, like those bubbles. She remembers the feel of his limbs, the solidity and goodness of him, how the weight of her child on her hip made her feel rooted and grounded for the first time in her life. The child was like ropes and ballast steadying a balloon. She was needed. She belonged to someone. Day by day, month by month, year by year he needed her less. She felt herself floating free, a bubble, a balloon rising, guy ropes loosening. 'Or is it him who is floating away?' she says under her breath. She thinks of the Saturn rocket, of floating in space, of freedom.

'I'm sorry?' Marco says.

'Would you go to the moon, if you could?'

'Of course.'

'Thank you!' she says, laughing. 'Kit thinks I'm quite mad.'

'But why? Can you imagine, seeing the earth from space. How perfect and insignificant it would all seem.'

'What would you miss, in space?'

'In space?' He hesitates. 'I would miss bonfires, and coffee, and the smell of lavender and jasmine. I would miss my dog. I'd miss my family, and friends, and watching the sunrise from my terrace in Florence, the way the sky turns from midnight blue to apricot, the way the light blooms.'

'It sounds beautiful.'

'You should see it.' He tilts his head. 'What would you miss, apart from Bobby, and your husband?'

You. It is the fist thing she thinks, as it begins to rain. *This moment.* This perfect moment. Marco rows towards the bridge, and they shelter there, cocooned, the boat rocking gently, rain falling beyond the shadows. 'I'd miss it all.' Tess rubs her arms, cold suddenly. 'Dancing, music, the beauty of it all.'

'You are cold,' he says, shrugging off his jacket. 'I think some memories are like the chorus of a song, repeated and repeated until they become the heart of your melody, the music of your life.'

'Thank you,' she says, gathering the jacket around her.

'It's a choice, which memories you play most, for good or for bad.'

I choose, she thinks, breathing in the scent of his cologne on his jacket. *I choose you. You are my melody.* 'I have this cottage, up in Provincetown, right on the tip of Cape Cod,' she says.

'You said. In the dunes?'

'Yes. I'd miss that.' She holds the thought of it now like a jewel - the clear, clear light, the view across to Long Point lighthouse. Her toes curl in pleasure at the thought of warm, rough silvered wood, sand, salt water. 'It's mine, you know, nothing to do with Kit, or Bobby, though he used to come up there in the holidays when he was smaller. I guess the sea is in my blood.' Tess shivers, and crosses her arms. 'My grandfather ran away to sea when he was fourteen, and my father was in the Navy-'

'And your husband.'

'Kit only joined up for the uniform.' Tess laughs softly and glances up at Marco. 'I'm not being disloyal, he's the first to admit it. He says he's seen enough of the sea for a lifetime. Kit loathes the cottage - or shack, rather. He doesn't do casual. The town closes up for the night by eleven, you have clams or fish or lobster for every meal. It's too bohemian for him, too shabby. I've got no electricity, and the water's brackish, but I love it.' Marco leans towards her, wraps his jacket closer around her shoulders. In the still shadows she feels the warmth of him.

'You surprise me.' He holds her gaze. 'I like that about you.'

Tess looks away across the water. She is lightheaded from the intensity of him. His close-ness. His warmth. 'It's real. You wake with the light, and curl up with candlelight after sun-set. I even love the sand getting everywhere - there's always sand in the bed.' She laughs softly, brushes a strand of hair from her face. *The bed.* She imagines Marco there. 'Most people abandon ship after Columbus Day.' She chatters on, trying to distract herself. 'But I go whenever I can, all through the winter, and swim in the ocean.'

'Is that safe?'

'Oh, sure there are jellyfish, and Portuguese Man O'Wars, and sharks.' Tess grins, glances at him. 'But mostly it's just cold. Very cold. It's crazy.'

'What do you do in the winter?'

'I normally close up the shack and rent a place closer to town, with a few more home comforts. I love it when snow fills the deck. You just load up the stove with logs and curl up in a nest of blankets. Maybe I'll buy a bigger place, one day, but I'll always keep the shack. I'd have moved there years ago if it weren't for Bobby and the dance studio. Now-' She hesitates. *Now I can do what I want.* 'Well, now Bobby has Frankie to take care of him my time is freer.'

'Will your husband not miss you?' Marco leans back. 'I know I would.'

Tess blinks. 'I - Kit's so busy with work. I'm sure he'd be glad to have me out of his hair more often. And I have wonderful Elaine, who can run the studio in her sleep.'

'So this is your time, now? Your third act.'

'Sorry?'

'You have been a child, a mother, and now you are free to be yourself.'

□

'This is me,' Tess says, pointing along East 79th. She is walking slowly, not wanting their day to end. 'I have a class.'

149

'Can I watch?' Marco says.

'You want to watch me teach?' *Please don't go*, she thinks. *Not yet, not yet ...*

'Sure.' He glances at her. 'Claudia said I need some lessons, didn't she? Maybe I can pick up some tips.' Marco shrugs. 'Besides, I just don't want today to end-'

'Not yet,' they say together, and laugh.

They walk side by side to the studio in silence, their arms, the backs of their hands brushing, the tension sparking between them like electric gold.

'Make yourself comfortable,' she says, gesturing to the row of chairs at the back of the studio. 'Can I fix you a coffee?' Marco shakes his head, and takes a seat. In the dressing room, Tess closes the door and leans against it for a moment, pressing the palm of her hand against the old, chipped paint. *My god.* Her stomach is taut with hunger, desire. She undresses, glancing at the door, the bare flesh of her arms, her legs alive. Tess hears the first pupils arriving and hurries, snagging the first pair of tights she pulls on. She picks out a second pair, and wriggles in to them, losing her balance, knocking against the locker. The thought that he is there, waiting, is too much. She looks at herself in the mirror. 'Get a grip,' she says under her breath, scraping her hair back into a bun. 'It's just a dance. He's ...' The thought of him rushes through her like a stone plunging down into sunlit water. She is liquid.

Golden. Tess closes her eyes, breathes deeply. 'What am I doing? You can't do this,' she tells herself. 'Yes. You can.'

She feels his gaze on her through the class. He sits among the mothers, a lion among a fluttering cloud of butterflies. He is impassive, unreadable. As Gladys leaves, switching off the light above the piano, she widens her eyes at Tess, a question, mouths 'my God.' The heavy door of the studio swings closed and they are alone.

'I hope you enjoyed the class,' Tess says.

'You are too good for them,' he says, standing. 'I can see it in your every movement. Why did you never dance professionally?'

'I should be getting back,' Tess says, not meaning it.

'Weren't you supposed to be teaching me to dance?' Marco says, shrugging off his jacket.

'Fair's fair,' she says, leafing through the albums. 'Do you know what you will be dancing to with Frankie?'

'Who knows. It is a tradition in our family. The bride's father has one last dance with his little girl before handing her to her groom.'

'I think that's lovely.' She slides a record from its sleeve, eases it onto the spike of the turntable. The hiss of vinyl fills the air, the opening notes of *'Take Good Care of my Baby'*. 'Appropriate?'

Marco shakes his head, and flicks through

the records. 'This one. *It's Now or Never*. Tess' hand trembles as she takes the needle from the record, and the song skips into silence. She steadies herself, places the record, the arm carefully, and flicks the switch. They walk in silence to the centre of the dimly lit studio as the needle hits the smooth edge of the track, a hiss of looping vinyl before the music begins, and he lifts his hand. Tess raises her palm to his, not touching. The air holds its breath, shimmering between them and they circle, gazes entwined, the music drawing them closer, his arm around her waist. Tess raises her chin, her hand resting lightly on his shoulder, his hand. At her nod, they move as one, an ease and lightness to their steps.

'I thought you said you couldn't dance?'

'I told you at the club, I don't dance.' He holds her closer. 'There's a difference.' He leans down to her, his lips brushing her ear. 'Anything you can teach me?'

'Let go,' she says. 'Trust me.' She closes her eyes. As they dance she remembers standing at the edge of a lake in China as a child, the mountain wind on the water. She felt the same then - weightless, limitless, at one with the air around her, a fleeting moment of grace. They dance on, even as the tune ends and the record falls silent.

'Dance for me, now,' he says.

'I can't. I mean, I haven't danced for anyone for years, not since-' She falters.

'Please. Let me watch you.' His head is

bowed, his lips brushing her cheek. She knows he is giving her a chance to run, if she wants to. He is giving her a last chance. Desire flows around them like the hum of a power cable. Tess backs away. *Last chance*, she thinks. In the dressing room, she glances at the back door and hesitates. She reaches into her locker and takes out the red pointe shoes. She kicks off her dusty black ballet pumps, and returns to the dimly lit studio with the red shoes swinging from her left hand, ribbons unfurling. She pads barefoot to the centre of the room, and sits on the floor to tie them to her feet.

'Do you know the story of the red shoes?' she says, not looking at him.

'The film? The woman who couldn't stop dancing?'

'In the fairytale, she cuts off her feet to escape the shoes.' Tess stretches, the red satin gleams. 'In the film the girl is punished because her desire is more important than her wedding vows.' She stands, strides over to the record player and selects some music, flicking through the sleeves. 'What do you think of that?'

Marco sits at the back of the studio in the shadows. She cannot see his face. His tie is loose, lying dark against his white shirt, his arms extended along the back of the seats. She thinks of a Pieta she saw as a girl, of the hot shame she felt, her desire for the luminous, languid, body in the shadowy still and the hush of the gallery. She remembers the visceral curve of muscle, skin, the chalice dip of collar bone. Tess slides the record onto the spindle, lifts the needle.

'That's the power of the red shoes. They reveal the truth about the wearer.'

'There is a penalty for every prize,' he says.

She looks directly at him, and lifts her chin, ready. The music swells, the yearning notes of an oboe concerto weaving around her arms, her legs, swirling between them like smoke. She dances as she has not danced for years, for a time when she was young, and free, and the future stretched before her as unblemished and full of possibility as the yards of silk she imagines unfurling at that moment in a tailor's in Queens. *And then the cloth is cut, and a decision made.*

Marco walks towards her and takes her in his arms. 'Tess,' he says. There is no hesitation now. She rises up to meet him, equal and sure. Overcome, she looks up at the skylight, at the night glowing city.

'We can't,' she says. 'What is happening?'

'We are happening. You, and me.' His hands are on her waist, her hips.

'Hello?' Elaine calls, her heels clicking along the corridor. Tess steps away from Marco, alert as a startled deer. 'Tess, are you in here?' Elaine stops dead as she sees Tess by the record player, turning off the music.

'Very good, Marco.' Tess lifts the record from the spindle, and turns to the door, sleeve in hand. 'Hi, Elaine? Is everything ok?'

'We were just driving by and I saw the lights were still on - I knew you weren't working so I got my darling husband to drive round the block so I could run in and check. Hello Mr Affini,' she says. 'Private lessons?'

'Tess is being kind enough to help me.' He gestures at his supple tan Oxfords. 'Ironically for a cobbler I have two left feet.'

'I'm sure you don't,' Elaine says, curling a strand of hair with her index finger. 'I imagine you're a marvellous-'

'I'll lock up, Elaine,' Tess says brightly. 'Perhaps you'd be kind enough to give Mr Affini a lift to the station?'

'Of course. Toodleoo,' Elaine says, raising her eyebrows at Tess, waving goodbye, her fingers folding one at a time to her palm.

'Thank you,' he says, tipping his hat to Tess and walking away. 'I look forward to our next lesson.'

Chapter 12

Kit Blythe plays a lot of sport. He plays hard. He rows at the club until he is dizzy with exertion, pulse racing, lights flashing in his eyes. He plays squash, hard, daring his heart to break, thinking with each whack of the ball of all the people who have crossed him over the years, of every demanding, tasteless client and recalcitrant bank manager. No slight is too small to be cherished like a gemstone in the glittering cavern of his memories. Kit thinks of himself like a goblet - a fine eighteenth century crystal goblet - full to the brim with anger and fear, the meniscus bulging, threatening to overflow. Exercise, unforgiving exercise is a release. Kit usually wins. It's a rare competitor who can match his lean, muscular anger. Afterwards he relieves his tension furiously, silently in the shower cubicle, his face contorted in agony, ecstasy. For a fleeting moment he forgets. For a moment he is at peace.

But not for long. He will not give in. He will keep himself in check. He will do what he promised. *I have been unfair to you*, he thinks, roughly towelling his hair dry, embellishing the scene he has imagined playing out with his wife a hundred times. Tess is seated in the window of the den, gazing away from him out across Central Park, her hair upswept, the early evening sun illuminating the fine gold hairs at the nape of her neck. *I knew how it would be when I married you, you did not. I have been ashamed of what I am my whole life and I can bear it no longer. I don't want to be ashamed any more.*

Kit takes a freshly laundered shirt from his locker, and dresses, tying his polished Oxfords so tight his feet hurt. There are no soft edges to his elegant, muscular body at all. His smooth stomach is hard, washboard ridged. Kit's trousers have the same slender waist he wore at Harrow. He keeps the same secrets he had at school as well.

Kit knows he will never have that conversation with Tess, or anyone, but still it is a release just to imagine telling the truth. He scrapes his fair hair into a precise side parting, setting it in place with a little wax. *I'm free*, he realises. *After the wedding, we will divorce. Of course, I'll see Tess and Bobby once in a while.* He pictures civilised Christmases, grandchildren, even. *I'll be free, soon.* Kit takes down a zipped leather portfolio from the locker, and tucks it under his arm, humming *At Last.* The metal tips on his heels click with military precision as he strides through the marble lobby. He pictures an open road. A sports car accelerating. He is so lost in his Technicolor future he does not notice Bobby entering the club just as he is leaving.

'Hey, Dad?' Bobby catches at his arm.

'Bobby? Sorry, I was miles away.'

'Thinking about that Hoffman job?'

'We've had a disaster with the swags.' Kit rolls his eyes.

'Hold the front page!' Bobby laughs.

'I had to sack my new assistant-'

'That pretty redhead? Shame.'

'I've sent the whole lot back to be re-stitched.'

'Boy, sounds like a life or death situation,' Bobby says, laughing.

'Details, Bob. It's all about the details.' Kit grins at his son. 'Are you still coming over at six tonight? With your new family-'

'Hey, don't be like that. They're swell.'

'*Roberto ...*'

'I like it.' Bobby shrugs. 'And yeah, we're coming over. They want to take you out.'

'What's the big surprise? Claudia left a message that they have some treat lined up. I loathe surprises.'

'Alright, alright,' Bobby says, giving in. 'Marco has tickets to some opera.'

'Oh god. The cobbler likes opera.' They step aside to let a group of men leave the club. The sounds of the street rise up as the plate glass door swings open.

'I never get why you don't like the opera. I

thought an old snob like you would be all over it.'

'It's so mawkish. So ...'

'Emotional?' Bobby looks his father in the eye. 'Anyway, it's not for you. He's arranged it for Frankie. Belated birthday present.'

'Did she like your grandmother's diamond ring?'

'Loved it. Thanks again Dad, it meant a lot that Mom gave it to us.' Bobby said as Kit checked the time on the clock above the reception desk.

'I must dash. We'll see you later. Your mother will be thrilled.' Kit calls over his shoulder. 'I'll be sure to pack a clean hanky for her.'

'Hey, Dad?'

'Yes?'

'Is everything ok?'

'Never better.'

'Say, can I come over to the Hoffman's after my swim? There's something I want to talk to you about.'

□

'Hoffman residence,' Kit says, picking up the intercom. He covers his free ear blocking the noise of sawing and drilling from the kitchen.

'Young man down here says he's your son, Mr Blythe,' the concierge says.

'Send him on up, Charles, thank you.' Kit hangs up and makes sure the door is on the latch.

Kit's immaculate white sleeves are rolled up, revealing smooth muscled, tanned arms. He busies himself untying the linen wrap of a Persian carpet in the empty living room as he waits for Bobby. 'In here,' he calls, hearing his son's footsteps in the hall. The floor to ceiling windows shed vast rectangles of light across the parquet floor.

'Jees, this place is something else,' Bobby says, crossing the room to take in the view of Manhattan. 'You could fit our entire apartment in this room alone.'

'Not bad, is it?' Kit nods his chin at the other end of the carpet. 'Here, give me a hand with this.'

'Don't you have serfs to do this kind of thing for you?'

'Usually. I like this part of the job, though. All the boring bits, the wires and pipes are done, all the paintbrushes have been cleared away. This is the fun bit.' Between them they unroll the lavish carpet, its jewel colours shining in the autumn light. 'Perfect,' Kit says, stepping back. He squats down on his heels and smoothes down the corner of the rug. 'Almost perfect. The weavers always drop a stitch, because nothing is as perfect as god.'

'You've told me that story a hundred times,' Bobby says, squatting down beside his father.

'Have I?' Kit runs his hand through his thinning hair. 'I must be getting old, repeating my-self.' He glances up as two porters in grey boiler suits appear at the doorway with an ornate tur-quoise silk sofa. 'Over there,' he says, indicating a spot at the far end of the room. 'Centre it be-tween the columns, please.' He chews the inside of his cheek watching the men. 'Wait. Let me see.' He strides over and rips back the protective polythene. 'I knew it! Take it away. This is tur-quoise, not teal. I specifically said to Maurice it must be teal.' Kit jabs a finger towards the Per-sian rug, pointing out the flecks of blue silk. The porters look silently at one another, biting their tongues and flex, lifting the sofa from the room.

'Dad, is there somewhere quiet we can talk?' Bobby insists.

'Honestly, I'm surrounded by halfwits and incompetents.' Kit watches the retreating por-ters. 'I heard that,' he yells after them.

'Dad, it's only a sofa,'

'Did you see on the news there's a huge fire sweeping across the Hollywood Hills? Burt Lan-caster's place has gone up, and Zsa Zsa Gabor's. Hundreds of homes destroyed.' Kit looks around the apartment. 'The Hoffman's have changed their minds so many times I've been tempted to put a torch to this place.'

'Can you take a break?'

'Good idea. Why don't we grab a sandwich round the corner,' Kit says, swinging his jacket from the back of a chair in the kitchen. 'Do you need some advice? Some running around money?' Kit reaches into his breast pocket for his wallet.

'No, it's not that. It's just I'm heading back to college in the morning, and we won't get a chance to talk tonight with everyone around.' He presses the brass switch for the lift, and waits, looking up at the lights illuminating the sign floor by floor. 'Dad, is everything ok with you and Mom?'

'Of course, why do you ask?' Kit is instantly on edge. *What's he noticed?* he thinks. *What's Tess said?* They step aside to let a porter wheeling a polythene wrapped armchair pass. Kit wrinkles his nose at the smell of Scotchgard. 'The Hoffman's do insist on letting their five - *five!* Shih Tzus sit on the furniture. Imagine living in a fabulous home like this and having to spray all your lovely new chairs with Scotchgard ...'

'Dad,' Bobby insists, stepping in to the lift.

'I swear, when those dogs attack it's like being mauled by a brace of mop heads.' Kit picks a stray hair from his sports jacket.

'Dad?' The doors sweep closed and they are alone.

'No,' Kit says eventually. 'Everything is not alright and it hasn't been for some years. In fact, I don't think it's ever been right.'

'But surely you can work it out?'

'I've asked your mother for a divorce. It's-'

'A divorce?' Bobby cries out. 'But you can't.'

'Bobby, I wanted to wait to tell you until after the wedding. We didn't want to spoil anything. And you mustn't tell your mother I've told you.' Kit looks at Bobby's crestfallen face, and cups his jaw in his hands. 'You always were an observant child. You'll make a fine lawyer, I think.'

'I can't bear it. The thought of you two apart.'

'Bobby, your mother and I care a great deal about one another, and we love you. But you have your own life now, your own family soon-'

'So this is my fault? If I wasn't leaving home-?'

'That's not what I meant at all.' The lift doors sweep open and they stride across the marble entrance lobby in silence. The doorman pushes the heavy brass and glass door to the street, touching his hat as they step onto the street and the noise of the lunchtime traffic, horns blaring, a jackhammer drill down the road engulfs them. 'It's time we all had a new beginning,' Kit says raising his voice. 'I can't make your mother happy, Bobby, and I'm tired of feeling like I am responsible for her unhappiness.'

'I'm not hungry, suddenly,' Bobby says. The sounds of the street, the crowds on the pavement roll around them, between them like two leaves swept away in a stream. Kit feels a gulf widening between them, a parting of the current.

'Perhaps I shouldn't have told you.'

'And what, just pretend we're happy families?'

'That's what your mother said.' Kit puts his hand on his son's arm. 'I promise, no one will guess a thing. You and Frankie will have the most perfect of wedding days-'

'I can't stand it, all this fakery. Keep up appearances, and then what? A discreet divorce, you go your separate ways?' Bobby shakes his head.

'Please, don't be angry-'

'Is Mom ok?'

'She'll be fine.'

'Sure she will-' Bobby puts his fingers in his mouth and whistles for a cab, stepping out into the traffic.

'We're a family, Bobby.' Kit feels helpless. 'All I want, all I have ever wanted, was for you both to be happy.'

'Happy?' Bobby laughs. A yellow taxi screeches to a halt beside him, and flicks off its light.

'Don't be like that. Maybe once you're a parent you'll see none of us are perfect. They don't give you a rule book when you marry, Bobby, nobody tells you this is how to be a good husband, a good father. We're all just making it up as we go along.' Kit's throat is tight. He digs his fingernails into his hand, pushing the emotion down with the same determination he rows, and hits, and runs. *I won't let it out. I won't.* Kit holds the taxi door open for Bobby. 'I promise, this changes nothing with the wedding.'

'Yeah, right. Mom's on board with this?'

'Don't worry, Bob. Nothing can possibly go wrong.'

Chapter 13

'Where are we?' Kit said, 'Do you know where we are?' He leant forward, peering through the grimy window of the yellow cab into the night. The tail lights of the car with Claudia, Frankie and Bobby swerved to the curb ahead.

'Kit. Stop it,' Tess whispered. 'You're drunk.'

'I am not,' Kit said, deliberately. He swayed a little as he sat back, taking a couple of attempts to flick his white silk scarf over his shoulder.

'We are in Little Italy, no?' Marco said, turning in the passenger seat to look at Tess. She sat way back in the cab, next to her husband, her cheek leaning against the cool steel door frame.

'I thought we were going to the opera?' Kit said. 'Why aren't we going to the opera?'

'Pay no attention to him,' Tess said, sighing. 'Kit comes out in hives the moment he crosses Park Avenue.'

'Here we are,' Marco said, as the cab stopped. He came round and opened Tess' door, offering her his hand. He squeezed her fingers gently.

'Thank you,' she said, not looking at him. She waited for Kit to walk on ahead, watched him steady himself on the doorframe of the bar.

'You look beautiful,' Marco said, his voice a breath on her skin.

'Marco, someone will notice-'

'Your husband never sees what is under his nose.'

'Welcome! Come on in,' Claudia called, ushering them in from the teeming pavement of Mulberry Street through the red white and green awning of a small bar. The 'closed' sign was turned in the window. 'Welcome, welcome.'

'Are we here? What is this place?' Kit said, his brow crinkling.

'This is where I first saw Frankie,' Bobby said, taking his fiancée's hand.

'I can't believe you arranged this for us,' Frankie said, standing on tiptoe to kiss Marco's cheek.

'It's nothing. Happy birthday. An old friend I grew up with in Florence sings with the company who are in New York on tour. When I told him you are getting married he wanted to give you a little performance tonight, just him and another singer.' Marco put his arm around his niece and squeezed her shoulder. 'It is less, of course - no orchestra, just a piano, some strings-'

'So we're *not* going to the opera?' Kit gestured at his evening suit.

'Oh good god, Kit,' Tess said under her breath. 'This is much more fun.'

'Relax, my friend,' Marco said, guiding him into the bar. 'Why don't you loosen your tie, get yourself a drink?'

'Oh goodie, a bar.' Kit walked ahead. The café door swung closed after Marco, and he stood behind Tess. The back of her silver evening dress hung down, a low v on her spine. In the dim shadows Marco traced the edge of the fabric, her shoulder blade with his index finger, unseen.

'Marco,' she whispered as the others chattered on, making their way to the bar. His touch felt like a flame to a gunpowder fuse, she was afraid the others would see her skin sparking, igniting in the shadows. The café had been cleared of tables, a row of six chairs simply arranged at the back, and a deep red velvet curtain hung from the ceiling at the end where a piano stood ready. Claudia gestured to the waiter, issuing orders in Italian. He raised a bottle of Prosecco from the ice bucket, eased the cork out.

'Now, Kit, we ain't got your fancy Beluga, but how about some bruschetta?' Claudia offered Kit a tray of antipasti.

'Mm, yum,' Kit said, wiggling his fingers above the tray, deciding which piece to take.

'Sit beside me.' Marco's breath warmed the curve of Tess' neck. 'I can't stop thinking about how it felt to dance with you. If I can't hold you in my arms, I must be close to you.' He led the way to the bar.

'So what are we being treated to tonight?' Kit said, turning to them. 'Verdi? Puccini?'

'Rossini. La Cenerentola,' Marco said. 'Cinderella.'

Tess smiled politely, taking a translucent sliver of Parma ham from the simple white platter Claudia offered her. 'Not my kind of thing,' Claudia said, 'but Frankie's always loved the opera and Marco reckoned you'd like it. Classy, you know.'

'Thank you,' Tess said. 'What a treat.'

'Classy,' Kit whispered to her. 'That's you to a T, darling-'

'Stop it.' Tess led him away to sit down. She noticed Bobby watching them. He wasn't paying attention to what Frankie was saying to him, but staring hard at Kit, a fierce look in his eyes. She winked, and mouthed 'don't worry', hoping to reassure him. 'Please behave, Kit,' she whispered. 'Don't spoil this for Bobby.'

'I may have many flaws, but I am not a bore when in my cups. I will behave perfectly, as always.' Kit's gaze followed the musicians as they stepped out onto the makeshift stage, and he clapped. 'Cinderella, might have guessed,' he whispered. Kit stretched out, and folded his arms as the lights fell. 'Shoes.'

□

In the darkness, Tess sat between Marco

and Kit, Rossini's aria shimmering around them. The intimacy of the music, the darkness, of Marco beside her was overwhelming. Marco leant back in his chair, stroking the smooth curve of her arm in the shadows. She felt him watching her, and she turned, a single tear coursing down her cheek. Her breath caught as she stifled a sob.

'Oh, goodness sake - here,' Kit said, shaking out a clean white handkerchief, not looking at her. 'Every time. Every single time.' He took another sip of Prosecco, spilling some on his shirt. His bow tie hung loose, his collar askew.

'Thank you,' she whispered, dabbing at her eye.

'Are you alright?' Marco said. 'Do you need some air?'

'It's just so-' The breath shuddered in her throat. 'So beautiful. So intense, like this. I can't bear it-'

'She's a shocking weeper,' Kit said under his breath, lurching across Tess to talk to Marco. 'I don't get it. Where's the glass slipper?' he said to Tess.

'It's the bracelet,' she whispered, forcing down the tight knot in her throat. Tess glanced over her shoulder once Kit settled back in his seat. The bar windows were full of faces, people on the street craning to see the performance.

'Allow me,' Marco said. He stepped silently away, and flung open the bank of glass windows, letting the cool air flow in while the music embraced the night. Tess imagined the perfect notes freed, rising away from the bar, the crowded street, on a shining silver stave, each crotchet and minim floating away from the piano, the singers' voices up to the stars, the moon. The music reached its climax, and the singers bowed, while the crowds on the street applauded. Frankie and Bobby leapt to their feet, clapping wildly.

'Bravo,' Marco said, stepping forward to embrace the prince.

'There we go,' said Kit, applauding politely. 'Happily ever bloody after.'

'Do you have to be so cynical?' Tess said, dabbing at her eyes. 'I thought it was beautiful. If you just took the time-'

'I'd what? Be swept away by emotion? No thank you.'

'Kit, Tess, another drink?' Claudia called. She gestured to the waiters to take a tray of glasses to the performers.

'Kit will have a coffee,' Tess said firmly.

'How do you take it?'

'Dark and bitter, like my heart.' Kit stuck out his bottom lip, rolling his eyes upwards to look at Tess. 'I don't see why I can't have one for the road?'

'I give up,' she said, standing. Kit moved away her chair, and swept a glass of wine from the waiter's tray as he passed. 'You don't see, do you? You've *never* seen, that's your problem, and now it's too late.'

Kit watched Tess walk to the bar to join Claudia and Frankie, his gaze drawn to Marco. *What does she mean, now? What don't I see? God, I'm sick of it.* Kit watched him watching Tess. *All this time, she still believes in fairytales. Would even that be good enough for Tess? Elizabeth always said I reminded her of Prince Charming.* Kit's mind drifted back across the years to Hong Kong, dancing with Tess' mother at their wedding. He caught his reflection in a mirror on the cafe wall, its silver foxing at the edges. *Just like me. I look tired, and old,* he thought. *Maybe I was Prince Charming, once, but not for Tess*. Kit closed his eyes, letting the bubbles of Prosecco fizz on his tongue. *Tess.* There was something on the edge of his consciousness. What was it? Kit's thoughts bubbled up from the darkness one by one. With a start, his eyes snapped open. He registered Marco's steady focus on Tess. Marco broke away from the group of singers to take a tray of champagne to the women. He gave a glass to Tess first, his fingers lingering on hers. *Oh, I see*, Kit thought. *I see it all. Who's keeping secrets now*?

Chapter 14

Tess is sheltering from the rain in Central Park beneath the bridge, the anticipation of another dance class with Marco at the end of the day as delicious a thought as sweet plums in the icebox. She lets her mind wander, thinks of bread, freshly turned out from the oven, golden, fragrant. She thinks of fresh asparagus tips dipped in warm melted butter. Her stomach quickens with hunger, she shivers with pleasure breathing in the smell of rain on the water. She thinks of the boat, the day she went rowing with him. She sees a man walking ahead of her, his collar turned up and fedora pulled low, and thinks for a moment it is Marco - he has the same broad shoulders, same animal strength, but as he turns she sees it is another man altogether. Tess registers the surge of life she feels as she thinks of him. His smile, as he turned to her in the doorway of the workshop. It was raining then, too. Her heart is in her throat, her hand rests there. *I'm in love. I'm falling in love with him*. She holds the secret like a first breath, urgent, pulsing, alive in her.

The rain is not letting up, but she does not

care. She runs, turns full circle, her face raised to the sky. Her feet dance above the slick pavement. She remembers telling him: *I wanted to be a dancer, once. Why? he said. Why breathe, she replied.* Tess had smiled at the recognition she saw in his face. He understood. *My parents, well, my mother wasn't keen. Then I married Kit, and I had Bobby ... and your body changes.* Now every nerve, every fibre of her hums and dances to its own secret melody. She remembers dancing with him at the club. *How funny, I'd barely registered him then,* she thinks. Sure, he was tall, and handsome, but there was no lightning bolt of attraction. *Slow burn,* she thinks. Marco, falling for him was a slow dance. She thinks of her hand resting against the hard muscle of his shoulder, how his arm encircled her narrow waist. She wants to be held, again.

She unclasps her umbrella and hurries on through the park, her basket over one arm. She thinks: *to the people I pass I look normal.* Just another New York housewife hurrying home from the market with steaks for tea and milk and bagels for the morning. All those years of changing nappies, and tidying rooms, and smiling at dinner parties, day after day of brushing her teeth and lining her eyes with kohl, tinting her unkissed lips with crimson, and wiping it away as the interminable lonely night stretched away. Day after day after day. And all the time she was burning inside.

You are too passionate, her mother used to say. *Too passionate? Is that a bad thing? How can you be too passionate in this short and crazy life? Oh God,* she thinks. *All these years of waiting and waiting to feel like this*.

He's family, she thinks. He's practically family. Her cheeks are wet with rain. She pauses at the crossing on 5th Avenue, looks up at the windows of the apartment glowing gold in the falling light. She thinks of how it had been described when they took on the lease. *Thirty foot living room, library, dining room, each with its own fireplace. Kitchen, pantry, servant's hall. Four baths. Four beds.*

And not one of them has seen any passion, any love. Tess thinks for a moment. *As far as I know*. She pictures Kit in his office, meticulously matching colours and patterns and tasteful faux antiques. *Conjuring stage sets for people's faux lives.* She instinctively tidies her hair, straightens the hang of her coat. *My faux life,* she realises suddenly. She imagines herself and Kit on a darkened stage, him seated at his desk, not looking up as she implores him. The walls of the study lift away, and she dances into the darkness. The magic is leaving her. She feels the quiet rhythm of her heart returning. She wants it back, the feeling she had running through the park. She wants to feel alive again.

At her desk, Tess flicks on the green glass

shaded lamp, and picks up a sheaf of papers, and the telephone receiver, dialling Kit's work number.

'Hello,' she says, crooking the phone beneath her jaw, extending one slim leg then the next onto the corner of the desk. 'I'd like to speak to Mr Blythe. It's Mrs Blythe.' She waits, twisting the flex around her index finger.

'Tess? Is everything ok? Where have you been? I called.'

'It's fine, I just took a walk to the market to clear my mind. Kit, I had a meeting with my lawyer and accountant this morning to go over the books at the studio.'

'Don't you mean our accountant?'

'No, my accountant.' Tess narrows her eyes, looking out at the sun setting over Central Park. 'You're divorcing me. I wanted to know where I stand.' She waits, the static on the line flaring. 'When were you going to tell me we're bankrupt?'

'Not the dance school,' Kit says. She hears the click of a lighter, he exhales slowly. 'That's yours. It was always in your name.'

'I mean the rest. My trust from mother and father, the sale of Aphra's house, the great Blythe estate in Somerset. Our joint finances. It's all gone, Kit.'

'I'm sorry. I'm truly sorry-'

'It's always been 'what's mine is yours and what's yours is yours', hasn't it, Kit?' Tess flung the papers on the desk. From her desk drawer she took a key and unlocked a drawer in her dresser. She slipped a yellowed letter headed 'Coutts" from an old photograph album, and tucked it into her handbag. 'Aphra warned me and by god she was right.' Tess slammed the phone down and swept her arms across the desk, piling papers into the large copper bin at her side, not resting until everything - the files, the paperweights, the staplers, the piles of utility bills had gone. 'There,' she said, standing and flicking off the light.

□

Tess has taken extra care with her hair. It falls across her shoulder in deep gold waves. Her eyes are smudged with kohl, gleaming emeralds. She lines her full lips with a nude shade, runs her tongue across her mint clean teeth. He is late. She closes her eyes, sashays across the empty dance studio in time with the Elvis Presley track. She is wearing a new dress, a simple black pencil sheath which clings to her curves. Her freshly bathed skin is electric, the warm breeze like a touch. She feels alive, quickened.

'Dancing alone, how sad is that?' Bobby cries out, tumbling through the door of the studio hand in hand with Frankie, Marco following behind.

'Bobby? Frankie?' Tess searches Marco's face for an answer but he is unreadable. She hides her shock in humour and puts her hands on her hips. 'Who are you calling sad? What a lovely surprise.'

'We thought we'd crash Uncle Marco's lesson. See if you can give us a couple of pointers for our dance, too.' Bobby wriggles out of his jacket, slings it over a nearby seat. 'What do you say?' He rolls up his sleeves and loosens his tie.

'Only if it's no problem, Mrs Blythe,' Frankie says, blushing.

'Of course I'd be delighted, dear. And I told you, do call me Tess. You make me feel like I'm a hundred years old.' Tess turns to the record player, hiding her disappointment behind a bright smile. 'Now, have you decided what tune you'll dance to?'

'The new one from Elvis. Frankie loves it - *Can't Help Falling in Love,*' Bobby says, reaching across and flipping the record over.

'It's our song,' Frankie says, reaching out to touch his arm. Tess wonders how it feels to have that unthinking intimacy with someone, to have that freedom to touch, to be touched. *I want that*, she thinks. *More than anything*.

'Oh, that will be lovely, perfect,' Tess says brightly. She closes her eyes, lets the tempo of the song pulse in her. 'Now,' she says, positioning Bobby in front of Frankie, and raising their arms. Tess holds their hands in hers, dances with them, Bobby moving between the two women. The kids can't help laughing, full of high spirits, tripping over one another's feet, but there's a tight knot in Tess' throat. She thinks how she used to dance with Bobby when he was small, resting his feet on hers, spinning round and around. The joy on his face. The spring brook laughter bubbling up out of him. How happy they were.

'There,' she says, releasing him, stepping back a little. She feels Marco watching them. 'Beautiful. Keep going. You're doing well. Bobby, raise your right hand a little, shoulders down.' She watches them, her hands clasped beneath her chin. 'Frankie, you're a natural.'

Tess backs away until she is standing at Marco's side. 'That was very moving,' he said. 'As I will give Frankie away at the wedding, it was like watching you hand over your son to her.'

'They make a beautiful couple,' Tess said, unable to look at him. Her throat tightened, fierce tears pricked her eyes. It was like he could read her emotions. 'I am so happy for them-'

'But?'

'You're right,' she says, exhaling with relief, the feeling welling up in her calming.

'Saudade? Happy sad?'

'I just feel like I did my best as a mother, and it still wasn't good enough.'

'But why? Why always the best? Do you think the world will stop turning if for once, just once, you are good enough?' Marco's eyes crease as he smiles down at her. 'Why don't you let yourself have some fun? Right now?'

Tess glances at him, and smiles.

'Shall we?' Marco offers her his hand and they join Bobby and Frankie on the lamp lit studio floor. 'When you dance, how do you feel?'

'It depends. Sometimes when I see something, or hear a snatch of music, it's like everything is all mixed up together. At the beach the other day, it was like the wind and the water and movement came together. I could see a dancer on stage, clearly. A dark stage with water, and every movement reflected, and the wind lifting her hair, her skirt. A new kind of dance.' Tess laughs. 'I don't know. Do I sound crazy? I have to dance or I'm lost.'

'I found you,' Marco whispers in her ear. 'You'll never be lost again.'

Chapter 15

'That was fun,' Frankie said running across the road hand in hand with Bobby, her glossy ponytail swinging. 'I love your mother. She's so gracious, and gentle-'

'Gentle?' Bobby laughed. 'Have you not noticed the red hair? She has her moments, I can tell you.' He flipped up the collar of his herringbone check overcoat, shivering.

'Well I think she's beautiful. She's been nothing but kind to me. A lot of women can get really funny with their daughter-in-laws, that's what Mama told me.'

'Nah, she's always wanted a daughter.' Bobby squeezed her hand. Nothing seemed to matter when he was with Frankie. Not his parents, not the squares at college telling him he needed to work harder, not Marco. *He hates me*, Bobby thought, striding across the road. *He thinks I'm not good enough for Frankie*. He glanced at her profile. *He may have a point*. 'Mom told me, she thinks you're swell, reckons you will be the making of me.'

'Is that so?' Frankie leant in to him, swinging her bag as they walked along the grey pavement. 'I can't wait, Bobby. I don't care if our apartment is tiny, and we have to sit on orange boxes. I just can't wait for it all to begin. To be with you. Really with you.' Bobby turned and kissed her at the crossing, and the night stood still around them. Evening traffic jammed the roads, red tail lights flaring in the deep blue night. Every cell in his body pulsed for her, urgent and longing. *I want you*, he thought. *I want you, I want you-*

'I love you,' Frankie said softly.

'Love you too.' Bobby leant his head against hers for a moment, his lips brushing the fine hair at her temple. *Torts,* he thought, wracking his brain for something dull enough to distract him from wanting her. Bobby thought of his mind as a series of filing cabinets stretching off into the dark corners, each one labelled: *Civil Procedure, Contracts ...*

'Where are we going?'

'A new place I heard about just off Times Square. I want to keep dancing.' He hugged her to him quickly before they ran across the road. 'Any excuse to have you in my arms for a while longer.' Frankie looked up at Bobby, her eyes dark with desire. Their steps slowed on an unlit, quiet stretch of sidewalk, the air shimmering between them like the strings of a guitar, and he pulled her into the forgiving shadows of a doorway. She raised her face to him, let him kiss her again, his tongue sliding, urgent.

'Be patient,' she said, breathlessly breaking away. 'Not long now.'

Bobby tucked his head down, holding her closer still, pressing the curve of her back to him. 'I'm burning up for you, Frankie. I can't wait-'

'Well you're gonna wait,' she said, dancing away, her hand reaching out to him.

'You're a hard woman,' he said, adjusting the seam of his trousers.

'Me? I'm hard?' she said, flashing him a quick grin.

They walked on, and Bobby checked the address on a slip of paper in his wallet. 'Should be there,' he said, pointing to a flickering neon sign above a fire escape leading down into the darkness. They joined the queue, sheltering in one another's arms, rock and roll pulsing the smell of smoke, perfume and beer out into the night from the blue lit doorway. 'The Office?' she said. 'I heard about this place. 'Where's your husband?' 'Oh, he said he's working late at the office.' She pulled Bobby into the club, laughing. 'What are we doing here?' she said. 'This place is ... it's got a reputation.'

'Live a little.' He paid the cloakroom attendant to take their overcoats, and put his arm around Frankie's waist, held her close at his side as they walked through the crowded club, his eyes adjusting to the darkness, the noise. 'No one will bug you while you're with me, your Ma thinks we're with my mother, and there's a great band playing tonight.' Bobby spoke to one of the hostesses and they settled at a table on the edge of the stage, a corona of red lamplight illuminating the dark grey cloth. Frankie looked around as Bobby ordered a bottle of Budweiser and a coke for her.

'Bobby,' she said, touching his hand. 'Isn't that your Dad? What's he doing in a dive like this?' Bobby squinted his eyes, looked across the room as the guitarist struck the opening chords of Del Shannon's *Runaway*'.

'Nah, he wouldn't be in a pl-' He paused. His father was seated with a group of young people and deep in conversation with dark haired man at his side. 'I'll be back in a minute.' He prowled around the edge of the dancefloor, stood at his father's side. One of the girls looked up and nudged Kit, who turned.

'Bobby?' Kit pushed back his chair, a steady smile on his face. 'What a surprise.'

'I could say the same.' He offered the young man his hand. 'We haven't met. I'm Robert Blythe.'

'My son,' Kit said. 'Alec and I are working on a project together. This is his girlfriend, Rita.'

'Yeah, we're doing a project,' Alec said, leaning back against the bar.

'It's been crazy today, thought we deserved to let off a little steam.'

'Couple of drinks before heading home. That's all,' Rita said, and hiccupped.

'You kids having fun?' Kit said.

Bobby glanced back at Frankie, waiting for him. 'Enjoy your drinks,' he said, turning.

'Bobby, don't be like that,' Kit said, catching his arm. 'This isn't how it-'

'Hey, you're divorcing Mom,' Bobby said, throwing up his hands. 'You want to hang out in some seedy pick up joint partying, knock yourself out.'

'Robert-'

'Oh, Robert, is it now. Don't be a bad boy, *Robert.*' Bobby shook his head, walking away.

'You remember Wednesday for supper?' Kit called after him.

'Sure.' Bobby raised his hand, not looking back.

'Everything ok?' Frankie said as he settled at her side. 'You look upset, baby.' Bobby drained his bottle of beer in one. He raised his hand to the waiter, two fingers.

'I'm fine,' he said. 'Don't worry.'

'Baby, let's dance,' she said, pulling him on to the dance floor. Bobby took Frankie in his arms, slow dancing to *Blue Moon*. 'What is it?' she said eventually, her lips against his ear. *What's he doing here? And who is that young guy?* Bobby thought, frowning. It looked like they were having some kind of disagreement. Kit was shaking his head. Bobby knew that expression. His father wasn't going to back down, but his friend seemed to have the upper hand, leaning back on the bar with a casual, animal grace. Every time Frankie and Bobby turned on the dance floor, his attention snapped back to his father. Bobby could tell Kit was watching him, too. 'Hey,' Frankie said. 'Hey, Bobby, I'm here.'

'Sorry, baby,' he said, holding her closer. Kit rose from his bar stool, slipping away into the crowd from the bar, and raised his hand in farewell to Bobby.

'What's eating you?' she said as they pushed their way through to their table.

'Nothing. It's nothing.' He chewed his lip. 'Tell me something, did your parents argue?'

Frankie frowned. 'How would I know? Papa died just after I was born. But Marco and Mama do.'

'Mine never do. Not a cross word in all these years.' The fresh bottle of beer rolled a little as he slammed it on the table. 'Oh they have their little spats, little barbs like fish hooks.' He shook his head. 'Their marriage looks perfect and pretty like spun sugar but it's hollow inside.' Bobby looked across the club to the place at the bar where his father had sat. 'You know, I didn't notice it so much, living with them all the time. You just get used to this low level tension. Like toothache, or - what's that ringing in your ears called?'

'Tinnitus?'

'Yeah. Like that. Just a general sense of something being off. Now I've moved away it's clear to see. Dad's always going on about how he hates fakes. He hates the clients he works for with their new money and zero taste. Sometimes I think he's the fakest person I know. He invented himself. Mr hand made shoes and suits from the tailor, and portraits of old guys in gilt frames we're not even related to. Try asking him about his parents, or where he came from. He invented this persona, this Englishman abroad.' Bobby waved his bottle of beer towards the space at the bar, the empty glasses. 'Sometimes I feel like I don't know either of them at all.'

Chapter 16

'We could have walked from the studio,' Tess said, pulling her red silk wrap around her shoulders. The taxi driver pressed down on his horn, blaring.

'I'm exhausted,' Kit said. 'It's been non-stop at the office all day.' He yawned, stretching, his hand brushing Tess' arm, her breast. Tess leant away. She felt claustrophobic, trapped in the dark cab, imagined the streams of stationary traffic clogging up the avenues of Manhattan. Kit had been staring at her for the last couple of minutes, too. I *want to get out,* she thought. *I want to run.*

'Do you remember that old saying, 'not safe in taxis'?' Kit said, sliding his hand along the cool banquette seat, and up over Tess' thigh.

'What on earth do you think you're doing?' Tess recoiled, pushing him away, but Kit's fingers gripped her thigh, he leant in to kiss her. 'Leave me alone,' she said, the heel of her wrist pressing against the shirt studs of his evening shirt. She turned her face. 'Stop it, Kit, stop it!'

'Say, lady, you ok?' The taxi driver said.

'It's fine, she's fine,' Kit said, sitting back and running his hand through his hair. 'Darling, I'm sorry. I just-'

Tess stared at him, horrified. 'What on earth has got into you?' She thought for a moment. *Marco. He's sensed something*?

'I saw that cobbler all over you the other night. The thought of spending another evening watching him drooling over you-'

'Is that it? You can't bear the thought of someone else finding me attractive?' She hugged herself. 'Now that you've thrown me out like a once loved toy, and you see that someone else wants me, you're jealous?'

'What's he got, hey? What can he possibly give you that I didn't? Sex? If it bothers you that much you should have said. We could-'

'Don't be ridiculous, Kit. I've always known you don't have feelings like that, for me.' Tess shrank back into the corner of the seat. 'Marco ... he's different.'

'Give me a break. I know I'm not him, I'll never be him-'

'Kit, you are the one who started all this. For God's sake, you asked me for a divorce. If you hadn't, we would have carried on quietly, just as we always have ...'

'All these secrets people keep. All these lives that might have been.' The taxi nosed its way through the traffic and pulled up outside the Metropolitan Museum of Art. 'Just do me a favour and don't embarrass me, or Bobby and Frankie.' He waved at them, waiting with Claudia and Marco on the steps of the Museum. Couples in evening dress strolled up towards the torch lit entrance, and Kit opened the taxi door for Tess. She stood, and the sheath dress of ivory satin slid into place, cool to her touch. She looked up and met Marco's gaze, watching her, drawing her to him.

'Hey, Mom,' Bobby said, jogging down the red carpeted steps to greet her. He glanced at his father and turned away. 'Everyone's here. What a crowd,' he said, putting his arm protectively around Frankie as they greeted one another and pushed their way through the milling audience in the lobby. The rock and roll music swelled as they walked through to the reception.

'Say, isn't that the young guy from the Peppermint Lounge?' Claudia pointed up at the stage.

'Joey Dee?' Tess blinked as a bank of flashbulbs sparked, photographers pushing forward to catch the dinner suited guests twisting.

'It looks like Mr Rorimer isn't happy.' Kit said, biting the inside of his lip.

'Who's he?' Claudia said, leaning forward, the light catching the heavy diamante jewels at her throat.

'The Director.' Tess watched as the man pointed and gesticulated towards the door. 'Someone's in trouble.'

'I heard these guys have played for balls at the Plaza and the Four Seasons,' Frankie said.

'And Mayor Wagner's Victory Ball,' Kit said. 'Look at them. All the stuffed suits love this stuff, they are lapping it up.'

'Stuffed suits?' Bobby said under his breath, and laughed. 'You're one to talk.' Kit glanced at him, warning him.

Tess felt the weight of Marco's gaze on her. He stood behind them, one tanned hand tucked in his pocket. She felt him, waiting for her.

'Look at this joint,' Claudia said, gazing around the room. 'It's beautiful. All these gorgeous dresses, the jewels-'

'I thought you might enjoy this evening,' Kit said, taking her elbow.

'Excuse me,' Tess said to Claudia. 'I'm just going to powder my nose.'

Tess waited in the marble atrium for Marco to come as she knew he would. She took a flute of champagne from a waiter passing with a tray, and leant back against a cool, smooth column, sipping her drink. The voices of the crowded party echoed up into the dark shadows of the soaring ceiling. She noticed Marco walking towards her but she did not turn. There were too many people who knew her, who knew Kit here.

'I must talk to you alone,' he said, leaning around the column from her, out of sight.

'But how?' She raised her chin in recognition of an elderly couple passing on the other side of the room who waved a greeting to her.

'Fall faint. I'll save you.'

Tess set her glass down, and walked across the crowded room, Marco following. She imagined the scene from a great height, the dinner suited men in their fine jackets and among them her vivid hair, her pale shoulders like an autumn leaf borne downstream on a dark river. And behind her somewhere he was following her, waiting to catch her. She raised her hand to her forehead and stumbled. She felt Marco's strong arms lift her clear of the crowd as her eyes closed and her head fell back.

'The lady is fine,' he heard her tell someone. 'A faint, that's all.'

He carried her into the quiet dark shadows of a side room. 'Oh god,' she said as he set her down, and her back pressed against the cool tiles. His fingers entwined with hers, pressed her hand to his lips. 'I can't bear it.'

'I think of little else but you. I have to see you,' he said, his lips grazing her cheekbone when she turned her head away. 'When can you get away?'

'Kit's suspicious,' she said. 'I feel so guilty, for feeling like this. I can't do this, not before the wedding. I can't do this at all. We've been together so long, I have to fight for our marriage-'

'If you have to fight, it's not worth saving.'

'You're wrong,' she said.

'Love is not a battle.' Her hip bone fitted perfectly in the curve of his palm. She felt his hand slide to the small of her back, his thumb and forefinger resting in the indentations of her spine, easing her forward, firm, sure.

'He made a pass at me tonight.'

'How dare he.' Marco stood taller, she felt the tension in him. 'The thought of another man-'

'He is my husband. He's a good man. He's just never had much luck. But he's always stood by me, and Bobby-'

'If you have to justify why you love him, you don't.' The silk of her dress slid across her stomach. She felt the edge of his jacket, the hard buckle of his belt. She felt how he wanted her. 'You deserve more, Tess. You need more.'

'I don't know what I need.'

'Look at me.' He waited for her to raise her face to his. 'Come with me now, I have something to show you.' He led her by the hand to the door, then ushered her forward through the crowd.

'There you are,' Claudia said, turning to them.

'Tess is unwell,' Marco said to Kit. 'I'll take her home.'

'How kind,' he said.

'I don't want to be a nuisance,' Tess said, wrapping her red scarf tight across her bare shoulders. 'It would be a shame for you to miss the meal.'

'You do look a little feverish,' Kit said to her, pointedly. 'Are you sure?' He turned to Marco.

'It is no trouble at all. Why spoil your party? You know I hate crowds,' he said, glancing at Claudia, tapping his ear.

'He's deaf,' she said to Kit, raising her voice. 'The noise bothers him.'

'Have fun,' Marco said to Frankie, and nodded at Bobby.

'You ok, Mom?' he said.

'I'll be fine,' Tess said and squeezed his arm, leaning in to whisper in his ear. 'Make sure your father doesn't drink too much, and that he dances with Claudia?'

☐

'Thank God,' Marco said, loosening the collar of his dinner suit as soon as they settled back in dark interior of the yellow Dodge taxi cab.

'It feels very wicked to be running away.' Tess flashed him a smile. 'Do you really not like parties?'

'Not like that,' he said, undoing his tie. 'Good friends, good food, good music - sure.' He gazed out of the window. 'But that kind of party when people are always looking over your shoulder while they talk to you to see if there's someone more important they should be sucking up to?' He shook his head.

'Where to?' the cab driver called back.

'The Empire State Building.' Marco turned to Tess and took her hand, their fingers lacing together on the leather bench seat. 'I have something to show you.' They drove on in silence, Tess watching the familiar lights of the city drift by.

'I'm afraid,' she said at last in the darkness.

'So am I.' His thumb caressed the side of her hand.

'I don't know why I'm telling you everything.' Tess turned to look at him. 'I don't know why I'm being so honest with you.'

'Because we let one another in. Because we are tired of spending our lives pretending everything is fine when it isn't. Fine's not good enough any more.' He raised her hand to his lips. 'I want to feel, and to give love, to feel alive again.'

Tess sensed the taxi driver watching them in the rear-view mirror, and glanced at him. 'This ok?' he said. 'Traffic's at a standstill further down town.'

Marco leant forward and paid him, before coming round to open the door for Tess. In the dimly lit maroon and grey marble Art Deco lobby, Tess waited while Marco spoke to one of the security guards on duty. She looked up at the gold leaf ceiling soaring thirty feet above them, her gaze tracing the lines of the sunbursts. The lobby felt womb like to her, warm and enfolding. She thought of the elevators bearing people up to the sky, to the viewing platform, and wondered if the astronauts launching into space in their rockets felt the same sense of peace she felt now. A sense that they were right where they should be, that it was all about to begin.

'Come,' Marco ushered her towards the elevators and they followed a burgundy suited doorman. The speed of the ascent took her by surprise. She felt her stomach fall away, the pressure in her ears.

'It's so fast,' she said to Marco, and he took her hand again.

'There is a long way to go.' They took a second elevator, and a third, until at the viewing platform the rest of the people got out. 'Follow me,' he said, his eyes sparkling. They went through a door, away from the public areas of the building, and climbed ever narrower steps and ladders.

'Did you plan all this?' Tess called back to him, climbing step by step above him. 'I feel like I'm climbing to the moon.' She lifted the hem of her evening dress to avoid tripping on it.

'No,' Marco said. 'But I like the view.' Tess looked down at him and widened her eyes, smiling. 'It is a happy accident that my old friend is working tonight. We are lucky. This is meant to be.' Eventually, Tess found herself at the entrance to a small circular room.

'Where on earth are we?' she said.

'Normally we only allow VIPs in here,' the security guard said, sorting through some keys.

'But my friend owes me,' Marco said.

'Anything for you, Mr Affini.' The guard ushered them in.

Marco swung open a small portal door, and gestured with his chin. 'Go on.'

Tess' heart quickened stepping out onto the 103rd floor parapet balcony. All that separated them from the night sky of Manhattan was a waist high limestone wall. 'Oh God, it's beautiful,' she said, overcome by the thousands of glittering lights below, mirrors of the stars above. 'We're on top of the world. It's like you've brought down the heavens.'

'I knew you would love it,' he said, standing close behind her.

Tess felt electrified, her skin sparkling, the cool night breeze around her. Her hair, her red silk scarf, the hem of her dress lifted - she felt if the wind were stronger it might carry her away into space. 'I feel alive,' she said. 'That's what you were talking about, wasn't it?' She raised her arms to the air. 'With you, I feel alive!' She closed her eyes and lifted her face to the stars. Her silk scarf freed, and blew away, catching on a metal girder just below the balcony. 'Oh no,' she said. Marco peered over the edge, reaching for it. 'Be careful!'

'It is too far away,' Marco said, his fingertips straining for the fluttering cloth. 'Forget it. I will buy you another.' He straightened up and slipped his arm around Tess' waist.

'There is no other. I can't possibly lose it. Kit will notice. It was the first gift he bought when we moved to New York.' Tess' brow furrowed. 'I was feeling homesick for Hong Kong, and he said the red silk would always remind me of home. He said it would be lucky.' Tess turned to Marco. 'Please, I have to get it, for Kit.'

'Kit? What does it matter if he notices?'

'It matters, of course it matters.' She burst out then: 'I can't have him and I can't have you? What kind of misery is this? I wish I'd never met you.'

'Misery? That's the last thing I want to cause you.' He looked down at his hand, hid the tremor in his fingers by slipping it into his pocket. 'You don't mean that. Tess, We all dream of the chance moment which changes our lives. The moment we feel we are truly alive.'

'Alive?' Tess shook her head. 'Oh, this is a beautiful moment but it will pass, won't it? Like everything. One day all this will be is a beautiful memory.' She looked down at the scarf fluttering in the breeze. 'I'm an almost person. Almost a ballet dancer. Almost a wife. Almost alive.'

'Before you, my life was orderly, and I was done. I was folding my life up neatly like a clean white sheet, and now ...' He looked down at the scarf, caught on the metal. Tess wished it would free itself.

'Now?' she said.

'You have come into my life like an explosion.' Marco took her face in his hands. 'It is a gift, don't you see? Our lives aren't ending, they are just beginning.'

'Before you I was reduced to a function,' she said and lowered her eyes. 'Wife. Mother. Not a person with feelings and needs and I was taken for granted. Completely taken for granted. They don't see me. You. You see me. You see me.'

'Tess,' he said, his lips searching for hers, but she turned from him.

'Fulfilment comes with a cost, though, don't you see? Are we going to pay the price? Are they?'

'Is that all there is? Duty? Have you never loved another man?'

'Never.'

'I wasn't looking for an affair, I wasn't looking for you.'

'But you found me.' She hesitated. 'You found what you needed. And I do need you. I need you.' Tess' voice broke. The realisation of how much hit her so hard she gasped for air like a diver, surfacing. 'I love you.' The truth of it pulsed in her, urgently. 'I'm falling in love with you. But I can't be with you. I love my family too much. I can't do this to Bobby, not now.' A tear rolled down her cheek.

'Then when? I know you. I know you have all this music inside of you waiting to come out. All this beautiful music. We can't spend the rest of our lives regretting that we didn't take a chance on one another.' He held her closer, his hands in her hair, fingers cradling her skull. 'I sensed the ache, the need in you the first time I saw you, because I see it in my mirror, in my own eyes, every day.' He leant his forehead against hers. 'I have been ... I've been so lonely. I've been ...' He hesitated. She sensed he was trying to tell her something.

'Marco? What is it? Was there someone?'

'No, no. It is not that.' He smiled sadly. 'It does not matter. I've been so restless. Burying myself in my work, my brother's family. When all the time, all I have been waiting for is you. You.' Marco thought for a moment. It seemed to her he was making a decision, and then he laced his hand in hers. 'If I hold you, you can reach your scarf I think.' Tess' eyes widened in fear. 'Trust me. I will never let you fall.' Tess stepped forward, looked down at the city swirling below. 'Trust me.' She braced her legs against cool stone of the balcony, reaching. She felt Marco take her weight, holding her. 'Trust me,' he said, and she leant forward, further. Her hand reached out, the fabric brushing her fingertips. 'A little further.' She was weightless then, powerless, leaning forward on the tip of her toe. She felt like she was floating free above the night city. If he let her go she would plummet to the earth.

'I have it,' she cried in triumph, waving the scarf like a banner. 'Don't let go!'

Marco drew her safely back to the balcony,

to his arms, and looped the scarf around her neck, gathering her to him, laughing with relief. And she kissed him then, captive of his heart, free at last.

Chapter 17

In the half light of the empty workshop, Marco worked with his head bent over the bench. Tess's new shoes gleamed. The pale leather had a pearlescent quality, a fine nacre sheen picked up in the shell buttons, the sea grey chiffon ties criss-crossing like a ballet shoe. The radio on the desk crackled, the opening notes of Peppermint Twist breaking the silence. Marco looked at the old leather chair, remembered Tess sitting there, how her hand felt in his when he helped her settle back for the fitting, the lightness and strength of it. He closed his eyes, remembering how it felt to kiss her the night before and the rain fell above him, pattering on the tin roof, rattling the casement window.

'You there, Marco?' He glanced round at the sound of Claudia's voice. 'You work too hard,' she said, shaking out the dark headscarf covering her hair. She swung a basket onto the counter, and lifted out a covered plate, setting down a soup spoon. 'Minestro-' she began to say, the word turning to ashes on her lips as she saw the shoes. 'They're beautiful,' she said quietly, lifting

one of the chiffon ribbons with her index finger. The shoe seemed to dance in the dim light,
shadows caressing the fine arch, the slender heel.
'They're for her, aren't they?' It sounded like
someone else speaking. He saw Claudia knew,
then. She looked at him. 'Marco?'

'She hates her feet. I wanted her to feel
beautiful.'

'Because that's what you think?'

'What if I do?'

'Marco, don't do this,' she said, her voice
crackling blue with static.

'Do what? I just want her to feel-'

'This is about Frankie,' Claudia said.

'You sure? You sure this isn't about you,
Claudia?' He swung round on the stool and
squared up to her. 'The good widow Affini.'

'How dare-'

'You want everyone else to be alone, like
you. What are you going to do when the last of
the boys marry, eh?'

'Don't.'

'You're happy enough having me around
the place like some eunuch.'

'Marco, I have never stopped you bringing
someone home. I want you to be happy, but not
like this.'

'Claudia, don't do this,' he said, throwing
down a small card box, diamante crystals scattering like stars on the dark bench. The simple
bowl of minestrone lurched and splashed.

'You screwed her, didn't you?' He saw she found strength in the familiar words. *Screwed her.*

'Is that what you want to hear? You want me to say it meant nothing?'

'So I'm right!'

'No-' Marco's brow furrowed. 'You're not. I haven't - we haven't. It wasn't like that.'

Claudia grasped the bench. 'How could you?' Marco wished he could help her. He knew that feeling, like the old boards of the workshop had lurched beneath her feet, had swelled and risen like the timbers of a ship casting anchor. The air knocked out of her. 'You've fallen for her.' She looked at the shoes. Marco took down the last for Tess' right foot, turned it over in his hands, the silence stretching between them.

'Yes,' he said without looking at Claudia. He set the last down on the workbench, his index finger tracing he curve of the toe. 'You happy now?'

'Her? Seriously. She's not your type.'

'Type?' He frowned.

'I want to hear that you made a mistake,' Claudia said, her voice shaking. 'I want to hear you say that you are breaking it off for the sake of Frankie.'

'This has nothing to do with Frankie.'

'This has everything - everything - to do with Frankie. What kind of a mess have you made between you? The mother of the bride and ... and-'

'And what?'

'The head of our family. It's-' Claudia's lip shook, baring her teeth. 'How could you?'

'I just wanted to feel like this one last time.'

'Does she know?' Claudia said. Marco shook his head. 'Then if you don't tell her I will.'

'How? How can I tell her I'm dying when she has made me feel more alive than I have ever felt before?'

□

Claudia dressed with care, laid out her corset and stockings on her pristine bed alongside her smartest black dress before bathing. Her hand, perfectly steady, slicked kohl across her eyelid, darkened the arcs of her brows. Finally, a determined slash of scarlet lipstick. She was magnificent. She carried the chiffon ribbon tied box before her on the bus to Manhattan, holding it on her lap like it would shatter. Once in a while she'd reach across and check the child sleeping in the Moses basket at her side.

She rang the bell of the apartment on 5th Avenue, and waited, heard the glide of the lift door, the distant whoosh of the elevator falling back to earth, muffled by the dense carpet, the polished wood and chrome. As she waited for the door to be answered she wondered what it was, the tangible sense of money in the air.

Where did it come from? It was more than simply quality - a better grade of stone or wood. It was as if the very fabric of the building was infused with status, a quiet sense of importance missing from her home.

'Good morning, is Mrs Blythe at home?' she said the moment the door opened. She stepped back as the old, one eyed Pekingese dog sped along the parquet floor, sliding to a halt by her feet, barking. 'She's not expecting me. I have something for her.'

'I'll check Ma'am, who may I say is calling?' Bessie looked uncertainly at the sleeping baby.

'Mrs Affini,' Claudia said.

'Claudia, is that you?' Tess swept into the entrance hall, a dusky apricot silk robe pooling on the marble floor behind her. She lifted the dog into her arms, 'Looty, behave. Isn't she adorable?' Claudia frowned as Tess scratched the dog's chin.

'I'm sure you're right,' Claudia said. Tess' good humour settled on her like snow on a cold, dark lake.

'Thank you, Bessie,' Tess said to the maid. 'Do come through, Claudia. Oh my goodness! Who have we got here.'

'This is little Carlo, my eldest's second child.' Claudia said, her face softening for a moment as she looked down. 'I was all ready to storm over here, and then I get landed with the baby. You can't storm anywhere with a goddamn baby in a basket can you?'

'Storm?' Tess registered her anger then, and stepped warily back. 'We'll take coffee in my study,' she said to Bessie, her voice light. She gestured for Claudia to go through a door at the end of the corridor, and handed the dog to the maid. 'What a lovely surprise,' she said, as Claudia sat on the edge of the sofa beside the baby, her back ramrod straight. Tess sat in the armchair opposite, folding her hands in her lap like origami.

'I can't stop for coffee,' Claudia said, her voice cutting the air like a steel tension cable. The baby stirred and mewled. 'Goddamn.' Claudia put the box on the table and scooped the tiny infant into her arms with practiced ease, draping it across her shoulder like a muslin cloth. 'I have something of yours, and you, I believe, have something of ours.'

'I'm sorry. I don't ...' Tess paused as the maid brought in a silver tray with a steaming pot of coffee. It stood untouched on the table between them. Tess's gaze turned to the box. 'I don't know what you're talking about,' she said the moment the door closed behind Bessie.

'One man wasn't enough for you?' Claudia said through her teeth, rubbing the baby's back to settle it. 'When I look at that good man you are married to. What is it? Sex?' She looked at the shoebox before shoving it across the marble table to Tess.

'Kit? You're talking about Kit?'

'Marco. Such a pair of shoes he designed

for you. But then, Marco has a magic to him. I have shelves and shelves of shoes at home, and still never enough. I still have the first pair he ever made me.' Her voice broke. 'They were simple, and good, but they will last a lifetime, you understand.' She stood, glared down at Tess. 'Do you understand? A lifetime.'

'I love him,' Tess said faintly. She rose and looked at Claudia eye to eye, one woman pale like the morning sun, the other dark as night. 'I love him,' she said clearly. 'And so do you. I'm right, aren't I?'

Claudia's eyes flinched, her face hardened. 'He is not yours to love.' Claudia looked her up and down.

'Nor is he yours. Your husband's brother? How long have you loved him.'

Claudia gasped. 'How dare you?'

'How long?'

'Forever,' she said finally, her voice a whisper.

'Does he know?' Tess asked quietly.

'Of course not.' Claudia said, surprised. 'Men like Marco don't notice a damn thing. The first time I saw him dance with you, it hurt so much I thought I'd die. It was a physical pain.' She clutched her fist at her breastbone. 'It felt like someone had cut me open, like I was carrying a great empty wound where I had carried him, had carried my love for him all the years.' Tess looked down at her hands. 'I was in love with him all that time.' Claudia laughed, shaking her head. 'Sure, I loved Carlo, but I don't think he had any idea what he threw away when he was unfaithful to me. I'd be in love with him, still, the fool. Even in death I'd never look at another man. Everything since, every happiness, every moment of joy has been muted. That's the real consequence. It breaks your heart, your spirit. Even if you carry on, after someone you trusted has lied to you, nothing will be that simple and true and good again.'

'I'm sorry.'

'We blew it, our chance. But I never let on to anyone. Do you know how many times I wanted to ask for help, to tell people I wasn't coping, that he had broken my heart?' Claudia's voice shook. She patted the baby's back, and wiped angrily at the corner of her eye. 'But I will not do that to our children. I want our sons to be better men than their father. Men with true hearts. I will suffer anything to make sure that they don't make the same mistakes.'

'Even not being with Marco.'

'What would they think?' she whispered, trying desperately not to stir the baby. 'Their uncle. Their father's brother.'

'He is a good man. Marco has sacrificed his own chance of a family, of children, to help you.'

'And now it is our turn to help him.' Claudia pressed her lips together tightly,

'What do you mean?' Tess folded her arms.

'Nothing. Just stay away, ok? He needs his family.' Claudia shook her head. 'He doesn't give a damn about you.'

Tess flinched, looked down at her hands. *Really? Is that true? Maybe he doesn't care?* 'We are family, or we will be.'

Claudia straightened her back. 'This is not about me, or about you, it's about the children, Frankie and Bobby. Don't ruin it for them.' She jabbed her index finger at her. 'Can you imagine everyone at the wedding gossiping and pointing? You don't get to do that to my Frankie, you hear?'

'I envy you, you know,' Tess said softly.

'You? You with your fancy Manhattan apartment and your furs and pearls? You envy me?' Claudia threw back her head.

'What does that all amount to?' Tess raised her gaze and looked at her. 'You have what I always dreamt of, a big, noisy, loving family. Bobby loves your home. I don't blame him.'

'Yeah, well as a grandmother you know how quickly this moment goes. I love them when they are babies. Such goodness in them.' She took the hand of the child sleeping on her chest and let its tiny fist curl around her index finger. Her eyes blazed, but she couldn't unleash her anger, not now. 'You stay away from him, you hear?' she said, soft enough not to wake the child.

Tess watched her leave. *He doesn't give*

a damn. Claudia's words circled around and around in her mind. She fell back into the armchair, shaken, the sleeves of her kimono backlit, sunlight streaming through them, a penumbra of light around her. She reached for the box and untied the ribbon. A sob caught in her throat when she opened the lid. She scooped the tatters of leather between her hands and leant her brow against her fingertips, breathing in the scent of the ruined shoes, her hopes and dreams defiled.

Chapter 18

It was a glittering day. Light sparking on the crested surf beneath a glacier blue sky reflected in the mirror in the kitchen where Tess checked her reflection by the back door. She thought not for the first time that the sand flats shone with fresh promise as she walked down from her cottage at dawn to the sea with Looty scampering at her heels, a gull's shadow skimming across the land. In Provincetown each day seemed like a make over. The sand whispering in the wind seemed to speak of another chance. Tess shielded her eyes and looked up at some swans riding high and fast together above the water, and her spirit lifted, flying with them. *He doesn't give a damn?* Perhaps Claudia was mistaken. Perhaps today it would all come good.

Tess had barely slept. She wondered if Claudia had told Marco what she had done. *Why didn't he tell me himself?* she thought.

Here, Tess sensed the turning of the seasons more keenly. She gathered in supplies - oil for the lamps, and driftwood for the fire. The summer crowds had gone home to the city. The beaches in their golden beauty were empty, the corona of light on the water felt like the edge of the world. Tess remembered back in April when she had been walking through Times Square and a test air raid sounded. The crowds evacuated the square, until only a police dog and handlers sat in the middle of the eerily quiet streets. For ten minutes, she waited. Then it felt like she had glimpsed the end of days. It terrified her, haunted her dreams. But here she did not feel lonely. *I feel* ... she thought, testing herself. *Relieved, here. Like I can breathe*, she thought as she swept the last of the fine white sand from the kitchen, and untied her hair. The town was going to sleep for the winter, and the thought of hibernating suited her just fine. Her red Cadillac was parked away from the dunes in the lot at Herring Cove, and she wheeled her bicycle around from the side of the house. She cycled through the brush and pines, breathing in the scent of sap, of salt.

Freewheeling down the narrow tarmac of Commercial Street, Tess' pale figure reflected in the windows of the stores advertising end of season sales as she sped by. She stopped at the market to buy a dozen eggs, and handed the man thirty cents. Tess stepped out onto the street and tucked the eggs into the basket on her bike.

'Hey, hey. Tess!' She looked up and saw a grey haired man in shorts raise his hand and wave as he and his companion approached her. A slim black man in a white chambray shirt at his side broke into a broad smile, and dropped his bag of groceries on the side of the road.

'Why, Ms Blythe, you look radiant!' Anton said as Tess put her bike on its stand and embraced them both. 'What on earth are you doing here?'

'I did something stupid.'

'Oh good,' Paul said, hugging her tightly. His thick grey hair smelt wonderful, of cinnamon and nutmeg. *I'm sure this is how it would feel if Father Christmas hugged you,* Tess thought, stepping back.

'What do you mean 'oh good',' she said, laughing.

'Makes the rest of us feel better about ourselves when even goddesses like you have clay feet.' Paul's cheeks dimpled when he smiled. 'I thought we had lost you for the winter. When did you get back?'

'Yesterday. I drove all night. I needed some space.'

'You've left him?' He stepped back, raising his eyebrows.

'At last.' Anton folded his arms. 'Thank god. Haven't we told you time and time again-'

'No, I - I just want to disappear for a while.'

'You're in the right place, honey.' Paul took her hand. 'Listen, you can't freeze out there in the dunes. Come and stay with us, we'll make up the guest cottage.'

'You are a darling. Maybe later in the year. I'm ... well, I'm thinking of moving up here permanently, but I'm fine now, tucked up with my fire. I just needed some peace and quiet before Bobby's wedding.' Tess pulled the sleeves of her old navy sweater down over her chilled hands. 'Why don't you drop by tomorrow?' She gestured at the eggs. 'Nothing fancy, just an omelette and a glass of wine.'

'We'll bring the wine, darling.'

'Say, Anton, are you still doing the exercises I recommended?' Tess said.

Anton turned a graceful, lithe pirouette, and bowed. 'They've saved my life. I've been telling the rest of the corps all about you. They're dying to meet you. I told them about your idea for a ballet-'

'Did you? It was just an idea, a silly idea, really.' Tess felt scared, uncertain. She stepped aside to let an old couple chattering in Portuguese climb the steps to the restaurant. In that moment she realised how badly she wanted to work with dancers. To see all the half dreamed ideas and movements she carried in her like a melody swell into life. 'When does your tour start?'

'Next month.' Anton leant his head against Paul's shoulder. 'I've persuaded this old guy to come with me. We'll be touring Europe through into next year and I didn't want to spend our tenth anniversary apart.'

'Say, I've just had the most marvellous idea,' Paul said. 'You need some space, we need someone to water the plants and feed the cats.'

'Are you sure?'

'Sure I'm sure!' Paul and Anton stepped back in time to a rock and roll tune pulsing from the open door of a nearby restaurant to let a pistachio green Chrysler cruise past.

'Come over for supper tomorrow. We can talk about it.' Tess swung her leg across her bike. '7.30ish?'

'It's a date.' Paul raised his hand. 'We'll bring sweaters and blankets.'

'The offer's there if you feel like running away.' Anton blew a kiss as Tess cycled on.

She didn't know where she was heading. *Just follow your nose,* she thought, and smiled, hearing Aphra's voice encouraging her to go exploring when she was a child. Tess cycled away from the town, feeling her limbs loosening and warming, her tension easing with the loop and whir of the tyres on the road. She explored beaches she hadn't visited for years. Tess remembered playing with Bobby, sun warmed and golden on summer days, clouds of Monarch butterflies rising around them, his tiny dimpled hands reaching to catch their orange and black wings.

As the sky bloomed gold and apricot, she headed back to town, and pulled up outside an old warehouse which had caught her eye years ago. It reminded her of barns she had seen in Connecticut and Vermont. There was something welcoming about it. *The kind of place you would have loved to play when you were a child. The kind of place you felt safe.* Then it was full of crates and pallets, fish being brought in to be packaged and sold on. *It's perfect*, she thought, looking up at the black clapperboard wall, laying her hand against it. Her touch was an overture, a promise. It was empty now, a 'to rent' sign swinging in the breeze. *One day, I will open a school in you,* she thought. *One day.* The bay was darkening, a far off green light glimmering on the water. At the sound of the foghorn from the breakwater, she turned back to the town, her shoulders hunched against the cold breeze rolling in from the sea. The lights blurred red and white in the gathering darkness. A storm was rolling in, fishing boats moored in the harbour's shelter like sea birds. At the water's edge, she looked back at the warehouse. She remembered buying lobsters for a party one summer. There was a raised platform at one end, and large north facing windows lining the hall. *A stage*, she thought. In an instant she could picture it. Modern, spare, light, beautiful. A workshop for dancers.

Tess remembered a collaboration between Balanchine and Stravinsky she had seen at the NYC Ballet. The dancers wore simple tights and leotards, there was no decor. It was all about the music, and the movement. She pictured lithe figures dressed in black on her stage, pared back, no stiff tutus or scraps of chiffon. Just muscular, precise bodies. Just perfect imperfection. *The Danceworks Center*, she thought. *Danceworks*.

Wheeling her bike back through town, the lights of Adams Pharmacy drew her in. 'Are you closing?' she said, pushing open the door, the brass bell ringing above her head

'Not for a while. What'll you have?' the girl behind the counter threw down her cloth and rubbed her hands, warming them.

'Vanilla milkshake, please,' Tess said, sliding up on to a chrome stool. 'I'm celebrating.' As the girl poured out the milk into a metal cup, Tess caught sight of her reflection in the ochre tinged mirror behind the soda fountain, and ran her hand through her hair, wild with salt spray and sand. *What would Kit think?* Tess laughed to herself, caught the girl glancing at her as she shook her hair free. *She probably thinks I'm mad. Maybe I am.* 'Thanks,' she said, sipping gratefully at the milkshake, closing her eyes. The taste of it brought back other summers, the years flying free like a calendar in the breeze. She remembered Bobby sitting beside her at the counter, brown summer feet in tan sandals swinging from the stool, his excited chatter. *We used to talk about everything,* she thought. *I was always the first person he ran to, always the first he told about his day. I hardly feel like I know him at all, these days.*

The old clock ticked on above the counter, its red hand purring away the seconds.

Maybe I should just take myself over to the Atlantic House? she thought, sipping at her drink. *I could just curl up by one of the fires and warm up, and have a brandy.* The thought of being alone in its dark embrace was not as comforting as she hoped. *Maybe if I move out here, I'll be one of those old girls who prop up the bar and watch the people dancing, and say: I used to dance, once. I remember seeing Billy Holliday and Ella Fitzgerald sing here ...* Tess was so lost in her thoughts she didn't hear the bell over the Pharmacy door ring. She did not see Marco step in from the cold street, take off his grey fedora, and run his hand through his hair, his gaze on her.

That morning she had seen a deer at the end of the Cape Cod road, in the dunes near the salt marsh. The gold sea grass blew in the wind, slivers of water reflecting the sky like shards of mirror in the rippled sand. The sound of the ocean roared beyond the dunes. *Where had the deer wandered in from?* she thought, remembering another time, another silent communion with a creature on the other side of the ocean. It seemed like a sign. A message. *Have you never loved a man?* Marco had asked her when they stood high above New York, on the top of the world. *Never,* she said. She lied.

Intermission

Q: Did you set out to shock with your performances, Ms Blythe? I refer to the near nudity of the dancers, to the sensuality of the scores. You are known for your celebration of what you call 'everyday miracles' - love, sex, birth - but you do not shy away from the baser human acts. I am thinking of the scenes of rape and war in *The Woods are Dark*. Some critics have found the violence, the bloodshed too much.

A: Shock? Never. I want people to feel alive, that's all. I want people to feel the performance viscerally. A physical response. And I want music that breaks your heart, that makes you fall in love. I want music that makes the fine pelt of your body rise, rise, rise ...'

- Interview with Tess Blythe, Dance Review

Chapter 19

Somerset
1939

I should be grateful, Tess thought, tucking her arm over her small suitcase. She wiped the steam from the rain streaked window and stared out of the bus, watching the houses of the market town roll by. *Is it this one? Or this one,* she wondered, hopefully, looking out at a cosy stone house whose windows glowed gold, inviting her in. Tess was exhausted from travelling, and she was trying to distract herself from the growing nausea she felt, lurching along in the crowded bus. There had been countless flights. So many countries. And then the shock of arriving 'home' to a world she barely recognised. *Pull yourself together*, she told herself. *I'm lucky. I have a kind husband who I love, who's my friend, who doesn't expect ... well, who doesn't ...*

I will have a beautiful home, she thought. They had little money, but she felt rich. Kit had told her all about the elegant house his grandfather would be leaving to him on the birth of their child. As long as he *is* a he, Tess thought.

'This is Midchester House,' the bus driver called out to her, and Tess scrambled out of her seat. 'Head up that track there,' he said, pointing to an overgrown, muddy lane.

'Surely this can't be it?' Tess said, setting down her suitcase on the road as the bus chugged away. She felt a faint movement in her stomach in answer. *This can't be the house Kit raved about.* She checked the address again, and stared forlornly at the modest brick house surrounded by overgrown lawns. Tess wiped the rain from her face. The grimy windows reflected the storm clouds faintly, and in an upstairs room Tess saw the figure of a woman, watching her, half hidden behind heavy velvet curtains. Tess raised her hand in greeting, but the woman let the drape fall closed. Frowning, Tess picked up her suitcase and strode along the weed choked gravel driveway. The doorbell didn't seem to be working, so she knocked loudly on the studded wooden door.

'Who is it?' a disembodied voice said after a time.

'Hello. Aunt Cally?' Tess heard bolts and a chain slide back. A small woman with the physique of a deflated balloon opened the door and peered at her from the gloom. She blinked her dark, myopic shrew eyes.

'I am Miss Blythe. And who might you be?'

'I'm Tess, Tess Blythe.' The old woman's face was unreadable. 'Kit's wife.'

'His wife are you? What do you want? I suppose you've come to turf me out and claim the family seat have you?'

'No, not at all-' Tess began to say, thinking: *yes, that's exactly what Kit wants to do.* She broke off at the woman's unexpected laughter. It was high pitched, unnerving. 'May I come in?'

'Help yourself my dear. I'll show you where the only dry bedroom is, and pack my bag. Maybe I'll head off to Lyme Regis and walk into the sea ...'

'I'm sure that won't be necessary.'

'Come in then if you're staying.'

'Are you not expecting me?' Tess followed her uncertainly, and closed the door. The house smelt of defeat and boiled cabbage. 'Did Kit not write?'

'I had a letter from Christopher. I wasn't expecting him to palm off his pregnant wife on me.' Cally slumped into the pink armchair. 'You've had a wasted journey. There's no room for you here.'

'But ... but this is Kit's house now.'

'So you expect *me* to leave?' Cally's eyes were pinpricks.

'No, not at all. But surely there must be a room-' Tess broke off at the aunt's hysterical laughter. Cally heaved herself out of the armchair and beckoned for Tess to follow her.

'A room? I'll show you, shall I? Let me give you the grand tour.' Tess' heart sank to her boots following Cally through the claustrophobic, must-smelling corridors, and stairs silted up with dying houseplants and piles of old magazines. 'I sleep in there,' Cally said, gesturing towards a narrow box room overlooking the garden. Kit's aunt stood on the landing pointing at each room in turn. 'This one the ceiling has caved in. This one has no electric. And this one,' she said, swinging the door open, 'leaks, as you can see.' Tess felt like crying. She blinked, staring at the rain dripping from the ceiling onto the sodden bed. 'You look disappointed.' Cally's eyes narrowed as she smiled. 'Let me guess. Young Christopher told you the Blythe family seat is heavenly.' Her mouth twisted in satisfaction. 'I knew it. Didn't I say it? I always said that boy lived in cloud cuckoo land. All his airs and graces would never do him any good.' She turned towards the back of the house and beckoned for Tess to follow her. 'Still. Where are my manners? A cup of tea, perhaps?'

'Thank you.' *I've travelled half way round the world,* Tess wanted to cry. *A cup of tea? All you're going to offer me is a cup of tea?* Tess followed the forlorn slap of the woman's slippers into the dark corridor. 'Have you lived here long?'

'Long enough.' Cally sank into an armchair by the coal range which sighed with defeat. She gestured at the overflowing sink. 'Be a love and wash a couple of cups?'

'Of course.' *Even better,* she thought, biting her lip to stop herself laughing in desperation. *I get to make my own cup of tea.* Tess took off her hat, and laid it carefully on the dresser. She rolled up her sleeves and gingerly rescued a chipped Royal Doulton cup from the oily bowl of water. She left the cups to drain and filled the kettle with water.

'While you're at it, why don't you boil a couple of eggs. The hens have laid this morning.' Cally poked a taper of paper into the fire and lit a Woodbine. 'It is a special occasion, after all.' She sank back into the chair. 'Don't get many visitors these days.'

I wonder why, Tess thought. She picked up the two small eggs from an earthenware bowl by the drainer, and turned to Cally. 'Boiled?'

'Yes. You do know how to boil and egg?'

Tess' cheeks coloured. 'I'm not hungry, thank you.' Her stomach rumbled in protest.

'You don't, do you?' Cally's eyes narrowed as she took a drag of her cigarette. 'I know your sort. Hot and cold running servants. I'm surprised you even know how to make a cup of tea.'

Hateful woman, Tess thought. She imagined throwing the eggs at her, one after the other. Instead she placed them back in the bowl, and calmly turned to the whistling kettle.

'You can just top up the pot on the stove,' Cally said. 'No use wasting new leaves when there's a good couple of sups left in that one. Anyway, make it easy for you.' Tess filled the brown china teapot in silence, and dried the cups.

'When was the last time Kit - Christopher was here?' she said, pouring a splash of milk into each cup.

'Oh, a long, long time ago. They all came over. My brother, his wife and the child. Our father was still alive then.'

'So the house was different, then?'

'It was never the Palace of Versailles, if that's what you're getting at.'

'I'm just trying to understand, It's not quite as he described.' Tess drained her cup and turned to Cally. 'I shall sleep in town.'

'Suit yourself if this isn't good enough for you.'

Tess collected her hat. 'Kit wrote to the family solicitor to arrange a meeting. I'm seeing him tomorrow morning if you'd like to be there? I assure you I have no intention of asking you to leave. This is your home.' *And it will never be mine.*

'In that case I have no interest in going to town. What would be the point?' The way Cally spoke it might as well have been the dark side of the moon. She heaved herself out of her chair and followed Tess to the front door.

'I shall be going to stay with my aunt Aphra on Exmoor,' Tess said, scribbling down an address in her notebook. She ripped out the page and handed it to Cally. 'If you hear from Kit, or need to contact me ...'

'I'm sure I won't. Good day to you, Mrs Blythe.'

Chapter 20

The scent of wild garlic is intoxicating, earthy. Through the acid green leaves on the trees she sees a vivid haze of blue. Tess dumps her suitcase by the side of the road and pushes her way through into the April wood, leaning down to touch the bluebells. Ahead on the hillside she sees azaleas, rhododendrons blazing cerise, scarlet. They make her think of bougainvillea in Hong Kong. They make her think of home.

Tess spun round, exhaling with relief, and let herself fall back onto the soft forest floor, her arms arcing, fingers reaching for the full stems of bluebells. A vivid filigree of glossy new leaves shimmers above her, the canopy of trees shattering the sun. She stretches deliciously, arms above her head, spine curving, easing out the tension of travelling. It felt like a day for new beginnings.

'I say, are you alright?' Tess rolled her face to the side at the sound of a man's voice, and running. 'Can I help?'

Tess propped herself up on her elbows. 'I'm fine, thank you.' She shielded her eyes from the sunlight filtering through the canopy of leaves, looked up at the dark figure of the man standing over her. 'I'm looking for Aphra Montgomery's house. I'm sure the lane was just off the High Street, but I haven't been here since I was a child.' Tess scrambled to her feet. 'I remember playing in these bluebells. I couldn't resist.'

'They are glorious,' he said, offering her his hand to help her up. His skin was pale, his grip firm and strong. *Quite unlike Kit,* she thought. Tess looked up at the man, her lips parting slowly. His thick dark hair waved back from his square set face, a bruise of five o clock shadow already growing at his jaw late morning. 'You're a friend of Aphra's?' His dark eyes danced with amusement. 'May I?' He gently took a golden beech leaf from her hair.

'Actually, she's my aunt.' Tess touched the side of her neck, hoping she looked less flustered than she felt.

'Any friend of Aphra's is a friend of mine.' Philip led the way back to the road and tucked Tess's suitcase under his arm. He gestured for her to follow him. 'We're neighbours, in fact. I rather envy her living in the old Rectory. Those were the days when clergy lived in style.' He pointed at a simple Edwardian villa up the road. 'That's me.'

'Oh? Are you ..?' Tess laughed in surprise as Philip unwound his scarf revealing a clerical collar.

'Reverend Philip Hardy,' he said, shaking her hand.

'Philip? Is that you?' A woman's voice boomed from the rhododendron lined driveway next door, and they turned at the sound of footsteps and barking. 'Time for a snifter and a spot of lunch? Sun's over the yardarm somewhere.'

'Aphra, you have a guest,' Philip called out. Tess felt herself exhale with relief. It felt like coming home. She could glimpse the corner of the white stucco rectory at the end of the curving drive, and saw her aunt striding through the trees towards them, a pair of Irish Wolfhounds at her heels.

'Guest? What guest? I'm not expecting-' She broke off at the sight of Tess. 'Tess? Little Tessie?' Aphra engulfed her in a bear hug. 'Oh, my dear. Can it really be you? When your mother wrote and said you were married, and expecting a child. It was too much to hope for.'

'Yes, yes, it's me,' Tess said, her voice muffled in the tweed. 'I wrote. Did you not get my letter?' *She hasn't changed, not at all*, she thought. She stepped back to look at her aunt. Aphra's sharp grey flapper's bob was just as she remembered. The hand-me-down tweed suit and brogues inherited from one of her deceased brothers remained the same.

'You'd be lucky with the postman here. Only last week they found a sack of mail slung behind a hedge. It would be quicker if I delivered the letters myself.' Aphra shook her head. The larger wolfhound reared up, placing its paws on Tess' shoulders.

'Hello.' Tess laughed, giving the dog's ears a scratch. 'Who's this?'

'Hebe, get down!' Aphra snapped. 'Most appalling manners, unlike Hero.' The dog sat beside her sister, and glanced balefully up. Aphra brushed a muddy footprint from Tess' jacket, and cradled her chin. 'Look at you. Just look at you. You do remind me of my mother.'

'Is this the Tess you've told me so much about?' Philip said, smiling.

'The last of the Montgomerys,' Aphra said. 'And isn't she a beauty.' She took Tess by the arm, and led her towards the house. 'Philip bring the case will you, dear heart? This calls for champagne.'

Chapter 21

September 3rd 1939

Here. Here is the sound of her heart, pounding. Here is the determined beat of her feet, walking through the forest, one step, two steps, pausing at each pain. Here is her breath in the silence, a steady cloud, exhaling. The trees are burning, autumn leaves blazing in the fading sun. The scent of bonfires, of scorched earth and leaves is sharp in her senses. Here is the drumming of hooves running fleet footed in the forest behind her, closing.

The river runs silver in the dusk light, mercury quick in the cupped palm of the dark valley. The stag and hind stand at the curve of the river. The hind is drinking. The stag stands watch over her, head alert, antlers piercing the rose flushed sky. Tess' frozen breaths hangs still, fades into air when she sees them. She has heard them bolving on the moor, rutting stags calling out their plaintive animal lament for a mate,

Tess' stomach hardens again, knocking the breath from her. *Here,* she tells herself, *I am here. I am. I am. One step. One, two, three* ... She cries out, grimacing, and the deer flee. It feels like every molecule in her body is contracting, coiling in on itself. *When it comes, think of the pain as a wave,* she remembers the district nurse telling her. Tess pictures herself adrift, pinprick small in a teeming dark ocean which is dragging her down.

The urge to squat down on all fours on the forest floor is overwhelming. She feels the core of her pulling down, down. It is as if the air itself is squeezing her.

In her pocket she carries a letter.

Dear Tess, Kit began.
This is the hardest letter I shall ever write.

Just thinking of how her excitement at hearing finally - finally - from him had turned to ice water in her veins at that line chills her again. Tess retches, doubling over. Once the nausea passes, she straightens up and wipes her mouth with the back of her trembling fingers. She stares along the valley path, squinting through teary eyes to set her next marker, an oak at the bend of the path. *Go to hell, Kit,* she thinks, making for it. *We don't need you.*

It had been months since she had heard from him, and she had written countless times. Their letters had crossed, it seemed. By the time Tess had settled at Aphra's and written to Kit to tell him her address, his letter had arrived at Cally's. *Who took her time forwarding it on,* Tess thinks, clutching her stomach and leaning against the nearest tree, riding out the pain. She strains her head back, a guttural howl rending the grey sky. A last burst of low sun cuts through the rainclouds, skimming along the pistachio green fields. Her fingernails rake the bark, and she leans her forehead against the mossy trunk, waiting for the pain to subside. *Cally, Cally, Cally* ... she thinks. The flap of the envelope was suspiciously wrinkled. Cally had clearly steamed open the letter before sending it on, and Tess felt humiliated that the old woman knew Kit was breaking with her before she did. She had already read Kit's letter several times since it arrived on Friday, and his words ran through her mind as if he were saying them to her.

I apologise for the radio silence. I have been wrestling with my conscience. This was a marriage of convenience for us both, I think. I had thought marriage might bring serenity, and yet I find the opposite. I am fretful without you here, and yet I believe I would be unhappier still were we trying to live as man and wife. I am too much a bachelor, Tess, to be a husband to you. If we had any time together before you left, perhaps it would be differ-ent, but I sleep alone on the linen we had initialled at the French Convent for our wedding, and wake to spend another day entertaining the notable bores of the Colony with trinkets to take their mind off the undeclared war between Japan and China which has been going on for two years already, and draws ever closer to us here.

You are well shot of Hong Kong, I am glad you are not here in the front row of the stalls for the coming war. Meanwhile I pass muster as a Bridge partner for your mother, a walker for the older ladies - and Mr Woo. Your mother says he still pines for you. Last week I arrived just after Tiffin with a lacquered box for an old girl who lives a few doors up from your mother on the Peak to find her in a silk kimono and little else. If you were here, I'm sure we would have had a good laugh about it all. The pace is pretty hot at many of the parties. I think many are having affairs - your friend Graves among them - while they can. I could pass as a gigolo with flying colours - instead I spend my nights drenched in whisky and gin.

Many have left, but this is our home, and your parents are in agreement too, that we shall ride it out come what may. It's impossible for you to return once the child is born as planned, and I cannot hold you to our vows, Tess. As I said, I fear I am too used to the bachelor life to be any good to you as a husband. I have let our little apartment, and the cook and the coolie go. I am content to lead a simple life, here, and have moved in with a couple of the chaps. I will of course take care of you and the acorn (or is he more of a walnut, by now) ..?

Tess laughs bitterly and strides on, breathing deeply, her hands supporting her stomach.

'Walnut?' she says under her breath. 'Try water-melon.'

You are under no pressure to divorce me un-less you wish. There will be no other Mrs Blythe. I hope all has settled well at the old homestead and you are comfortable with Aunt Cally. When this damned mess is sorted out, I shall take some leave and come and see you and young Master (or Miss), Blythe. I care for you, Tess, always know that. I am sorry I am not the man you deserve.

Forgive me.

Kit

Tess cries out in pain and doubled over.

'Tess?' She raises her head at the sound of a man's voice, and hooves pounding along the leaf strewn track behind her. 'What is it? Are you unwell?' Philip leaps down from his horse, and takes her arm.

'No I'm not unwell,' Tess says, grimacing. 'I'm having a baby.' She cries out, holding on to his shoulders, the comforting warmth of his thick wool jumper.

'What can I do?' Philip holds the reins tighter, his horse pawing the forest floor. 'Why don't you jump up, and you can ride back-'

'Jump up?' Tess snaps, a cry catching in her throat. 'Jump up? I'd like to see you jump on a horse if-' She digs her fingers into his arm, her agonised howl muffled in his tweed jacket. His eyes widen in pain as he holds her, waiting for the contraction to subside.

'I'm sorry,' he says, smoothing back her hair from her glistening brow. 'Lean on me. It's not far now.' He hooks his arm around Tess' waist, supporting her. 'What on earth are you doing out in the woods by yourself?'

'I had backache all night, and couldn't sleep. I thought it was too soon, for the baby. I thought ...' She breaks off, panting.

'It's not due 'til later in the month, is it?'

'Tell that to the baby,' Tess says. She clutches her side, and feels Kit's letter crinkle in her pocket. 'I ... I had a letter ...'

'From your husband?' Philip says gently.

'He ... he says he doesn't love me-'

'Oh, Tess. That can't be right.'

'He says I'm free to do as I wish. That it was all a mistake.'

'It's the distance talking. They're so brave, our boys on the front line.'

'Boy? Kit's no boy-' Tess winces, a sharp pain stabbing her hip. 'And I don't want him to be brave. I want him here, with me, when the baby's born-'

'Tess ...'

'I don't mean that. Of course I'm proud of him. I'm proud of all our men.'

'Of course you are, really. You're in labour. You don't know what you're saying.'

Tess rounds on him. 'Don't you ever tell me I don't know my own mind. Ever, ev-aaargh,'

Tess says, her words rising into a siren cry, her fingers digging in to his arm.

Philip holds his breath, teeth gritted until it passes and she releases him. 'There,' he says, and they stumble on. 'The world is full of uncertainty at the moment, but everything will be different when he sees you, and your baby,' Philip says, holding her closer.

'He's not the father,' Tess says, grimacing.

'Are you sure?'

'Perfectly sure.' Tess cries out, gripping Philip's shoulder for support. When she catches her breath, she goes on. 'I'm telling you because I think Kit realised he couldn't cope with it after all. I don't want there to be any more lies. I'm tired of pretending.' Tess glances at him. 'Are you shocked?'

'Surprised, but ... You're terribly brave, to do this. To have the baby.'

'Brave? I'm not brave,' Tess says, gasping as another contraction hits her. 'You just have to get on with it, that's all.' *It's my fault. It's all my fault.*

'There,' he says, pointing. 'Not far now. Can you see the smoke from Aphra's chimneys?'

The trees thin towards the road, a copper carpet of leaves leading them home. Tess stops at the edge of the woods and turns to him. 'Will you stay? I don't think I can do this by myself. If I know you're near by ...'

'Of course I will,' Philip says. 'I'll wait as

long as you need.'

'Tess? Philip? Where on earth have you been?' Aphra says, running from the driveway of her house.

'I went for a walk,' Tess says. 'I think it's time.' Aphra takes her other arm, and they guide her home. 'I think the baby is coming.'

'Never mind the baby,' Aphra says. 'We're at war. 'Chamberlain has declared war.'

Chapter 22

October 1940

The light is jaundiced, the sky a mottled bruise. Tess looks up at the scattering cries of a murmuration of starlings, swooping low above her. The dark birds rest for a moment in the shimmering branches of a golden sycamore, before flying on as one pulsing form. She wishes she could fly away with them, away from this earth, this war. Tess pulls the collar of her coat around her and lowers her head against the push and pull of the wind, carrying the pail of milk to the house from the stable. Aphra had taught Tess how to milk the placid Jersey cow soon after she arrived, and now she looks forward each day to the task, the warmth of the hay, the comforting animal's golden hide.

Tess has learnt to make butter and cream. To cook with the eggs from the chickens. 'The finest omelette in Somerset,' according to Aphra. She has learnt to dig and hoe the vegetable garden, to tend the orchard. They have eaten simply but well through the summer, in spite of the war, on asparagus and figs, and honey from Aphra's bees. Tess has grown lean and strong, working the land and keeping the house, and her child is bonny, plump limbed and rosy cheeked. Aphra taught her to cook simple, wholesome meals, and in the evening when the dining room is lit by candles and firelight, and Tess looks around at the faces of her son Bobby and the children from London they took in as evacuees, at Aphra and Philip, eating the food she has made, chatting and laughing, Tess thinks she has never been happier. This is the family she has always longed for, that is her secret. *Does it matter that it's make believe, that one day it will come to an end? We are all just playing a part.* She feels ashamed, sometimes, that she has found such simple contentment when the world is at war. When she said this to Aphra, how guilty she felt that Kit and her parents were in such peril, Aphra said 'We must find happiness where we can. They made their choice, to stay in Hong Kong. You made your choice to come here,' and she looked pointedly at Philip, playing with Bobby on the white crocheted blanket on the lawn. 'We will pray for them, but your husband has clearly decided married life is not for him. You must think of your future.'

Find happiness where you can. Tess loves her child, but it is a relief to be free of him, for an hour. She feels exhilarated, unsettled by the storm. She walks alone on the church path, windblown yew berries scattered before her like coral beads. Tess reaches for the tumbling gold leaves, trying to catch one. *We could do with some luck.* She has had a letter from her mother. Kit has clearly not told her about the break. *Has he changed his mind?* Tess wonders. *Perhaps it was simply a whim?* The men had met at the Peninsula hotel a few days before to discuss evacuations. It was decided that those who had chosen to stay in Hong Kong could stay put. Those who were away on leave could not return. It felt like another door closing, reading her mother's words. However fanciful it was, the thought that perhaps Kit might change his mind had sustained her. They had been friends for so long, she had hoped there might be a chance he would change his mind and give their marriage a chance, and send for her after the war.

I am a married woman. And yet. And yet. Kit has cast her aside. She is not a free woman, but the future seems full of possibility. At first she grieved for her marriage, for everything she had hoped to share with Kit. Philip was there to counsel her, console her. He was there, the first man to hold Bobby when he was born. He was there at her side once she was strong enough to go on long walks across the moor. *He's been a good friend to me,* Tess thinks. Her stomach blooms, tight petals unfolding, thinking of him. *Is it wrong,* she thinks, *that when I look at him with Bobby I wish we were a family?* The conversation she plans to have with Philip has been playing in her mind on a loop: *do you care? will you ask? when? when?* Tess flings her arms wide, dancing with the wind. *When?*

A red sun hangs in the grey sky, clouds scudding fast and high above the church like smoke. The stained glass windows glow in the dim light. Tess pauses by the gate to Aphra's orchard, watching a blackbird swoop from the path to the wall in triumph, a red berry clasped in its gold beak. The bird turns a quick glass bead eye over her, and flies on to the orchard. Tess remembers standing in the middle of the trees in the spring, blossom falling on her like confetti, how she longed to dance again. *What does he see? What do I look like to that bird, standing here in my dull beige Mac?* Tess pictured herself dancing on a darkened stage, spot lit, her arms rising up with the plumage of the Firebird, her feet a blaze of red satin. She lifts one hand, turns it in front of her face. *Oh god, it's hopeless.* The first drops of fresh, cool rain sparkle on her skin. She has a nagging sense that she has missed her moment, somehow. That her chance with Philip has been and gone. *Or never was?* They have settled into an easy familiarity. *Too familiar. I don't think he looks at me, like that. He doesn't see me. He doesn't feel ...* Tess sighs with longing. *He doesn't feel that hunger.*

It begins to rain steadily and she runs to the lych-gate, her hand resting on the wood frame slick with water as she shelters there. Desiccated acorn cups and conker cases crunch beneath the sole of her shoe, rain coursing down the turning leaves above her. She loves the trees around her aunt's Regency home, watching the changing seasons of the ash, the beech hedges, the hazels, the elegant sway of the willow by the pond. She loves the golden rain, tumbling leaves of copper, ochre, gathering burnished conkers with Bobby in the autumn, easing them from their prickling felt hearted husks. She loves the white geese on frozen pistachio coloured fields in winter, the indignant flash of their gold beaks. She loves the catkins heralding the spring. She loves the bluebells in their woods and the buttercups in the pasture, the cowslips and dandelions, the ferns. She loves the heron, stalking the shore of the mill pond, the fat newts, the cygnets gliding after their stately parents. She loves it all. If she closes her eyes, she can sense the adders sliding silently between the strands of heather and ivy, the nectar coursing in the flowers, the balls of mistletoe in the hawthorn waiting for the winter. She imagines herself gliding through the rain flecked water like the otters. She is the quicksilver flash of the kingfisher at the edge of the water, the soaring song of the lark, the ripples on the lake, expanding.

'Mrs Blythe!' a voice calls brightly, and she turns, wrenched back to the present moment. Her heart plummets like an anvil from a cliff. She was so close to home, but Mrs Filby, the church warden's wife is bearing down on her, wide galoshes splashing in the puddles. Tess imagines the anvil, a cartoon, falling, stopping Mrs Filby in her tracks, galoshes splayed beneath its edges. 'What a day,' she says, tilting her umbrella to fit beneath the lych-gate. 'It's almost pitch black. They say there's sand in the air.' She looks up at the red sun. 'Look at that mucky sky. When I imagine the apocalypse, this is how I picture it. And I just cleaned my windows.'

'It's rather thrilling,' Tess says, running her hands across her forehead, pushing back her hair wet with rain.

'Not the word I would have chosen, but then you do tend to see *la vie en rose*, Mrs Blythe. I find the atmosphere most sinister,' Mrs Filby says. Tess feels claustrophobic. The woman smells of sweat and talcum powder, musty and cloying. 'But where's your child?'

'Aphra offered to babysit for an hour so I could have a break.' Tess hates her need to explain. What business is it of this woman's.

'A break? Why both of mine never left my side for a moment.' Tess thinks of the chronically awkward Filby twins and says nothing. 'So you came to church?' The question hangs. 'How is your Aunt? I must talk to her about the flower rota.'

'I'll remind her once I get back from the village.'

'Have you heard from your husband, Mrs

Blythe? Is he still in Hong Kong?'

'It's rather difficult as you can imagine getting any news. His aunt forwarded on a letter he wrote in September-' Tess clenches her jaw, remembering Kit's stilted, formal note, wishing Bobby a happy first birthday. He spoke of their friends, that all the women were being evacuated to the Philippines, and many on to Australia. 'He's keeping a stiff upper lip, and-'

'It's terribly brave of you, under the circumstances.'

'Sorry?'

'Venturing out into the village.'

'I don't-'

'I've said enough,' she says, shaking her umbrella. Raindrops fleck Tess's coat. She sees the orchard gate behind her, only a few paces - could she make an escape? It feels like the hedge is receding as the woman talks on. 'I just know if it was me people were gossiping about, I'd want to know-'

'Gossip?' Tess' focus snaps back to the woman.

'Always the last to know.' Mrs Filby purses her lips. Tess notices her lipstick has bled into the bitter little ravines encircling her mouth. They hear the church clock stirring and wheezing in the tower, the bells silent.

'If you have something to say.' Tess steps forward, challenges her, angry suddenly. *Not with this woman, she is nothing, no one, a bored and lonely bitter old woman.* She is angry with Kit, with herself. She sees alarm flicker in the woman's eyes.

'Consider your husband,' she says, hurrying on. 'People are talking. You're a married woman. It's my duty to let you know.'

Tess waits, rain pattering on the tiles of the lych-gate above her. *Duty?* Once the woman has disappeared, she thumps the wall in frustration, and leans her head against it for a moment. *Oh, go to hell. Hateful woman.* She walks on, deliberately, swings open the gate to the old Rectory. She does not stop to remove her boots at the porch, but walks on through the house, dripping water, leaving wet footprints across the slate floor.

'Aphra,' she calls up the stairs into the dark silence. She stands in the centre of the hall, turning slowly in a circle beneath the oval glass dome, looking for a clue, a sign. Everything is perfectly normal. The cases of butterflies, the modern paintings from Aphra's Paris days aligned just so. The crimson velvet sofa waiting in the silent drawing room is a vivid, rebellious slash. She wishes her aunt's taste had rubbed off on her. Even Kit had tried at first to educate her, but no. The electric light in the ceiling rose flickers on briefly, and Tess looks up.

'Bastard!' Aphra's voice drifts up from the cellar stairs.

'Aphra?'

'Down here. Ruddy electrics are on the fritz again with the storm.'

'You should get them looked at, it's not safe,' Tess says, rummaging in the hall drawer for a torch. She picks her way gingerly down the worn stone steps. The cellar smells of the earth, of dust and old newspapers. The faint beam of light sweeps across the shelves stacked with jars of chutney and preserved vegetables she had helped Aphra prepare for the winter. She sees her aunt crouched beside the fuse board.

'There!' she cries triumphantly, throwing down her screwdriver. The hall lights cast a golden rectangle down the cellar stairs and Tess flicks off her torch.

'Aphra you must be careful. The wiring in this place is shot.'

'It's been perfectly serviceable since my parent's time, and has a good few years in it yet. It only plays up when it rains.'

'Where's Bobby?'

'Sleeping with the cat, he's fine.' Aphra slams the fuse cupboard door shut triumphantly.

'Aphra, are people gossiping about me?'

'About you, about me, about everyone. People will always gossip.' She wipes her hands on her tweed trousers. 'Now, what time is it? We'll be late for choir practice. Run along,' Aphra waves her hands, shooing her up the steps.

'I was just on my way when I bumped into

Mrs Filby.'

'Oh, that woman spits poison like a cobra. Ignore her.' Aphra slams the cellar door. 'Run along, now. We'll catch you up. Don't keep young Philip waiting.'

The weather vane on the solid grey church tower swivelled this way and that, a whirl of indecision. *Will you? Do you? When?*

'Hello,' Tess said, shaking out her umbrella in the porch.

'Come in and close the door,' Philip said, forcing the door closed against the wind. 'What a day. The children in the kindergarten were a nightmare this morning, your two evacuees included. They ran amok in assembly.'

'It's the wind.' Tess remembered running along the shore of a lake in China, arms outstretched. She felt no edge to her at all. She was the wind, the water, and they were part of her. She felt like a bird in flight, she felt like flight itself. 'It always makes children wild. Can't you feel it?'

'The wind? Don't be ridiculous.'

'I'll have a word with them at supper.' Tess dug her hands into her pockets. *Ridiculous?* 'I think they're settling rather well, after all they've been through.'

'Don't get too attached.'

'I'm not!'

'They're not like puppies or kittens. You'll

have to give them back.' Philip gestured she should sit down in the front pew. 'I see the way you look at them sometimes.'

'The flowers are lovely,' she said, changing the subject. She pointed towards the altar. She felt wounded, as if her hopes and dreams had been held up to the light and exposed. *Ridiculous?. I'm not ridiculous.*

'There was a wedding. The usual rush job, the chap was shipping out this morning.'

Tess let her head fall back as she sat in the pew, and her eyes closed, letting the silence and stillness seep into her. The fibres of her hummed like a power line, insistent, waiting. Her arms extended along the pew back, hard wood beneath her bones. She thought of her own wedding dress, the last time she held it. It was the spring after Bobby was born. The quiet desperation of the days, of small things, the neediness of the child had quite exhausted her. Then came another letter from Kit saying he wouldn't be coming home, that he was making a new life. That he wanted a divorce.

She retaliated by getting rid of the wedding dress she had so carefully carried to England to make into a christening gown for Bobby. It would be bad luck, she thought, to be christened in silk from that ostentatious dress her mother made her wear. There was enough silk over, anyway, sitting in the bottom of her trunk to make a gown. To make a whole new wedding dress, perhaps.

It was at a WVS tea dance she heard they were collecting dresses.

'One of the Welfare Officers, Mrs McCorquodale, is gathering a wardrobe of dresses so that all the girls who would miss out on a white wedding will have their dream day,' the woman told her. Tess paused in wiping out the tea cup. 'She's a terribly elegant lady herself. I hear her ATS uniform was tailored by Worth. I think it's terribly romantic.'

'Is that Barbara McCorquodale? Are they taking donations?' Tess said.

'Absolutely. There are so many women in uniform at the moment I believe she is travelling the country to gather hundreds of dresses together.' The woman reached across and handed her a copy of *The Lady*. 'Look in the Classifieds. There's an advert in there with the telephone number.'

□

'May I use the telephone, Aphra?' Tess said that afternoon, popping her head into the kitchen.

Aphra looked up from the financial pages of the newspaper. 'Of course, dear. Good day?'

'It's getting better,' Tess said, marching through the house. She dug the torn out classified ad from her pocket and picked up the receiver on the hall table. She dialled the number and leant against the wall, waiting to be put through. 'Good afternoon, I understand you are collecting wedding dresses?'

'That's right, you may sell your old wedding dress to us free of coupons. We are gathering dresses for an ATS pool, and also for the RAF. Women apply to their Company Commanders to borrow the dress for one day, and we supply the dress of their choice. So much more romantic than marrying in khaki.'

'Do you need to see the dress, or would I just be able to post it to you? I'm in Somerset.'

'As long as it is in good condition, send it along.'

Tess remembered sitting on the floor of Aphra's living room some weeks later, one leg extended, her cheek resting on her knee. She had read Kit's letters so many times they were falling apart at the folds, and as she threw the last one to the floor beside her, the sections of paper lifted like wings. *I don't love you*, she saw, Kit's looping blue words fading already. *It was a mistake. I want to be free.* She watched Bobby's pram on the lawn, saw a tiny hand reach up to the sunlit branches shading him from the morning sun. The phone in the hall rang, and Tess leapt to her feet to answer it.

'Hello? Montgomery residence,' she said, crooking the receiver to her ear.

'May I speak to Mrs Blythe?'
'Speaking.'

'My dear, this is Barbara McCorquodale. I have your absolutely divine wedding dress in front of me.'

'Oh good. I was worried it might not arrive safely.'

'Are you sure you wish to part with it, my dear? It's terribly generous of you - this beautiful silk.' Tess heard her pause. 'My maximum budget is normally £8 but I'll give you a little more out of my own pocket. I realise that dresses like this are made of more than silk; they are made of dreams.'

'Dreams,' Tess said softly. 'Yes, I suppose it was. We married in Hong Kong,' Tess said, letting her fingers run over the skirt of her simple cotton dress.

'That explains the fine quality of the silk. How romantic.'

'It was.' She remembered it all. Kit's proposal in the Repulse Bay Hotel. Sunsets and pink gins. 'We had our reception at the Peninsula. A Rolls Royce picked us up from the church for the wedding breakfast.'

'Oh, how glorious. I can picture it all. What a wonderful romantic story that would make. The marble lobby, the gilt, and you in this glorious dress. So romantic.'

'It is rather, isn't it. I remember feeling terribly awkward at the time.'

'There's no hurry. If you change your mind-'

'No, I like the idea of the dress bringing joy to someone else, rather than being shut away in some trunk.'

'You don't want to keep it for a christening gown?'

Tess looked at Bobby's pram on the lawn. She felt the ache in her, the space which might never be filled by the child of someone she loved, by all the children she had dreamt of having. *Stop it* she told herself, feeling her love for her son rise up in her fierce and protective. *You are lucky to have him.*

'No, we won't be having any more children,' she said, smoothing down the skirt of her dress. 'I hope it brings someone ... just as much happiness as we had.'

'You're terribly brave saying goodbye to the dress.'

A small smile flickered over Tess' lips. She liked Barbara. '

'Thank you.'

'I always think it's like saying farewell to who we were, once. Which is no bad thing.' Tess heard Barbara beckon to one of the girls chattering in the background to come and take the dress. She imagined a young woman, a customer, eyeing the dress. Tess remembered then. 'Wait! Do you have a seam picker?' she said.

'Yes, of course.' Barbara called someone over.

'Tell them to feel along the left arm.

There's a pin.' Tess waited, picturing a seamstress reaching through the neck, turning the dress inside out, exposing the arm seam until she felt the rigid metal. She imagined a close up, a couple of stitches worked free, exposing the unforgiving head of the pin, and then it is eased out.

'There,' she heard someone say. 'Now it will be perfect.'

'I think we have a young lady interested already, Mrs Blythe,' Barbara said. 'It would suit you beautifully,' she said to the girl. 'When are you getting married?'

'Saturday,' the girl said, blushing. 'Hugh's shipping out on Monday.' Tess imagined her reaching out, stroking the heavy oyster silk. Perhaps a tiny gold band with diamond chips on her finger.

'I'm so glad,' Tess said, her throat tight with tears. Such innocence and hope. 'Thank you. Please wish them every happiness.'

☐

'Tess?'

She looked up to the wagon roofed nave, found her favourite boss, a mermaid, comb and mirror in hand. *I have heard them calling,* she thought.

'Are you alright?'

'Yes, perfectly alright. I was just thinking about my wedding.'

'Are you happy here?' Philip asked.

'Me?' Tess said. 'I haven't really stopped to think about it.' *Am I? Am I happy?* 'I suppose I never expected to feel so lost, coming home. Does that make sense?'

'Not really.'

'I've only been 'home' to England once every four of five years, growing up. I sometimes feel like I don't belong in my own country.' *That's it. I feel like a stranger in the place I was born.* She pointed up at the mermaid. 'How old do you think they are?'

'Twelfth century, probably. Beautiful, aren't they?'

'That one was always my favourite, when I was little,' she said.

'The mermaid?' Philip slumped down in the pew beside her, ran a hand through his rain darkened hair, looking up at the roof. She could smell the cold air on him, the earth, the hills. 'Rose among the thorns.'

'Or green men, at least,' Tess said, settling back to look at the ceiling. The clock in the tower ticked steadily, keeping time with the patter of rain overhead. 'I gave them all names when I was a child. That's Seth,' she said, pointing at a primitive carved face, garlanded with vine leaves and fruit.'

'Appropriate,' Philip said, glancing at her.

'Years and years of Sunday school.' Tess hugged herself.

'You know,' he said, leaning closer. 'In

medieval theology the head was thought to be the seat of the soul.' Philip took a fragile gold leaf from her hair. Instead of dropping it on the floor, he slipped it into his pocket. 'These images were incredibly potent. The mouth was the gate of the soul.'

'Taste of forbidden fruit?' Tess paused. 'Philip, Mrs Filby-'

'Oof. What does she want now?'

'The usual, I expect,' Aphra said, striding up the aisle towards them, the wheels of the pram hissing slick and wet on the tiles. 'To make everyone else as damn miserable as she is, the old bitch.' Aphra mouthed 'sorry' towards the altar, and sat next to Philip, stretching her legs into the aisle and crossing her ankles. The sole of one ancient tan brogue was coming away from the scuffed toe.

'She said everyone is talking,' Tess said.

'About you two, I imagine?' Aphra looked at them out of the corner of her eye.

'I can assure you, Aphra, we are friends. Nothing untoward-' Philip began.

'Then it damn well should. You've been dancing around one another like fireflies for a year now. You're young-'

Tess inhaled sharply. Philip was looking at her, his eyes questioning. 'I'd - I'd better get ready for the choir practice,' he said, and went to the vestry.

'Aphra, you're dreadful,' Tess whispered,

digging her in the ribs. 'You've embarrassed him. Look at the way he shot off.'

'Poppycock. Sometimes people can be terribly slow. He needed a push in the right direction. As my namesake said,' Aphra whispered once the vestry door closed, "one hour of right-down love is worth an age of dully living on'.'

'Aphra!' Tess said.

'There's a war on. You've already lost one chance of happiness. If you lose any more it will look like carelessness.' Aphra reached across and squeezed her hand, glancing up as the church door opened and the other members of the choir filed in. 'What are you waiting for?' she said under her breath. 'You've done your grieving. Kit told you he wanted out of the marriage, and lord only knows what is happening in Hong Kong. He could be alive or dead. Are you going to stay faithful to a ghost your whole life?'

Chapter 23

Christmas 1945

The hill rose high and dark behind the house, an eyelash fringe of bare trees brushed the Prussian blue sky. Philip and Tess walked in companionable silence back to the gold glowing lights of the Old Rectory, arms full of logs and kindling, their breath hanging on the frozen air.

Tess had been dozing in front of the fire after lunch when Philip returned from serving lunch at the soup kitchen. She was, as usual, still hungry after picking at the simple meal, but Aphra's special occasion whisky warmed her throat. She looked at her child sleeping peacefully on the sofa next to her aunt and the dogs. Aphra was wearing an old pair of cords, belted in, and a darned fisherman's sweater, a jaunty red polka dot scarf tied at her throat the only concession to Christmas.

At a soft knock on the door, Tess had stirred. Philip poked his head in, and seeing Aphra sleeping beckoned for Tess to come to the hall. It was freezing there, and Tess pulled her cardigan around her, shivering. 'Finished for the day?' she whispered. Philip nodded, and lifted a small sprig of berryless mistletoe above her head, kissing her chastely on the cheek.

'I wondered if you felt like a walk?'

'Love to,' Tess said, and grabbed her coat and wellingtons from the boot room.

'Is that Philip?' They heard Aphra call from the drawing room.

'Happy Christmas, Aphra,' he said, pushing open the door.

'Jolly good sermon,' she said, struggling to her feet.

'Don't get up,' he said. 'We're just going for a walk.'

'Are you alright with Bobby for an hour?' Tess said.

'Run along, take as long as you wish,' Aphra said. 'Why don't you come for supper, Philip? We can get plastered and play charades.'

'Are you leading me astray, Aphra?'

'No, but someone should,' she said, looking at Tess.

'What a glorious day,' Tess said now, leaning in to him. 'You know, Bobby's gift was far too generous.'

'The National Savings certificates? Nonsense. It's good to think of the future, at last.' Philip put his arm around Tess' shoulders. 'Besides, the poor little chap only had an orange, three nuts and a penny in his stocking.' Tess laughed. 'It will be different next year, you'll see.'

'How long do you think we will have to wait?'

'To be together?' The pale cloud of their breath melded between them as he turned to her. 'We must do this properly. Now that the war is over, we must wait for official notice that your husband is dead. God knows, there's a hell of a mess to sort out. We just have to be patient.'

Tess turned the thin silver band Philip had given her in the summer as a promise on her right middle finger. It had been too large, but she treasured it and wore it always. 'I don't understand how it can be taking so long. We heard soon enough about Mother, and Father.'

'But that's different. Your mother managed to write one last time from the internment camp, before she died. And then there were people around her when she went.'

'I'm so glad she wasn't alone, that she had friends.' Tess' voice caught. 'I'm so glad I found out what happened to them, soon after. It's the not knowing, with Kit, that's so dreadful. I feel like we are in limbo. I hope he survived, but I just wish he would let me know that he's alright, if he is, so that we ... Oh, god that sounds so awfully selfish, when so many don't have a future to think of.'

'It's still raw, darling, I know.' Philip held her close and leant his cheek against the top of her head. 'Give it time. Just as soon as we know what happened to your husband, we can make plans.' They walked on down the hill towards the lights of the village.

'I do wish we'd had snow this year, wouldn't that have been perfect?' Tess looked up at the darkening sky as it began to rain again. 'I love Christmas. It's like you said in the sermon today, all the parties and paper chains aren't an escape from reality, they just show how we can transform it.'

'I must admit I stole that idea from the Archbishop of York.'

'You are wicked.' Tess grinned at him. 'It feels like this year we have that chance anew.'

'Do you know what I love about you?'

'No, tell me,' Tess said, turning to him and taking hold of the collar of his overcoat.

'You always see the positive in every situation. I think you will make a marvellous vicar's wife.'

Tess' expression fell a little. *Doesn't he find me beautiful? Or fun to be with?* she wondered. *Doesn't he lie awake at night aching to be together, really together, as I do?* For some time Tess had longed for a glimpse of passion in him, a flash of sunlight among the clouds. 'Well, someone needs to keep an eye on you,' she said as they hurried along the drive. 'Stealing sermons, indeed.'

Tess kicked off her wellingtons in the porch and Philip held open the door for her. The wreath she made from branches of pine and holly smelt green and fresh. She paused at the sound of voices, one her aunt's the other a man's. The lamp lit hall was warm, rich with wood smoke. Tess paused to drape a strand of ivy back across a painting, frowning at the sound of the voices, trying to work out who might have called round. She walked on towards the drawing room, her stockinged feet padding silently on the Persian carpet.

'No, no we didn't get your letter,' Aphra was saying, her back to the fire. She was talking to someone in the high wing backed armchair. Tess could not see who it was, only a grey suited trouser leg crossed elegantly at the knee. Bobby sat on the floor behind Aphra. He was in his pyjamas and dressing gown, ready for bed, his dark hair damp and cheeks rosy from the bath. He was casting wary glances at the man, pushing a toy car again and again along the floor.

'Tess?' Aphra said, her face ashen. 'Marvellous news, darling. Look who's here.'

□

'Tess? Tess?' When she came round, it was Philip's concerned face hovering over her.

'Did I ..?' She struggled to sit up.

'You fainted.' Kit's voice drifted over from the armchair. 'Perhaps I should have called ahead. I thought it would be the most splendid Christmas surprise. It seems you have a surprise or two of your own.'

Tess struggled up and looked at him. She hardly recognised her husband. He huddled in the armchair, still wrapped in his greatcoat. Kit's hair had thinned, his skin was a waxy grey, his hands skeletal. It was as if his cornflower blue eyes had frozen to an icy blue. Where was he? Where was the tall, heroic, golden hero she first saw on parade in his white uniform. Where was the elegant, athletic man she adored?

'That's enough, Christopher,' Aphra said firmly. 'I was just bringing him up to date with how busy we have all been, with our evacuees, and the ballet classes you have been running in the village hall. Tess has been quite the hit in the village-'

'So I can see,' Kit said, running his index finger along his chapped lips. 'You do look well, Tess. I don't think I've ever seen you look so lovely.'

'Thank you. You-'

'I look like the walking dead,' Kit said laughing. He broke off into a hacking cough, and lit a cigarette. 'I had pneumonia. Lucky to be alive.' There was an elegance to the way the blue smoke curled around his fingers, cigarette aloft, that Tess remembered. It was like hearing a favourite melody out of tune.

'Are you sure I can't get you anything to eat?' Aphra said, frowning. 'I'm sure there's some plum pudding left, or a bit of cold roast pork.'

'Good god, no.' Kit wrinkled his nose. 'The

smell of roasting flesh makes me quite sick. I'll never eat it again, after everything ...' He trailed off. 'Let's not talk about the war.' Kit's eyes were too bright as he turned to the child. 'Look at the size of you, Robert. I somehow imagined you as a baby all these years, and here you are, quite the young man.' He slapped his knees. 'Well, what are you waiting for? Come and sit with your father.'

Bobby shook his head, tears welling in his eyes, and ran to Philip, hiding behind his legs.

'You'll have to give him some time, Kit,' Tess said, struggling upright on the sofa, pushing her hair away from her face. 'Philip is ...'

'We haven't met,' Kit said, ignoring her. He jumped up and strode across the room towards Philip, bristling with such manic energy Tess thought of the RKO Radio Pictures mast at the cinema. Tess half expected blue sparks to fly from his extended hand. 'I'm Kit Blythe. Tess' husband.'

'How do you do? Philip. Philip Hardy.'

'Philip's our vicar,' Aphra said carefully. 'He has been a great support to us all.'

'I bet. I bet he has.' Kit's sharp glance at Tess stung like a wasp. 'Vicar, eh? Well, well. You don't look like a vicar. Though the dog collar is a bit of a giveaway,' Kit said, swaying as he reached for the back of the red Knole sofa for support. The upholstered peg came away in his hand and he lurched forwards, the sofa wing collapsing.

'Steady, old chap.'

'I'm perfectly fine.' Kit said, snatching his arm away as Philip went to help. He sank back into an armchair opposite the fire, doing a quick double take as he spotted the drinks tray. 'I say is that brandy?'

'Allow me,' Philip said, pouring him a glass.

'Thanks, *old chap*.' Kit drained it, his eyelids flickering. 'Isn't this cosy? A real Christmas scene. The kind of thing you dream of when you're overseas. Merry old England.' He patted his knee. 'Come on Robert, be a good boy. Come and say hello. Daddy's home.' The child shook his head.

'You're not my Daddy. I don't have a Daddy. I have Philip. Philip is my friend.'

'I see we shall have to teach you some manners, young man.'

'Kit, don't-' Tess said, her skin prickling at his tone.

'It's alright, Bobby,' Philip said, stooping down to the child's height. 'I have to go now.' He turned to Tess and forced a smile. 'Happy Christmas.'

'I'll see you out,' Aphra said, striding from the room.

'Well,' Kit said, turning to Tess.

'I can't believe it,' Tess said, sitting on the edge of the sofa. Bobby scrambled up and curled in to his mother's side, eyeing Kit warily.

'I should have called.'

'It's just ... such a shock. We thought you were dead. I'd heard nothing ...'

'Let's forget all that.' Kit tilted his head. 'Have you had a good war? That's what people say, isn't it? I think you have. You look terribly well, and the boy. And the house is quite charming. I stopped off to see aunt Cally-'

'Kit I explained about that-'

'I can quite see why you prefer it here. The old bag really has let the place go dreadfully. I fear there shan't be much to inherit once she pops her clogs.'

'Kit-'

'Yes, it is quite charming here,' he said, leaping to his feet and pacing in front of the fire. 'And such delightful company.'

'Don't.'

'How long has it been going on?'

'I don't know what you mean.' Tess whispered in Bobby's ear and the boy ran from the room to find Aphra. Tess smoothed down her skirt as she stood, and she walked to the drinks cabinet, collecting Kit's empty glass on the way.

'Him. The Vicar.' Kit gripped her wrist and grimaced. 'Philip.'

'Let me go.' Tess waited for him to release her hand. 'Nothing happened.' She calmly poured herself a brandy and refilled Kit's glass.

'Nonsense.' He looked up at her and took the drink.

'What do you care, anyway?' Tess sat back

on the sofa and crossed her legs. 'I got your letters, Kit, the ones you sent before the war. You told me it was a mistake, that we were a mistake, that you wanted something different, to be a bachelor again-'

'That was then.'

'And now?'

'And now I can't believe that while I've been rotting in a PoW camp you have been playing happy families with Philip.'

'Stop saying his name like that, you sound ridiculous-'

'Philip ...' Kit said, wheedling. 'Philip, Philip-'

'Stop it!' Tess cried, putting her hands over her ears.

'I'm not angry,' Kit said. 'God knows, there was a war on. And you're right, the last you heard from me I was working through some ... doubts.'

'And?'

'I'm disappointed that you are lying to me.'

'Disappointed? *You're* disappointed?' Tess forced down her rising sense of panic. All her dreams, the future she had imagined with Philip seemed to be caving in like a house of cards. 'Nothing happened, you have nothing to be angry about-'

'I'm not angry that you deceived me. I'm angry that I can't trust you ever again.' Kit's sunken eyes blazed, a cold fire. 'I believed in you, in the idea of you, and the child, and building a life in England with you. I carried you in my heart all these years, and you, meanwhile you-'

'I never made love with Philip. I am still your wife.'

'But you fell in love with him, I can see it. You say nothing happened, but everything happened. You fell in love with another man. How do you think that makes me feel? I thought I was loved-' Kit's shoulders hunched, and he buried his face in his hands.

'I love you, Kit, I've always loved you,' Tess paused. 'But you never made love to me. I've spent all these years feeling I am not enough. That I'm not good enough for you.' She forced down the tight knot of disappointment in her chest. 'It doesn't matter to me, the sex, I mean,' she lied. 'I know I've made a mess of all that-'

'Tess, don't blame yourself.'

'But haven't we always been friends? Oh, darling, what is it? You know you can talk to me, don't you? You know you can always tell me anything.' She sat on the arm of the chair and folded herself around him, stroked his fine blonde hair back from his brow. She realised with surprise how painfully thin he was beneath his coat. It was more like cuddling Bobby than embracing Philip.

Philip. Tess forced the thought of him away, for now, running her thumb against the silver band on her finger. 'Come, sit with me on the sofa.' She plumped the cushions for Kit, and pulled a moth-eaten tartan blanket over their knees. Tess turned to him, her legs folded beneath her. 'Tell me everything. Tell me about what happened.' At her kindness, Kit's shoulders shook, and he buried his face in his hands. 'Oh, Kit,' she said, holding him.

'I'm sorry,' he said. 'It's just - it's a relief seeing you, Tess. Our life, everyone and everything we knew is gone. I feel like a fool,' he said, wiping at his eyes with the heel of his hand. Tess pulled a clean hanky from the sleeve of her sweater and gently wiped away his tears. 'Thank you.' Kit regained his composure, letting himself relax into the sofa while Tess stroked his hair. 'We all carried on with our tennis matches and tea parties and drinks at the Jockey Club, right up to the bitter bloody end. There was even a regatta at the Hong Kong yacht club not long before the Japanese attacked.' Tess felt him tense. 'Churchill wouldn't leave a bunch of volunteers to defend Hong Kong, would he? Surely troops were on their way to see off the Japanese.'

'Oh darling.' She held him closer, feeling his arms tremble.

'The last time I saw your parents was at a charity ball at the Pen, two days before the invasion.' He glanced up at her. 'How did we know as we were sipping our gimlets that the Japanese were swarming twenty miles away at the border? We danced on regardless. I was dancing with your mother, as it happens, when the call came at 11pm. The orchestra was playing *The Best Things in Life Are Free.* I'll always remember it. All naval personnel had to return immediately to their ships. That was it. That was the last time I saw your father.' Tess buried her head in the dip between Kit's neck and collar bone. 'So it was up to the rest of us. We weren't going to let the bastards take our home without a fight. There was ...' He paused. 'There was a unique spirit among the volunteers.' He fell silent. 'But it was hell, Tess. The brutality of them. I still have nightmares about the things I saw. The smell-' He pressed his fist to his lips as if he was trying to stop himself retching. 'Aphra and her bloody roast pork. The sheer thought makes me want to-' She waited, letting him gather his thoughts. 'It's hard to describe how intense a time it was. How it brought people together. We weren't sure if we were going to live or die.' Kit paused. 'The thing is, I met someone, too.'

'I know. I guessed from your last letter. You seemed to have regained something of your old self.'

'You always knew me well. You must think me a terrible cad.' Kit pushed the cuticles back on his bitten fingernails with this thumb in turn. *He had such beautiful hands,* she thought. Tess took his hands in her own, warming them. 'It was wrong of me, to break with you in a letter. And then I didn't feel able to explain more. There aren't a great deal of amusing anecdotes to share from POW camps.'

'You were saying, you met someone?'

'A while before the invasion.' Kit's eyes filled with tears 'I lost them, in the camp-'

'Oh, Kit. I'm sorry. I don't need to know the details.' Tess held Kit as he wept. *Philip*, she thought. All this time she had waited and waited, doing the right thing while this hunger ate away at her heart. She had fought her feelings, and Kit had been having an affair?

'I'm so sorry darling. It was pointless, all of it. This bloody awful pointless cruelty all around us. People raped, mutilated, butchered like dogs.' He paused. 'We found some comfort in one another-'

'We'll never talk of this.' She swung her legs from the sofa and leant over her arm, her head bowed in the shadows, hiding her face from him. She was not weeping. She was angry.

'I just want you to understand.' Kit reached out and touched her back.

'I feel sick, like I've been eviscerated.'

'Can you ever forgive me?'

'I can't.'

'But you must. For the sake of our marriage, and the child. We can start again. We can comfort one another.'

But I don't want you, she longed to cry out. *I want Philip. I want a man who loves me, who can really love me.* Kit's touch unnerved her. She knew immediately it was over with Philip, she saw it in his eyes. 'The only person I want to comfort me is the one who has broken my heart,' she said, thinking of him.

'Darling, don't. You'll make me cry too.' Kit reached onto the coffee table and picked up the Mason Pearson brush Aphra had been brushing Bobby's hair with when Kit walked in. 'It will never happen again, I promise.'

'I don't care about the affair. Don't you see, it doesn't matter now,' Tess said, closing her eyes as he brushed her hair. 'Now I know it's me. It's me that you can't love.'

□

'... five, four, three, two, one! Happy New Year!' Aphra shouted, throwing her arms into the air. Everyone at the party cheered and clapped, embracing as balloons and confetti rained down. 'Happy New Year, darling,' she said, hugging Tess. 'I just know 1946 will be a good year.'

'It won't. I can't bear it.' Tess hung her head, and Aphra held her tighter.

'Yes, you can. You're a Montgomery. Your forefathers have survived wars and shipwrecks, shark attacks and mutinies. You can survive a broken heart, trust me.'

'Aphra, Philip is on the other side of the room and it may as well be the dark side of the moon.'

'If he doesn't have the guts to stand up and

fight for you, he doesn't deserve you.' Aphra took Tess' face in her hands. 'You can bear this, and you will bear this.'

'I can't-' Tess broke down.

'Stop it. Stop it right now.' Aphra turned her away so that no one could see Tess' face, her tears. 'Pull yourself together. No man is worth your tears, take it from me.'

'I love him-'

'So let him go. Release him back into the wild, and in your old age you can imagine him settled down with a wholesome, good woman who will serve him and the church, and know that every so often when the moon is full, or he sees a beautiful sunset, or hears a piece of music which moves his heart, he will think of you. And think of everything, everything that might have been.' Aphra closed her eyes, steadying Tess as she composed herself. 'Let him go. You must do the right thing. You chose to marry, you chose to keep the child. Honour those choices.'

'I need him. I miss him-'

'You do not need him. You don't.' Aphra stepped back, and shook Tess' shoulders gently. 'You will get over him. Trust me. You will get over him, and he will become such a distant memory you will surprise yourself.' She stroked a strand of hair that had stuck to Tess' cheek away, dried her tears with her soft, wrinkled hand. 'Philip is already your past. You will do your duty, to Bobby, and Kit, and once they are on their feet you will have your chance. Just wait. My thirties, my forties were marvellous. You have such adventures, so much happiness ahead.'

'Let's hope so,' Tess said, looking across the room to where Philip stood. He raised his glass in a toast, smiled sadly. 'Thank you,' Tess whispered, kissing Aphra's cheek.

Kit watched the silent exchange, and flicked his cigarette into the fire. He took his glass of whisky from the mantelpiece and pushed through the party towards Philip. He held out his hand. 'I haven't had a chance to thank you for looking after my wife, Reverend Hardy.'

'Please, call me Philip.' He took his hand, holding it firm.

Kit waved at the sofa. 'Shall we?' He settled back in the armchair, pulling his heavy cardigan around him in spite of the warmth of the fire. 'It's most reassuring to know someone was looking after her, and my son.' Kit held his gaze. 'The thought of my family kept me going.'

'I only did what anyone would have done.'

'For us chaps fighting our greatest fear was that some bounder would take advantage of your girl. And she does have history. Tess is a vulnerable woman.'

'I don't know what you mean, Mr Blythe.'

Kit coughed productively, convulsing. He

wiped his mouth with a yellowed handkerchief. 'She was damaged goods when I married her.'

'Damaged?' Philip frowned. 'Tess ... Tess told me you are not Bobby's father.'

'It seemed like the Christian thing to do,' Kit said, draining his glass. 'She was in a spot and I helped her. You see, Tess and I have history and nothing will come between that.'

Philip folded his arms. 'You wrote to Tess,' he said. 'You told her you had made a mistake, that she shouldn't return to Hong Kong.'

'Ironic, eh? She couldn't have returned if she wanted to.'

'Tess thought you were dead.'

'And you comforted her?'

'I have absolute regard for Tess. She is a re-markable woman. I hoped-'

'And that is why I married her,' Kit inter-rupted. 'Why I *am* married to her.' He sneered, leaning forward in his seat. 'You know, under normal circumstances Tess wouldn't have given you a second glance.'

'I'm sure you're right.' Philip held his gaze steadily. 'You are a lucky man, Kit.'

'I don't need your sort to tell me how lucky I am.' The vein in Kit's temple pulsed. 'You make your own luck in life.' He raised his chin and stood, looking down on Philip. 'It is a small pond, here, Reverend Hardy and people talk. If we are all to get along, I think it best if you see as little as possible of Tess and Bobby from now on.

Do I make myself clear? Tess is a married woman. You have your position, your career to think of.' Kit's eyes glinted. 'How cosy it must have been. A vulnerable woman, heir to the lovely Old Rectory.'

'I assure you, my intentions were pure. My feelings for Tess-'

'If the Bishop were to-'

'That's enough. Don't demean yourself with threats and blackmail, Mr Blythe.' Philip stood, squaring up to him. 'You have made yourself perfectly clear.'

'Crystal, I hope.'

'I imagine your experiences have tried your faith.' Philip looked him in the eye. 'I meant what I said. You are a lucky man, in spite of your suffering. You have a remarkable wife and a beautiful son. You have everything to believe in.'

'Oh,' Kit said vaguely, looking across the room to where Tess was watching them. 'I believe in God, alright. I simply don't believe in man.'

Chapter 24

1946

'Kit, don't you think it's time you thought about a career? About how you are going to support your family?' Aphra stood in the French window looking out across the dark, rain lashed lawns. A scattering of brave purple and ochre crocuses shone in the rectangles of light from the drawing room, bright beacons of hope. She turned to Kit, glancing up as the pendant light at the heart of the drawing room dimmed for a moment.

'Support?' Kit shook out the newspaper, chewing the end of his pencil.

'Dear boy, if you weren't here - and please don't misunderstand, I love having you all here, god knows the house is far too large for me - but you couldn't survive on what Tess earns from her dance classes, could you? You couldn't afford to run a household. I'd hate to think you are burning through her inheritance.'

Kit cast aside the Times crossword and hung his head. 'I'm trying, Aphra. We're terribly grateful for your support. It's just ... every time

I try to think about the future, about working for some firm, I can't get my thoughts together. I can't.'

'Dear boy, I can't begin to imagine what you have been through, but you have a family relying on you.'

'Please don't tell me to pull myself together.' Kit leapt up and strode across to the drinks trolley. 'It's my fault. It's all my fault,' he said, his hand trembling as he reached for the decanter.

'Heaven's sake, Kit. Look at me. You have responsibilities - and do you really need another drink?'

'Stop nagging, Aphra.'

'This is not about you. This is about Tess, about her happiness. Frankly that is all I care about. You have treated her very cruelly, casting her aside and then rising from the dead expecting her to pick up the pieces.' Aphra folded her arms. 'It says a great deal about her strength of character that she has put aside all her hopes and dreams for you.'

'You're talking about the vicar.'

'She could have been happy-'

'She owes me.' He emptied the last drizzle of brandy into his glass, and peered into the decanter hopefully.

'She does not *owe* you,' Aphra said, unable to hide her irritation. 'If we are going to get along, you have to know I loathe self pity.'

'Is it cold? Are you cold?' Kit wrapped his cardigan tighter and flopped onto the sofa.

'- and profligacy,' she said under her breath. 'Tess is working every hour that god sends teaching. Why don't you go and chop some wood while she's at work?' she said, flicking at the switch on the electric fire. 'That will warm you up and get some colour in your cheeks.' Aphra knelt and peered under the drinks trolley. 'Who unplugged that?' She reached forwards, fumbling for the frayed flex, her fingers brushing the dusty pile of the Axminster carpet.

'Can I help?' Kit's head lolled towards her.

'You can help by getting off that ruddy sofa and bringing in some logs.' Kit sighed and forced himself up, loping off towards the kitchen. 'The thing is,' Aphra continued, 'Tess deserves to be happy. Do you really want her to stay with you because of guilt?'

'Guilt?' Kit said over his shoulder. 'I want her to stay with me because we made vows to one another.' He swung open the kitchen door.

'Since when have you given a damn about your vows?' Aphra called after him, jabbing the plug at the socket in frustration. 'Vows? I-'

Kit jumped in shock at the bang, the spark, the smell of burning. 'Aphra?'

The lights in the house went dark just as Tess turned in to the drive, running hand in hand through the rain with Bobby, singing *You Are My Sunshine,* the beam of her torch swinging in time with the melody. They kicked off their boots in the porch, and called out 'hello', Bobby skipping through the house looking for the dogs.

'Aphra?' Kit called again, flicking at the hall switch, stumbling over the umbrella stand in the darkness.

'Kit?' Tess called out, directing the beam of light around the hall, looking for him. She strode through to the drawing room, following the sound of the dogs' frantic barking.

At Tess' scream, all the dark birds rose from the ploughed field beside the house as one, wheeling up, up to the sky.

□

Kit closed the front door of the Rectory after the last of the black suited guests left, and stood side by side with Tess, only the ticking of Aphra's long case clock breaking the silence. 'You made far too much food for the wake. We'll be eating sausage rolls for days.'

'I wanted to, for Aphra.' Tess hugged herself. 'I couldn't boil an egg when I turned up here, do you know that? All those years of having cooks and house boys, I never had to lift a finger. Aphra taught me everything she knew about cooking, and being a good hostess.'

'I noticed you'd put on a couple of pounds.'

'Oh, shut up, Kit.' Tess turned on her heel, and kicked off her patent shoes.

'Do you really want to let yourself go,

stuck in this backwater? I can't live like this,' Kit said, picking them up and placing them neatly beside the front door, side by side.

'Neither can I.' Tess strode back through the house to the drawing room and fell to her knees by the hearth. She felt hollow, as light as bark driftwood, all life scooped out of her. She struck the match again and again, kneeling in front of the cold fire. It sparked finally, and she held it to the pile of damp newspaper and kindling. *I feel nothing,* she thought. *I feel dead inside.* It seemed impossible to think she would ever be happy again.

'We need a fresh start, somewhere we can make our fortune.' Kit spun the globe on the bookcase, his finger landing on America.

'But where? We've already failed in London, tried Hong Kong. Where on earth are you supposed to go after that?' Tess squeezed her thumb tight in her fist. 'The thing is, Kit. I love it here. Bobby loves it here.' Her chest tightened at the thought of never seeing Philip again. He had barely looked at her during Aphra's service. He had said exactly the right things - made sense of the senseless, heartbreaking accident that had taken Aphra from her. She still expected her aunt to walk through the door. The dogs lay in the kitchen, watching and waiting for her return. Tess knew how they felt. Philip had shaken her hand after the service when she thanked him, Kit at her side. He *shook my hand*, Tess thought, hugging her arms to her stomach. *Like I was a stranger. Like I was just another bereaved member of his congregation.* It was the first time in weeks he had looked at her, and she longed to embrace him. She missed him. Missed his company. But it was enough, almost enough, to wake each day with the hope of bumping into him in the village, of counting down to each church service just so she could sit and listen to his voice.

'New York,' Kit said softly. 'New York.'

'What about New York?' she said incredulously, wheeling round on her heel to look at him. Tess stood slowly and leant against the wall beside the fireplace.

'You know, in 1942 they let the American internees go, from the camp.' He spun the globe again. 'What a lottery life is. If I'd had an American passport, I could have gone home. Instead we were left there to rot for another three years, eating rat infested rice congee and dreaming of beef and Yorkshire pudding.' He tilted his head, and jabbed at the globe. 'New York it is. Pack your things, we leave in the morning.'

'Kit, we can't. What about the house, all of Aphra's things?'

'I've made an inventory of all the most valuable things and contacted a house clearance service.'

'But it's not yours to-'

Kit pushed back his chair and stood unsteadily. 'You are my wife.' He walked slowly over to her. 'What's mine is yours and vice versa.'

'But you have nothing. You never did have anything, did you? That - that wreck of a house? Your great inheritance. You married me for my money. That's what we are burning through.'

'The sale of this place will give us a nice little boost.' Kit put his hands on his hips. 'Down-payment on the lease of an apartment overlooking Central Park, the chance to start up a design firm for me, a dance school for you ...'

'You have this all figured out, don't you.' Tess rounded on him. 'What about Aphra's dogs, what about Hebe and Hero?'

'I thought your vicar would take them on and find a home for them. Least he can do.'

'But-'

'No buts. Our passage is already booked,' Kit said, his face still and fierce. 'Do you really think I'm going to live here with you and that - that excuse of a clergyman conducting your vile affair?'

'How dare you! Don't you talk about Philip like that. I couldn't have coped without him and Aphra. They were good friends to me, and that is all.' Tess' face contorted. 'Now they are both gone. It feels like all the music in my heart has gone too.'

'You wanted it to be more, didn't you?' Kit seized her by the throat, his fingers pressing against her jaw. 'What did he do, hey?' Kit ground his hips against her, his other hand grabbing her thigh. 'Did he make love to you like this. Did he?' Kit's fingers scrambled at Tess' stocking tops. 'Is this what you want?'

'Kit, stop it!' Tess cried out. 'Stop it, please.'

'Did he make you want him?'

'Please, don't,' she said, turning her face to the wall, a sob catching in her throat.

'Mummy?' a small voice said from the doorway. They turned, breaking apart.

'Bobby-' Tess straightened the skirt of her dress, stumbling past Kit.

'Why is he hurting you? Why is father hurting you?'

'We were just play fighting,' she said, rushing over. She knelt down and hugged her child. 'Don't be scared,' she whispered. 'Go to bed, darling. Go to bed.' She watching him clamber up the mahogany staircase, waited for the close of Bobby's bedroom door and the golden light to extinguish on the landing.

'Tess, darling, I'm sorry.' Kit reached out to her.

'Don't touch me,' she said, recoiling. Tess scrambled to her feet, feeling her way up the doorpost. 'Never touch me again.' She backed away from him and turned, running through the kitchen corridor, Kit following her.

'Where are you going?' he called, his voice plaintive now. 'Are you going to see him?'

'I'm not leaving here,' she said, thrusting her arm into her overcoat. 'We can divorce, take the money if that's what you want.'

'I want a family. I need you,' Kit said. 'You owe me, Tess. I married you, saved your reputation, saved your and Bobby's life by sending you home.'

'I will always be grateful for that.' Tess hesitated. She opened the door and the dogs raced out into the night. 'I felt so guilty. I feel guilty.'

'You owe me. Do what's right.' His eyes gleamed darkly. 'If you leave me for him, I'll drag you through the courts. I'll take the money and I'll take Bobby. You'll never see him again.'

'You wouldn't do that!'

'Who do you think they would believe? Upstanding war veteran or a silly girl who got herself knocked up out of wedlock, and had a wild affair with a vicar while her husband was in a POW camp-'

'Don't ...' Tess felt sick.

'Go on. Run along,' he said, swinging the door open wide. Kit bent low in a courtly bow ushering her out into the night. 'Go and say your goodbyes.'

Tess ran through the grounds of the Old Rectory, gasping for breath. Sodden branches of rhododendrons caught at her as she slipped around the driveway into Philip's garden. The rain plastered her hair to her head, mingling with the tears running down her cheeks. She flung open the kitchen door, and leant against the frame, catching her breath. She heard Philip's footsteps coming through from the living room.

'Who's there?' he said, peering into the darkness. 'Tess?'

'Oh, Philip,' she said, falling into his arms.

'What on earth is it?' He held her close as she sobbed. 'Has he hurt you?'

'He wants us to leave.'

'Leave ..?' Philip said softly.

'In the morning.' Tess looked up at him, her eyes streaked with kohl. 'He's had it all planned for ages. I can't bear the thought of never seeing you again.' She kissed him then, crushed her lips against his. They fell back into the shadows of the corridor, her arms encircling his neck. In the living room the jazz record he had been listening to ended, and silence shrouded them. Her breath seemed loud. She could hear her blood pulsing, singing in her ears.

'Tess,' he said, breaking free. 'We can't do this.'

'Darling, please.' Tess held his face in her hands, looked up at him. 'Don't let it end like this. He's making me sell the house, but I could get a little cottage nearby. Then when the divorce comes through-'

'Tess, you know I could never marry a divorced woman.'

'But ...' Tess recoiled, staggering back into the darkness. 'Then all these months, what was that-'

'Darling,' Philip said gently. 'I'm a vicar, not a saint. I thought you were widowed, Tess. That in time, I hoped-'

'But surely, if you love me, you could stop being a vicar, you ... you could-'

'It's a vocation,' he said, gently wiping back the hair from her face. 'I love you, Tess, but this is my calling.' He held her head in his hands, kissed her on the forehead. 'I miss you so much. I will never forget you, Tess.'

'Forget me?' Shocked, angry tears pricked Tess' eyes. 'Is that it? You're just going to let me walk out of here? You'll never see me, or Bobby again.' She pulled the collar of her coat across her chest. 'You were there when he was born. Who does he run to when he is hurt?'

'Tess, I love Bobby, but-'

'I love you,' she cried, her voice breaking into a sob. 'I love you.'

'Don't. Please don't say that, Tess. It's breaking my heart,' he said. 'Don't think for a moment it isn't.' Tess stumbled back into the shadows, away from his open hands. In the open doorway with the rain falling silver in the porch light she stood up straight, composing herself. She looked back at Philip, certain this was the last time she would ever see him. Tess imagined a stage behind her, not a windswept English garden. The porch light became a spotlight. Her chest rose as she straightened her spine and raised her chin.

'Goodbye, then,' she said. 'I'm glad - so very glad, to have known you.'

'Tess, I'm sorry,' he reached out to her, but Tess raised one hand, an elegant farewell.

'So am I.' She imagined the rapturous applause of the audience at the end of the dance, the fading score. It felt like someone was binding her heart with wire, tighter and tighter, but her face was impassive now.

'Will you write, let me know you are safe?'

'I don't think that's a good idea.'

'Tess, please-'

'Goodbye, Philip,' she said, and closed the door. Tess leant for a moment against the cold wet wood of the porch, her eyes screwed closed in distress. She ran wildly down the driveway, rain lashed and weeping, calling for the dogs. She fell against the trunk of a cedar tree and doubled over, her arms clutching her stomach in a silent howl of pain, the night falling around her. In the distance, she heard Hebe and Hero barking, and she headed towards them, her feet slipping on the wet grass.

'Hebe,' she called, following their cries to the church yard. She found them lying on Aphra's grave, heads lying on the freshly turned soil, whimpering and crying for their mistress. 'Darlings,' she said, kneeling beside them, stroking their rain soaked fur. 'I miss her too.' Tess raised her face to the sky. 'I promise you, Aphra, I will make you proud of me. Thank you-' The breath shuddered in Tess' throat and she screwed her eyes closed. 'Thank you.'

Act 2

'With *'Bring Down the Stars'*, I had this idea of a complete work of art - a *gesamtkunstwerk.* I wanted a perfect synthesis of dance, theatre, film, music. I wanted the stage alive with the elements - fire, air, water, earth in the form of sand piled like dunes in a ruined room of high, white arches, glass walls. I wanted audiences to feel like they were there, out on the water with the dancers, escaping to Cythera - swimming, drowning, clinging to life and one another. When I was younger, I swam with my husband in a phosphorescing sea. It was like the stars were underwater. I wanted to share that beauty, to immortalise the moment. So I had a clear vision of a plain backdrop where projected images danced in time with the music. I wanted to show people kymatic forms, the hidden secret beauty of sound waves revealed in water, rippling, dancing just like the performers. You see, I think we all have this rhythm, this music pulsing through us. We sense it, just out of reach. We just have to listen, to trust it. We just have to let it flow from our hearts.'

- Interview with Tess Blythe *Dance Now*
1979

Chapter 25

October 1961

Marco walked across the Pharmacy towards Tess. She blinked in surprise, registering his reflection behind hers. 'There you are,' he said, brushing her hair aside, revealing the pale curve of her neck, a sickle moon above the black bateau neckline of her sweater. He closed his eyes and lowered his forehead, resting there.

'You?' She said like a sigh. The memories of the past, the tight ball of pain in her chest dissolved like ink in water.

'Where were you?'

'Somewhere far away.'

'Never run from me again,' he whispered, his lips brushing her ear. 'You told me once you are always looking for home. Well I'm here. You found me. I am your home.'

'Then why am I afraid,' she said.

'Of what?'

'Of you. Of falling in love with you.' She felt him exhale.

'Falling ...' Marco said. 'When do you think we become afraid of falling? When I was young,

I used to climb mountains, and trees, I rode wild horses without a thought.'

'You bounce, when you're young,' Tess said, laughing softly.

'I see old men who fall going to collect the post, and they never get up again.' Marco exhaled. 'I'm not ready for that, yet. I want that-' He struggled for the word. 'That spontaneity. That glorious confidence. I want to feel physically, emotionally invulnerable again.'

'Like when we were young?' Tess looked up at him. 'Me too.'

'So we fall together. Hand in hand. Forever.' He embraced her, his forearm across her chest, and she leant in to him. 'You're afraid. I'm afraid.' He shrugged.

'You asked me once if there had ever been anyone else.'

'It was not my business to ask. The past is another country.'

'There was someone, once. But nothing came of it.'

'Oh, Tess.' Silence embraced them. 'He must have meant a great deal to you.'

'He - my heart broke into so many pieces, I don't know if I'm capable of trusting anyone again.'

'Trust me.'

'I can't.'

'Know what I think? After this guy, after Kit, you gave up on yourself, on your happiness

when you should have given up on your marriage. All these years you've put all your love,
all your desire into dancing. But you've kept
it small because you're afraid. You're afraid of
putting yourself centre stage and getting hurt.
That's why you never performed. Am I right?'

Making a spectacle of yourself. The phrase
came to Tess again, her mother's voice. That old
hot feeling of shame and fear.

'No good ever came of being less than you
can be,' Marco said. 'Let go, Tess. Trust me. I
won't rush you. I can wait for you.'

'But you're leaving soon, after the wedding.' She waited, trying to sense whether Claudia had told him about their conversation.

'Is that what's stopping you?'

'I can't ... I can't bear the thought of giving
in to loving you, only for you to leave.'

'Tess, don't you see? Where you go, I go. I
don't care. Come with me to Italy. Come here.
None of us-' He paused. 'We don't know how long
we have.'

'I know.' She took his hand in hers, laced
her pale fingers in his like willow around staves.
'I'm not scared of them, of what everyone thinks.
I'm scared of losing you.' She gazed out of the
window at the dark harbour lights. *Do I tell him?*
'Kit wants a divorce, you know that?' She looked
up at him, her eyes fierce. 'Are you shocked?'

'No.'

'I have been a good wife, all these years. I

would never -' She hesitated. 'No matter how at-
tracted I was to you, I would never have let this
go so far if Kit hadn't told me he wants to end the
marriage. He wants me to pretend everything is
hunky-dory. He says it's so we don't ruin Bobby
and Frankie's day, and that's the last thing I
would want to do. I love Bobby, and Frankie will
be so good for him, I just know it.'

'Bobby will be good for her too. She is too
serious, too good. She needs a little passion in
her life.' Marco smiled. 'You know, I fell for you
before I met you?'

'How?'

'Bobby carries a photograph of you in his
wallet, do you know that?' Tess shook her head.
'He's so proud of you. He carries one of Frankie,
and an old photo of you.'

'You fell for a photograph?'

'I found it charming. It says a lot about
your son, how much he respects you and loves
you.' Marco tilted his head. 'You are a little
younger. It is in England I think. You are sitting
on the lawn of an old white house.' *Aphra's home*,
she thought. 'You look happy. When I met you,
I saw that had changed.' Marco cupped her face
in his hand. 'I want to make you look like that
again, Tess. I want to see you lit up inside. I want
to make you happy.'

'I've pretended for so long,' Tess said, shaking her head. 'I don't know how to be happy. All
Kit cares about is saving face. I hate it. I hate the

deceit. And all the time, all I can think about is you.' She leant in to his embrace. 'And now I'm going to lose you, too.'

'Hey, hey,' he said softly, cradling her in his arms. Marco closed his eyes. 'I am not going anywhere, yet.' He ran his hand over the stubble bruising his jaw. 'What were you thinking about? You were very far away.'

'I was ... I was thinking of the War.' She raised her face to his. 'And you. I was thinking of you. What are you doing here?'

'I wanted to check you are alright.'

'You came all this way?'

'I felt like a drive.' Marco put his hat on the counter and leant against it, his arms trapping Tess. 'And Claudia told me what she'd done. I had to see you. I went to your apartment and your maid told me you had driven up here.'

'Well you've seen me, I'm alright.'

'I don't think you are,' he said, smiling. 'I think you are in love with me and you don't know what to do about it.' He kissed her then, cradling the blade of her jaw in his palm. Marco stepped back, blinking. 'Vanilla,' he said, biting his lower lip.

'Want some?' Tess offered him the cup, buying some time. Marco swung his leg across the stool beside her and rolled up the sleeves of his white shirt. She felt a sense of peace settle on her just having him close.

'Pretty good,' he said, gesturing to the

waitress. 'Espresso, please.'

'How did you find me?'

'I asked around. A couple of guys - a young black guy and his boyfriend told me where your cottage was, but it was closed up. I hoped you'd just gone for a walk in town, and then I saw you here.'

'So what do you think of this joint?'

'The town? I like it.' He nodded as the waitress slid a steaming coffee cup in front of him. Marco sighed, blowing the steam.

'Kind of like you, I fell in love with it from a photograph.' Tess leant on the counter, resting her chin on her hand. 'I read a book - *The Outermost House*. Have you heard of it?' Marco shook his head. 'I'll lend you my copy. It was so beautiful, so full of passion, the way the man described his home, the Fo'castle. I remember sitting on the wall of the library in New York, reading about how he swam in the sea with bioluminescent plankton.'

'Plankton?'

Tess laughed. 'It doesn't sound very romantic, but I drove out here the next day, and bought my little shack.'

'And have you swum with bio ...'

'Bioluminescent,' she said, laughing. 'Yes, I have, many times. It's just as he described.' Tess swept her arm in a graceful arc. 'It's like swimming with stars.'

'How about we lose ourselves here for a

while?' He leant his head on his hand. 'Maybe for a lifetime.'

'Marco, I can't-'

'What? Can't love me? Can't let yourself feel something?' His smile creased his eyes. 'Live dangerously.'

'We can't do this to Bobby and Frankie, not now.'

'Then when? When it is too late? When your idiot of a husband realises what he is losing. There are a thousand reasons not to be together and only one to be. We love one another. That is enough.' Marco held her gaze. 'I know you, Tess. I know how hungry you are for life, and for love. I know you, because I am the same. I sensed it in you the first time I saw you, that hunger for love.' He drained his coffee cup and put on his hat.

'Where are you going?'

'Back to the city.'

'But it'll take hours-'

Marco stooped and kissed her cheek. 'I said, I just wanted to make sure you are alright.' He ran his thumb along her lower lip, the tip of her tongue brushing his skin. 'When you are ready, call me.'

Marco closed the door of the cafe behind him, and strode along the street to his car. 'Wait for me here,' he said to the driver, tossing his hat onto the back seat. He glanced back through the golden window of the Pharmacy and saw Tess leaning back against the marble counter, ship-wrecked, one elegant arm extended. He closed his eyes, committing her beauty to memory like a poem.

Marco smiled to himself as he walked on through the darkening night to the beach, drawn by the sound of the crashing surf, the lament of the foghorn. *Pazienza*, he said to himself over and over again. *Patience.* The hulls of the boats gleamed like bones on the black water beneath an ink blue sky, streaked with the green flash of the aurora borealis. *I cannot give her happily ever after,* he thought. *But I can give her happiness.* The wind blustered against him, buffeting his overcoat, lifting his hair wild and free. Marco stopped suddenly and closed his eyes, inhaling the good clear air. He raised his hands to the sky and his face, arching back. 'Give me time,' he cried out to the wind. 'Give me time.' He screwed his eyes closed. 'That is all I ask. Give me enough time to love her, to bring her back to life.'

Chapter 26

'I'm looking for Marco Affini.' Marco looked up at the sound of Kit's voice. He saw him standing in the open doorway of the gym, silhouetted against the sliver of daylight spilling into the dimly lit interior through the rough metal door.

'He's just finished in the ring,' the owner said, pointing towards the spot lit heart of the gym where two men were dancing around one another, trading punches beneath a bare light bulb.

I think the fight is just beginning. Marco breathed in the familiar smell of the gym, of sweat, and dust, and liniment. He tossed his gloves aside, and clapped the young man beside him on the back. 'Well done, Rocco. That was much better.'

'How come I still can't beat you?' Rocco said, doubling over to catch his breath.

'One day soon, you will.' Marco took a long drink of cold water from the bottle on the side of the ring, and wiped his mouth. 'Just be sure you don't tell Claudia-'

'Don't tell Claudia what?' Kit said, strolling over. His crisp white shirt and immaculate grey coat looked out of place in the grimy gym. 'Are we keeping secrets?'

'She doesn't like me fighting.' Marco said, wiping his face with a towel. 'She thinks I am too old.'

'What are you? Forty?'

'I am forty five,' Marco said. 'Old enough to know better.'

'I was just in the neighbourhood,' Kit said, glancing around the gym. 'I called in at the house, but Frankie said you were here, coaching.'

'Yes, that's exactly what I have been doing.' Marco gestured for Kit to follow him, and he held open the door to the changing room. 'If Claudia were to ask.'

'So,' Kit said once the door swung closed.

'So.' Marco opened his locker and unwound the wraps from his hands. 'I went to see Tess.'

'You did?' Kit sat on the bench seat, and crossed his legs. 'Where is she? I suppose she ran off to that god awful shack in Cape Cod?'

'That doesn't matter.'

'It matters to me.' Kit waited for Marco to look at him. 'I believe my wife is in love with you.' Marco hesitated for a moment, then kept on unwinding the wraps, pooling the fabric on the floor at his feet.

'I think you should talk to Tess.'

'Have the decency to deny it, man.' He looked up at him, the tendon in his neck taught as a violin string.

'I can't do that,' Marco said carefully.

'How do you feel?' Kit leapt up, pushed his chest. 'Do you love her? Or is this some kind of sordid holiday romance? Is that why she's run off? You've used her and cast her aside?'

'Don't do that,' Marco said, not moving an inch as Kit shoved him again.

'I'll do what I damn well like,' Kit said, tossing his head, a lock of blonde hair falling forwards.

'I would never treat Tess badly. I have too much regard for her.'

'Regard? You have the nerve to talk about respect?' He wiped the back of his hand across his lips. 'How long's it been going on, hey? How long? Christ, we only met you a couple of weeks ago, and here she is driving off into the night like a lovesick teenager.'

'Nothing is going on.' Marco held his ground, held Kit's gaze. It felt like the air between them was shifting, contracting.

'But you'd like that, wouldn't you?' Kit sneered. 'As if someone of Tess' refinement would fall for a washed up old bruiser like you. The very thought of you-'

'What would you like?' Marco looked down at him, blinked slowly. 'Tell me. Do you find me attractive?'

'How dare you suggest-' Kit's expression tightened, a drum skin stretched taut. 'Think what you like. I care little for your opinion.'

Marco shrugged. 'My opinion - that you do not value - is that your wife is unsatisfied.'

'Why you-' Kit rounded on him, furious.

'I do not know who or what you are. I don't believe people fit as easily into little boxes as they would have us believe.' Marco folded his arms. 'What I do know is that Tess is a beautiful woman with much love to give.'

'You think I don't love her?'

'You are not in love.' Marco rubbed his palms together slowly.

'Has she told you-' Kit put his hands on his hips. 'What is it these days? Sex is the be all and end all. What about a long and contented marriage built on friendship and-and-'

'Tess is burning, and you don't see it.' Marco rolled his head from side to side, easing his neck. He did not want this confrontation with Kit right now. He was weary, and sore from sparring with Rocco. He daydreamed of a hot bath, Tess, a bed ...

'Is there anything else you'd like to tell me about my wife of over twenty years?'

'She is the kind of woman every man desires. But not her husband.'

'Go to hell.'

'I think you do not desire your wife, and you are surprised - jealous even - when other men do.'

'Jealous? Of you?' Kit tossed his head, laughing.

'It's none of my business.' Marco shrugged. 'Who am I to judge? We are all as bad as one another. If women knew what men think of in our secret hearts, I think they would never talk to us again.' He gestured at a dog-eared glamour shot pinned to the flaking window frame of the dressing room with a rusted drawing pin. 'We are wolves at the hearth of our women.'

'Wolves? Far worse than that.' Kit regarded Marco steadily. 'Did you fight? During the war?'

'Of course.'

'Do you ever talk about it?'

'No. The only men who bang their drums and talk of war are those who have not lived through it. Men who have not seen how bloody, sad and pointless war is.' In the silence that settled on them, he offered Kit his hand. 'I will do nothing to spoil the wedding. There will be no scandal, no scenes, you have my word.'

'Stay away from her.' Kit's skin was pale, washed green in the subterranean light.

'Don't threaten a man who has nothing to lose.' He released Kit's hand.

'You have *everything* to lose. How can you say that? Think of your family. Think of Tess.'

'Talk to her.' Marco held Kit's gaze. 'It is Tess' decision. She is not some prize for us to fight over. She is her own woman, but I am in love with your wife.'

'In love?' Kit laughed. 'Moons in June? Red roses and romance? Love doesn't last.'

'You're wrong. And if you are changing your mind about divorcing her-'

'She told you?' Kit raised his head in surprise.

'-I intend to take her from you.'

'Like hell you will.' Kit slipped his hand into his breast pocket. 'Have you told Claudia?'

'No, and I won't. Frankie and Bobby are young, and very much in love. Nothing must spoil their day.'

'Talking of which. For the wedding.' Kit reached into his breast pocket and threw down a roll of banknotes on the table. 'Bobby is our only child. I insist we help.' Marco saw him hesitate.

'I don't need your money, Kit.' He handed the roll back to him.

'But I insist.'

Marco raised his palm. 'No one need know.'

'I will take care of the rehearsal dinner then. It's the least I can do. Where would Frankie like it to be?'

'Orsini's,' Marco said. 'She's been going there since she was a kid.'

'I'm sure it's charming.'

'You don't think much of us, do you, Kit?' Marco stared at him. He dismissed him with a wave of his broad palm. 'It doesn't matter what you think.' Marco turned to the window and looked up at the sky. The locker room door slammed closed behind Kit, and Marco exhaled, carried on rolling up the wraps from his hands, the slanting light from the basement skylight illuminating the white material. He loosened the ties of his satin shorts, and undressed, padding across the room in a white t-shirt and boxer shorts to his locker, rubbing his ribs where Rocco's jab had hit home. He took out his sketchbook and flicked through the pages until he found the design for Tess' shoes. He could picture them already, perfect and supple, sparkling on her feet as she danced. *Think of Tess*, he remembered Kit's words. 'Lately I think of little else but Tess,' he said under his breath.

Chapter 27

In the distance he sees her, sweeping sand from the house onto the bleached boards of the porch and out into the wind. Tess' house cups in the hollow of the dune like a pale egg, shadows arcing like scimitars above. It is just as he imagined it would be. Simple, perfect, true. The sea glitters beyond the fringe of sea grass, the light is dazzling in its clarity. Her hair flames in the dark doorway, a tongue of fire leaping free. He thinks of the fire he has just read of in the Algerian desert, six hundred foot flames leaping from the earth, the world's largest fire. It is nothing compared to her, the effect she has on him. She has not seen him. She closes her eyes, raises her face to the sun. She is the most beautiful thing he has ever seen.

He has walked for miles through the woods to find her, it seems. His shoes are dew wet and caked with sand. He sits down to take them off, balling his socks inside, and rolling up the cuffs of his fine wool suit. Nearby a shed snake skin caught on the sea grass stirs in the breeze, silver, fine. The sand feels good beneath his feet as Marco walks on, his prints breaking the pale dry film to leave dark marks leading to her door. It feels like a pilgrimage. She has gone inside, the open door an invitation. The charcoal rectangle set against the storm blasted silver timbers seems a black hole, infinite, pulling him to another world. Tess appears at the upstairs window, a white sheet billowing from her hands like a sail, a surrender. Marco's pace quickens, he breaks into a run, and waves his hand in greeting.

These are the moments he will think of at the last, the moments when it all began, the moments his entire life was leading to. The sand in the bed. The taste of salt on her lips. The whiteness of the sheet in the sunlight, reflection of the mares' tail clouds above the sea. Her body. The surprising, supple strength of her. Her love. Her.

He had stopped in town, and he unbuttons his jacket as they kiss, chastely, in the simple living room. Through the door, he sees a wide, white bed, waiting. He sets aside the parcel he is carrying, and from his coat pockets he pulls two bottles of red wine, a loaf of bread, some salami and cheese like a magician. He loves her laugh. He raises one finger, and from his breast pocket he takes a single, perfect tomato. It is warm from his skin when she takes it. And then, a peach. She cannot wait. She sinks her teeth into the felt soft skin, and when he kisses her she tastes of the lost summer, of home. He drinks the nectar from her lips, her tongue. She bathed before he came as best she could, and her hair is damp and scented with lilies. Her fingers curl around his neck, coral tipped like stamens dripping pollen. There is no hurry now. The anticipation is exquisite.

The night stretched before them, inviting as the dark sky scattered with stars. She felt alive with him. Alive for the first time. She was aware of it all - the sunrise bloom to the light, the ozone fresh air on her skin, every touch, every move closer, closer still. She looked at him leaning against the rough wood counter, his starched white shirt, the sharp crease running down from between his shoulders. He was shipwrecked with her.

The sun blessed them, gilded everything - the simple coffee pot on the stove, the knife, two glasses on the table. She noticed every detail, not wanting to miss a thing: the breeze weaving among her outstretched fingers as they walked to the sea together, the cuff of her old cashmere sweater brushing the inside of her wrist, her bare feet grounding her on sand and wood. She felt electrified, her hair rising, searching and wanting. She was the deer in the forest, sensing the stag, close, coming for her.

The oil lamp guttered in the wind as Marco pushed the door to, the flames leaping. Night was falling, the gold light of their windows shining alone on the shore.

'You know, I've been trying to get a message to you for days.' He slid the shoebox onto the kitchen table. 'I called the pharmacy, left messages for you there. Did you get them?'

'Yes, I did. But she told me to stay away from you.' Tess was peeling apples, the blade sliding beneath the skin, her mouth watering. A bowl of freshly rinsed cranberries gleamed like rubies beside her.

'Claudia? And you listened?' She sensed him standing just behind her, and she lay down the knife. 'Tess,' he said, her name a breath, a sigh, his lips against her ear. *Tess. Tess.*

She knew if she turned to him now, it would all be over.

She turned.

'What do you want from me, Marco? I'm just learning to be by myself. I don't need some kind of rebound romance, only for you to leave.'

'I love you.'

'Prove it.'

'I don't want you,' he said, his lips hovering above the tendon in her neck. 'I need you.'

'I don't need you. I don't need anyone. I'd be just fine alone.'

'You've been alone for years. You've been waiting your whole life to feel this.'

'We can't,' she whispered. The sunset glinted on the blade, she rested her hand against the counter. 'It would break too many hearts.'

'We are all adults. They will get over it.'

His hand cupped the bone of her hip, slid flat across her stomach. 'Lives look smooth from a distance. Up close there are many cracks, many breaks.'

'And this would just be another break? Another change of course?'

'I wanted to fight, once, just as you wanted to dance,' he said, his lips tracing the taught tendon at the side of her throat. 'I lived for boxing, refused to go into the family business. Shoes? Why would I make shoes like my father?' Marco closed his eyes. 'Then my brothers died, one by one.'

'In the War?' Tess felt Marco nod, and she reached for his hand.

'All but Carlo and me. We were the lucky ones. Then Carlo left for America with Claudia, and my mother - well, she just died of a broken heart.'

'She still had you.'

'I wasn't enough. I was the great disappointment to them, a street fighter, a punk. They were ashamed of me.'

'And that's why you've been making it up to them ever since?'

'I owe my family everything.'

'Even your happiness?'

'I had to learn the business, learn how to take care of my father, of Claudia's family.'

'And you? Who took care of you?'

'There was someone, for a long time. But

she wanted more, she wanted a family, all of me. She wanted more than I could give, then.'

'And now?' Tess pressed against the sink, the steady weight of his hips against her waist. 'What is this?'

'Now I give you everything. All of me, all that I have left.'

There is no waiting now. No time. He swings her easily into his arms, and carries her to the bed. The wind swirls around the shack, sand grains hissing against the wood, whispering secrets to the night. It is cold, they shiver as the air finds their skin.

'Are you sure?' he says.

'Yes. Yes,' she says. His body thrills her. This. This is how she always hoped it would feel. His warmth, the breadth and strength of him. She traces the hard line of his collar bone, the groove of his sternum. She helps him shrug off his white shirt, and pulls at her sweater, longing to be with him, to feel skin on skin. Even the thin silk of her camisole is too much, and he slides it over her head as if she is shedding a skin. She is reborn. He lowers his lips to her shoulder, her breast.

'Your beauty,' he murmurs, awestruck, looking down at her where she lies back on the bed, her hair golden fire in the lamplight, burning on the white pillow. The storm snatches at the house, jealous of their warmth. Tess buries down in the bed, pulling the blankets over his shoulders, keeping them safe.

'Nothing can touch us here,' she whispers to him, her back arching beneath him. 'No one can find us.'

'We are like two animals in a burrow, in a cave,' he says, his eyes closing as her hand slides down his spine, his hip. 'See? Do you feel how I want you?'

'I don't want to wait,' she says, her face buried against his neck. 'Do you want me?'

'Yes,' he says, 'yes.'

□

'Open it,' he said, placing the box in her hands. Tess laid it on the rough pine table beside the bed and slid off the black lid, leaning it against a new copy of *Catch 22*. She peeled back the layers of white tissue paper to reveal a flash of scarlet silk.

'Oh, Marco,' she said, her fingertips touching her lips. 'I can't-'

'Yes, you can.' He took her hand and helped her sit on the edge of the bed, her auburn hair falling around her naked shoulders. He moved aside the simple black ballet pumps by the nightstand and brushed the sand from the arch of her foot. He eased her right foot into the first shoe.

'They are too beautiful,' she said. 'You made them again, for me?'

Marco shook his head. 'I designed them

but there was little time - the boys in the workshop made for you.' He held up his hand, to help her stand and she saw the tremor in his fingers.

'Are you ok?'

'Me? I'm fine.' He kissed her gently. 'It's you, you were marvellous, wonderful. You exhausted me. After a rest I will be fine again.' Tess felt her cheeks colour, and she looked down at her pale legs, the red shoes. She thought of fruit on the vine in warmth and sunshine, her skin singing with his touch, with him. She covered her mouth with her fingers, stifling laughter bubbling up in her joyous and free.

'I'm sorry,' she said. 'It's just - god, I had no idea it could feel like that. How you made me feel it's-' Her gaze met his and he grinned, shrugging.

'Hey, so I still got it. But maybe I need to take it easy.' Marco turned his hand over, flexing the fingers. 'Too many fights, maybe.' He raised his gaze to her.

'You,' she said, touching his face. 'God, I'm forty. Forty! I've waited my whole life to feel this.' *This*, she thought. *This is happiness.*

'The red is right, I think? For your dress. I thought of what you said about the scarf. How the red silk makes you feel.'

'Yes, yes it's perfect.' She flung her arms around him, laid her forehead against his. 'Thank you.' She stifled a laugh. 'Kit will be scandalised. I adore them, but I can't wear them, what will people say?'

'Nonsense.' Marco sat back on his heels and slid the other shoe onto her foot, his hands sliding along her ankles, her calves, and rose up until his face was level with hers again. He leant in to her his hands on her thighs, her hips, pulling her to him.

'Wear them,' he murmured, kissing her throat. 'What are you afraid of? Your own power? Wear them. Own them. Own your power.' He touched the hollow below her jaw, traced the curve of her throat to her collarbone. She shivered. 'When I touch you, I feel everything you have hidden away. All of your passion. All of your desire. I can feel it, waiting to break free in you.' Tess gripped the edge of her bed, her knuckles white. 'I have to be with you. I don't give a damn who knows.'

'We can't let people know, Marco. I'm still married.' She gestured at her new book on the bedside table. 'It's an impossible situation. It doesn't matter how-'

'You are wasted on that man.'

'Does it make a difference if I am divorced?'

'No, why?'

'There's a stigma to divorcees.'

'Nonsense.'

'And perhaps you like the idea of being with me with no strings, no expectations? If I am free-'

'I want to be with you, it is that simple.' Marco dragged her forward to him, hip against hip. 'If you are free to be with me, then that is better. If not, I will take you from him.' Tess was breathing hard as Marco traced the pearl bones of her spine by one. She closed her eyes, her head falling back at the warm touch of his palm sliding round, felt the pull of the pale sheet against her skin. 'Has he ever made you feel like this?' Marco let his head fall forward to her shoulder, waiting for her reply. 'I won't rush you, Tess, but what are you waiting for? I told you, nothing good ever came of being less than you are. I want to be with you, always. Be everything you were meant to be.'

'I'm afraid, Marco,' she said, burying her hands in his thick hair, tracing the bones of his skull with her fingertips as he kissed her stomach. She felt the tension in him.

'What do you have to be afraid of?'

'You. I've been waiting for you, all these years. And now you're here it feels like I've conjured you from my dreams. I'm afraid you might disappear, when I wake.'

'I'm not a dream.' Marco lay beside her. 'I am here. I am.' Her head turned, the dazzling flames of the fire blurring, her eyes closing as he touched her. 'And now I am going to make love to you 'til dawn.'

'This is too perfect, too much happiness ...'
'Trust yourself. Trust me.'

'What we are doing is wrong. We are going to hurt the people we love the most.'

'How can something that feels like this be wrong? You and I ...' Marco paused, enfolding her in his arms. 'We have always done the right thing. We've taken care of them all. And yet we are both so lonely. I told you that day in the workshop, we are two lonely hearts who have found one another. What can be wrong in that?'

'You know, I envied you.' Tess laid her cheek on his chest, resting, listening to his heart beat. 'I always wanted that, a big family, all that love and noise. One day last summer, just after Bobby met Frankie he came home. I overheard him saying to Kit: 'I love their family. You should see it, a table full of people talking and laughing. That's the kind of family I want for me and Frankie.' Tess closed her eyes and turned in to Marco, burying her head against him. 'Something in me died. You see, I'd always wanted that and instead I had this life full of ... of silence.'

'I will give you children,' he said, stroking her hair. 'If that is what you want, we will make the most beautiful-'

'I don't think I can,' she said, her voice catching.

'Tess?' He rolled back in the bed, making her look at him. 'What is it? Tell me what hurts you so.'

'They told me I probably can't have any more children.' She smiled, her lips pressed tightly together. 'When Bobby was born, I almost died. I thought-' She pressed the heel of her hand against her eye, stemming a tear. 'I thought - oh it doesn't matter.'

He kissed her forehead. 'You were only a child yourself.' Marco stood, and helped her to her feet. She stood naked but for the red shoes beside the fire burning bright, and beyond the window the sea. 'You make me think of Botticelli,' he said, 'of Venus.' He handed her her sweater. 'Come, let's take a walk and you can tell me all about it. We have all the time in the world.'

She dressed beside the fire, and hesitated, slipping her wedding ring into its usual place on her finger. She placed the red shoes carefully in their box, and pulled on a pair of old white sneakers. 'My pearls?' she said, looking for them among the clothes cast aside on the floor.

'Here, I warmed them for you,' he said, turning her to the mirror and pulling the strand of pearls from his hip pocket. He fastened them around her neck. She noticed a tremor in his hands, his determined frown sliding the gold catch closed. 'When we are together, I will always do this for you.' Marco held her close. 'Now we are going to make a flask of coffee, and go and see the sunrise on the beach, And when you are ready you can tell me all about it. Tell me the truth, Tess.'

Chapter 28

Kit slowed his pace to a jog and turned, hands on hips, waiting for Bobby to catch up with him. Central Park was busy with weekend walkers, children playing, kites buffeting above the golden, windswept trees. *Happy families,* Kit thought, leaning against the statue of Alice in Wonderland to catch his breath. Bobby ran towards him, weaving through the walkers.

'Jees, Dad, what's got into you?' Bobby said, gasping for breath. He leant down on his knees, coughing. 'You went off like a goddamn rocket. I thought we were heading up to the track round the reservoir?'

'Changed my mind. I've always loved this statue. It was my favourite book when I was small. I always hoped I might fall down a rabbit hole.' Kit tilted his head. 'See the patina? All those little hands climbing over it. It feels loved, don't you think? A beautiful memorial to a loved woman.'

'Memorial?' Bobby wiped the sweat from his brow on his sleeve.

'Delacorte dedicated it to his wife a couple

of years ago.'

'Would you do something like that for Mom?'

'What were we talking about just now?' Kit said, changing the subject. He leant against the statue, stretching out his hamstrings. 'The Rembrandt. Did you see the Met have just paid over two million dollars? The most expensive painting in the world-'

'Dad, where is she?' Bobby folded his arms. 'Where's Mom?'

'Oh, she just felt like a break, before the wedding. She's gone up to close the shack down in Provincetown.' Kit ran his hand through his hair as they walked on towards the lake. 'It's an emotional time for her. Only son getting married. The empty nest is feeling ... well, empty.'

'Thing is, Dad, Marco has gone awol too.'

'Has he?' Kit stepped aside to allow a young woman pushing a large pram glide past. 'Feels like yesterday we were pushing you around in a pram.'

'You never pushed me in a pram, Dad. I was born during the war. You were in Hong Kong when I was born.'

'You know what I mean.'

'Dad, talk to me. What's going on?' Bobby stopped walking.

'Such a lovely building,' Kit said, looking over his shoulder at the Loeb Boathouse. 'I always said I'd take your mother rowing. I never did. Perhaps that's the problem-'

'Dad?'

'I bet he does things like that,' Kit said, high spots of colour burning on his cheeks. 'Moons in June.'

'No? Hold on - are you saying Mom, and Marco?' Bobby's eyes widened. He stormed on ahead towards the lake, only to turn on his heel and stride back to Kit. 'How long has this been going on? Christ, they only met a couple of weeks ago.'

'Whirlwind romance.'

'It's ... my god, it's disgusting.' Bobby grasped the air. 'What are you going to do about it?'

'The thing is, I asked her for a divorce, before they ... they-'

'She's still your wife. Jesus, what a goddamn mess. This is going to ruin everything. What the hell is Frankie going to say?'

'Must she know?' They walked on and Kit looked out across the water. 'I think it would be best to turn a discreet blind eye to your mother's ... crisis. There's no need to upset Frankie, or Claudia for that matter.' Kit grimaced. 'The thought of that woman on the war path. Not a pretty picture.'

'How can you be so calm about this? Don't you care?'

'Care? Of course I care. It's humiliating. I feel ...' Kit paused, wondering what it was that he felt. Jealous? No, not exactly. He remembered picking up an exquisite seashell from the beach when he was a little boy. It was so beautiful, he couldn't bear to take it from the beach. He put it safely back where he had found it, saving it, a secret to return to later. Another child spotted it, and took it, chattering excitedly. Kit was incensed. He grabbed the shell back from the child, pushing them over. That was how he felt. 'He beat me, that night,' he said under his breath.

'What? Who beat you?'

'Oh, nothing.' Kit bit a piece of loose skin from the side of his thumbnail, rubbing it smooth. 'The thing is, your mother is her own woman. I've always admired that about her. She's an independent spirit.'

'That's what drew me to Frankie, you know. I think she reminded me of Ma.'

'If your mother has chosen to have a fling with this ... this cobbler, then I am not in a position to be jealous, or try to stop her because I have already broken with her.' It felt like Kit's insides were being wrung out like a wet cloth. 'I want her to be happy.'

'But she was happy, with you. You were both happy.' Bobby picked up a pebble and skimmed it out across the lake.

'No, Bobby, she wasn't happy with me.' Kit glanced at his son, wondering how much to tell him. I'm tired of all these secrets. All these lies. 'You see, we've never had a full relationship as man and wife, and that's not fair on her-'

Bobby turned to Kit in surprise. 'You mean you've never ...' Kit watched him carefully, waiting for Bobby to catch on. 'But you had me.' Bobby's voice shook. 'Didn't you? You had me.' He backed away from Kit, shaking his head. 'That whore-'

Kit slapped him.

'What did you do? Why did you do that?' Bobby said, cupping his jaw.

'Christ, Bobby, I'm sorry,' Kit said, tears pricking his eyes. 'I'm sorry.' He took his son in his arms, holding him. 'I never hit you. All these years, I promised I'd be a better father, that I'd do better than him.'

'You're not my father?' Bobby screwed his eyes closed.

'I'm sorry,' Kit said, holding him fast. 'You're my son. I have raised you as my son.'

'Then who was he? Who did my mother screw-'

'Bobby, stop it.' Kit took his face in his hands. 'You never talk about her like that, do you hear? This is not my story to tell you, but Tess gave up everything to have you. She gave up everything for us.'

'I can't believe she had an affair, and you still married her.'

'She was beautiful, and smart, and I loved her. We were friends, Bob, and I thought we could help one another out of a spot.' Kit smiles, remembering. 'I went up to take her and her parents out to dinner the night the engagement was announced and she was playing tennis, bouncing balls against the back wall of the yard trying out her new name in time with the bounce of the balls: Elizabeth Blythe, Elizabeth Blythe ...'

'The whole damn thing has been a game to her all along, a sham-'

'Bobby, you don't know what you're talking about. She was a child, really-'

'How many other men has she screwed, hey?'

Kit gripped Bobby's collar. 'Don't you ever, ever talk about your mother like that.'

'Get away from me.' Bobby pushed his father away.

'You have to keep this a secret, for Frankie's sake,' Kit called after him. 'It will all blow over, once he goes back to Italy. You'll see. I'll always be here, for you both, and your mother. Please don't let Tess know I told you. Don't ruin everything, Bobby.'

Chapter 29

'You were dreaming,' Marco said, turning to her as Tess stirred in the crumpled white bed. They had made love again, after walking on the beach, and they had dozed contentedly for a time. He stood up and closed the stove door, gold flames illuminating the glass, gilding the walls, his skin. Looty stirred sleepily in her basket by the fire, and sighed contentedly, closing her eyes. Marco let the grey wool blanket around himself slip, and he walked naked to Tess, the peach sunrise reaching out to paint his limbs through the bare windows. He draped the blanket across the mattress and slid back in to bed beside her.

'Your feet are like ice,' she said, sleepily. 'How long have you been awake?'

'A while.'

'Is there something you need to talk about?' Tess propped herself up on her elbow.

'You know what Claudia said to me the other day?' Marco stared at the ceiling, his hand behind his head. 'Your problem is you never want to let anyone in. You never let anyone help you.'

'Is that true?'

'Maybe.' He looked at her. 'It doesn't matter.' Marco opened his arm to her, and she curled in close to him. 'Tell me what you were dreaming about.'

'No,' Tess said, sharply. 'No, I'd rather not.'

'You were having a nightmare,' Marco said gently. 'I wasn't sure whether to wake you.' He stroked her hair. 'You were crying out: no, no, no ...' Tess screwed her eyes closed and buried her head in the warm safe dip of his arm.

'Oh, I have lots of nightmares.'

'Tess, what is it?'

'I haven't thought about it for a long time.' *That's a lie,* she thought. *I've thought about it every day for the last twenty years. Every damn day.* Tess took a deep breath. She felt safe with Marco. She didn't want to have any secrets between them. 'Something happened to me, a long time ago.'

'Tell me.' Marco held her closer, waiting for her to go on.

'I was seventeen. A child, really. Kit and I had been dating for a while. Everyone said he'd propose at New Year. I suppose I was feeling a bit high, and happy.' She thought for a moment. 'I felt light, in a way I've never felt, since.' Tess frowned, annoyed to feel tears pricking at her eyes. 'It was a wonderful night,' she said, clearing her throat, 'a Christmas party at my parents' house in 1938. Kit was on a trip, up country sketching some mountain or another with his friends.' Tess paused. 'My mother made me dance. I wanted very much to be a ballet dancer, then, you see. It was my life. I spent every hour I could practicing in the studio. When I was dancing, I felt carefree, and elegant, not this awkward bullied child. *Stand up straight*, my mother always used to say. *Shoulders back ... you take after your father with your huge feet.* She made me dance. I wanted her to be proud of me, so desperately. I never, ever felt like I was enough.'

'But why?'

'She had a son, before I was born, you see. He was still born.'

'I'm sorry. That must have been hard for you all.'

'She never talked about it, of course, but he was always there. Always perfect.' Tess laid her cheek on his chest, tracing the warm line of hair to his navel with her fingertips. 'Not only was he perfect, he was dead, so he could do no wrong. Whereas me ...' Her voice trailed off. 'Everything I did, everything I was wasn't enough.' Tess fell quiet. 'I wonder, sometimes, if it would have happened if she hadn't made me dance. I heard her telling her friends 'oh yes, Tess has a promising career as a ballet dancer, but of course Kit and their family will come first.' Tess paused. 'There was a band, and she asked the pianist to play the *Dying Swan*.' She laughed softly. 'The bloody dying swan.' Marco kissed the top of her head, held her safe in his arms. 'I felt .. I suppose I felt flattered by the attention. I changed, afterwards, into a white silk dress.' Tess imagined the walls of the shack falling away, and she was there again, in the garden in Hong Kong with the strung lanterns glowing in the darkness. 'I remember how happy Mother looked after I danced, and everyone was applauding. It was the night I stopped waiting for everything to go wrong. Ironic, isn't it?' Tess wiped her eye. 'Clive made a beeline for me at the bar, said 'come on then, dance with me, Tess. Show me how to do it'. He was terribly charming, you see, a marvellous dancer. I remember he gave me glass after glass of fruit punch. I had no idea how strong it was. I remember very clearly thinking: *I should go to bed, I'm tired.* But then I heard him saying my name. By the time he asked me to dance again, and we were turning around and around on the dancefloor, the music was distorted and the whirl of the lights and the lanterns, my head was spinning, spinning ...' Her voice trailed off. 'I think I must have blacked out. I don't remember how we got from the dancefloor to the gardens. The house was on the Peak, you see, the gardens were beautiful. Lots of hiding places. It was dark and misty. I remember feeling cold, the taste of earth in my mouth. He was kissing me.' She felt Marco grow still. 'He said afterwards, 'what did you expect, flaunting yourself in front of everyone wearing next to nothing? There's not a man at the party who didn't want to do what I've just done."

'Flaunting yourself?' Marco breathed through his teeth. *'Bastardo.'*

"Why are you crying?' he said. 'Good god, don't say you were a virgin?' He laughed in my face and lit a cigarette. 'Come on, tidy yourself up." Tess bit her lip. 'I said: 'How ... how could you? Why did you choose me?' I remember he looked at me like I was an idiot. 'Because you were the one every man wanted tonight,' he said. 'You were the beauty. You were the prize.'

'The prize?' I said.

'No need to tell anyone, there's a good girl,' he said.

'I hate you.'

'Hate me? You should thank me. Think of it as a parting gift,' he said. 'God knows if you are marrying Kit Blythe you should thank me.'

'I don't understand-' I said.

'I won't tell a soul. Your honour is safe with me. There's a good girl.' Tess began to shake. 'Before he went he said: 'here's a tip. For your husband to be's sake, it's good form to at least pretend to enjoy it. *'There's a good girl.'* A single hot tear trickled from her eye to Marco's chest.

'It meant nothing to him,' she said. 'I know how he envied Kit, envied his popularity, his position. Everything. You have to understand, Kit's a shadow of the man he was before the war. When I first knew him ...' Tess fell quiet. 'He was golden. That's the only word for him. He was like a golden Adonis figure. All the women had terrific crushes on him. He was brave, and funny, and kind.' She fell silent. 'Kit's a mystery, really. I can't imagine him as a child. There are no photographs of him before 1934.'

'You still love him.'

'Of course,' Tess said, looking up at Marco. 'But not like this. Not like you. I have never felt like this with Kit.' She took Marco's face in her hands and kissed him. There was nothing between them now, no secret in her heart eating away at her. 'Kit and I should have remained friends, that's all,' she said. Tess laid her chin on Marco's chest and pushed her hair back from her face. 'Like I said, I think it wasn't really about me at all, that's the awful thing. Clive was jealous - he just wanted to take something from Kit. It wasn't even really about me.' She exhaled, it felt like a tight band around her chest loosening. 'I wondered, sometimes, if he ever thought of what he did to me. I remember seeing his name in the paper, among the war dead, and I was glad - is that awful? I thought: *Good, at least he won't be able to do that to another girl.*' Tess stared into space. 'I wonder how many others there were. There's hardly been a day in my life when I haven't regretted agreeing to dance with him.'

'It wasn't your fault.'

'Nobody forced me to dance with him, or drink so much. I take responsibility for that, for being unable to-'

'He was a rapist. It doesn't matter if you were drunk or not. You were incapable and he raped you.' Marco paused. 'Bobby? He looks so unlike Kit.'

Tess nodded. 'He doesn't know,' she whispered. 'He must never know. It would destroy him.' She lay back on the pillows, her hair spilling around her. 'Sometimes when I look at him, and his easy charm, I see his father in him. I love him so much, but at those moments, my stomach turns.'

'Tess,' Marco said, rolling over to look at her. He stroked the side of her jaw with the back of his fingers. 'I am so sorry, for all you have suffered.'

'My mother found me,' she said, staring at the ceiling. 'She found me weeping in the drying room.'

'Drying room?'

'Every house on the Peak had one. It was so damp and misty all the time. It was where everyone kept their linen, their papers. I went there to try and clean myself up. I - There was ... there was blood on my shoes.'

'Oh, Tess.' Marco held her closer.

'I refused to tell her who did it, at first. I didn't want a scene. Clive's family were friends of my parent's you see. Mother idolised the Graves.' Tess tucked her hand behind her head. 'The thing is, he wasn't even a significant person.

I'd never ... He was like a piece of the scenery at parties: 'oh, there he is, good old Clive, a bit of a cad, rather 'NSIT' - not safe in taxis. But he had always been kind to me. Perhaps that's what men like that do. He was a friend. And then, he ...' Her voice broke as a sob caught in her throat. 'He destroyed my peace of mind. No matter how happy I have been, no matter how many perfect moments there have been in my life, since then, it marked them all. There is always a part of me which is broken, and I want to feel whole again, more than anything.' Tess rubbed her eyes. 'Mother could never believe the great Clive Graves would have done that. I was sobbing, but instead of comforting me, she just took my by my shoulders and shook me, slapped my face. She was ... she was so angry.' Tess thought for a moment. 'No, she was afraid. She was afraid it was all falling apart, the wedding, her glittering, fragile plans.' Tess closed her eyes and passed her palm across her cheek. 'She told me to get used to it. That that is what happens to women who don't watch out.' Tess took a deep breath, exhaling slowly. 'What a dreadful thing to say to your daughter. I never forgave her for that. What kind of a way is it to live - always vigilant, always afraid. Why the hell should we get used to that?' Tess frowned. 'Why should we be afraid of walking down a dark street, or learn to go out in the city with keys between our fingers, just in case?' Tess imagines herself walking alone, head high, defiant. She imagines flames, torches, lights in the darkness drawn to her. She imagines a river of women, burning, a river of light. *To hell with the men who made us feel less, the women who made us feel culpable. To hell with them. Bring on the light.* 'She told me I must never talk about this,' she said. 'And I never have, until now. She said that Kit must never know.'

'But you told him what had happened? That you were attacked.'

Tess nodded. 'Eventually.'

'What did he do?'

'Knowing Kit, he probably took the high road, told Clive to run along, and shook his hand.' Tess pressed her lips together. 'I saw them talking at our wedding. I could tell Clive was trying to get a rise out of Kit. I was terrified Kit was going to punch him, but he just walked away.'

'I'd have killed the bastard.'

'What good would it have done? Pour violence on violation?' Tess sighed. 'I blamed myself, anyway. I was too innocent, too trusting.' *Too much.*

'It wasn't your fault-'

'I know that, now, of course. Then, I did. I thought it was all my fault. I was in shock, I think. Mother smuggled me through the house, to my room. She brought me a brandy, ran a bath for me, told me to go to bed. In a way I think she relished it - that she was right, that I had messed up yet again and only she could keep the show on the road. Downstairs I could still hear the party going on, the countdown to midnight.' She tucked her arm beneath her head. 'I made up my mind never to dance for anyone again. And I didn't, until I danced for you.' Marco lowered his lips to her hair. 'I just wish I was whole, Marco. I wish I wasn't damaged-'

'We all think we are broken and damaged, that's our secret. We're all the walking wounded.' His eyes softened. Tess wondered what he had been through, what secrets he carried. She hoped he would tell her, in time. 'Let go.'

'It's not that easy.'

'It is. You choose. Nothing is broken in you. This man is dead, yes? Only your memory keeps this pain alive. He can't hurt you any more. So let go of it all, choose to be free. This is a new day, a new life.'

'You make it sound easy.'

'Does Kit know? About Bobby, I mean. That he isn't his?' Marco stroked the hair away from her face. 'Is that it? Is this why it haunts you so? You had to tell him that his son is not his?'

Tess remembered bumping in to Kit on Hollywood Road. *That was the day he proposed.* He had ordered sacred heart tea for her in a café on a grimy side street. It was dark inside, scented with incense, light slanting through the plantation shutters. The street, the city, bustled on outside, but they were the only people at the bar. She felt safe with him. Kit told her to watch as the tightly sewn ball of leaves blossomed in the glass teapot like magic. *'Marry me,'* he said. *'It's the obvious thing to do. We're friends, love will come later.'*

'Oh, Kit knows,' Tess said to Marco at last. 'The thing is, Bobby couldn't possibly be his.'

Chapter 30

Kit leant his throbbing head against the cold steel panel of the elevator, a pair of Ray Ban Wayfarers shielding his eyes from the relentless fluorescent light of his office building. He had always imagined his mind to be a network of subterranean caves, some filled with glittering diamonds, rubies, emeralds, others with seams of pure gold. Some were fathomless, dead ends pitch dark with despair. Today, he pictured an army of tiny men with pickaxes mining determinedly in the tender region of his right temple.

He stepped out on his floor and strode across the open plan communal lobby. It was modern, clean lined with wood veneer panelling and a pale green fitted carpet, a suspended ceiling with square lit panels above. A couple of banana and parlour palms in steel pots were the only decoration. Kit nodded a greeting to a couple of men in dark suits chatting to a secretary in a pink dress and white gloves by the elevator. He recognised them from one of the other offices on his floor, but had never spoken to them. Passing through the plate glass doors etched simply with 'Christopher Blythe' in an elegant Baroque font was like going back in time through several centuries. Two gold Corinthian columns flanked the reception area, and a passable copy of a Titian landscape in an ornate gilded gesso frame hung above the walnut desk. Kit's receptionist stood to say 'good morning', and give him a list of all the calls, but Kit held up his palm to stop her and strode down the Persian carpeted hall towards his office, ignoring the greetings called out by his designers and assistants. He tossed his sunglasses onto his desk blotter, and picked up the telephone, dialling a number from memory. He flicked through a swatch of rich purple brocades waiting for the line to connect.

'It's me. I feel terrible,' Kit said, crooking receiver beneath his jaw. He hung his hat on the coat stand and pushed his office door closed, quieting the noise and chatter from the studio. He rummaged in his desk drawer and dropped two Alka Seltzers into a glass of water. 'I just feel such guilt. If I'm not ghastly to her, now, Tess won't cut loose. Tess is so *good*.' He raked his hand through his hair, and slumped back in his office chair, swirling the glass impatiently. 'It's infuriating how understanding she has been.' He listened for a moment. 'Yes, she knows, but not who. I have to break it to her gently.' Kit pressed his lips together. 'I must admit, I didn't expect her to run off to that shack with the Italian. But then Tess always did surprise me. It's one of the things I love about her.' He picked up a heavy silver paperknife and spun it round on its tip. 'It hurts, I can't deny it. I love her, you see. I always will. Just not as I love you. It's been disastrous, ever since our wedding night.' He squeezed the bridge of his nose, remembering their room in the Manila Hotel, the high white walls and arches, the smooth dark wood floors. He remembered how beautiful she looked, and how helpless he felt.

'Darling, I have to tell you something, a secret,' Kit had said, folding his dressing gown closed with the precision of origami. He had just done his nightly hundred push ups, and his body hummed with exertion, tense, taut muscles glowing with a light sheen of sweat. The sounds of the Manila street below drifted up through the closed shutters. Tess stared at him in the dim, humid light, the fan looping leisurely above their bed.

'I've had lovers, but I'm not like most men.'

'Oh, thank god,' Tess said, sitting up on her knees in the bed.

'Thank god?'

'You see, I thought you would be terribly disappointed.'

'In you? Never. I knew about Clive.'

'I didn't want it, you have to understand.' She began to shake, and Kit pulled a velvet throw from the armchair, wrapping it around her shoulders.

'There,' he said. 'You mean he did - he forced himself on you. I knew it.' He lit a cigarette. 'But you can be flighty. Did you lead him on?'

'No!' Tess sat up, the red velvet blanket pooling around her. 'How can you even think that?' She reached out for Kit's hand but he wouldn't look at her. 'Oh god, this is a terrible mistake.' Tess buried her face in her hands. 'You don't love me. I can't let you throw away your life on me, on us-'

'Us? You mean you and me?' Kit looked at her, realising. 'You're pregnant, aren't you? Is it his?'

'Who else's would it be?' Tess yelled, her face contorted with anguish. 'I think I am. I don't know. The day I bumped into you on Hollywood Road, I'd gone to get some herbs, just in case. I couldn't drink it. The smell made me sick.' Tess grimaced at the memory. 'It killed me,' she said. 'Standing there in church making my vows to you, knowing he was there in the congregation, watching, knowing.'

'It makes sense now,' Kit said, pacing the room. The harbour lights glimmered in the darkness behind him like fireflies. 'At the reception your mother was fawning all over him. She stayed close, so he couldn't say anything, of course.'

'You must hate me.'

'I adore you,' he said, sitting on the edge of the bed, leaning forward for her hand. 'Darling it's perfect. I need an heir, you need the security of marriage for you and the baby.'

'Security?' Tess said. *What about joy, and passion, and love.*

'You can't let this moment define you. You can't allow this sadness to settle on you, do you hear? Or you will wake up in five, ten, twenty years and realise you have wasted the best of your life. Don't let Clive take that from you as well.'

'You're right, of course,' she said, trying not to cry.

'Don't upset yourself.' He offered her a clean handkerchief from his breast pocket. It smelt of lemon verbena. 'It's not good for you, or the baby to be this unhappy.' Kit squeezed her hand. 'Let me take care of you both. Let me make you happy again.'

'But you don't love me.' She looked up at him, beseeching. 'I wanted it all, Kit, intimacy, passion, commitment.'

'Contentment is underrated, old girl,' he said, making her laugh.

In his mind, flickering image of the hotel room took on the austere beauty of a monk's cell. He moved the receiver to his other ear, and took a cigarette from the silver box on his desk, tapping it on the lid. 'From that moment, I never touched her.' He flicked the lighter, listening. 'Why?' Kit sat back in the chair, blowing a long plume of blue smoke to the ceiling. 'Tess must know, in her heart.' He picked up a postcard of a gondola from the desk drawer. 'How was Venice? Perhaps we'll go together, next year.'

Chapter 31

The week without him is a penance. Tess thinks of him the moment she opens her eyes. She dreams of Marco at night. When finally he walks in to the beach house at sunset on the Friday night he is earlier than she expected. She has not dressed yet. Her hair is wet and her skin is fresh from the sun and sea air, pink from hot water, perfumed with good soap. She looks up in surprise from the stove, and throws down the gingham cloth. She goes to him without a word , and embraces him. They fall on one another like water on dry earth.

'This. This is a welcome,' he says, lifting her onto the counter, her legs around his hips.

'Oh god, I've ached for you all week.'

'See?' he says, 'see? Now you are alive.'

They take the meal she has cooked down to the beach where he has built a fire, and wrapped in blankets they feed one another - clams, warm bread, wine.

'This is living,' he says, leaning back against a driftwood log, silver with age.

'It's different in winter. It's getting colder.'

'What do we care? We have each other, a fire, a bed. What more do we need?' He holds her closer, growls into her neck until she laughs. 'We will hibernate like bears, watch snow fall on the veranda.' Tess blinks, a grain of sand in her eye. Marco tells her to trust him, licks the sand clear with the tip of his tongue, tastes her tears, her eyelid fluttering butterfly light.

When they walk home late that night after a drink with Paul and Anton, they see two white horses standing face to face, flank deep in grass in a dark meadow. The horses are perfectly still, contented, together. *That is how I feel when I am with you*, she says. *It's like I can finally breathe.*

The next afternoon they take a boat out at Race Point, huddling together in the cold, eyes stinging from the sea breeze. Tess wants to suck the marrow from every moment, to remember everything in case it all stops just as quickly as it began. In case all she has is memories. She imagines sand slipping over the smooth hip of an hourglass.

A couple of hours out from shore, a school of dolphins racing and leaping by the boat, they see them. Marco jumps to his feet. 'They are there - see? See?' The humpback whales break the water. Their hides are covered with barnacles, their grey underbellies are scarred and freckled. The whales smell of oil, of the sea. 'They are beautiful!' he cries, holding Tess firm at his side.

'Isn't it sad that the whales felt they had to

move all the way out here?' she says. 'There were so many whales here once upon a time, they used to harpoon them from the shore.'

'Really?'

'So they say.'

'No wonder they left.' Marco holds her closer, keeping her warm and she leans into him. They rest against the bough of the ship, watching the sun sinking low over the horizon. 'This,' he says quietly. 'When I think of this moment it will be with your saudade.' Marco rested his chin on Tess' head. *'Era già l'ora che volge il disio ai navicanti e 'ntenerisce il core lo di c'han detto ai dolci amici addio ...'*

'What does that mean?'

'It is Dante.' Marco lowers his head, his lips by her ear. 'It was the time that melts the hearts of men at sea, that wakes fond desire ... in the morning they bid sweet friends farewell.' He pauses, thinking. 'The pilgrim newly on his road thrills if he hears the vesper bell from far.' Tess feels him exhale, the lift of his chest, the swell of the boat. 'That - that is saudade.'

'Are you missing your home?'

He holds her closer. Her cheeks are cold, his lips are warm, salt spray blesses them like a benediction. 'You are my country. Wherever you are is my home.'

'You're leaving, aren't you? You're going tomorrow.'

'So must you. The wedding is in a few days.

Frankie and Bobby need us.'

'And Claudia, and Kit, and all of them.' Tess screws her eyes closed.

'Kit is a good man. It takes a big heart to raise another man's child as your own.'

'It suited us both.' Tess looks out at the whales. 'We were both drifting, both at sea. I was in an impossible situation and Kit needed an heir to inherit his family home.' She laughed softly. 'Family debts as it turned out. Perhaps keeping secrets runs in his family.'

'Your parents - what happened to them?'

'Kit's are still alive, I think. Retired to the Home Counties. Mine ...' Tess takes a deep breath. 'Didn't I tell you already? I was an only child. My mother and I joined my father when he was posted to Hong Kong. We took the Canton Belle-' Her face softens at the memory. 'I remember Aphra waving us off. It felt like such an adventure. These beautiful green and silver railway cars taking us all the way from Paris, Berlin, Moscow to our new life.'

'Your parents remained in Hong Kong, like Kit?' Tess nods.

'They died there,' she says. 'Oh god, I can't bear it. I can't bear the thought of you going away so soon. Sometimes it feels like everyone I ever loved has left me. I wish this moment would go on and on forever. What's going to happen? I can't stand the thought of not being with you.'

'We have this moment.' He turns her to him, kisses her. 'I love you, Tess. I want to give you everything. I would bring down the stars for you.'

'Marco-'

'But whatever happens we will always have tonight.'

'Always.'

Chapter 32

'Mm, oh - Claudia, men write sonnets to women for less than this puttanesca sauce.' Vittorio leant over his bowl, guzzling the spaghetti. 'Whore's pasta,' he said, laughing. 'That's what my wife always used to say.' He took a sip of wine and looked over at Claudia, who was standing by his sink, halfway through washing down the draining board, gazing out of the window. 'Say, I'd marry again for this sauce. Less sex these days, but lots of spaghetti. What do you say, Claudia? Can you resist?' He waited for her to laugh. 'Claudia?'

'Sorry?' She came back to the moment, and finished wiping down the sink.

'What's up? Why's a beautiful young woman like you so blue?'

'Young?' she said laughing. Claudia took away his plate and washed it up.

'Hey, come on. Stop working.' He patted the seat beside him. 'Come and tell an old man your worries. It's not like I'm going to run around telling anyone.' He gestured at his legs. Claudia hesitated. 'Come on. You've got a heart of gold, Claudia. You come up here every day to make sure I'm still alive-'

'Somebody's gotta do it.' She said, raising her chin.

'The least I can do is try and make you smile a little. What's up? Is it the kids?'

'Nah. They're all good.'

'Then you, what is it? You sick?'

'I'm not sick.'

'Pregnant?'

'Vittorio.' She swiped him with the tea towel, and he pretended to flinch. 'I haven't been with a man since my Carlo died.'

'Waste of a woman,' he said. 'If I was twenty years younger ... thirty, then, I'd marry a woman like you in a heartbeat.'

'Who's gonna marry me? Eh? Eight kids ...'

'Is that it? You in love with someone and he doesn't love you.' Vittorio waited for her to answer. 'That's it, isn't it? Some chump has broken your heart.'

'He doesn't know I'm alive,' she said quietly, a tight knot swelling in her throat. 'Not like that. He just looks through me, like I'm just a mother, a part of the scenery.'

'He takes you for granted?'

'It's complicated. He ... he just doesn't see me as a woman.' She blinked away the tears pricking her eyes, turned away to wipe down the table, her face crumpling.

'He must be blind. Fool.'

'I just want to take care of him. He's ... he's not well.' Claudia's voice shook and she covered her eyes with her palms.

'Hey, hey ...' Vittorio rocked a couple of times, getting up the momentum to push himself out of his chair. 'It's serious, eh?' He shuffled over and put his arm around Claudia. She buried her head in his frail shoulder, sobbing. Vittorio smelt of washing powder, hair oil, peppermints. 'What's he got? Heart? Cancer? Parkinson's?' Claudia nodded, her sobs muffled in his sweater. 'Madonna ... An old buddy of mine from the Fire Station had that.' He held his hands out ahead of him, trembling. 'He'd just retired when they finally figured out what was wrong with him. Maybe for him it would have been better not to know. He went from being a little shaky to slowing right down. I don't know.' He hunched his shoulders stiffly. 'We all gotta go some way or another. How old's your guy?'

'Late forties, fifty.' Claudia sniffed, and wiped her eyes with a lace edged handkerchief. 'That big bruiser of a man. What's it about, eh? Life make no sense to me sometimes.'

'Ah, he's a kid. People can live with it for years and years.' The old man's face brightened, hearing a key in his door. 'Say, Claudia, you remember my youngest, Johnny?'

'Hey, Pa, Mrs Affini.' A man with thick dark hair and a kind, open face pushed through the door carrying two brown bags of groceries. His jaw bloomed with blue stubble, and the collar of his fireman's uniform was open at his throat, a clean t-shirt white against his olive skin.

'You been working round the clock again?'

'Yeah, Pa, it was a long night.' He looked at Claudia and smiled, bashful. 'The kids are with their grandparents.'

'Johnny's a widower too.' Vittorio raised an eyebrow at Claudia.

'Pa!' Johnny said, laughing.

'Just saying,' the old man shrugged. He gestured at the serving bowl of pasta and leant towards his son. 'Try her puttanesca sauce. *Then* you'll have the balls to ask her out on a date.'

□

Frankie and her youngest brothers are lying on the floor in the lounge, applause from Dick Clark's American Bandstand rippling over them with the shimmering light from the TV. Frankie's legs are crossed at the ankle, her foot tapping in time with Chubby Checker. She is filling circles of net with sugared almonds, tying them with satin ribbons for wedding favours.

'Hey, Ma,' Frankie says, jumping up and taking the tray from her. 'How's Vittorio today?'

'Trying to set me up with his son,' Claudia says, touching her hair. Could her heart take it? A new man. Her good heart, her heartbreak. What if she was hurt, again? 'Talk to him,' a friend said to her the other day when she confided her feelings about Marco. 'Tell Marco how you feel.

What have you got to lose?'

'Only everything. I can't.' Claudia had said. 'If I do, it's out there. It will all break. I can't. How do you put something back together after that?'

Claudia turns slowly to find Marco sitting alone at the dining room table. Every surface in the room is littered with bags of sugared almonds, piles of wedding presents, orders of service. Claudia's sewing basket is a cornucopia spilling lace and pearls onto the table. A needle lies tucked into the hem of a bridesmaid's dress, waiting for her to continue sewing. Eight starched shirts hang from the banisters, and Frankie's wedding gown is draped in its garment bag from the picture rail, ready to be taken upstairs. Claudia gestures for Marco to follow her to the kitchen, and she waits in silence until he closes the door behind them.

'So you came back to us, then?' she says. 'Where is she? Still up on the coast?'

'Why did you do it?' he says without looking at her. 'Why did you cut up the shoes?'

'Why do you think?' Claudia stalks the kitchen, to and fro beneath the window, wiping down the already clean counter.

'I never knew,' he says quietly.

'I never told you.'

'I had no idea how you felt about me.'

'Because I could never tell you,' Claudia says, fighting to keep her voice low so the others didn't hear. 'I never expected anything from you.

I never meant anything to you.'

'That's not true.'

'But not like that. You never loved me.' Claudia paces, wringing the cloth between her hands. 'I suppose she called you, did she? Tell you I've been over there?'

'No.' Marco wipes his hands. 'I went to her.'

'Why? Phone call not good enough?'

'She doesn't have a phone in Cape Cod-'

'How bohemian. I guess you love all that-'

'I love the peace and quiet.' Marco rubs the heel of his hand between his eyes.

'So why do you go see her? To screw her?' Claudia grabs a chipped white plate from the table and flings it at him. Marco swerves to the side without moving his feet.

'Stop it Claudia,' he says.

'Stop it? Stop it?' she cries, sweeping aside the place settings. One of the boys opens the kitchen door a crack, and Marco gestures for him to go.

'I just made another pair,' he says, lifting his jacket from the coatstand.

'Then I'll cut those up too, if I get my hands on them.'

'Too late. I took them to her.' Claudia's shoulders slump as she leans on the sink. 'Don't do this.' Marco looks at her steadily. 'You got me to make shoes for her, so I did. And I'll make pair after pair if I have to.'

'What's she got that's so special, hey?

What's she got that you'd ruin your niece's happiness?'

'She needs me.'

'We need you,' Claudia cries, clutching her chest. 'I need you. Your nephews and niece need you.'

'You don't need me. You haven't needed me for years-' He thumps the table in frustration. 'She wants me, really wants me. It's - oh god-'

'What? Passion? Love?' Claudia leans across to him. 'What do you think you are, Marco? Some big hotshot Renaissance man? Lover, fighter, artist? Is that it? Have you forgotten how it was before I married Carlo, how we set the night on fire?'

'That was a mistake,' he says quietly. 'It was one night-'

'You were the first man to touch me. Have you forgotten how we hungered for one another?' She steps close to him, her breath on his neck. 'I drank you in like cold water on a summer day.'

'Claudia, don't. We were kids-'

'All the things we loved,' she says, forcing him to look at her. 'I knew everything about you, once. If I died tomorrow, you'd only know after the fact what I loved, what made me happy. You never bothered finding out. One night. Just one of the many, eh? You never cared about me-'

'I was here, wasn't I? I stayed, took care of you after Carlo died. Isn't that enough?'

'But I *loved* you,' she cries, her fist balled on her heart. 'We could have had it all, Marco. We could have had it all.'

Rocco pushes open the door. 'Ma is everything ok? Why you crying?'

'It's fine, baby. It's just the wedding. All these preparations - it's getting to me.' Claudia smiles, reassuringly. 'Go on. Let me finish talking to your uncle.' She waits until the door closes. 'You don't get it do you? I want nothing to do with you if you go with her. We don't want you, we don't want your money.'

'Claudia, don't do this-'

'You lose all this - all of this, everything that fills your heart that has made your life. You lose it all.' Claudia falls silent, her chest rising and falling. 'We just want to take care of you now.'

'Care? I don't want to be cared for. I want to live. I want to feel alive, really alive. To love.'

'This is different, isn't it, with her? It's not about sex, not like me-'

'Maybe, just maybe if you had let me near you years ago instead of going off with Carlo the minute he clicked his fingers, it would have been different.' Marco's brow furrowed. 'He always took everything I wanted, you included.'

'Don't pretend this is my fault, Marco!' Claudia cries. 'It ain't been easy with Carlo, let me tell you. He didn't believe in birth control. Oh no, he liked it the old fashioned way. How many more pregnancies? How many more miscarriages-' She inhaled sharply, forcing down the pain. 'All those babies, Marco, all the babies I lost.'

'Claudia-' He steps towards her, his arms open. She pushes him away, hugs her arms around her waist, keening softly.

'So you love her, do you? Don't do this to us, Marco, don't do this.' She folds in on herself, slides down the kitchen wall to the floor.

'It wasn't something I could stop.'

'But why? Did we not love you enough? Were we not grateful? Is that it?'

'No,' he says gently, kneeling down beside her. 'None of that.'

'Then what?' She looks at him with red rimmed eyes. 'You know how I feel about you.'

'Claudia, it would never - could never have worked. You were, you always will be, my brother's wife. You chose him and there's an end to it.' Marco takes her hand. 'We're the past, Claudia. Frankie loves Bobby. I promise nothing will spoil this wedding.'

'I was just a child ...' Claudia leans her head back against the wall. 'I thought I was marrying for love and look how well that turned out.'

'Carlo was an idiot.'

'He couldn't help himself.' Claudia pulls herself up and turns to the sink. She runs the tap and rinses each wine glass in turn. 'So many women. Sure, he always came home to me but when you marry for love it breaks your heart.' She shakes the water from the last glass. 'My marriage - Carlo, it was more than just him and me. It was all of this.' She gestures at the empty dining table. It was the family. It was you.'

'Which is why I supported you all these years. I know what Carlo put you through.' His hand shakes as he reaches for the first glass, and it tumbles to the floor, smashing on the terracotta tiles. 'Damn.'

'Leave it. I'll get it,' Claudia says, stooping and gathering the broken pieces. 'Why am I - why is all this not enough for you?' She shakes her head. 'I don't need you, Marco. You want to go, go. Screw around. Go home to Italy if you want, like you always talked about. Frankie'll be married soon, she has her own life ahead of her. Me and the boys will be fine without you.'

'That's it,' he says. 'Don't you see? You don't need me.'

'And she does?' Claudia lifts the lid of the bin and drops the broken shards in.

'Yes. She didn't make me feel like some big kid, some washed up guy who might have been something, once, might have been someone.' He rubs his face wearily and looks down at his shaking hands. 'She needs me.'

'We need you,' Claudia says, thumping his arm.

'You just said you didn't.'

She pushes him away, exasperated. Footsteps echo down the hallway, the front door bangs shut. She hears Frankie calling out a greeting to one of her brothers. 'Say nothing,' she warns him, smoothing down her hair, her apron. She grabs a broom and begins to sweep away the last of the glass from the terracotta floor. 'Go. Stay. I don't care. I'm not going to spend the rest of my life feeling like I'm not enough for you.' She raises her chin and looks up at him. 'You feeling worse?'

'Yeah. Not such a good day today.'

'You told her yet?'

'No. I'm waiting for the right time.'

'Whatever you decide, nothing happens until after the wedding. Agreed?'

Rocco pokes his head round the kitchen door. 'Say, Ma, there's someone at the front door.'

Claudia unties her apron and smoothes down her hair. 'Hello?' she says, swinging open the door. 'Johnny?'

'I'm sorry to disturb you, Mrs Affini.' He clasps a small bunch of pale yellow roses in his hand. 'I just wanted to say thank you for your kindness, with my father.'

'It's nothing. I love the old guy,' Claudia says. She takes the flowers, and touches the nape of her neck.

'I appreciate it, knowing you're keeping an eye on him. He can be ...'

'A handful?' They both laugh.

'Say, I wondered - maybe, I mean, say no-'

Claudia tilts her head, giving him time to get the words out. 'Maybe you'd like to take a walk, some time, have a cup of coffee?'

'I'd love to,' Claudia says, glancing back over her shoulder at her home, her family. 'Things are kind of crazy now, but after the wedding?'

'Sure,' he says stepping back into the dark hallway, smiling like she has just promised him the world.

Chapter 33

The city seems hard to Tess now, sharp-edged with steel and glass. She has grown used to the whisper of sand and sea, and cloud. Her home for so many years feels like that of a stranger. She has already moved on.

Bessie is out, interviewing for a new position, and Tess made sure Kit is at work. She has the apartment to herself. Her key in the lock sounds loud, the hall echoing. She follows the sound of Looty's claws tapping on the parquet floor.

'Looty,' she says, scooping the dog into her arms. 'Let's get out of this joint.' The Pekingese turns delighted circles as she sets her down. 'The shack is all ready, and then we're moving in to Paul and Anton's for a while.' The dog follows her as Tess strolls from room to room. The apartment is, as usual, immaculate.

Tess is meeting Bobby across town for an early supper, but she has a little time. She flicks through the records, picks out a Nina Simone album and sets it playing on the turntable by the window. Tess looks out across the city, saying goodbye, the lights flickering on one by one at dusk. She kicks off her shoes and dances across the room, sliding in her stockinged feet, singing *My Baby Just Cares for Me,* the dog dancing around her. In the drawing room she opens the old red lacquer wedding cabinet, and fixes herself a Martini, twisting the lemon peel, fine zest spraying her skin, her mouth watering.

In her dressing room, her old cedar trunk lies empty, ready for her, just as she asked. Ready for the next journey. She is grateful that Kit is making this easy. *I can do this*, she thinks, flicking through her clothes: *keep, Bessie, thrift store ... It's easy*, she thinks, when all that remains in her wardrobe are empty hangers clattering like fortune sticks in a canister.

Shoes next. Photograph albums. Paintings? She hesitates. *Kit chose them all. He can sell them, or keep them, I don't care.* Looty looks up from the bed as Tess strides through the apartment to turn the album over. The music swells, and she turns in a slow circle, her mind running through the contents of cupboards and drawers, the silt of a long marriage, like a mouse looking for a golden grain.

I don't need any of it, she realises. She thinks of a hot air balloon she saw once, taking off from a field in Connecticut. She had stopped driving to watch it lift, the guy ropes straining. That is how she feels, like she is rising, rising.

But then she spots the framed photographs on the console table, and her breath catches in her throat. *Bobby,* she thinks, picking up his baby photograph. *Our wedding.* What do you do with framed wedding photos when you're divorcing? Do you throw them out, pretend it never happened? Do you use the frame for something else, when every time you look at it the ghost of the old photo is there behind the glass? Tess' breath shuddered, and her vision blurred, looking around their home. Suddenly she wants it all. She wants it all to be just the way it was.

Pull yourself together, she thinks. She packs the photographs anyway. At her dressing table, Tess picks up the telephone, and dials the workshop. 'Hello,' she says. 'May I speak to Marco Affini? Thank you.' She waits, imagines the leather chair, the workbench. She remembers the first time he touched her.

'Hey?' Marco says.

'It's me.'

'Tess - I was thinking of you. Are you ok?'

'I'm just packing. Meeting Bobby later.' Tess winds the flex around her finger. 'I had to hear your voice.'

'You sound sad.'

'I'll be ok. It's just hard, you know. It's ...' She looks around the room. 'A whole lifetime. You know.'

'Did you ever read Gibran?'

'Nope.' Tess tilts her head, and wipes away

a run of mascara beneath her tear bright eye.

'He said something like grief scoops us out so that there is more space for love, the next time.' Marco laughs softly. 'I miss the poetry in translation, but you get the idea?'

'I like that. Is that what we are? The next time.'

□

At the chime of a carriage clock, Tess looks across the room. 'I've got to go,' she says to the dog, closing the trunk. 'I promise, just as soon as I'm back we'll go to the park.'

Tess runs through the lobby, and the doorman hails a cab on the street for her. She is wearing a simple navy pencil shift dress and a pale coat which swings out as she jumps in to the taxi. On the way across town, she checks her make up in a gold compact. She does not want Bobby to see she has been crying.

While she waits at the bar, she looks at a photograph of a fishing boat in the travel magazine she is flicking through. Her heart swells with longing. *Part of my heart will always be in New York,* she thinks, *but it's gone, I've already gone.* She remembers sitting in Dr Hiebert's study in Provincetown the day before. The wallpaper had scenes of an English fishing port in maroon on cream.

She had climbed the steps to his surgery on Commercial Street full of hope. She was late, this month. She hoped, dreamed that she might be pregnant.

'Mother,' Dr Hiebert called after he told Tess the news. 'Mother! Better make some tea for Mrs Blythe, please.' He pushed a box of tissues towards her. 'Please, don't upset yourself. It's not unusual to take some time when you decide to expand your family later in life. You're only in your late thirties I think, but it can take months, years even to fall pregnant. Your husband will understand, I'm sure-' He paused. 'Ah, not your husband's?'

Tess shook her head. 'My husband and I have never had a sexual relationship, Dr Hiebert.' She looked at him, her eyes blazing. 'All this time, all these wasted years.'

'Mrs Blythe,' he said gently. 'Your marriage is not of concern to me, but your health is.' He scanned her notes.

'It's not fair,' she cried. She looked up as Dr Hiebert's wife brought in a cup of steaming tea for her.

'Thank you, Mother,' he said.

'When I had Bobby, they said it was un-likely that I would ever have children but not impossible. When I missed my period, I thought-'

'Mrs Blythe, you are an extremely slender woman. Am I right in thinking your monthlies are irregular at best?' Tess nodded. He looked through the file of notes in front of him. 'I see you suffered some complications during the birth.' He took off his glasses and rubbed the bridge of his nose. 'The truth is, Mrs Blythe, it's in the hands of God,' he said, lacing his fingers together and leaning towards her. 'There's little I can do. But miracles happen.'

'You must think I'm terrible, wanting another man's child so desperately when I am still married. We are divorcing. I'm very much in love-'

'It is not my place to judge your behaviour.' Dr Hiebert closed the file. 'That's between you and Him. I suggest you allow yourself to relax a little, Mrs Blythe. Eat well, for you and your hoped for child. Plenty of fresh air. Plenty of love. You never know.'

□

Who am I? Tess thought, looking at herself in the mirror of the Grand Central Oyster Bar. *I am a mother. I am a wife. I am a lover. I am ... I loved to dance, once.*

'Hello, Mom,' Bobby said, sliding onto a stool next to Tess at the bar. It was rush hour and every red check table was full, He leant over and kissed her cheek. 'It's good to see you.'

'I promised I'd be back in time.' She tilted her head.

Bobby stared down a dark suited man at the end of the bar who had been watching Tess. 'You look beautiful. Not safe to leave you alone in a joint like this,' he said. She detected an edge to Bobby's voice. *What's going on?* she thought.

'Nonsense,' Tess said, laughing.

'I've always loved it how you turn heads, have I ever told you that?' Bobby said, sitting back in the stool. 'I remember being so proud of you when you came to pick me up at school, and walking home each day. You were always the most elegant of the mothers at the school gates. I'd count how many men turned their heads to look at you.'

'You're making me blush,' Tess said.

'I think I've always felt a little protective of you.'

'Are you ok? Did you have fun at your Stag?'

'Me? I'm fine.' Bobby set a beer mat on its edge and spun it round on the bar. 'Kind of a sore head, but I'm fine.' She saw him struggling. 'Are you ... do you feel better, after a break?'

'Yes. Much. I just needed to get away for a while.' She nudged him. 'You and I are alike. A couple of hot heads.'

'Needed to cool off, eh?' Tess couldn't work out Bobby's expression. She knew it - it was the same when he wanted something he was afraid to ask for when he was little. 'So what's up?' he said, looking down at his hands.

'Do I need an excuse to grab a bite with my son when he's in town? I just thought it would be good to see you before we all get swept up in the wedding,' Tess, said, swinging round to face him.

She cupped her chin on her palm. 'I've ordered a platter-'

'With bluepoints? And a lobster?'

'Of course,' she said, laughing. Tess swirled the olive in her Martini.

'Got to have the lobster.'

'How many years have we been coming here?'

'Forever.' Bobby shrugged off his jacket and hung it on the back of the stool. He beckoned to the bartender and ordered a beer, and a glass of sparkling water for Tess. 'That won't ever change. This is our place.'

'Oh, it will. Everything's changing.' Tess patted his hand. 'You're at college-'

'I'm in Massachusetts, not the other side of the moon,' Bobby said laughing. 'Besides, you spend half the year out in Provincetown. We'll spend just as much time together as we ever did.'

'You'll have a wife soon, Bob, and a family no doubt.' Tess leant back as the waiter slid a gleaming platter of shellfish between them. 'Has your father talked to you-'

'Mom!' Bobby choked on his beer. 'For heaven's sake. It's the 1960s.'

'Bobby, I'm serious,' she said, touching his hand. 'Be kind to her. Be kind to Frankie.'

'Ma-'

'I mean it. You have so much joy ahead of you, but be understanding, if-'

'Hey?' he said quietly, his brow furrowing.

There was so much she wanted to tell him. It was killing her not being able to tell him that she was leaving, that Kit had asked for a divorce. 'Don't get upset.' He handed Tess a handkerchief, and she dabbed at her eyes.

'Oh, ignore me.' Tess wanted to tell him everything. To tell him about Kit, about their life together, about how she stayed because she loved her son so.

'Getting sentimental in your old age?'

'Not so much of the old,' she said, nudging him.

'I love Frankie,' Bobby said, and gulped down an oyster. 'You know, she reminds me of you.'

'That's sweet. So it's not just the money, then?' Tess smiled sadly. She glimpsed the future, then. Her charming son, evenly tanned and burnished gold, cushioned from hardship in his cashmere life. A cottage in the Hamptons, perhaps, a law practice in town, and Frankie and a troop of dark haired children in a charming house somewhere up and coming. And where would she be? Where did Tess fit in to this future? An occasional lunch for old time's sake? Thanksgivings and Christmas? Christenings and funerals? *Not so much of the old.*

Bobby paused, his glass half way to his lips. 'No. It's not just the money.' He sipped his drink. 'Although it's nice, of course. Not much gets past you, does it?'

'I just want you to be happy, Bobby.'

'So do I. And I can't be poor.'

'I spoke to Frankie the other morning.'

'She said.' Tess felt the edge in his voice, a defensive tone she recognised.

'I like her.' Tess took his hand. 'I always wanted a daughter-'

'And now here's one, ready made.'

'Don't be like that. You were always enough. You know, I heard you talking about Claudia's family, how much you love them. I think that's just swell.' She swallowed down the tight knot in her throat and waited for him to look at her. 'You and Frankie, make the family and home you dream of, Bobby. But she's a bright girl. Let her follow her dreams as well as yours.'

'She is.' Bobby let his head fall into his hands.

'Bobby, what is it?' All of Tess' worries swept away with concern for her son. 'You're not having second thoughts?'

'About Frankie, hell no. It's just ...' He flinched. She knew that look. Ever since he was small if there was something wrong, if he had been caught out, that was the look he gave. 'I did something stupid, Mom, and I don't know whether to tell her.'

'Oh, Bobby,' Tess said, and squeezed his hand. 'What did you do?'

'It was the Stag, you know. We had too many drinks. There was this girl - everyone knows she's easy. She'd been knocking back the drinks, she was asking for-'

'Bobby, I never want to hear you talk about a girl that way, do you understand.' He looked up in surprise at her fierce tone. 'Never.'

'Sure, Mom, I'm sorry. I shouldn't have told you.'

'No, I'm glad you did.' Tess exhaled. *Oh god, my son, my beautiful boy*. Like father like son? She forced down the thought, and nodded, encouraging him to go on.

'The thing is, should I tell Frankie?'

'Is she likely to find out?'

Bobby shook his head. 'The guys would never let on, and this girl ... I doubt Frankie would ever meet her. But what if they did?'

Tess pressed her lips together, looking at the guilt and fear written across her son's face. 'You know,' she said, pushing his heavy dark fringe out of his eyes. 'When the doctor handed you to me, and I held you for the first time, I never felt love like it. It was like I'd waited my whole life for you. When I looked into your eyes it was like you knew the secrets of the universe. You were so perfect, so beautiful.' Bobby looked down at his hands as she went on. 'You always want to make the world perfect, to protect your child. To make their life perfect in a way your own hasn't been, or isn't. But you can't. It's part of being human, and part of growing up. Life is messy, and beautiful, and it fills your heart with love, and sometimes breaks it. But you know what, I wouldn't have it any other way. Nobody is perfect, Bobby. No love is perfect. If Frankie will never find out, don't tell her. It will only hurt her. But promise me, once you are married-'

'I'd never,' he said, looking up quickly. 'It's just I'm so crazy for Frankie, and she's made me wait-'

'Yeah, well, good for her,' Tess said, draining her glass. 'I adore Frankie. I look at her and she is just so ...' Tess sighed, squeezing her fists tight. 'She's got such goodness in her, such innocence. You can see she thinks she knows it all, knows everything about love, but she doesn't know how it hurts. There's no edge to her - nobody has disappointed her, nobody has hurt her. She doesn't just love you, she's in love with you, actively lost in the magic you have made together.' Tess realised Bobby was staring at her, incredulous.

'I've never heard you talk like this.'

'Oh, I'm just feeling old, and bruised.' Tess pulled on her gloves. 'I love that about her. Her heart is fierce and good and true. I see the person I was, once, in her. She has such light in her. Don't disappoint her before you even begin. Don't break her heart.' Tess jabbed her index finger in his chest. 'And you - you are lucky to be loved like that. Do you have any idea how rare it is, and how lucky you are? Buck your ideas up. Be the man I raised you to be. You have your whole lives ahead of you. She wanted to wait and you should have, but now you'll have this little pin-prick of conscience every time you think of it. Learn from it, Bobby. That's what mistakes are for.' She patted his hand, and took out a sheaf of bills from her pocket book to pay the bill, toss-ing them onto the counter. 'Be the man Frankie deserves to be her husband.'

'You're not mad, are you Mom?'

'Mad?' Tess laughed softly. 'I've never been able to stay mad with you for long, you know that.' She punched him on the arm. 'You have a great future ahead of you, just don't mess it up before you've even started.'

'Who knows what the future holds.' Bobby shrugged his jacket on. 'I don't like the way things are shaping up in Vietnam one bit. We've got thousands of men out there already, and more will follow this year, mark my words.'

'Oh god, I hope not. I can't bear the thought of another war.' Tess looked at her son, her stomach twisting at the memories bubbling to the surface.

'Me and the guys were saying at my Stag that when the draft comes-'

'When? What makes you so sure?'

'We'll fight for a better world for all of us.'

'Bobby, you're young, and idealistic-'

'Just because I still believe in fighting for something?'

'What do you mean?'

'I believe in love, and family, I promise I do-'

'Bobby?'

'I believe in making a better world. Is that so wrong?'

'No, no it's not wrong, to believe in love.' Tess slid down from her stool, and embraced her son. 'I love you, Bobby,' she whispered, screwing her eyes closed to stem the tears as she hugged him.

'Mom ...' he said. She felt he was struggling to ask her something.

'Yes?'

'Oh, it's nothing.' Bobby frowned. 'It can wait, until after the wedding.' He hugged her. 'I do understand, I promise. I've been thinking about it all a lot. I understand.'

'Good,' she smiled brightly, confused, and they walked on. 'As long as you're happy. That's all I care about. Now, that's enough talk of war. Before you save the world, you have your future with Frankie to think about first.' They stopped at her exit and she brushed down the lapel of his jacket. 'See you at the rehearsal dinner tonight?'

'Seven at Orsini's. It's just round the corner from the church in Howard Beach. Do you think you'll be ok finding it?'

'Your father has had his office organise everything.'

'It's really generous of you guys to shell out for tonight. You don't - you don't think he's gone over the top do you?'

'Kit, go over the top?' she said, smiling slowly. 'We'll see. And he's driving. We'll be fine as long as he doesn't get a nosebleed crossing over to Queens.'

'5.30pm at the church. Don't forget!' Bobby waved, walking backwards, then turned and strode off into the afternoon crowds on the concourse.

Don't forget. Don't forget ... she thought, walking away. *That's just the problem. I remember too much. All these 'what ifs' and regrets looping round and round.* She dug her hands into her pockets, weaving through the crowds spilling in to the station. *Maybe it's time to draw a line.* Tess stopped at the crossing and looked up at the lavender evening sky. *I have to forget the past. Bobby is his own man, I've done what I can, and now it's time for him to make his life. It's time for us both to look forward.*

Chapter 34

'Kit. What have you done?' Tess stood in the doorway of Orsini's private dining room. Her hand slipped from Kit's arm, her eyes widening in horror. She could hear Frankie and Claudia talking behind them, walking through the entrance hall: *Baby, be sure when you walk down the aisle you hold your bouquet, low down, like this, so everyone can see the beading on your dress ...* And further back, Marco, talking to Bobby. *Everything is arranged for the honeymoon. You'll be met at the airport by my assistant and taken to your hotel in Florence ...*

Florence, Tess thought. She wished she could click her fingers and be in Florence at this moment. The entrance hall filled with more voices, Frankie's brothers, their wives, the bridesmaids.

'Perfect,' Kit said, rubbing his hands together. 'Marcel, you've excelled yourself,' he said to a young man in a dark suit who stood as they entered the room.

'It's too much, Kit,' Tess whispered, turning to him.

'Bobby is our only child,' Kit said, his gaze taking in the swathes of white chiffon pinned to the centre of the room, billowing out like the roof of wedding tent. 'This is the one chance they gave us to contribute to the wedding and I wanted it to be something special. They chose the restaurant, I took care of the decor. It was the least I could do.' Towering arrangements of lilies on wrought iron pedestals scented the air, and hundreds of candles illuminated the round tables. Above the end table, Tess spotted photographs of herself and Kit, Claudia and someone she assumed was Frankie's father in huge silver heart shaped frames, and between them 'Frankie and Bobby: Happily Ever After' glittering in silver around photos of the couple.

Bobby strode across the room, ignoring the decorations and headed straight for the bar. Tess overheard Marco talking to Frankie: *Why does he not escort you in to the dinner? He is too busy talking to his friends and getting himself a drink to care for you? He's not good enough for you, I tell you.* And then Frankie: *Stop it. It's too late, I'm marrying him and I love him.* Tess strained to hear Marco's reply: *I wanted for you someone who will treat you like a princess.* She smiled, hearing Frankie's reply: *He'll learn.* Tess turned, waiting for Marco to look at her. He and Frankie were a few paces behind Claudia. *There is always one who loves more, who sacrifices more in a marriage. I wanted that to be your husband. Bobby thinks of himself first. If he doesn't treasure you now, what hope is there?*

Marco joined Tess. 'Well, Kit has his day,' he said quietly, taking in the ostentatious decorations.

'I'm torn,' Tess said. 'Part of me wants to stand up for Bobby.' She watched her son at the bar. 'Part of me thinks you have a point.'

'Don't worry, I won't make a scene. But for the rest of her life, Frankie will put herself second - to your son, to their children. That's what mothers do. That's what real love is. You care more about someone else's happiness than your own.' Marco looked down at her. *Is that what you think of me,* Tess thought. There were too many people around. She kept her distance from him, though she longed to fall into his arms. Tess could tell from his steady gaze holding her, drawing her to him that he felt the same.

Tess glanced out of the corner of her eye at Claudia's expression as she drew abreast with them. In a matter of moments her face expressed shock, anger, control. 'Kit, you shouldn't have,' Claudia said, placing her hand on his arm.

'My god, it's ... it's more beautiful than the wedding.' Frankie said, joining her mother. She started in surprise at the coo of the doves in the gilded cage by the entrance.

'Nothing will be more beautiful than that,' Marco said, putting his arm around her. 'This is ... very generous of you. Thank you, Kit.'

Frankie glanced over her shoulder at the family crowding in to the lobby. 'But what are we going to do?' she said under her breath. 'When they see this, tomorrow is going to be a let down.'

'Please, let me show you to your seats,' the maitre d' said to her.

Claudia nudged Frankie's arm and nodded at Kit and Tess. 'Thank you,' Frankie said, smiling. She kissed them both in turn. 'It's beautiful.' She walked ahead, alone and Bobby joined them, giving Frankie a glass of champagne. Tess turned to Marco and raised an eyebrow: *See? He thinks of her.*

'What? What have I done now?' Kit said.

'You just couldn't resist, could you, Dad?' Bobby raised his glass and went to join Frankie.

'What?' Kit ushered Tess to their table.

'You've upstaged the wedding,' Tess said under her breath, batting aside a silver heart shaped balloon.

'A few metres of white fabric and balloons?' Kit clicked his tongue.

'Doves. There are doves,' Tess said, sitting as he pulled out her chair for her. Tess glanced down at the menu. 'And seven courses?'

'Stop being a spoilsport,' Kit said, taking a knife and tapping the edge of his champagne glass.

□

'That was some meal,' Marco said, joining

Tess at the bar.

'I'd have been happy with a bowl of spaghetti,' she said, sipping her Martini.

'Tell me something. Why only one Martini? Why don't you let yourself relax?'

'Why?' Tess glanced at him. 'My parents were alcoholics.' She swirled the olive in her glass. 'Though they would never have called themselves that. Everyone in Hong Kong drank like fish - gin was the cure-all for every expat problem. I'm the same, addictive. If I have one, that's perfect. If I have two, I want three, or more ...' She pressed her lips together. 'I've always been careful, ever since ... after-'

'After what he did to you?'

'Yes.' Tess sipped her drink. 'This is my daily treat, my daily test of character. It's far more useful to be addicted to exercise, and work, and dancing.' They turned to watch the couples twisting to Chubby Checker on the dance floor. *And you*, she thought. 'I miss you,' Tess murmured, not looking at him. She felt his index finger brush the side of her hand. 'How are you?'

'I'm fine. I have to see you.'

'Dance with me,' she said, leading the way through the swirling couples on the parquet floor, lights of the glitter ball sweeping around the hall.

'Tess, I must talk to you,' he said, raising his arm to take her hand. She saw him flinch.

'What is it?'

'I'm fine. Just a little pain.'

'Marco, talk to me. Claudia told me to stay away from you. She says it's up to the family to look after you, what does she mean?'

'Claudia is wrong,' he said. 'I just - It's ... I've never felt like this before. I need to talk to you, but not here. Not now.' He took her hand in his, and they moved together to the music. 'Let's run away, Tess. We can leave, go somewhere new, where no one knows our name.'

'I can't,' Tess said. 'I'm sorry. I can't do that.' She broke away from him, and pushed open a fire door, heading for the empty dark terrace. She heard him following behind her, his footsteps tracing hers to the quiet shadows. The lights of Manhattan spread before them in the distance, a glittering blanket of stars. Tess laid her palms on the cold stone balustrade.

'Wait, Tess,' he said. 'You can't just walk away.'

'I have to. You see, I love you, Marco, but I love Bobby and Kit too. I can't do this to Bobby, and to Frankie. I can't destroy their happiness for the sake of ours.' Her lips trembled as she tried to smile. 'Bobby's been acting strange. Maybe it's nerves about the wedding, but I can't help thinking he suspects something. I don't want to ruin this for them. Their life is just beginning, and-'

'And ours is ending?' Marco bowed his head

and he rested against her shoulder. She leant in to him, pressing his skull into the hollow of her throat, stroking the fine dark silk of his hair. 'Don't say that. It's not. This is just the next act, Tess. A third act for you. You have been a child, a wife and mother, and now it is time for you to be who you want to be. This is your time. What do you want, Tess? I will give anything, do anything to make you happy.'

'I wanted to dance, once upon a time,' she said, looking at the lights across the water, her hand pale against his glossy black hair. 'I wanted to be the greatest prima ballerina in the world.'

'So dance.' He looked up at her. 'I would never stop you doing anything.'

'You're crazy. I'm too old.' She tilted her head and smiled sadly.

'Then help others just starting out. Create this workshop you talk about. Choreograph new ballets.'

'I can't-'

'Of course you can.' Marco raised his head. 'You can do anything you want to. Learn. Do something new. You are a young woman still.' He glanced back to make sure they were alone, and kissed her, crushing her lips beneath his. 'What are you waiting for?'

In the restaurant, Bobby laid his palm against the cool glass window, his face setting hard.

□

'Thing is, I don't know how you can sit there, pretending,' Bobby said some time later, lurching forward to grab the bottle of Sangiovese.

'Bobby, what are you doing?' Frankie said, touching his arm. 'Don't you think you've had enough?'

'Enough?' He filled his glass, slopping wine onto the tablecloth. 'No, I haven't had enough wine if that's what you mean, but yes, yes I have had enough of them-'

Claudia dabbed at the stain, splashing soda water on. 'Leave it,' Bobby said.

'Don't talk to your mother in law like that,' Marco said his voice low. He leant across the table.

'You -' Bobby said, pointing at him. 'You don't even talk to me.'

Marco pushed back his chair from the table and stood slowly. Tess looked up at him, imploring. 'If you have something to say, say it.'

'Please, don't-' Frankie said. Claudia looked from her daughter to Marco, to Tess, her face unreadable, dignified, alert.

Bobby leapt up, leaning on the table to steady himself. He strode round to Marco, and pushed him in the chest. Marco stood firm. 'I'll tell you what I've had enough of - you. You've never thought I was good enough for your precious family, and all the time-'

'Robert, sit down,' Kit said sharply. 'You're

causing a scene.' He glanced around the restaurant. Every face turned their way like sunflowers in a field.

'A scene? God forbid I'd cause a *scene.*' Bobby said, rolling on his feet. He pointed at Marco. 'Outside.'

The moment Marco stepped onto the slick pavement Bobby swung for him. Marco sidestepped, the blow skimming his jaw. 'You don't want to do that,' he said. His nephews spilled out of the restaurant after them, trying to keep Bobby apart from Marco.

'I want to knock your damn head off for screwing my mother,' Bobby said, lunging towards him. Blow after blow rained down on Marco. Bobby's fists pummelled his stomach, and Marco blocked him again and again, not fighting back.

'For god's sake,' Kit said. 'Stop.' One of Frankie's brothers stepped between them, pushing Bobby away.

Marco's face set, grim. He patted his nephew's arm. 'You all go back inside, make sure the women are ok. This is between Bobby and me.'

Bobby lurched blearily towards Kit. 'Someone has to make a stand. Why the hell you aren't, I don't know?' He lunged at Marco, who sidestepped. 'Damn it. He screwed your wife.' Bobby's face contorted as he looked at Marco. 'You and her. You - she disgusts me.'

'Don't you talk about Tess like that,' Marco said, his fist clenching.

'Or what? You and my whore of a-' He staggered back as Marco knocked him on the jaw, an elegant jab, just enough to send him staggering back.

'That's enough,' Kit said, catching Bobby.

'We're just getting started,' Bobby said, scrambling forward. Marco shook his head. 'Fight me, damn it.'

'No!' Frankie said, pushing past Kit. She wrapped her arms around Bobby. 'I don't know what's going on, but we are getting married tomorrow. Stop it. Stop it,' she said, breathing into his hair, his jaw. Bobby pushed her away, his eyes wild, and he strode off into the night.

'Let him go,' Kit said, dusting off the sleeves of his blazer. 'I know Bobby. He'll cool off, don't worry. He'll be there in the morning, I'll make sure of it.'

'Marco!' Claudia shouted, shouldering her way out of the restaurant. She spoke quickly in Italian, a machine gun volley of words punctuated by gestures which needed no translation. He hung his head. '- and you couldda given one another a black eye for the wedding. I suppose it's all come out has it about you and her?' She turned from Bobby's hunched, retreating figure - who raised a hand, batting away her shout like a fly, back to Marco. 'You shouldda known better -' she said, jabbing him in the chest. 'You shouldn't be fighting in your condition.' Marco glanced at Tess as she walked out of the restaurant.

'What does Mama mean?' Frankie said.

'Marco?' Tess said. 'What is she talking about?'

'See? See! I knew he hadn't told you.' Claudia turned to her triumphantly. 'As for you. Don't you think you've done enough? Go home with your husband.'

'We're divorcing, if that makes any difference,' Kit said.

'You're *divorcing*?' Claudia said, her voice rising.

'Thanks, Kit,' Tess said.

'Just trying to help,' he said.

'Claudia,' Tess said. 'What do you mean? What condition?'

'I told him.' She jerked her thumb at Marco. 'I said *tell her* - then we'll see if she's so keen to throw it all in for you.' Claudia tossed her head back.

'Claudia, don't do this-' Marco began.

'He's sick,' she said, her face close to Tess'. 'You've fallen for a dying man.'

'Tess-' Marco said, as she stepped back. Tess felt ice water coursing through her veins, the street falling away around her.

'No. You're lying.' Tess shook her head, backing towards the restaurant.

'Why would I lie to you?' Claudia said.

'No,' Frankie said, running to tell her

brothers. 'You're lying. It's not true!'

'You couldn't wait,' Tess said under her breath, pacing forward suddenly. She leant in to Claudia. 'Really? This is their moment, not ours. This is Frankie and Bobby's night. Look what you've done.'

'Ah, Frankie's tough. She'll get over it. Anyways, you can talk. What I've done?' Claudia laughed. 'At least I tell the truth. Not all of us are buttoned up like you.' Claudia hissed, and raised her chin at Kit. 'Not all of us keep a lid on our emotions-' Tess turned on her heel and swung back the door to the restaurant.

'It's called being a grown up,' Kit said. 'You should try it. Tess, are you alright?' he called, following her back inside the party.

'Leave me alone,' she said, gathering up her red silk wrap and bag from the table. 'Give me the car keys.'

'I'll drive you.'

'Forget it. I'll find a taxi.' Tess pushed her way out through the chattering crowd, staring resolutely ahead, feeling their curiosity picking and pulling at her like brambles.

'Tess.' Outside on the teeming pavement, Marco grabbed her arm, took her aside.

'How could you do this?' She felt nauseous, as though the floor swayed beneath her feet. 'How could you let me fall in love with you, when I'm going to lose you?'

'I did not want to hurt you, Tess. I wanted

to give you something you had lost - passion, a sense of being alive.' He paused. 'I didn't expect to fall in love with you. You made me feel more alive than I have ever felt.' He glanced back to the doorway, to the crowd of family and friends watching them. 'Believe me, I never meant to love you.'

'But you do, you do love me.' Tess wiped an angry tear from her eye. 'So why didn't you tell me? I told you everything, Marco. Everything.' She balled her fist and laid it against his heart. 'Why didn't you tell me?'

'I tried to, when we were in Province-town. The night I couldn't sleep.' He took a deep breath, turning his back on the crowd. 'But then you woke up and told me about what happened to you, about Bobby. It just didn't seem like the right time to burden you with this, when you had been brave enough to be vulnerable.' Marco glanced over his shoulder. All eyes were on them, still. 'I want to hold you, but I can't.'

'It's hopeless, Marco.'

'Don't say that. All my life,' he said quietly, 'I have taken pride in caring for others. For the people who work for me, for my family, my brother's family. To become a burden to them, to you is unthinkable.'

'What's wrong? Is it your heart? Cancer?'

'What condition do I have? Parkinson's.'

'But people live with that for years-' Tess gazed up at him. 'We have time.'

'The thing is, it's not if but when I will grow weaker.' Marco shrugged. 'Who knows. Maybe the boxing is to blame. I've known ...' he sighed. 'I've known for a long time. I hid it pretty well.' He looked into Tess' eyes. 'I'm getting shakier, stiffer, every month. One day, I won't be the man I want to be for you.'

'One day,' she said, taking him in her arms. 'One day - we can deal with that, together.'

'I came to New York to make sure everything was in order for the family. I came to say goodbye to them all, while I was still well enough to travel. I want them to remember me like this.' He gestured at his chest. 'I thought I was slowing down, but now you.' He buried his face in her hair, not caring now who was watching. 'You, you've broken my life open. In a way I wish I'd never met you. I was ready, but now I want so much. So much I can't have.' He fell silent. 'I want you to be free, for the first time. I don't want you to be tied to me-'

'I am free,' she said fiercely, raising her face to him. 'I choose you. We'll face whatever is to come, together.'

'Are you sure?'

'Yes. When you get sick-'

'I will decide.'

'What do you mean?'

'When the time comes you must let me go.'

'I don't know if I can,' Tess said, her voice

catching.

'Claudia wants me alive at all costs. She would happily feed me like a child, helpless and bedbound.' The street lights flashed gold in Marco's eyes as he turned. 'I will not live like that. I live on my own terms, and I die on my own terms. If you cannot accept that, then I set you free.'

Tess saw the light of a taxi approaching and she waved her arm, hailing it. Kit stood beside Marco, and watched her leave.

'What have we done?' Marco said, as Frankie pushed past, a dark suited brother on either side.

'How could you?' she said to him. 'With her?' Frankie shook her head. 'You should have told me. Why didn't you and Ma tell us you're sick?' She held her head high, but a single tear coursed down one cheek.

'What have we done? We've made a bloody mess of it, as usual,' Kit said, leaning against the wall beside Marco, and lighting a cigarette.

'How could I tell them I am dying,' Marco said.

'Oh, blah, blah, blah. We're all dying, what makes you so special?' Kit said, exhaling a plume of smoke. 'Some of us will get there quicker than others, that's all.' He turned to Marco as Claudia and the other brothers swept past after Frankie. 'One for the road? Why don't you tell me the whole story, and we'll figure out how we are going to make this right for everyone.'

    'I don't know what to do.'

    'You're going to get on with it before you lose her.' Kit waited for Marco to look at him. 'I love her. She's chosen you. I want Tess to be happy. It's as simple as that.'

Chapter 35

Kit waited up for him, pacing before the window overlooking the dark heart of Central Park. 'Bobby?' he said, turning at the sound of the key in the door.

'I'm home,' Bobby said, slinging his jacket onto a chair in the hall.

Kit strode over to him and hugged him tightly. 'I was worried about you. Where were you?'

'Over at the Pep.' Bobby swayed, negotiating the wide open plain of the hall, and Looty, racing delightedly around his feet. 'Rocco and a couple of Frankie's brothers talked me down.'

'Good. Marco sent them off to look for you. Come on, let me make you some tea.'

'Marco? I'd rather have another drink.'

'Tea,' Kit said firmly. He looked at his watch. 'You're getting married in twelve hours. He swung open the door to the kitchen and flicked on the light. The smell of gas filled the air, the click of the stove. Bobby slouched at the kitchen table, laid his head back against the wall. 'Why are you so late? The club must have closed some time ago.'

'They made me go round to the Affini's. Rocco got some busker he knows to play *Moon River*, and made me sing to Frankie.'

'Sing? Poor girl - did she agree to marry you to make you stop?'

'Yeah. Maybe.' Bobby laughed, and rubbed his bloodshot eyes. 'There I was on my knee, singing up at her window at midnight and all the lights were going on in the houses. She shouted out: *It's bad luck if you see me before the wedding.*' He shook his head. 'I said: Oh, so you are going to marry me, then?' *Maybe I'm just covering myself, she said, just in case.*'

'What did you say to that?' Kit poured boiling water into the teapot, and swirled it round, emptying it, steaming, into the sink.

'I said I'm sorry-'

'Good for you.' Kit spooned leaves into the pot, and filled it up. 'It takes guts to admit when you are wrong. Sometimes 'sorry' is all you need to say.'

'I told her that Marco thinks I don't deserve her. Nobody is good enough for him-'

'You're doing a damn good job of proving him right.' Kit glanced at him. 'Look at the state of you.'

'But she is? Mom is good enough for him.' Bobby wiped his mouth against the back of his hand. 'Anyway, I begged her. I said: let me spend the rest of my life becoming the man who deserves you.' He raked his hands through his hair.

'Good for you.'

'What's going on, Dad? Why aren't you mad as hell? I know I am. I can't believe she's done this to you. To us.'

'Mad?' Kit busied himself with the teapot, setting out two cups. 'Of course I'm mad. Our marriage may be ... unconventional by some standards, but she is still my wife, for now.'

'For now?'

'I told you, I asked your mother for a divorce a few weeks ago.'

Bobby spun round to look at him. 'But that's got to change. It's not too late for you both.'

'Perhaps.' Kit settled down opposite Bobby, a pool of light over the yellow Formica table illuminating their faces.

'It's revolting. The thought of her, with him-'

'Bobby, you mustn't be too hard on your mother.'

'Why the hell not?'

'You see, we had what is quaintly termed a marriage of convenience.'

'What do you mean?'

'We were - we are - friends. Nothing more.'

'Ever? I don't understand.'

'Oh, Bobby. Think.' Kit poured him a cup of tea. 'I was in something of a spot - financially - in Hong Kong. So was your mother, in a spot, I mean. It suited us both. Marrying Tess gave me security, financial and social, and marrying me gave her ... Well, it gave her a father for her child.' He looked up at Bobby. 'For you.'

'Yeah, I still haven't worked up the guts to ask her about that. You know who my father is?'

'I do-'

'So tell me!' Bobby's voice rose. 'A hell of a night this is turning out to be. She won't, I know it. If she's kept it secret this long. She's too busy with her new life, with him-'

'Never, ever talk about your mother like that do you hear?' Kit paused. 'It's not my tale to tell.'

'Tell it to me anyway.' Bobby sank back in his chair. 'This is a damn mess. Jesus. You know, I look at Frankie's family, and I love it. They fight and they yell and then they make up, but they talk and it's ... it's real. Whereas you - you two,' he said, making the shape of a ball with his clenched fingers. 'I said to Frankie, it's like some spun sugar sweet. Looks great on the outside but it's brittle and hollow, and it's not real. Was any of it real?' His voice cracked, pleading.

'When you get back from your honeymoon, you need to talk to Tess. But before you do, I want you to know two things. I love your mother, and I love you. That's real.' He reached over and took Bobby's hand. 'You are my son.' He glanced at his watch. 'And right now, you need to get to bed.' Kit stood, scraping his chair back on the tiled floor.

'Where are you going?'

'Me?' Kit glanced over his shoulder, pulling on his overcoat. 'Now I know you're safe, I'm going to find your mother.'

Chapter 36

Kit unlocked the door of their apartment, and strode along the marble corridor. Looty stirred in her basket, let loose a volley of barking. 'Bessie?' he called above the din. 'Bessie?' She appeared at her bedroom door by the kitchen in a hairnet, pulling a blue wool dressing gown around her.

'Yes, sir?'

'Has Mrs Blythe been home?' He lifted the receiver of the telephone in his study, and flicked through his address book. Who should he call at this hour? Where might Tess have gone? Think.

'No, sir. Is there anything I can do?'

'No, thank you. Go back to bed, and for pity's sake take that dog with you. I'll call if I need anything.' Kit slumped back in his burgundy velvet chair, the telephone dangling from his hand. His head was throbbing. It felt like he was pulling each thought from chewing gum. He had checked the studio, the all night café they both loved. *Elaine? Would she have gone there?* Elaine would never tell him if Tess was sitting across the room from her, nor would Gladys. They were both too loyal to her. Kit rubbed his temple. *Marco?* Maybe she has gone back to that godforsaken shack in Provincetown? He frowned. *She'd never do that to Bobby, not with the wedding in a few hours.*

Kit dialled a number, and as he waited for it to pick up he paced his study. He poured a glass of scotch into a heavy cut glass tumbler from the antique decanter in the Tantalus on his dresser.

'Hello? Did I wake you?' Kit's face softened. 'Oh, I'm ok. I just needed to hear your voice.' He took a sip of his drink. 'It's tomorrow.' He checked his watch. 'I mean, today. Yes, I'm going to leave straight after.' He looked out at the dark heart of the park beneath him, fringed with glittering lights. 'I've made a terrible mess of things. I don't know what to do.' He closed his eyes, listening. 'Yes, you're right, of course. I've just got to get through the day.' He nodded. 'I love you too.'

Kit dropped the phone back into its cradle. *Where is she?* he thought, looking into the night. *Christ, it's all my fault.* Suddenly he hated the perfect glass in his hand, the opulent tastefulness of the furnishings. He threw the glass against the wall, and it smashed, rebounding into the softly lit cabinet of eggs. Kit pulled out drawer after drawer of carefully catalogued specimens, flinging them against the walls, the floor, not resting until every last egg had broken.

As the pendant light swung, it glimmered across a silver framed picture on his bookshelf, and Kit's eyes narrowed. He stepped over to it, the broken shards of glass and wood crunching beneath his shoes, and picked up the old black and white photo, turning it to the light. It was of Tess, not long after they had met. She was dressed in a simple white shirt and light cotton skirt, white ankle socks bright against her barred shoes. *She was so young,* he thought.

He remembered the night of their wedding in Hong Kong.

Clive Graves had swaggered over to him at the crowded bar in the Peninsula. 'Congratulations, Blythe.'

'Thank you.' Kit had wanted to punch him. He longed to see his satisfied, puffy blue eyes widen in shock. He took a long drag of his cigar, and tapped the ash into a glass ashtray.

'Gallant of you,' Clive said, swirling his glass.

Kit raised his hand, catching the bar tender's eye. He knew Tess was watching every moment. 'I don't know what you mean, old boy.' He watched their reflections in the mirror over the bar. Clive was shorter than him, half the man. He loathed the thought of his hands on Tess, beautiful Tess. It repulsed him in the way the story his father had told him as a child about a snake eating a litter of puppies in India repulsed him. Clive turned his stomach. The idea of him with

Tess was against the natural order of things. Kit wanted to protect her. He felt impotent that he wasn't there when she needed him. He glanced across the room and saw from the flush of her cheeks she was close to tears, her look beseeching him not to make a scene. Clive turned to him, the mean coal of his cigarette glinting.

'I know you've had your eye on her for a while. Quite a prize, our Tess. Striking girl, and an independent income. Some would say she's loaded. But really, it's terribly good of you, taking on damaged goods.' Without missing a beat, Kit turned, Tess' fresh glass of champagne in one hand, and his cigar stubbed hard against Clive's hand in the other. 'Jesus, watch out man,' Clive cried out in pain.

'Sorry old boy.' Kit leant down to him. 'You are the damaged one, Graves. You think you're it, don't you? Life and soul and all that. You're just the spoilt only son of a tradesman, that's what you are. You're used to taking any pretty thing which catches your eye. But people like you will never know happiness, never know contentment or love. You use people up to try and make your hollow heart feel something, anything, but it never will.'

'I felt Tess, alright.'

'Oh you had your way with her,' Kit said, his voice low and quiet. He glanced at Tess, saw the distress on her face. 'You're no kind of man, in my book.' He leant closer, said under his breath.

'You stay away from her, you hear? If you come anywhere near her, I will destroy you.'

'I'd be careful if I were you, *old chap*,' Clive called after him, nursing his hand. 'We all have our secrets, don't we?' He raised two fingers to his lips and blew a kiss.

'Secrets?' Kit glanced back at him. 'Tess won't tell anyone, and neither will I. In fact, she refuses to talk about it, so you really can't have been that memorable, Graves. I wouldn't brag about it, if I were you.'

'How did he know?' Kit said under his breath now, wiping a film of dust from the photo. *Bessie is slacking now she's been sacked*, he thought. Beside his thumb, he saw the words 'Star Ferry'. Tess was leaning against the balustrade of one of the boats, Hong Kong harbour lit up behind her. *The ferry. Of course*. Kit flung the photograph into his half packed suitcase and grabbed his coat, running towards the elevator.

'Where to?' the cab driver asked, swinging out into the traffic.

'Staten Island Ferry Terminal,' Kit said, drumming his fingers on the door frame. 'If you can get me there in ten minutes I'll double your fare.'

Kit sat back in the car, watching the lights flash past. *Hong Kong*. It felt like a different life-time. *Where did it all go wrong?* What happened to him and Tess?

'I do love her,' he remembered telling Tess' mother Elizabeth at that final party in December 1941.

'If you love her, why have you broken her heart?' Elizabeth said with all the imperious warmth of her namesake.

'I wrote to her to tell her to make a life without me, to set her free. I told her I had found someone else.'

'Oh, Kit, but why?' Elizabeth took his hand.

He looked up at a red balloon floating towards their table, and batted it towards the jostling dancers. The band was playing Glen Miller's Moonlight *Serenade*. 'Tess loved this song,' he said. 'I hope she's still dancing.' He looked at Elizabeth. 'She's safe and so is our child. They have the protection of marriage if she wishes. They are safe. That's what matters. I've suspected for some time that things will not go well for us here.'

'I'm scared pink, if I'm honest,' she said calmly. 'I feel like a canary in a cage with a hungry black cat pacing at the flimsy bars.' Elizabeth looked out across the terrace. 'I can't bear much more of this strain, the boredom and drinking. This hideous pretence that everything is normal. I spent the day playing golf at Deep Water Bay you know, just as we always do. And tonight we are dancing, while the Japanese are massing their forces somewhere out there, so close, so close ...'

'I can't believe they would hurt the women,' Kit said. 'There are rules, even in wartime. We're prepared to fight to the death, and god knows I'd rather a quick end, from what I've heard of their troops.' He lit a cigarette. 'Anyway, who are you calling flimsy? You have the finest members of the Wavy Navy here to defend you, Elizabeth, even if Churchill has hung us all out to dry.'

'Of course, dear boy.' She took his hand. 'Don't give up on Tess. She loves you. If you make it out of here-'

'That's rather a big 'if' Ma-in-law.'

'When. When you make it out of here, go to her. Give yourselves another chance. You have a child to think of.'

'They are all I think of. But what good would it do, her grieving for me if I die? Why waste her life. I want Tess to be happy. Let her hate me. Let her be angry with me for abandoning her. Some young fellow will snap her up, if they haven't already.'

'You mustn't think like that.'

'I love her, that's all.'

'And when you explain, she will fall into your arms, and you will live happily ever after.' Elizabeth stood. 'Shall we dance?' Kit escorted her to the dance floor, and they shuffled sedately near the open terrace door. 'I know,' Elizabeth said quietly, and Kit leant down to hear her better. 'I know what happened to Tess.'

'Don't upset yourself,' Kit said, squeezing her gloved hand.

'I found her in the drying room, trying to clean herself up after ... after that cad-'

'Hush, now. There's no need for any of us to ever look back,' Kit said.

'You are a good man, Christopher Blythe, to take on Tess and her child.'

'I love her,' he said for a third time, just before the band stopped playing and the war came home.

□

Tess leant against the railing of the Staten Island Ferry, watching the lights of Manhattan retreat, dark water churning beneath her. *The night before Bobby's wedding,* she thought. She remembered her own wedding night. Tess had felt as if she was playing dress-up. She remembered standing in the dressing room of their suite in the hotel turning this way and that, looking at the young woman in the mirror, wearing a Crepe de Chine nightgown her mother helped her pick out from the Harrods General Catalogue. Tess wished she had put her foot down and bought the pure silk pyjamas she had really wanted. The nightgown felt insubstantial. She reached for her new Tortoiseshell hairbrush on the dressing table. *Finest quality veneer rather than solid tortoiseshell, darling,* her mother had said, *but no one would ever know*. Growing up, Harrods had seemed the whole of England to Tess. She had spent hours thumbing through the catalogue each year, longing to Telephone Sloane 1234 ('Day and Night'). Ordering her trousseau seemed like a right of passage, sending the Telegram to: *Everything Harrods London*.

'*Choose a few luxuries from Home, to help you set up your home*,' her mother had written on a pale blue sheet of airmail paper, tucked into the cover. Reading by lamplight in the narrow bed she had slept in every night of her childhood, Tess had paused at the page for the World Wide Service: '*Expeditions completely equipped for all parts of the world.*' That is what marriage felt like to her: it was as if she were setting out for uncharted territory. She turned down the corner of the page of watches, choosing a silver Rolex Oyster with plain leather strap, £5 15 0 for Kit as a wedding present. She had spent enough time with him already to know that he considered gold watches 'too much'. '*All Rolex Oyster watches are immersed for several hours in water as a final test*' she read, and gazed up at the looping fan on her ceiling, imagining Kit swimming an elegant breaststroke in a large fish tank, tapping the watch and giving her the thumbs up.

Tess flipped on through the catalogue turning down page after page: Mrs Sykes' Housekeeping Accounts book 3/-; a new Pukka cabin trunk for their honeymoon in the Philippines;

Leda silk stockings in Mist Grey. She paused at the pages of dolls' prams and Sunbeam racing cars, trying to imagine buying toys at Christmas, and filling stockings, trying to imagine being a mother.

Tess closed her eyes now, remembering how terrified she had been at the thought of going to bed with Kit. The long rope of wedding pearls around her neck was heavy, warm. Tess cupped the gentle swell of her stomach in her hand, felt her child's answering kick. *I can do this*, she thought, hoping desperately that Kit had already gone to sleep. She stepped from the hotel bathroom into the suite and her heart sank at the sight of Kit, sitting reading in bed in a pair of starched white pyjamas. He looked impossibly handsome, his gold hair brushed back from a wide, tanned brow and high cheekbones, the white cotton setting off the perfect symmetry of his collar bones.

She thought of the cheery taffeta bedspread she had bought from the catalogue for their new home ('A Beautiful Bedspread Adds Much to the Charm and Restfulness of a Bedroom'). It was still wrapped in brown paper at the bottom of the tea chest in their new apartment in Hong Kong waiting for her to dress their bed. She knew instinctively at that moment that Kit would loathe it.

'How lovely you look,' he said, marking his page. He turned back the heavy linen sheet on her side, making room for her.

'What a glorious day it was,' she said, slipping off her gown. She went to take off the pearls, but Kit stopped her. 'Keep them on?' she said.

'Yes. They are so beautiful.' He patted the bed.

'I'm on the wrong side,' Tess said, thinking of her bedside table at home. 'Or is this my side, now?' Kit, leant in to kiss her suddenly, and their noses bumped.

'Sorry, darling. I just - oh, you are so beautiful,' he said. Tess lay back, rigid with fear, staring at the ceiling as Kit kissed her, fumbling with the edge of her nightgown. She screwed her eyes closed as he kissed her again, and she felt his hip nudge hers. She tried desperately not to think of before. 'Tess? Tess you look scared half to death. Darling, you do want to, don't you?'

'Of course.' She blinked, looking up at his kind, handsome face smiling down at her. 'I want to be a real wife to you. I want to please you. I just-'

'I'll be gentle,' he said, untying his pyjama bottoms. Kit wriggled out of his pyjama jacket. Tess had never seen him naked. Even swimming, the bathing costumes were substantial. His kisses were flaccid, like damp tissue paper pressing against her skin. She had not expected the body beneath the sharp suits and stiff creases to be hairless, his skin soft as a girl's. *I can do this*, she told herself. *It will be over soon.* She tried to push away the memory of Clive's fierce biting kisses which left her lips swollen and bleeding, the marks his teeth left on her neck, her breast.

Then he was on top of her, and she felt Kit struggling to put himself inside her. There was suddenly so much of him, all skin and frantic pushing. Where was the urbane man she knew, his tailored suits, his manicured nails?

But then Kit laid his hand on her stomach, and the baby moved. He recoiled from her like he had been stung, his limp penis hiding in its downy nest.

'Your - good god, is that the child? Is that what it feels like when you're pregnant?' Kit grimaced. 'I - oh god, it's no use.' She felt him, soft, flaccid, slipping away from her. 'I can't,' he said, rolling away. 'I can't.' He sat on the edge of the bed, his back curved, and Tess' lips parted in shock. She touched the indentation of his spine, afraid that the silver filigree of scars still hurt.

'Kit? What happened to you? Who did this?'

'Don't,' he said, shrugging her away. 'Make a man of you, it will,' he said lowering his voice. Tess lifted up the white sheet, gently wrapped it around his shoulders and laid her head there.

'Don't close me out, Kit, please.' She waited, hoping he wouldn't push her away again. 'My poor darling. Tell me in time, when you are ready.'

'What's to tell? Just another tale of childhood brutality?' She felt him closing off again. 'You may have noticed I don't keep in touch with my family.'

'We'll have our own family now.' Tess held him, rocking gently.

'You know, the first time he hit me I was small enough to think his belt was a snake. I couldn't conceive that father would hurt me, so my young mind convinced itself I'd been bitten by a snake. For years I was terrified of them.'

'Poor Kit.'

'I remember I wet myself. My pyjamas were sodden.' Kit began to shake. 'I went to bed convinced I was going to die. I was so afraid, that if I closed my eyes-' He made himself sit upright. 'Christ, look at the state of me. What kind of a man have you married?'

'Darling, I want to be a wife, a real wife to you,' she said, forcing away the thought of Clive, of how he had hurt her.

'Do you? Still?' She felt the quickening of the child in her stomach, sensing her anxiety as Kit turned and took her in his arms. Tess tried not to recoil at the feel of Kit's tongue in her mouth, less urgent now, steady and pressing, the sudden weight of him on her, the touch of his hip on her thigh. She felt him trying again to enter her, his frantic fumbling.

'Damn it, it's hopeless. I'm sorry, I just can't,' he said, rolling away from her as if he'd been stung. Kit pulled on his pyjamas, his dressing gown. Tess couldn't understand it. She was sure that Kit would be a man of the world, that he'd know what to do. She had carried a romantic image of him and her, together, in her heart for so many years. It was impossible that someone as attractive and charismatic as Kit hadn't had lovers before, surely?

'It's me, isn't it?' she burst out, a sob catching in her throat. 'Oh god, I've just realised.'

'Please, darling, don't-' He reached for her hand, not looking at her.

'I disgust you, don't I?' She pulled the sheet up over herself.

'No.' He sounded more certain. 'No.'

'Is it the baby?'

He hesitated. 'Yes. Yes, of course that's it. I've had too much champagne so the old chap isn't quite up to it, and I'm afraid of hurting the baby.'

'I don't believe you. I disgust you, don't I? Because of what he - what Clive did to me.'

'Hush now,' Kit said gently. 'When he taunted me tonight, I felt impotent.' Kit laughed softly, and gestured at his lap. 'Ironic, really.' He buttoned up his pyjama jacket and smoothed down his dishevelled hair. 'God, I wanted to thump him. He said it was a bit late to be defending your honour, the cad.'

'I'm sorry, Kit,' Tess said, curling up in a foetal position. 'I'm so sorry.'

'You have nothing to be sorry for.' He

turned out the lamp on the nightstand, and leant over to kiss her forehead. 'Don't cry, darling. This is the happiest of days.' He wiped away the tears from her cheeks with the clean sleeve of his pyjamas.

'I'm so lucky to have you, Kit. Please don't leave me.'

'Hush,' he said, laughing softly. 'Why would I leave you?'

'Mother was saying, I heard her talking to someone at the wedding breakfast: 'how extraordinary that Tess should land someone as cultured and handsome as Kit. What a catch. What a day.' I could have screamed.'

'It's me who's lucky,' Kit said. 'I adore you, Tess. Never doubt that. As for this,' he said, gesturing at the rumpled bed. 'It will be fine, later, I'm sure. Right now, I think the best thing is for you to go home.'

'To my parents?' she said, alarmed.

'To England, silly.' Kit sat cross legged, buttoning his pyjamas. 'I've been thinking about it. I've written to my aunt in Somerset, already-'

'When? When did you write to her?'

'A few days ago.'

'What? Why didn't you ask me? I don't want to go to Somerset. This is my home, here, in Hong Kong.'

'Hear me out. She's been looking after the family estate, Midchester - she's a housekeeper, really. Now that we are married, I inherit, and you can take care of making sure the house and accounts are in order while you wait for this little chap-' He pointed at Tess' stomach.

'What if she's a chap-ess.'

'We'll deal with that if it happens.' He calculated quickly, ticking off the months with his fingers. 'The child must be born in Somerset-'

'Is that why you married me?' Tess edged away from him. 'You don't love me. You're just using me and the baby.'

'Don't be silly, Tess. I adore you. We've always been good friends, haven't we? The rest will come, I'm sure.' He settled back against the plush headboard and opened his arms to her, waiting for her to curl up against him. 'I do love you, Mrs Blythe.'

Tess hesitated, and lay down in his arms, warily. 'I love you, too, Mr Blythe.' Tess wondered if this was love why it was that she felt so lonely.

'And Master Blythe will be born in September. You can tell everyone there he's a honeymoon baby, and everyone here will be none the wiser, Tess.' He paused. 'What were you going to do, if I hadn't bumped in to you on Hollywood Road? You knew I was going to ask you to marry me. We'd talked about it. Did you plan to pretend it was mine?'

'No. No I was going to tell you. Mother told me not to, but I couldn't have married you under false pretences. I hoped - I hoped you loved me enough that you would be gallant.'

'Gallant.' Kit laughs softly, sinking back on the plump white goose down pillows. 'What a marvellously old fashioned notion. No, I wasn't being gallant. I was looking after myself, as I always do. *I've never known such a selfish boy.'* That's what my mother said the last time I saw her. Dear mother.' Kit's face twitched. 'I wonder if we will do a better job as parents?'

'I hope so. I feel terribly guilty that I was going to get rid of it.'

'Until I came along like a knight in crumpled linen? I guessed the herbs were for an abortion. Very enterprising of you.' Kit lit a cigarette, and crossed his legs. 'You're right, I'm playing with you. Of course it made no difference to proposing to you.'

'And it doesn't bother you, still?'

'In fact it amused me. That's why I thought it was worth trying ...' He waved his hand with distaste at the bed.

'I amuse you?' Tess said, her cheeks colouring. 'Do you really think so little of me?'

'I adore you. We're good friends, aren't we? I think you are bright, and beautiful, and the perfect wife for someone of my status. It suits me, if you want to know the truth. If I am to inherit Midchester, that is contingent on providing an heir. As it is ...' He gestured vaguely at the bed. 'Well, I am more than glad to accept yours. We can help one another out, until the child is old enough to look after himself-'

'Or herself.'

'Of course. A marriage of convenience.'

□

'What ho, Tess,' Kit said, standing in the shadows on the ferry deck. 'Tess?'

She turned, startled, the night and the water rushing away behind her as the ferry surged forward. 'How did you find me?'

'You were upset.' Kit cupped his lighter in his hand, lit two cigarettes. He exhaled a slow plume of blue smoke to the breeze. 'I remembered how you used to ride the Star Ferries all night when you had something to think about. Where else would you go but here?' He passed a cigarette to Tess. 'Do you remember, we came here on our first night in New York?'

'I was just thinking about our wedding night.'

'Good God, why?' Kit leant against the railing next to her, gazing out at the retreating lights of Manhattan, scattered across the dark water like a thousand flames.

'Kit, why did you write that letter to me, in Somerset.'

'When?'

'During the war.'

'I ...' He ran his thumb along his lower lip. ' I wanted you to have a chance to leave me. Just as I do now, with this divorce. You're my best friend,

Tess. You deserve better.'

'I love you, Kit, you know that, don't you?'

'Even now?' Kit looked down at his hands and cleared his throat. 'But we both want something the other can't give.' He wiped quickly at his cheek. 'Don't leave me, Tess. I've made a terrible mistake.'

'Kit - don't. It's too late.' Tess screwed her eyes closed, trying to stop the tears. She looked at him, her eyes shining. 'I want it all, Kit. I want the fairytale, the happily ever after.'

'I know. I know you do. It's what you deserve.' Kit nodded, his brow furrowed. 'Damn it, this cold wind makes your eyes water.' Tess laid her hand on his arm without looking at him, let it rest there. 'I can't blame you, for choosing him. I'm bankrupt, Tess. I live a lie ...'

'Or a beautiful fiction?' She leant in to him.

'You always did see the best in me.' He kissed the top of her head. 'I liked the me I saw through your eyes. God knows, I was no good before, and I doubt I shall be after you.'

'After? You think you're getting rid of me that easily? Divorce me by all means, but I loved you then and I love you now.'

'Tell me something. How long was it before you realised I wasn't the dream lover you'd projected on to me?'

'How long? The first night - actually the whole honeymoon in Manila was a bit of a giveaway.' Tess burrowed closer in to the warmth of his heavy wool coat. 'I adored you from the first moment I saw you in 1934 in your dazzling uniform and pith helmet at the King's Birthday Parade in Hong Kong. You were the most handsome officer I'd ever seen.'

'Was I?'

'You know perfectly well you were. All the girls adored you. You paid me no attention whatsoever-'

'You were a child.'

'-until you saw me playing tennis.'

'You've still got a serve like a scalpel. Such elegance and fury.'

'I thought we could be happy.' Tess sighed. 'Perhaps if you hadn't always compartmentalised your life, if you'd let us in-'

'I learnt early on at boarding school not to show emotion,' Kit said, laying his head against hers. 'It's hard to let people in after that. I don't have the facility for happiness.'

'We've had our moments of happiness, I think.'

'After all we saw during the war it was more than I could have hoped for.'

'Do you remember when I came to your dressing room, not long after you came back from the War,' she said. 'You hadn't been in my bed again since our wedding night ...'

'I remember,' he said, taking her hand.

'I couldn't bear the distance. I understood that I repulsed you-'

'No, never that.'

'You have a true heart, Kit. You couldn't pretend to feel something you didn't.' She leant her head against his shoulder. 'I respect you for that.'

'You said you missed me,' he said, looking out across the water.

'We did. We had a good marriage, in our own way,' she said, thinking of their contented nights, of falling asleep listening to Kit reading to her from Kipling and Graham Greene in their pristine bed.

'We could still have a good marriage. Start again. Not like before, everything open and honest, and-'

'Open? You take lovers and so do I?' She shook her head.

'You're right.'

'I want more than that, Kit. I want the fairytale. The dark and the light, not just the glitter and the sparkle.' Tess gazed steadily at him. 'You just want to be the perfect man. A golden couple envied by everyone around.' She laughed. 'If Fabergé had designed nests they would have looked like that gilt edged mausoleum you designed for us.'

'Whereas you want to hook up with some aging, damaged, dying-'

'Don't.' Tess stood up straight, and flicked her cigarette butt over the side of the ferry, watching the pinprick arc of light.

'I can't bear the thought of you throwing away your chance at happiness on this man. I can't bear the thought of you having to bear another broken heart.' Kit turned to her. 'Do you intend to marry him?'

'I don't know. Let's get the divorce out of the way first shall we?'

'I don't want to fight anymore.' Kit looked out across the water. 'I was thinking about the last conversation I had with your mother on the way here.'

'Mother?'

'I told her I had written to you because I loved you. I wanted you to be free, to be happy.'

'But I broke it off with Philip when you came back, didn't I?'

'Oh *you* did, did you? Are you sure that prig with his eye on Aphra's house didn't run like billy-oh once the husband miraculously rose from the dead.'

'Don't be cruel.' She touched his shoulder, and Kit looked away. 'Surely you still care enough for me that you still want me to be happy? After over twenty years of loving marriage-'

'I don't think I ever truly loved you.'

'What do you mean?' It was as if the floor swayed beneath her. She remembered taking Bobby to the boardwalk when he was small, a house of fun on Coney Island. The floor boards lifted, cycling, creaking, carrying him away from her outstretched hand. She remembered how while he had shrieked in fear and delight she had fought to hide her sheer terror. It was like her most secret nightmares made real seeing her child borne away from her. She steadied herself now, placed her hand on the cold railing. 'You're lying again, to push me away. You don't mean that.' She raised her chin. 'You didn't mean it then, and you don't now.'

'When I was in the internment camp, in Shamsuipo, I envied you. It's very hard to remain noble when you are living in hell. I hated you, do you know that? I didn't want you to be happy, in Somerset, let alone with some clergyman with ideas above his station. I wished I hadn't sent you away. I wished you were suffering with me.'

Tess' stomach lurched with nausea and hunger. 'I felt - I feel - such guilt, still. That you had sent me home, and then you couldn't get out of Hong Kong.'

'The war ruined so many of us.' Kit turned away from her, his thumbs tapping against his fingertips. 'The horrors I saw.' Tess placed her hand on his shoulder, rested her head against his back. 'I almost died of dysentery.'

'You never talked about it,' she said. 'People in the camps managed to send a letter a month, I know Mother did, until she died.' Tess smiled sadly. 'Hers were as agog with scandal as her peacetime letters, always licking her chops over some Colony woman's misfortune.'

'I expect she was trying to hide the truth of how grim it was in Stanley from you. You would never have understood. War takes you far from home, and you never return. The only ones who understand are the ones who walk at your side.' The tendon in Kit's neck flexed. 'Besides, why talk about it when I relive it every night?'

'Still?' she said. She took one of his hands, forced him to stop the old familiar tapping. He snatched his hand away. 'It's gone-'

'It will never be gone. It's always a part of me. I'll never be happy.'

'And you want me to be unhappy too? Is that it?'

'Of course not,' he said quietly.

'I'm leaving, straight after the wedding,' Tess said.

'What? What about the studio, all those years building up your business?'

'Elaine is-'

'Like a daughter to me?' Kit said, mimicking Tess' voice. 'Elaine is a woman in search of a personality.'

'Kit, stop it. You've always been jealous-'

'Me? What about Bobby? If only he'd married her. Wouldn't that have been neat.'

'Happy families?'

'Not something I know about or aspire to.'

'It's all I ever wanted.' The silence stretched between them. 'I found one of my teenage diaries the other day. Do you know what

I wrote: *I want a home full of colour, light, love and laughter, full of children and happiness* ...' Her voice trailed away.

'That's why we have to make a break, now, while there's still a chance for you.' Kit took her hand in his, and turned it over, tracing the lines. 'Have you ever seen the way you look when a baby carriage goes past?' He laughed and shook his head. 'No, of course you haven't.' He held her close, and kissed her head, blinking away the sting in his eyes. 'I'm not enough for you. Is that any way to live, knowing you can't give the person you love what they need? We want different things, Tess.' Kit stroked her hair, she felt him breathe in her familiar scent of lilies. 'I am going to miss you so much.' His voice broke. When he spoke again, Tess knew he was crying. 'I rather hope after all of this, we'll find one another again.'

'All of this? Oh, Kit. You mean when Marco dies?'

'Who knows.' He laughed through his tears. 'I'd just always imagined us tottering around Somerset together.'

'Somerset?' she said, looking at him in surprise. 'What an extraordinary idea.'

'One must go home, eventually.'

'I don't even know where home is any more,' she said, realising in that moment she did. *Marco. Marco is my home.* 'It's done now. I've made Elaine my partner. I feel confident leaving the studio in her hands.'

'Wait,' Kit said, wiping at his eyes with the heel of his hand. 'What do you mean, leave? Leave where?'

'I have plans, Kit. Big plans. With the money Elaine's given me for half the dance studio, I'm starting again, in Provincetown.'

'That end of the world-'

'I love it there.'

'But how will you support yourself while you're getting started?'

'Oh,' Tess said, smiling to herself. 'I'll manage.'

'Will you?' Kit frowned.

Thank you, Aphra, she thought, looking up at the stars. *'You need a war chest, dear girl,'* she remembered Aphra saying to her one evening after Kit had returned from Hong Kong and he had gone to the village pub so they were alone. Aphra handed her a letter with details of a bank account at Coutts set up in Tess' name. Her eyes widened when she saw the figure deposited. 'Always have some running away money of your own, Tess. That way you know you are staying because you want to, not because you have to. It's very important for a woman to have choices, and the option to be independent, and to do that you must have your own money. Never, ever tell Kit about this account, do you understand? I don't care if you are both on your uppers and eating beans, this is yours, not his.'

Tess smiled, looking up at the North Star. She remembered Aphra sitting back in her favourite threadbare armchair by the fire, a crocheted rug across her knees and one ochre wool sock in need of darning resting on the back of the hound curled up near the hearth. 'The problem with Kit is he looks like a matinee idol,' Aphra said, 'and everyone projects their dreams on to a man like him. The reality often falls short.' *She was right,* Tess thought, glancing at Kit's profile. 'People like him come to expect the best as their due because that is all they have ever received. Everyone smiles when they enter a room. Everyone hands them money, and jobs, and gilded laurel wreaths. Kit will burn through your inheritance, I warn you now.' Tess remembered Aphra holding up her hand. 'He has gaps between his fingers. Sure sign of profligacy.'

'What are you laughing at?' Kit said now.

'Nothing.' Tess smiled and looked down at her hands. 'I was just thinking of Aphra. What she'd make of all this.'

'Aphra would be cheering you on.' Kit pulled his collar up around his ears. 'Will he go with you? It will never last.'

'You think so? Maybe I'll just prove you wrong.' Tess raised her chin defiantly.

'Why don't you. Then when you've made a complete fool of yourself, you-'

'What? Did you think I'd end up like one of the atrophied Upper East Side old broads, returning to my little studio and a cat and a tin of soup each night once you'd gone?' Tess put her hands on her hips. 'Do you remember that argument last Christmas you said I was weak for putting up with our sham of a marriage all these years, that I was afraid to live my own life. That's not true.' The river shimmered silver beneath them and the wind billowed her coat like a sail. 'I stayed with you because I was strong, not because I was weak. But this is just the beginning for me. I loved you both, you and Bobby. I gave you all I had. I'm sorry that wasn't enough for you.'

'God, you've never looked more beautiful than this moment,' he said quietly.

'Oh, Kit.'

'I'm sorry. I don't want to fight anymore. We did our best, for our marriage and for Bobby.' Kit put his arm around her shoulders and they turned to watch the Statue of Liberty, the lights of Manhattan pulling away from them. 'Marriage is more than a state. You always said marriage is an unexplored country. We did our best charting it together. We just got lost, that's all.'

Chapter 37

Tess slept little before the wedding, the restless hours filled with thoughts of Marco, Bobby, Kit. She showered at seven, gasping as she turned the dial to cold and plunged her face beneath the jets of water, trying to wake up. Wrapping a white waffle robe around herself, she stepped out onto the cool marble floor, and swept her hair up in a turban. Tess wiped away the steam on the mirror, only clearing her face. It surprised her, as always, how small the clear patch of mirror was. *Faces are so important*, she thought, widening the patch, swirling her finger round and round. Her eyes were red with sleeplessness, dark circles blooming beneath them, and Tess grimaced, sticking out her tongue. *Come on,* she said to herself. *Pull yourself together, woman*. She glanced at the door as she heard the water running in Kit's bathroom, and her face softened. It was the last time she would get ready in the morning and hear him next door. After all these years of living parallel lives, their paths were diverging.

In her dressing room, Tess settled before the mirrored table, and looked from her reflec-

tion to the familiar view of the New York skyline through the tall windows behind the mirror. She applied her foundation cosmetics with
practiced skill, not looking away from the view,
and swept a large powder brush around the
planes of her face. She turned to the mirror,
and caught sight of her gown hanging from the
empty wardrobe rail behind her, in its garment
bag. Beneath it sat the plain black box Marco had
given her with the shoes.

Tess licked the tip of a fine brush and
swept it through the kohl palette. Her hand was
steady, marking a fine line across her eyelid like
a blade on ice. She swept dark mascara over her
eyelashes, leaning in to the magnifying mirror.
From a silk pad on the table she took a needle,
and separated out her lashes one by one until
she was satisfied. At last, she rifled through her
drawer of lipsticks until she found the perfect
coral shade.

Tess set her hair, and padded across the
thick pale carpet to her chest of drawers. She
let the robe fall to the floor, and picked out
her underwear with care, before emptying the
rest into the cedar trunk. She discarded the new
set of lingerie she had bought for the occasion
and chose instead an old favourite which always
made her feel wonderful.

'Tess, are you almost ready?' Kit's voice
drifted through from the hall. She glanced across
at the rattle of the handle. 'Why have you locked

the door?'

'I wanted a moment to compose myself.' Tess slipped the oyster silk strap of her slip over her bra strap and checked her reflection.

'The car will be here in five minutes.'

'I'll be there.'

'Shall I check your outfit?'

'No. I think I need to do that for myself, from now on.' She glanced at the door, imagining Kit's intake of breath. She heard his footsteps retreating along the parquet and she smiled.

Tess took down the garment bag, unzipping the plain black to reveal a sumptuous jade gown fashioned like a cheongsam, with intricate coral embroidery at the neckline. Her wide brimmed straw hat was understated, simply trimmed in jade and coral silk. Finally, she carried Marco's shoes to the velvet banquette, and she sat, her feet tucked beneath her in anticipation.

'Tess, we are going to be late, what will people-' Kit said, turning to her at the front door of the apartment. The intercom buzzed insistently. Bessie opened the door for them, nodding her approval at Tess as she passed.

'Goodbye, Bessie. Thank you for everything,' Tess said, hugging her.

'Thank you, Ma'am,' Bessie said, dabbing at her eye with a white handkerchief.

They stood before the gold elevator

doors, waiting, and Tess pulled on her pair of soft suede eau de nil gloves.

'You look ... breathtaking,' Kit said.

'Thank you,' Tess stared upwards, waiting for the lift.

'The shoes.' Kit blinked as Tess clicked her heels together. 'They're red.'

'Coral, really,' Tess said, twisting the rope of pearls looped around her throat.

'Is that entirely ...'

'Suitable? Who gives a damn.'

'Is this your idea of a joke?' he said, lowering his voice, aware of the maid listening. Tess strode into the elevator. 'What? Do you think you're like Vicky, in the film, forced to choose between her passion for dance and her husband?'

'Perhaps.' Tess rolled her eyes and sighed. 'If you must know, they were a kind of nude originally, a pale, pale suede. Claudia cut them up.'

'In jealousy?' Kit stared at the shoes. 'He remade them in red for you.'

'Marco knows I love red.'

'It's like the fairytale, then. Hans Christian Andersen,' Kit said as the elevator plunged downwards. 'They're about magic, aren't they? Passion, and escape.'

The elevator pinged, and the doors slid open, autumn sunlight spilling across the lobby, drawing her out to the street. 'Now you are talking, old boy,' Tess said.

Chapter 38

'Frankie, phone,' Rocco called up the stairs of Claudia's house.

'Coming,' she called, wincing as the hairdresser pinned the last roller in her hair. A make up artist added a final slick of mascara to her eyes. Frankie's bridesmaids were squeezed in to her small bedroom, chattering canaries in lemon yellow gowns, touching up their make up, smoking, fastening stocking tops and buttons. Tulle and chiffon spilled across the dark bed like clouds across a mountain top. Frankie wrapped a plain pink dressing gown around her corset and petticoat, and ran downstairs to the hall, weaving past the little page boys playing with tin soldiers on the steps. 'Hello?'

'It's me,' Bobby said.

'Are you ok?' Frankie stepped back to let the florist squeeze by with a large white box.

'Whatchyou doing down here?' Claudia said, shooing her upstairs. 'The cars will be here soon.'

'Just a minute, Ma,' Frankie said, turning her back and covering her other ear. 'It's a madhouse,' she said. 'I can't wait to be alone with you, somewhere peaceful and quiet.'

'So you are still marrying me, then? I was just checking you hadn't changed your mind.'

'Yeah, Ma's calmed down a bit.' Frankie watched her mother storming through the kitchen firing orders at her brothers like a machine gun in shot silk and patent stilettos.

'What am I going to do, Frankie? Mom, and your uncle. If Dad hadn't got this stupid idea of a divorce into his head, none of this would have happened. And *he's* not my Dad.'

'Don't you ever say that. I'd die rather than think of one of our kids saying that about you.' Frankie clasped the receiver to her other ear, trying to hear above the hubbub of voices. 'Who raised you? Who put a roof over your head and food in your stomach and money in the account of that fancy prep school of yours, Mr Ivy League?' She smiled, hearing him laugh. 'Who held your hand, and wiped your tears, and read you all those stories you've been talking about reading to our baby, when he comes?'

'He did.' Bobby exhaled. 'What a mess, Frankie. Why did they have to do it, and wreck everything for us before it even began? Why? Couldn't there just be something perfect, one thing?'

'It makes no difference to us,' she said. 'No one knows but the family. 'This afternoon we are going to walk down that aisle as Mr and Mrs Robert Blythe and the world can go to hell.' She blew him a kiss down the line. 'Just wait ... one more day, Bobby. One more day and we can be together. If you get blue, start counting down the hours, baby.'

'I love you, Frankie,' he said. 'We're going to go away from here, from all of them. Hell, forget law school, let's stay on in Italy. We can open a restaurant together.'

'We have all the time in the world, baby.' She glanced at the clock on the wall. 'But now I have to go. Go on, Bobby. Tell your Mom and your Dad you love them, and that everything is going to be ok, because it is. Their lives are their lives, and ours is ours, and it starts today.' Frankie hung up the receiver, and turned to see Tess silhouetted against the screen door, standing in the doorway. 'Hello,' she said, smiling brightly.

'Frankie, I don't want to intrude-' Tess glanced into the house, uncertain. Frankie looked over her shoulder, and gestured Tess should step out into the yard. Frankie closed the door behind her.

'Think it's better if Ma doesn't see you right now. I was up most of the night calming her down.'

'Frankie, I'm so sorry.' Tess' brow furrowed. 'I wanted to come and apologise to you. I hope - I really hope we haven't ruined your day for you. What must you think of us?'

Frankie stood on tiptoe and hugged Tess, breathed in her scent of lilies. She was surprised how slight Tess felt in her arms. She remembered holding a wounded blackbird in her hands when she was younger, feeling the light bones beneath the glossy plumage. That was how Tess felt to her. Fragile. 'You know what, good people make bad mistakes. People fall in love. It's ok.' Tears welled in Frankie's eyes. 'It's killing me, about Uncle Marco, of course, but I get it. I get why he didn't want us to know, and I get why you fell for him. He's a mess, by the way. I don't think he's slept at all since you walked out of the party. Talk to him. He needs you.' Frankie stepped back, smiling, and Tess gently wiped away the tear in her eye with her gloved thumb.

'You mustn't cry on your wedding day. You'll set me off,' she said and smiled. 'I'm sorry. I am so glad, so very glad that Bobby is marrying you. I'm sorry it's all begun like this. I promise, I will make it up to both of you.'

'Bobby's pretty mad, with you both, and Marco.'

'He'll get over it.' Tess glanced up, hearing Claudia calling Frankie in the house. 'You'd better go. I'll see you at the church. I just wanted to say I'm sorry, and I'm so happy that you are going to be my daughter.'

'Me too.' Frankie smiled, pulling the sash of her dressing gown tighter. 'We're going to do better than all of you, you wait and see.'

'Oh, Frankie ...'

'Bobby loves me. He really loves me. We've got passion, you know. He would never cheat on me, or run out on me, not like-' Frankie stopped, seeing Tess' face crumple. 'Hey, I didn't mean to hurt your feelings? I just meant we're going to do all we can to make this work.'

'Good for you,' Tess said, looking at her, her eyes shining. 'Good for you.' She handed her a battered silk box. 'I wanted you to have these,' she said. 'They were my mother's.' Frankie opened the lid to see a fine set of jade jewellery.

'Oh, it's beautiful,' she said, hugging Tess. She started like a deer, her dark eyes widening at the sound of Claudia yelling: *Frankie.* 'Thank you,' she said, backing away. 'Gotta run. We've got a wedding to go to.' She watched Tess' slender figure walking down the path to the waiting limousine, and saw Kit step out to open the door for her. Kit raised his hand to Frankie, and she waved. *What a mess,* she thought, waving back. *It all looked so perfect, the two of them. Why'd they make such a mess of it all?* She thought of her wedding gown, waiting for her upstairs. She had modelled it on Tess' wedding dress. *That photo of the two of you, in Hong Kong. You looked so happy. I want that. I want to keep that, for the rest of our lives.* Frankie watched their car drive away towards the church. *We are going to do better than you.*

Chapter 39

Frankie is everything Tess wished she had been on her wedding day. She is poised, confident, revelling in her moment. *They look impossibly young, impossibly in love,* she thinks, looking at her son and his wife side by side beneath the altar. The oyster silk gleams in a way it never did on Tess. The fabric undulates over Frankie's curves like water. The tailor has perfectly fitted the pattern to her. A row of tiny buttons, no bigger than the pearls at Tess' throat line Frankie's spine.

There is a briskness to Bobby she has never seen before, an intensity. *He wants this over with. He wants to be alone with her, of course*, Tess thinks. *They are half gone, already*, she realises. Tonight they will be on their way to Europe, to Italy, as man and wife. Tess closes her eyes, her heart full of longing. All that lies ahead for them is behind her now. She glances across the aisle at Claudia, who is sobbing, Rocco's arm around her. Marco stares ahead at the altar, his gaze on the window behind.

After the service *The Arrival of the Queen*

of Sheba pipes up from the organ, and the family walk down the aisle behind Bobby and Frankie, pausing as the congregation reaches out from the packed pews to congratulate them.

'Well,' Claudia says under her breath to Kit. 'The universe has some sense of humour, hey?' Tess and Marco walk behind them, she hears every word.

'It certainly does.' Kit puts his hand over hers. Once the congregation thins out, he turns to her, speaking softly. 'Are you alright?'

'We will be.' Claudia holds her head high. 'It'll take more than this to break up my family. The life we built together is more than him, and more than her.' Tess senses Claudia watching her and she looks across. Claudia's eyes narrow, her gaze travels from Tess' face to the red shoes. 'I got eight children, to think about. Eight living.' She touches the fine gold cross on a chain at her neck. 'Oh, it's tempting to say: fine, you go ahead and screw up your lives and we'll just carry on without you.' She glares at Marco. 'But I stay because I believe there is more to all this than us, and I believe in my vows, and I believe in family, and because I believe that love is more than who you screw. I believe in loyalty, and if you say you are going to love someone til death us do part, if you promise you are going to do something you damn well do it right and see it through even if they go and die on you.' Claudia and Kit pause in the church doorway, watching Frankie and Bobby laughing, confetti and rice showering down on them. 'I wish Carlo was here,' she says to him. 'I wish he could see how beautiful his daughter is, and how happy your son has made her.' Her face softens, and she takes Tess' hand. 'Look at them. Look how happy they are.'

□

'Dance with me,' Kit says to Tess, smiling and waving to the Hoffmans across the room. 'Fuchsia marabou is really a most unfortunate choice of trim for a woman of her colouring,' he says through his teeth.

'I think she looks fun.'

'Fun? Really? Have I taught you nothing?' He offers Tess his hand. 'Come. We must keep up appearances-'

'If you say 'old girl' I'll kick you in your shins, and I don't give a damn what blessed Mrs Hoffman thinks.' Tess says, striding ahead of him onto the dance floor. 'I thought Frankie and Marco did well with their dance, didn't you?'

'Hm? I suppose so. All these songs,' Kit says, taking her in his arms. She moves, light as a chiffon scarf on the breeze, barely touching him. 'All these songs of love, huge and simple.' His gaze follows Bobby and Frankie, dancing to-gether, lost in one another. 'It's just an animal de-sire to love and be loved.'

'What else is there to live for?' Tess says. 'That's where we always differed. I loved you, I loved Bobby.'

'Whereas I never loved anyone but myself? I am the archetypal Englishman, Elizabeth, repressed in every way-'

'You're drunk,' she says under her breath.

'My only son has just got married. Of course I'm drunk. I'm entitled to be a little maudlin.'

'May I have this dance?' Bobby holds out his hand to Tess, cutting in.

'Francesca!' Kit says brightly, swinging her away.

'You don't have to,' Tess says, smiling bravely. 'I'm so happy for you, darling.' Her voice shakes. 'I'm so sorry.'

'You have nothing to apologise for,' he says. 'It's me who owes you an apology. Can you ever forgive me for behaving like an idiot, Mom? I don't understand, but I want to.'

Tess hugs him as they dance. The years fall away between them. Now, he towers over her but she still remembers holding him for the very first time, the surprise of him. She remembers all the nights she rocked him to sleep in her arms, sitting in Aphra's old plantation chair in the nursery, singing softly to him in the lamplight. Her child, her boy is a man now, with a wife, and a new life stretching ahead of him. 'I'm so proud of you,' she whispers. 'I love you, Bobby.' She remembers it all.

'Come on,' he says, and leads her to the

front of the dance floor. Frankie smiles reassuringly at Tess. At Bobby's signal, the band strikes up *The Way You Look Tonight.*

'Oh, our favourite,' Tess says, lifting her head to look at him, tears filling her eyes.

'I asked for it especially for you.' Bobby leads her round the dance floor, and the room fades away for her.

'How much do you know?' she says quietly.

'All of it. I know everything, I think,' he says. 'But I need to know something. When you look at me, do you see him? Do you see my father? What was he like, were you in love?'

'No,' she says truthfully, touching Bobby's cheek. 'I was very young. When I look at you, I see you. I see the wonderful young man you are.' *He doesn't know*, she thinks. *Thank you, Kit. He doesn't know Clive forced me.*

'It was so brave of you, to keep me.'

'I wasn't brave. It was your father who helped me hold it all together. I was in pieces. If it wasn't for him ...'

'I know. I know you were going to get rid of the baby. Me. Dad said he proposed and you changed your mind. I'm glad you did.'

'I'm so sorry. I'm so ashamed.'

'Mom, you were a kid. A scared kid.'

'I was so afraid.' She looked away. 'So ashamed.'

'But you kept the baby.' Bobby squeezes

her hand.

'We did. Your father very much wanted you, too. He wanted it all, I think, then - marriage, a family.' Tess smiles, her brow furrowing. 'Just not me. He never wanted me.'

'Dad's explained all that, too,' Bobby says, lowering his voice. 'I understand now. I'm sorry. I made so many assumptions.' He glances across to Marco, watching them. 'You can thank Dad and Marco for all this, by the way.'

'Marco?'

'He made me see sense. Knocked it into me, in fact,' Bobby says rubbing his bruised jaw. Tess' eyes widen, and he laughs. 'Don't worry, I was asking for it.' He spins Tess around, the light from the glitter ball catching the diamond crystals on her shoes. 'He's a good man.' Bobby looks over as Claudia taps her watch. 'I gotta go. I want you to be happy, Mom. I don't like it one bit, that you and him are together, but you've got to follow your heart.'

'You don't - you don't mean that?'

'I love you, and I love Dad, and nothing is ever going to change that. If you don't love one another then go! I hope it works out with you both. And now, I have to take my wife on honeymoon.' He hugs his mother. 'I love you, Mom.'

'Excuse me,' Marco says. 'May I cut in?' He and Bobby stare at one another for a moment, until Bobby nods and backs away. Marco takes her hand, and she settles into his arms.

'Tess, I-'

'We mustn't do this, not here, not now,' she says, her eyes closing. 'Everyone knows. Everyone is watching-'

'Claudia told me to dance with you.' She looks up in surprise. 'She said it would be more suspicious if we didn't dance together as the mother of the groom and the proxy father of the bride.'

'True.'

'Tess, come away with me. Once the kids leave for the honeymoon-'

'But you're leaving soon, aren't you, after the wedding? I can't let myself love you, only for you to leave. I've lost-' Her voice catches. 'Everything is changing, but now you will go back to Italy, and you won't let me help you.'

'Like I said, all my life I have taken pride in caring for others.' Marco holds her close as they moved to the music, their bodies a perfect fit, no air between them. 'To become a burden for you is unthinkable.'

Tess remembers the Empire State Building. The scarf, slipping from her fingers. 'But you want to live?' she says quietly.

'Yes.' He closes his eyes. 'More than anything. I want to live forever, with you. But you must let me go, when the time is right.'

'Marco, I can't. I can't let you-'

'Claudia wants me to live at all costs. She wants me to stay here with them and baby me, repay me for all the years I have cared for her family.' For the first time she hears the rage in him. 'I am a proud man, Tess. I won't have them drag my life out until I am no longer the man I am in here.' He balls his fist against his chest. Tess lays her palm over his hand, waiting in silence for his anger to pass. Marco's lowers his forehead slowly to hers. 'I want to live my life as the man I am. I want to live the rest of my life, as long as I have, with you by my side.'

'Marco-'

'And then I'll die on my own terms.' Tess nods. 'I love you, Tess. I'd reconciled myself to dying, but you - you've given me new life. I've waited my whole life to find you, and whatever time we have left together let's not waste it.'

'I love you,' she says, longing to kiss him. She glances at the wedding guests turning to stare at them as they pass, like pins drawn to a magnet. 'I love you.'

'Your marriage is over. Your son has his own life now. What are you waiting for Tess? The right moment?' He turns to walk away. 'There is no right moment. There is only now.'

Chapter 40

Tess thinks of Bobby and Frankie on their way to the airport. Watching Bobby wave and turn, helping Frankie into the going away car decked with ribbons and cans, she realised that her son was not just going away, he was going out into the world without her. She would never really know him as himself, as a man, he would always be her son, and that love bound them, and kept them apart. *The love gets in the way*, she thought. To her, he would always be her child. She would never know the music in his heart. That was for him alone. *I am so proud of you*, she thought, watching him drive away. *I wish you joy, and that life full of children and noise and laughter you want so badly. That we both wanted. I wish you both love.*

She can picture the room waiting for them in Portofino, the pristine white linen glowing, expectant in the velvet night. 'I love you, Mrs Blythe.' She had heard Bobby lean across and say it to Frankie as the band struck up *Stand By Me* for their first dance. She realises now that Kit had never said it to her, not once, not like that. She wants to be loved freely, completely, just once in her life. To really belong to someone, for a time.

'Goodbye, Claudia,' she says, stooping to kiss her once, twice, a breath light brush of the cheek. 'The wedding was beautiful. You made our families proud. She looks around the empty reception room.

'If you're looking for Marco, he's gone,' she says. 'Went earlier.'

'Gone?'

'He did his duty, gave Frankie away, and now it's over.' Claudia squares up to her. 'See, I told him we gotta do the right thing. You put your family first. We're done.' She brushes the palms of her hands together. 'If you want, you and me don't have to see one another again until the first christening.'

'Claudia, I don't want it to be like that.'

'What? You think we can be friends, after all you've done?' She laughs, her head thrown back, hands on hips.

'I never planned any of this, you know.'

'Yeah, but you just couldn't help yourself, could you?' Claudia's lip curls. 'I don't care if you're getting divorced. You should be ashamed, a married woman.'

'Ashamed?' Tess says quietly. 'I've been ashamed all my life. Of who I am. Of what happened to me.' She stands tall, her spine straightening, each bone rising. 'But you don't know about that and you don't know me. Who are you to tell me I should be ashamed?' Claudia takes a step back, the colour draining from her face. 'I've been ashamed of many things, but I'm not ashamed of loving him.'

□

The limousine drops Tess outside her building, but instead of going in she takes her keys from her bag and heads to the garage. It is raining, so she runs, holding on to her hat, the lights of the traffic washing the grey pavement gold beneath her red shoes. The garage is quiet and dim, scented with oil and petrol. Tess stops at the attendant's office, and collects Looty from him. She walks quickly along the line of cars, and unlocks her red Cadillac, lifting the dog onto the seat. She checks her trunk is in the boot, and settles in to start the engine.

Kit taps on the window and Tess turns in surprise. 'Room for one more?' he says.

'I thought you were going straight to the airport. Did you change your mind?'

'Gentleman's prerogative,' he says, walking round to the passenger side. 'Oh, I think I'm just having a moment. It's good to be afraid, I think.' Kit tosses his hat onto the back seat. 'You're the only home I've ever had, really, Tess. I can't imagine living without you.'

'Then come with me,' Tess says as he clambers in and shuts the door. The rain is muffled now. 'I'm heading up to Provincetown.'

'With the Italian?'

'There's no rush.' Tess' brow furrows. 'He left without telling me where he was going, but he'll come when he's ready, I'm sure.' *Am I?* she thinks. *Where did he go?* 'Can I drop you somewhere?' she says.

'Let's drive for a while. Head over to 42nd.' Kit winds down his window. 'Let's play that game we used to play with the Atlas.' Kit leans his head against the frame. 'A new start. A new life, for both of us. Not together, but as friends. Let's go somewhere no one knows who we are.'

'Paris, perhaps?' Tess shakes her head, playing along. 'No, somewhere warm. I want to feel the sun everyday.'

'Not Provincetown, then?' Kit laughs. 'You're going to freeze spending the winter up there.'

'California?' She starts the engine.

'San Francisco? Come with me.' Kit hesitates. 'It's easier to be broke if the sun is shining. And ... I know someone. A friend. It's different there, apparently. Things are changing.' He looks at her. 'We can be who we were meant to be all along.'

'Who we were meant to be?' Tess takes off her hat and tosses it onto the back seat beside Kit's fedora. She rests her pale gloved hands on the white steering wheel and turns the ignition, the engine throbbing into life. 'Do you ever think we are exactly who we were meant to be? It just takes the guts to stand up and say 'this is me'. It doesn't matter whether we are in San Francisco or Italy or Timbuktu. You and me and Bobby we are always linked, whatever happens.' She reaches across and squeezes Kit's hand.

'I always loved how much you adore our son. I hope Bobby knows how lucky he is.'

'Oh, parents always love more than they are loved. When you have a child, you lose a layer of skin - you're alert to danger, to beauty, to life in a way you never were before. You lay your heart completely open.'

'Perhaps for you, because you have a capacity for love some of us lack.'

'I love more than I'm loved, I know that.' Tess waits for him to look at her. 'That's my blessing and my sadness. You should see it, Kit, this world, this life I see. You should see yourself through my eyes. You are wonderful.' Kit raises her hand to his lips and presses her fingers to him. 'Go on. I dare you.' He lays his cheek against her palm for a moment, and closes his eyes. *Surely, he's not crying?* Kit takes a pair of Wayfarers from his breast pocket and raises his chin, looking at the dark road ahead.

'Show everyone, Tess,' he says. 'Choreograph shows which make everyone sit up and take notice of this crazy, beautiful world of yours, and I'll be able to say to them: 'yes, I knew Tess Blythe. Once upon a time, she loved me.' He looks out at the city streets drifting by, the night air cold on them. 'It is extraordinary, isn't it, how two lives become linked. How can someone you've never met before become the centre of your world?'

The drive through Manhattan she knows is a last goodbye. She wonders if she will ever see Kit again. They talk of Bobby, of all the times they shared, moments frozen and cherished, snapshots of a life together. Several times she breaks off to wipe at her eye. *The wind,* she says, rummaging in the glove box for a tissue. She steers the red Cadillac along 42nd Street, the street lights glinting on the fins. Kit turns to her. 'Can you drop me over there,' he says, gesturing towards Grand Central Station.

'Aren't I dropping you at the airport?'

'No, I'm travelling light. I'll catch a bus.'

'A bus?' Tess says, surprised.

'Needs must, dear heart.' Kit stares towards the park. 'I've instructed a removal company to store the best of the Chinese furniture for you. The bank can take the rest.' Kit swings his hat from the back of the car. 'Frankly I have no intention of hanging around for the bailiffs.'

'Can't I drop you at the bus station?'

'That has no romance, does it?' Kit laughs. 'One must say goodbye at Grand Central. I've always loved train journeys. Do you remember the Canton Belle?'

'I'll never forget it,' she says, parking up. 'All those wonderful cities. Moscow, Berlin,

Paris. We have seen some marvellous things, haven't we, Kit?' She squeezes his hand. 'At least let me see you off.'

'Just walk me to the station.'

Tess steps from the bustling night pavement into the familiar marble hall, the high arched windows above are dark now, but she imagines them sending shafts of light across the station like spots on a stage, illuminating one by one, the commuters turning to one another, dancing below. She turns to her husband. 'Goodbye, Kit. You will ... oh, god it feels ridiculous to say you will keep in touch. You've been such a huge part of my life. I don't know how I shall miss you.'

'You'll manage,' Kit says, looking beyond her to where Marco stands beside the steps. 'You'd better hurry, you have a plane to catch too.'

'A plane?'

Kit gestures at Marco. 'You're taking off from New York International in a couple of hours.' He smiles at the confusion on her face. 'You can't drive all the way to Italy, darling. Leave the car at the airport. Let the bloody bank deal with the parking tickets,' Kit says, screwing his eyes tightly closed as he kisses her one last time. 'I spent my last sou on Looty's ticket.'

'Oh, Kit.'

'Don't say goodbye, I couldn't bear it.' He holds her tight in his arms. 'We are nomads, Tess.

One day our paths will cross again.'

'But what if they don't?' she says, stifling a sob.

'Then I'll miss you, and you'll miss me.'

'We will find one another again,' Tess says. 'We will.'

'I'm sorry, I messed up,' he whispers. 'Be happy, darling.' He jogs down the steps, pausing to shake Marco's hand, and Tess imagines a soaring score full of hope and new beginnings, every person in the station dancing, dancing towards the future. 'Good luck, Tess,' Kit calls. 'It's never too late for your happy ending.'

The crowds on the concourse clear and Marco steps towards her. He draws her to him like gravity. There is in that moment everything: the melody, the memory of the sun, the sea, the past, the future. The next step in the dance.

Act 3

I admired Tess' elegance, her beauty, her brav-
ery. The last ballet she choreographed before she
died was *'Third Act'*. It is pared back, but rich
with her familiar signature touches from other
ballets, such as *'Red Shoes'* - it is elemental, with
fire, earth, water, wind. The dancers rise up from
the city to escape to forests, to the seashore. She
told me once: 'there is a profound link between
your body, your mind and your soul. My work
is full of joy because my heart is grieving. But
love never leaves you. Your body, your spirit remembers them. When I dance, I remember him.
I remember our love. I want to conjure joy, happiness from the air. I want to remember how it
feels again and again. Each ballet is a new beginning ...' *Third Act* had an aching beauty to it, a
longing. She said 'I wanted to dance all my life.
That's all I dreamt of. I missed my chance, which
is why I poured all that love, all that longing into
choreography. I wanted to help other's dreams
come true.' Tess was like a composer, really, and
we were the notes of her melody. I remember her
saying to me once: 'One day, all this will be mem-

ories. What are you waiting for?"

- Anton Gerard Jones, Principal dancer, Prov-
incetown Dance Company

Epilogue

I found Tess' diary hidden in a shoebox with the beautiful pair of shoes Marco had made her for my wedding. They were stored carefully alongside an elegant but robust pair of ballet flats he had made for her before he died, which she wore every day and polished each night.

In the diary she poured out her heart and I learnt the full truth about Hong Kong, her marriage to Kit and her love for Marco. It was only when it was too late that I found out how my mother had sacrificed her own happiness for me, and I wish I had the chance to say sorry to Tess for being so harsh. There was always a distance between us. I never quite forgave her for hiding the fact that Kit wasn't my father, but now I know why. I am glad that though Kit and Tess lived separate lives, they both found happiness with other people and remained friends to the end.

My parents were unconventional but they taught me about sacrifice, and love, and working for something bigger and better than yourself. They believed in excellence and beauty and that there are many ways of loving one another, many kinds of families. While I was fighting in Vietnam, the whole family came together to care for Marco. Everyone put aside their differences. Forgiveness. Sacrifice. Love is as much about that as moons in June, as Kit often said.

With Marco my mother found the love of her life. Tess and Marco lived in great happiness and devotion, splitting the time left to them between Tuscany and Provincetown. Marco encouraged her to train as a choreographer, to build a life ready for a time when he would no longer be there at her side. She nursed him alone at the end, that is what he wanted, at their home in Provincetown, and he died in her arms.

It is the greatest regret of my life that I wasn't there for her, then. I wish I had been more accepting of their all too brief marriage. I tolerated it rather than embraced it, to my shame. We grew closer towards the end of her life, and I am glad of that, but she never remarried, never loved again. I hope this book gives some idea of her capacity for love, the woman behind the ballets so many adore, and that it is never too late to find happiness - if not forever after. Tess and Marco called their life together the Third Act. That is why my younger half-brother Angelo and I have named the women's refuge we've established in Tess' memory 'Third Act'. If our mother taught us anything, it is that it is never too late to change your story and create a happy ending.

No wonder so many people loved her. If Tess was lonely after Marco died, she never complained, and she was never alone - there was always work to be done or friends to see, and her ballet company spent months every year on the road performing in London, Paris, Rome, Tokyo. Everywhere she went, Tess carried her love for Marco with her, watching it play out on stage night after night in the stories she crafted. And in turn, everyone loved Tess.

The congregation spilled onto the sidewalk at her funeral a couple of months ago, men in light suits and women in a rainbow of dresses. *No black*, she'd said. Typically ironic as Tess had spent her life in black. People came all the way from Europe. It was simple, and beautiful, and full of music - the Beatles, Billie Holiday. The only flowers were a spray of white chrysanthemums tied with scarlet silk on the plain wooden casket. A young violinist played 'Lark Ascending' as the coffin was lowered, and I had to smile through my tears, it was so typical, again, of our mother. That delicious contradiction even at the last. I had to carry Tess' little dog away from the grave. She didn't want to leave her. She just lay down beside Tess, and cried and cried for her. But the teal sea glimmered beyond the bay like the angels had scattered the skyline with diamonds just for Tess. She'd have liked that - glimmering and glittering at the last. It was so beautiful, her final curtain. A clear Spring day which spoke of beginnings.

There was a Dictaphone tape, found among the pages of my mother's diaries from which this book is drawn. It was wonderful to hear her voice again. In life Tess was always there, always ready to listen to you. Perhaps it's only fair that in the story of her life the last word should go to Tess.

Robert Blythe - February 2018

❑

Q: One last question, if I may Ms Blythe. What advice would you give to a young dancer just starting out?
A: Advice? (Laughter). None. None at all, my dear. Why, everyone has the answers within them. Keep going, that is all. Love is coming. Listen - can you hear the music?

THE END

Acknowledgements

I would like to thank Sheila Crowley, Emily Harris, Katie McGowan and all at Curtis Brown Books. At Piper, I thank Michaela Sappler and her editorial team, and Elke Link for her sympathetic translation. I am grateful for the help of Jim Moske, Metropolitan Museum of Art, the Parkinson's UK Research Team, and Gloria de Santis and Paolo for teaching me Italian and bringing my attention to Dante. As always, my love and thanks to my family.

Printed in Great Britain
by Amazon

43633947R00258